I0949699

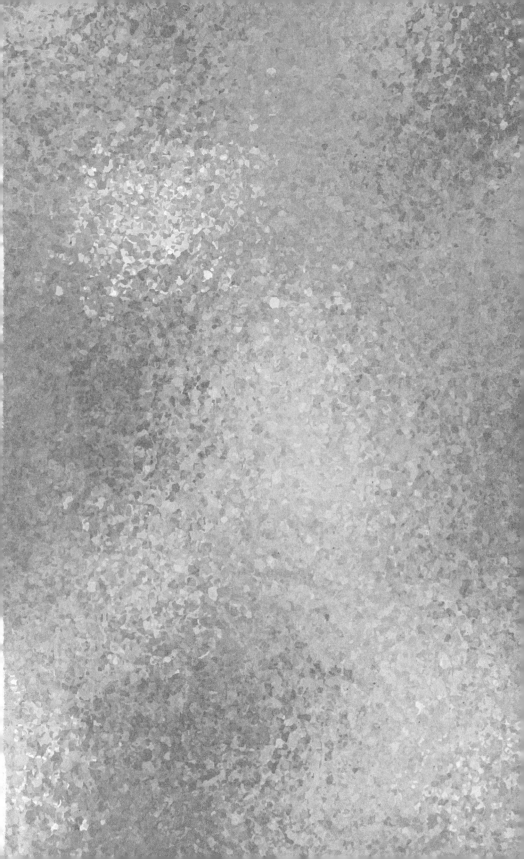

Advance Praise for
TRIAL

"A death in the dark, a young life on the line. From the backroads of rural Georgia to the halls of Congress, this riveting novel draws on Richard North Patterson's years as a trial attorney as well as his insider knowledge of Washington DC. Intricate, compelling, and timely, it may be his best book yet."

—**Geraldine Brooks**, Winner of the Pulitzer Prize for Fiction
and *New York Times* bestselling author of *Horse*

"It is no overstatement to say that *To Kill a Mockingbird* for the 21st century has arrived. *Trial* grapples with the biggest issues of race and justice and does so in a meaningful and engrossing way, page after page. You cannot help being moved by this story and it illuminates the biggest issues we face in our nation today."

—**James Stavridis**, former Supreme Allied Commander of NATO
and *New York Times* bestselling novelist

"For all its timely discussion, *Trial* is first and foremost a novel of irresistible suspense. This is a barnburner of a book whose huge drama, large characters, and elemental conflicts grab you from page one."

—**Scott Turow**, #1 *New York Times* bestselling author
of *Presumed Innocent* and *Suspect*

"This is a portrait of the America I know. It is compelling, contemporary and thoughtfully researched truth telling. *Trial* might be fictional but it is real. Allie, Chase, Malcolm, Jabari, and Janie are real people. I know them. Their experiences are real. I've lived them."

—**Bruce Gordon**, former CEO of the NAACP

"For many years, my law practice representing Black men and women struggling for justice in a Jim Crow environment took me into the courthouse and among the people of the area depicted in this novel. As a Black native of Southwest Georgia and based on my professional experience, Richard North Patterson has done a commendable job of capturing the spirit of the place and its people."

—**Judge Herbert E. Phipps**, Georgia Court of Appeals (Ret.)

"Richard North Patterson has written another excellent novel which rings with authenticity. He captures virtually all the racial subtleties I would expect from a Black author, and knocks the politics out of the park."

—**Judge Thelton Henderson**, US District Court (Ret.), former US
Department of Justice attorney, Civil Rights Division, Voting Section

TRIAL

TRIAL

RICHARD
NORTH
PATTERSON

Post Hill
PRESS

Post Hill Press
New York • Nashville
posthillpress.com

Published in the United States of America
1 2 3 4 5 6 7 8 9 10

For David Cooke
and for the dedicated people
of the New Georgia Project

PART ONE

The Killing

1

In the pitch darkness of an unlit road in rural Georgia, Malcolm Hill drove with the windows cracked open, hoping that the humid crosscurrents would diminish the torpid semistupor of too many beers.

It was past midnight. At eighteen, Malcolm was three years short of the legal drinking age—a young Black man who, he dully realized, had rendered himself vulnerable to mischance. There were no streetlamps. Around him he felt, more than saw, the open fields stretching between dense stands of pines or oaks that blocked the thin silver light of a quarter moon.

As he oscillated between hyperattention and slackness, Malcolm lost the sensation of time passing, and the asphalt road in his headlights seemed to recede before reappearing in sharper focus. Abruptly recalling the pickup truck that, perhaps an hour before, had slowed as it passed the front porch where he sat drinking with his friends, he glanced in the rearview mirror, searching for the beam lights that—in reality or imagination—had appeared in the ghostly distance before vanishing again, conjuring from his subconscious the decades of bad history that had made Cade County, once a cradle of slavery, so dangerous for Blacks.

As he often did, he remembered his mother's catechism: *Don't play loud music. Don't violate the speed limit. Don't drink and drive. Don't give them any reason to stop you.* As if in defiance, Killer Mike was rapping on his sound system, rapping an anthem to resisting the police.

In Malcolm's mind, the words provoked both fresh anger at rogue cops and the odd sense of himself as a seriocomic figure, a recent honors graduate of Cade County High School living on the edge of criminality by edict of the Georgia state legislature. On the passenger seat beside him was the proof: piles of absentee voter applications that, Wednesday through Sunday, he passed out to the county's Black electorate—his summer job before going off to college.

But though his ultimate boss was his formidable and demanding mother, the enterprise she ran was no family business. In 2020 the Blue Georgia Movement had persuaded unprecedented numbers of African Americans to vote absentee or by mail, helping to make Joe Biden president and elect two senators, one Black, who had given Democrats control of the United States Senate. Too many people despised her for it.

In response, the legislature had barred election officials and organizations like Blue Georgia from mailing out absentee ballot applications, making it harder for Blacks who worked long hours or were burdened with childcare to vote. Now the election of November 2022 was only five months away. Until September, Malcolm's job was to knock on doors or go to fairs, churches, concerts, and barbecues—anywhere Black people gathered—to pass out applications.

This, too, might be illegal in the minds of Allie Hill's enemies. There was just no telling—since the election of 2020, there was so much hatred that she had stopped counting death threats. Instead she had stepped up her warnings to Malcolm: *If somebody hassles you for canvassing, don't get mad; just try to defuse the situation and get out of there. We're not in the business of creating martyrs—our movement had too many of those long ago.*

Once again, Malcolm looked in the rearview mirror.

Nothing but darkness.

In fifteen minutes or so, he would be home in bed, the only consequence of his carelessness her sharply worded disapproval for driving too late at night on a lonely road. Bed would feel good. He was not only borderline drunk but stone tired.

The neighborhood he had worked today was deep in poverty—shotgun houses maybe eight hundred square feet, with aluminum shades outside the windows and, too often, tarpaulins or garbage bags or cardboard covering leaks in the roof that spawned mildew and mold. Most of the postage-stamp yards were dirt or untended grass; the people who lived in these hovels often did not own them—the owners of record, his mom had explained, were parents or grandparents or other dead relations who had passed away without wills or any notion of probate. One wizened old woman had asked Malcolm to check the overhead light in her kitchen; when he unscrewed the bulb, cockroaches fell on his head. The house was clean enough; she simply could not afford to maintain it.

His mother knew everyone in these houses. Sometimes she went there in her old flatbed truck, the one she kept for carrying packets of food to the people she knew needed them most. *You don't just ask folks to vote*, she had told Malcolm, *unless you care about their lives. Still*, she always added, *changing lives is impossible unless enough people cast ballots.*

Deep down, Malcolm knew his mother had not wanted him to do this work. But he had insisted and, rare for her, Allie Hill had relented. What followed were still more warnings: *Once it gets dark, try to have company. You don't want to be alone if you can help it, at least not anywhere no one can see you. There are still a lot of people in Georgia who hate Black folks, and too many have guns. A few wouldn't think twice about killing you because you're my son, or just because you're a Black man.*

Glancing behind him, Malcolm thought again of that truck slowing down, as if to mark the group of young Blacks and whites chilling out after a long day spent putting the power to vote in the hands of their neighbors. In the distance behind him, new headlights slowed and then disappeared as he entered the last stretch of solitude. In ten minutes or so, he would reach the long driveway running through the parcel of land where his mother and grandmother kept up old family farmhouses, the place his grandfather had lived until that heart attack took him so fast that he was dead before he hit the grass where he had been pitching horseshoes with Malcolm in the dusk after supper. The memory felt like lead in Malcolm's heart.

In the rearview mirror, Malcolm realized with a start, a blue flashing light had appeared.

He felt the dampness of sweat on his T-shirt and forehead. As the light came closer, the shriek of a police siren pierced the night.

Reflexively, Malcolm remembered his mother's instructions for dealing with cops who could snuff out a life in a moment of fury or fear. *Be respectful; don't move quickly; make sure they can see your hands.*

Malcolm had not told her about the gun.

The used Glock 19 was concealed in his glove compartment. He had bought it two weeks ago after starting this work, remembering all the videos of Blacks killed by police. He had imagined a moment like this, but the reality of this moment jolted him fully awake. The squad car loomed behind him, filling his rearview mirror, sirens screeching.

Heart pounding, Malcolm pulled over to the side of the road, wheels skidding on gravel before he jammed on the brakes. The old Honda jolted to a stop, its headlights streaks of white-yellow that evanesced in the infinite black of featureless grassland.

The car stopped behind him. The siren stilled; the blue beacon ceased flashing; the headlights disappeared. Everything around the car became silent and dark.

Malcolm's stomach knotted. In a panicky reflex, he took out the gun and hid it beneath the papers beside him, the tools of democracy.

2

Pacing the living room of the weathered farmhouse she shared with her son, Allie Hill paused to check her cell phone for texts.

Nothing.

Pacing from room to room, Allie recommenced her restless pursuit of nothing save to kill time. She was slight and intense, gifted with a kinetic energy that fueled a swiftness of thought, speech, and movement so marked that—so her mother said—she seemed to burn calories just by being herself. Waiting for Malcolm, she gazed at the photographs that they had hung on the walls: her parents and grandparents at her kitchen table; a Hill family gathering on the green farmland outside; Malcolm watching his grandfather slip his ballot into a drop box; the faces of ordinary Black people from hard times past. *It's good to remember*, she had told her son.

Aimless, she went to the kitchen for a drink of water. Opening the refrigerator, she realized they were down to a loaf of bread, cold cuts, English muffins, and a quart of milk. *I've neglected my shopping*, Allie reproved herself. Malcolm inhaled food, and she didn't want him eating junk. Tomorrow she would squeeze an hour from her schedule to buy groceries.

She stopped, pensive. Through the window screen she could hear the sounds of a spring night in Southwest Georgia—crickets, wind rustling the leaves of trees—but not the one she awaited, the hum of a motor coming up the drive. Gazing into the darkness, she inhaled the scent of the crape myrtle trees she fitfully tended; felt the moist, lingering heat of a spring day that augured another sweltering summer that would breed mosquitoes as big as dive bombers; sensed the coming of a thunderstorm, perhaps bearing the jagged, shimmering bolts of lightning that, when Allie was small, had split the night sky and announced the awesome nearness of God. All that was missing from the remembered sensations of her childhood was the drone from a television as Wilson Hill watched his favorite team, the Atlanta Braves—Hank Aaron's team, he had later explained to seven-year-old Malcolm, and then Dusty Baker's, a Black man with a baseball mind so keen that he was still managing in the big leagues. Sometimes Allie would leave off helping her mother clean dishes after supper to peer into the living room and watch Malcolm sitting in her father's lap, the boy's head on the man's broad shoulder, her father's masculine warmth serving Malcolm's need for a father of his own.

But now his grandfather was gone. Across the darkened fields where she, then Malcolm, had played as children, Allie saw the porch light of her mother's home—as if she, too, would wait until Malcolm returned. Janie Hill's heritage of worry had long ago become her daughter's.

But she was far from Janie's equal as a mother, Allie knew. During election season, Allie worked ten to twelve hours a day, seven days a week, supervising over one hundred employees in eight offices across the state—many of them canvassers not much older than Malcolm. In three months he would be off at college, and she felt her time with him slipping away.

Through sheer will, she stopped herself from calling him. He was touchy and proud, too aware that the major force in his life was a woman others viewed with something akin to awe. He was on the cusp of adulthood, searching for an identity all his own, and he felt her anxieties and desires for him as a burden. But she would have suffered them in better times than these: He was an eighteen-year-old Black man in Georgia who was sometimes too quick to anger, and one moment of misjudgment could change his life in ways he could not yet imagine.

Tonight, as often, she felt alone. *This is how things are*, she reminded herself, *and much of that is my doing*. But no matter the air of certitude she adopted for Malcolm, as a mother she had made her share of mistakes. Tonight she worried yet again that allowing Malcolm to share in her work was another. But in the end, she could not diminish her son out of fear. To stand up was what her family had always done, even back when it could have meant a casual death at the hands of racists that would likely go unpunished and, except by their community, unmourned. Standing up was what she knew, the only way forward. She could not separate Malcolm from three generations of Hills.

Perhaps more than any single person, a columnist for the *New York Times* had written, Allie Hill had shifted the balance of power in American politics. The price was raising ever more money to buy security for the offices where her people worked insanely long hours for too little money. But Georgia, its northern counties especially, was crawling with militia and white nationalists who carried assault weapons or knew how to build bombs, and hated anyone who had "stolen" the White House from the one "rightful" president.

Now her work meant living with all the hatred welling up from the fever swamp of fanatics who believed she was bent on replacing white Christians with brown and Black people who would destroy their primal America. The fact that Allie, too, was a Christian meant nothing. After the 2020 election, armed white militia had massed in front of her offices in Freedom, right-wing extremists had posted her picture, and then, more ominously, photographs of her home on the internet.

Waking up that morning, she had discovered another voice message from an unknown caller. His ungrammatical threats of sexual violence and asphyxiation would have been almost comical if not for the venom seeping through the honey-dipped inflections. She had given up wondering how these people got her cell number; though she had always loathed firearms except for the rifle her father used for hunting, lately she had considered buying a handgun.

But the fear she felt most profoundly was not for herself. Yesterday, for the first time, a particularly virulent website had posted Malcolm's high school yearbook picture with the caption "Allie Hill's illegitimate son."

Once again, she checked her cell phone. Still nothing.

Stepping outside, she stood in ankle-deep grass, gazing up at the sliver of moon suspended in the darkness above Cade County. Then she snatched the phone from her pocket and called Malcolm.

3

In the thin silver light through the bedroom window of his gracious home in Georgetown, the rising public servant known as Congressman Chase Bancroft Brevard, Democrat of Massachusetts, contemplated the slender back of the woman sleeping beside him, his girlfriend of the moment.

Kara McGuire was twenty-nine, an Irish Catholic from Boston who had worked her way through BU—the people's school, she would remind him wryly—before becoming a political consultant of considerable promise. She was smart and perceptive, with a keen sense of humor, attuned to the vicissitudes of the world they shared. Politics was in her blood; her father, a plumber, had volunteered for Ted Kennedy, and she had grown up hearing long and colorful stories about politicians whose devotion to the old neighborhood sometimes outran their ethics. Every now and then, inspired by a glass of wine, she made Chase laugh by telling him a couple that were particularly droll.

In their way, at least for now, they were perfect for each other. She was neither a reporter covering the Hill—which would have been an inherent conflict—nor, even worse, a congressional staffer whose involvement with a congressman would have raised the very real question of sexual leverage. If anything, she was mining him for insights helpful to her career and profited from the cachet that came from showing up at social events with a politician most people not only liked, but had marked as someone to watch. Though Kara was younger than he, she was more than old enough to be good company, and he enjoyed her cultivation of an affected cynicism she would one day earn. Chase expected her to thrive.

But though she was ambitious, as was Chase, politics was not all for her. She was the last of five daughters, close to her family, and when the time was right she meant to have children of her own. That time was coming, Chase knew. Last night, over the candlelit dinner that had preceded their lovemaking—her favorite: Dover sole, prepared by Chase himself; a California chardonnay she particularly liked; crème brûlée he'd been smart enough to buy—they had celebrated the final birthday of her twenties, and Chase had felt the first premonition of the unwelcome but inevitable end of their time together

Now, as she slept, Chase wondered about himself yet again.

As a professional matter, he did not mind people knowing that he liked women, and the patina of glamour that came from dating the occasional politically obsessed actress or high-profile journalist had not hurt him with the constituents who kept returning him to office with ever-greater margins. But he was approaching the time when the absence of wife and family was beginning to seem curious, if not emotionally arrested. Damning him with the very faintest of praise, a disappointed ex-lover had told him: "I'd take you for Peter Pan, but you're not nearly that narcissistic or screwed up. It's more that you don't seem to need anyone enough to inconvenience yourself by getting married." Though that troubled him, then and now, he could find no good way to tell her that only once, too long ago, had he found a woman so compelling that he could imagine sharing something so important as a lifetime, so profound as the love of a child rooted in his love for her.

Beside him, Kara stirred but did not awaken. Admiring her ability to sleep despite his restiveness, Chase pondered how it might feel when she no longer occupied what had become, in their transient monogamy, Kara's side of the bed.

Perhaps, he acknowledged, he had become so elusive that he had begun to elude himself. "I know what you are," the woman before Kara had told him, "but not *who* you are." But maybe the *what* and *who* were one and the same: a man who had been born lucky and, except for one painful passage, had stayed that way.

Chase came from a wealthy Boston family, made so several generations back by a somewhat predatory financier on his mother's side, great-grandfather Bancroft. Chase had acquired his surname from a French professor of literature who had met Caroline Bancroft while she was studying at the Sorbonne before, as he sardonically put it to tease her, he had followed the money to America. Chase was an only child, more than enough for Jean Marc and Caroline Brevard, and shortly after he turned fourteen they had packed him off to Middlesex with no more sentiment than Caroline's parents had displayed when they dispatched her to Rosemary Hall. Chase did well on his own, academically and socially; after prep school came seven successful years at Harvard—college, then law school. Looking for a challenge that might prefigure a career in politics, instead of striving for money he did not need, Chase became an assistant district attorney in Boston.

Once more, he had been lucky. True, he had worked hard to become a skilled trial lawyer. But when a daunting but high-profile case had appeared—the fatal shooting of an unarmed Black man by a white cop under ambiguous circumstance—Chase had asked the district attorney to give him the case. A year later, after Chase had decimated the policeman on cross-examination, the jury returned a verdict of second-degree murder.

The police union detested him for it. But the profile of a privileged young man turned progressive prosecutor was ideal for the affluent congressional district near Boston where his parents maintained their principal home. After a blistering primary contest, Chase entered Congress at the age of thirty-two.

Politics, too, continued to reward the gifts that came to him naturally. Like any good politician with adequate self-awareness, Chase knew what they were: He was attractive, likable, a smooth but compelling speaker gifted with a pitch-perfect public persona and the instincts to match. He seldom spoke precipitously or let passion outrun good judgment: Ask Chase Brevard a question, a veteran reporter had said of him early on, and he could see the implications in a heartbeat. He was, in short, a talented and reliably mainstream Democrat well-liked by the House leadership, which increasingly abetted his blossoming ambitions.

He was forty now, and among the younger Democrats who forecasters believed could someday become president. But Chase dismissed such talk as a distraction, even a curse. He had resolved to focus on the as-yet-unannounced goal that lay immediately before him: a race for the Senate from Massachusetts in 2024. Lose that race, and idle dreams of occupying the White House would be not merely speculative but absurd.

"It's way too early," he had told Kara over dinner. "Start to obsess on that, and you risk breaking your own heart. I've seen too many ambitious politicians who think they can only become themselves by becoming president. It's a form of psychic suicide. Before you even think about running for president, it might be good to have some experiential basis for imagining yourself as a colossus astride the world stage. Besides," he had finished with a smile, "there are a few barriers standing between me and historic greatness. Some of whom are my colleagues."

Amused, Kara had raised an eyebrow. "Let me take a wild guess. She's Black, about five foot two, has a wicked tongue, and thinks you're white bread in an Armani suit."

Which had brought Chase back to the problem Kara had identified so astutely: the ardently progressive Black congresswoman from a far more modest district in Boston. Lucy Battle was outspoken, charismatic, and an unapologetic class warrior who mesmerized the activist left. Chase's mild mockery of Lucy's call to "defund the police" had provoked her caustic rejoinder that putting one bad cop in jail was a moment, not a vision. Lucy barely concealed, when she bothered at all, her view that Chase was an overly privileged trust fund baby who would never understand people of color. She knew in her bones that she was as worthy of becoming a senator from Massachusetts as Chase Brevard was not.

"She's kind of getting to you, isn't she?" Kara had ventured over dessert.

Chase shook his head. "She'd like to think so. Actually, I sort of like her—way more than she'll ever like me. Four hundred-plus years of racism seem to have curdled her disposition. But what gets to me is how much running against Lucy would become about race, like it or not. No matter how I feel about that."

The amusement surfacing in Kara's eyes, Chase had long since learned, augured mischief. In the abrasive tone of a particularly obnoxious Fox News anchorwoman, she had demanded: "So tell me, Congressman Brevard, is America a racist country?"

"Of course it is, Laura," Chase had answered without skipping a beat. "That's why your all-white audience is so paranoid about Blacks. How else could a bleached-blonde sociopath like you make ten million bucks a year for saying that the only discrimination left in America targets fundamentalist Caucasians?"

Kara laughed. "That's certainly *one* way to go viral."

"And lose all those suburban swing voters Lucy petrifies?" he inquired with mock horror. "Don't you want me to become a senator?"

As Kara had smiled at this, he'd regarded her familiar features in the candlelight: thick brunette hair, large brown eyes, generous mouth—the look of a smart and very pretty soubrette. "It's fine with me, Congressman. The House is way too small for a man of your vast talents. But the Democratic primary is two years away. Tonight is my birthday, and we've got other things to do."

And so they had, slowly and sweetly. Afterward, as Kara fell asleep, with a tinge of melancholy Chase had imagined her as someone else's wife.

4

Hands on the steering wheel, Malcolm waited. But for the streaks of his headlights converging, he was surrounded by fathomless night. Thick, lowering clouds had begun obscuring the quarter moon; Malcolm could barely discern the cop's shadowy form approaching in the rearview mirror. Then it disappeared, and the crunch of footsteps on gravel grew louder.

Malcolm tensed, sweat stinging his eyes. His mother's warnings slowly surfaced in his brain: *If police stop you, do what they say. Never show anger. Don't reach for anything; don't move unless you have to. The wrong cop could kill you in seconds.*

He heard the stranger approaching the driver's side window, saw his flashlight as a blinding circle of yellow. Malcolm averted his eyes from its brightness. His first fleeting impression was of a big man with an over-sized head beneath the visored cap of authority.

What kind of Black man would the cop imagine seeing? Malcolm wondered. For at least some white people, he knew, he wasn't the menacing predator of their most fearful imaginings. His skin was lighter than his mother's or grandparents'; growing up, he had learned that all kinds of girls liked his face. But that only put other guys on edge, white and Black, and so did his musculature—that of an athlete. Malcolm lifted weights until his sinews ached, the better to ward off sports opponents or whoever might confront him in a place with no rules. Maybe tonight that time had come.

The cop rapped the glass with his flashlight, thrusting its beam in Malcolm's face. "Open the window," he ordered.

The insinuating molasses drawl of a backcountry white speaking to an inferior underscored that Malcolm was alone in the darkness, subject to whatever this man cared to do. Slowly raising one hand from the steering wheel for his faceless captor to see, Malcolm pushed a button.

With a quiet shudder, the glass between them lowered.

Wordless, the cop reached through the window and switched off Malcolm's headlights, turning the night that enveloped them pitch black. "Get out," he said in the same quiet, contemptuous tone. "Time for your breath test."

Malcolm's stomach clenched. Stupidly, he had licensed his own entrapment, and now he was invisible on a backroad in Cade County. Struggling to separate reality from fear, he realized that the cop had not asked for his name or driver's license. Malcolm remembered that the new sheriff, a Black man, had required his deputies to turn on their body cameras before making an arrest. But Malcolm saw no light on this man's chest, nothing that suggested a functioning camera.

"Follow me home," he managed to say. "We can talk there."

His own voice, Malcolm heard, sounded like he was frightened or drunk. But the muted laugh through his window seemed oddly contented. "We're staying where mama can't help you," the man answered, and Malcolm grasped with terrible certainty that the cop already knew who he was.

"I've got the right to call her," Malcolm said tautly.

From the darkness came a sigh of feigned sorrow. "Afraid it's just you and me, Malcolm—a respected law enforcement officer, and the bastard son of a socialist whore who'd fuck any man who didn't mind watching her fuck three other men first."

Malcolm tensed with caged anger, torn between the pain of a wound scraped raw and rage at hearing the sick loathing and desire that went back to when white men like this could treat Black women as they pleased. Thinking of the gun, he tightened his grip on the wheel.

"Sad you've got no father," his predator continued in a conversational tone. "You're just a mama's boy, rounding up people too stupid to vote on their own."

Glancing in the rearview mirror, Malcolm hoped for anyone who might see them by the side of the road.

Nothing but darkness.

Suddenly, he felt his cell phone vibrate in the pocket of his blue jeans—his mother, he felt certain. "I need to answer that, Officer."

"Just keep your hands on the wheel, Malcolm. Out here you've got no phone privileges to help you."

In the suffocating stillness of the car, Malcolm's phone kept buzzing. The man thrust his flashlight toward the passenger seat. "Tell me what you got there."

Malcolm froze. In his silence, the phone went still.

"Answer me, Malcolm."

Malcolm's throat was dry. "Absentee ballot applications."

"Seems like you've been violating the voting laws of the sovereign state of Georgia. Hand those to me. Slowly."

He couldn't, Malcolm knew, without uncovering the gun. "I don't want any trouble," he implored. "Please, just take me to Sheriff Garrett."

"You'd like that, wouldn't you? 'Please take me to my mama's friend.' But that's not how your life is going tonight, Malcolm." The man's voice hardened. "First, you refuse a breath test. Now you're defying a lawful order to turn over evidence of a crime. Unless you're fixing to die, stay where you are."

Slowly, the deputy backed away from the window. Paralyzed, Malcolm heard his footsteps on the gravel, saw his shadow circling the car. As Malcolm turned, the man's form filled the passenger window. Reflexively, he slid his right hand down the wheel.

The man jerked open the passenger door, switching on the inside light. For Malcolm, time stopped. As the deputy leaned inside and stretched his hand toward the papers, Malcolm took both hands off the wheel.

Beneath the overhead light, the Glock 19 showed dull black on the passenger seat. In a rush of adrenaline, Malcolm grabbed it.

The deputy wrenched it from his grasp. Desperate, Malcolm gripped the man's wrist with both hands, struggling to turn the barrel. They fought for leverage in the tight space of the car, their heads inches apart, the deputy using his bulk to push Malcolm down.

Malcolm's skull struck the steering wheel. Lights flashed through his vision as the deputy twisted the barrel back toward him.

Grasping the handle, Malcolm used all his strength to turn the weapon away from his face. All at once he felt it wrench, twisting in the big man's hands.

A sudden, percussive pop sounded in the car. The man's head seemed to lift, and something wet spattered Malcolm's T-shirt.

Shocked, he recoiled, hands dropping to his side. In the dim light, the deputy toppled sideways, sliding down the passenger seat, his eyes staring, mouth agape. His hair was close-cropped, his face broad and florid. A piece of his forehead had disappeared, and his skin was streaked with blood and brain matter.

Turning in horror and revulsion, Malcolm opened the door, stumbling from the car before falling to his knees.

The night was dark and silent. Head bent over the gravel, Malcolm vomited, the sour smell of beer filling his nostrils. The cell phone vibrated in his pocket.

Too late, he told her. *It's too late.*

5

In numb despair, Malcolm sat motionless beside his car.

The shrieking siren grew louder. Breaks squealed behind him, spitting gravel, and blue streaks of light shimmered on the asphalt. A car door flew open, followed by swift footsteps. Malcolm did nothing. He no longer cared what happened.

A man shoved Malcolm's face forward into the gravel, cutting his skin. Wrenching Malcolm's arms, the cop cupped his hands behind him.

Malcolm lay in the gravel, silent. Turning his face sideways, he could see a second cop walking toward the car, a dark figure in blue phosphorescence.

The man stopped, staring through the open door. Squaring his shoulders, he slid inside Malcolm's car.

For a moment all was silent. Then Malcolm heard the cop speaking in an urgent rush, "It's Nick Spinetta. Officer down on Old County Road."

Manacled, Malcolm could not move.

More footsteps. Then Spinetta knelt over him and put a gun to his temple. The feel of metal reawakened Malcolm's fear of death. "It was an accident," he said dully.

Spinetta drew a deep breath. Holstering the gun, the cop rose to his feet, standing over Malcolm as dueling sirens split the night. More cars skidded to a stop, their headlights bathing Malcolm in yellow.

"It's George Bullock," Spinetta told someone in a low voice. "He's dead."

Two deputies jerked Malcolm upright and then pushed him into the back of a squad car. Both deputies sat beside him, their faces like stone. Two more jumped into the front seat. The car started, its radio crackling with taut voices.

Malcolm closed his eyes. Hunched forward, he could feel the trapped hatred inside the car. *It was an accident*, he wanted to tell them, but could not speak.

Opening his eyes as the car finally slowed, Malcolm saw the featureless rectangle of the Cade County jail, its metal fence topped by barbed wire. Every window was illuminated, and sheriff's deputies waited in front.

The two deputies in back pulled him from the car, pushing him through a gate, down a cement path flanked by more armed men, through the door to the jail.

Malcolm had never been inside. He stepped like an automaton across a bare tile floor, deputies gripping both arms, and was swallowed by a process that separated him from everything he had known.

Uniformed men prodded him to recite his name, address, the birthday he'd celebrated with his mother and grandmother a few months before. Then they booked him; took his fingerprints and his picture; bagged his wallet, cell phone, and keys; swabbed his hands for soot and blood. Sticking a needle in his arm, they watched his blood flow through a tube into a plastic bag. Then they stripped off his clothes, gave him the orange jumpsuit of a convict, took him to a windowless room, sat him alone at a long Formica table, and closed the door.

Alone, Malcolm struggled to comprehend what was happening to him. He had drunk too much beer, and his gun had blown a jagged hole in a white man's forehead. Now he was here.

For some indeterminate time, he stared at the table. Then two keen-eyed white men in nondescript suits entered the room, introducing themselves as special agents of the Georgia Bureau of Investigation.

They were a different species, Malcolm realized.

He forced himself to focus. Calmly, the big man wearing a blue-striped tie recited the daunting catechism Malcolm knew from crime shows: "You have the right to remain silent. Anything you say can and will be used against you in a court of law. You have the right to an attorney. If you cannot afford an attorney, one will be provided for you." Leaning forward, the man said, "Do you understand that, Malcolm?"

"Yes."

"Does anyone live with you?" the agent in a white shirt asked.

"My mother. Allie Hill."

The man paused. "Your father live hereabouts?"

"I don't have a father."

His interrogator sat back, appraising him. In an even tone, he said, "You killed a man tonight, a law enforcement officer with a wife and two kids. This is your chance to tell how that happened."

Malcolm's mouth felt like cotton. *It was an accident*, he wanted to say. *Please, you have to believe me. The man who died was looking for me because he hates my mother.*

Malcolm stopped himself. He imagined his mother waiting up for him, the way she always had. Then he remembered the warnings she had given him when he learned to drive. *Don't think cops are your friend*, she had told him, *or that you can talk yourself out of trouble. Somebody arrests you for anything, I don't care what they say to get you talking. Tell them you want to call me and want a lawyer. Anything else is too many words.*

Malcolm sat straighter. "I'm not answering any more questions, all right? I need to talk to my mother. She'll get me an attorney."

The agent closed his notebook. "We'll be letting her know soon enough."

6

Just before two a.m., a thunderstorm struck Cade County.
Waiting for Malcolm on her screened front porch, Allie could hear
the sheets of rain pummeling the ground, and the thunder that followed
jagged bolts of lightning shook the floorboards. *Even the weather here feels
primal*, she often thought.

But tonight its furious assault deepened her fear that something
terrible had reached out for Malcolm. She remembered her own fright
at such storms as a child, when her mother or father would come to her
bedroom; remembered holding the infant Malcolm before he grew to
understand that this was nature's way in Southwest Georgia. When shimmering headlights suddenly appeared from the torrential gloom at the
foot of her driveway, her heart swelled with sudden hope.

She ran to the door, ready to stifle any rebuke out of sheer gratitude
that Malcolm had come home safely. Abruptly the car stopped in the
driveway, and two shadows emerged in the pale illumination cast by
her porch light. They scrambled toward her, head and shoulders down,
hunched against the rain.

She drew back, apprehensive. "Mrs. Hill," one called out. "We're from
the Georgia Bureau of Investigation. Freedom office."

Allie hesitated, then opened the door and backed away to give them
a small space inside before blocking their path. They were both white,
she saw, wearing caps and dressed in blue windbreakers. The taller one
fished out identification from his pocket and said, "I'm Special Agent
Moss," before inclining his head toward the squat man beside him. "This
is Special Agent Tanner."

Taut, Allie did not move. "Has something happened to Malcolm?"

Gravely, Moss nodded. "He's in custody, ma'am, for killing a sheriff's
deputy during a traffic stop. He's asking for you and a lawyer."

Allie was whipsawed by conflicting emotions—her son was alive, but
in the worst kind of trouble a Black man could face. "Where is he?" she
demanded.

"County jail." The agent placed some papers in her hand, adding with
quiet authority, "This is a warrant to search his room."

She forced herself to stay calm, be the parent Malcolm needed. She
scanned the warrant, then directed, "Don't move. I've got a phone call
to make."

She looked from one man to the other, assuring their compliance.
Then she went to her bedroom and called Jabari Ford.

* * *

Standing in the doorway to Malcolm's room, Allie watched the man called Tanner put on gloves and slide her son's computer and e-reader into a plastic bag, while Moss searched his desk, drawers, and closet. The two men seemed like alien presences in a sanctuary she had always known better than to disturb—the unmade bed; the clothes strewn in a corner before Malcolm troubled himself to throw them into the washer-dryer; the orderly desk that reflected his meticulous side; the barbells he hoisted in front of the full-length mirror that, to Allie, reflected both the vanity and insecurity of an eighteen-year-old still searching for his own identity.

To Allie, it was as if these men were claiming pieces of him, passing their own skewed judgment on a boy they didn't know. The bigger one, Moss, paused to contemplate a photograph of Malcolm X on the wall, seemingly of greater interest than the picture of the nine-year-old Malcolm Hill standing with his grandfather in front of the stadium where the Atlanta Braves played; the debate citation he had won in eleventh grade; the gold-plated trophy for Athlete of the Year at Cade County High; the acceptance letter from Morehouse College she had insisted on framing, just as her parents, overcome by pride, had framed her own college acceptance letter years before. She could not yet fathom how the course of Malcolm's life, once defined by these artifacts, might have changed.

Moss turned to her. "Did he have any more guns, Mrs. Hill?"

He doesn't own a gun, Allie wanted to protest. But she already knew better than to betray what Malcolm had not told her. "Take what you've got a warrant for," she said, "nothing more. Then get out. I need to see my son."

As soon as they left, she called Sheriff Al Garrett. Then she hurried to her truck and drove through the deluge toward the county jail, face damp with rain, her headlights illuminating the glistening asphalt roads where no one else dared venture out. When she arrived, the sheriff had two deputies waiting for her. Fortifying herself for whatever would come next, she followed them inside.

* * *

Sheriff Garrett was waiting in his office. Tersely, he thanked the deputies who had brought her, then closed the door behind them.

Allie felt a moment's relief at the familiar sight of him: a tall, dark-skinned man with a big chest and shoulders, his mass made even more imposing by the erect posture of the military policeman he once had been. She had known Al Garrett nearly all her life. But now his usual impassive gaze had softened with worry, and after the briefest hesitation he reached out his arms and let Allie rest her face against his chest, his embrace at once sheltering and respectful.

After a moment, he led her to a chair, pulling up another to sit beside her. "I would've called you," he said, "but the GBI took over in minutes."

She looked at him intently. "What happened to Malcolm?"

"I don't know much. One of my deputies, George Bullock, pulled him over. Apparently, Malcolm had a gun. He told the arresting officer it was an accident."

Shaken, Allie imagined how alone Malcolm must feel. "Can I see him now?"

"Of course." The sheriff took Allie's hands in his. "I know you're going to worry for him, being locked up here. So I'm making you a promise. The GBI may be running this case, but I'm still king of this jail. No one's going to complain about whatever I do to keep your child safe." He paused for emphasis. "I've put him in a windowless cell, away from the other prisoners. There's a deputy posted at the door. He'll have a television to watch, everything reasonable to keep him from going crazy. He'll shower alone, with a deputy standing outside. If he needs to talk to me, he can tell whoever is looking after him."

In mute gratitude, Allie nodded. "If you wake up afraid for your boy in the middle of the night," Garrett continued, "just call me, and I'll see to it he calls you right back. Starting tonight, you won't have to talk to him through a plastic window. He'll be in a separate room for contact visits from friends and family, whoever he wants to see. Thirty minutes is all I can do. But at least you can put your arms around him, and he'll feel like a human being with folks who love him. I'll call Janie in the morning to tell her the same."

Allie's throat constricted. "Was Bullock a white man?"

"Yes." Garrett stood. "I need to say one last thing, Allie. He was one of my deputies, and whatever I thought about him, I've got duties to perform. A lot of things are going to happen in this case that I may not hear about right away. But any information I get that may help Malcolm, even suspicions about where to find it, I'll make sure the district attorney knows about that—no matter what."

Standing, she gave him a last swift hug, and then began preparing to see her son as a prisoner.

* * *

Malcolm was waiting in the contact room when the sheriff let his mother inside.

The door closed behind her. Even in his despair, the first sight of her made Malcolm heartsick. Despite his resistance to her seeming omnipresence in his life, more than anything he had wanted her to be proud of him. Now all he could do was try to be stoic for her sake, just as she was doing for him in the first silent moment of their new existence.

As he stood, she hugged him fiercely. "I'm here for you, baby. Whatever this turns out to be, we'll get through it."

Malcolm wished he could believe her. Silently, he put his arms around her.

They stayed like that for a time, embracing without speaking. Then she sat beside him, taking his hands, and looked deep into his eyes as if willing him to be all right. Even though she was small, to Malcolm she always had seemed bigger than she was, maybe because of the space she took up inside him. She had always been there, at least until she began traveling so much and his grandmother Janie stepped into her shoes. But in his memory she was still making him lunches, driving him to school, rooting for him at games, supervising his homework, laying down the rules, cooking so much that there were usually leftovers, even when she claimed to fear that he'd swallow the refrigerator because they'd run out of food.

Outside the house, she was still big. Everyone looked up to her. Malcolm was afraid to fail because, as near as he could tell, Allie Hill never had. She had been valedictorian of her high school and a graduate of a college that, for most folks he knew, might as well be on Mars. He had long since stopped counting how many people her age or older told him that his mother was the smartest person they'd ever known, unless they were saying she was the most determined or, with rueful affection, the most stubborn. She willed people to do what she wanted—her son included.

But in jail she seemed smaller. Her features were stiff, as if she were afraid of losing control, and she bit her lip, an uncharacteristic gesture that betrayed her rare moments of confusion. It made him feel even more vulnerable.

When finally she spoke, her tone was softer than he ever could remember. "Just take your time and tell me what happened."

In his fatigue and confusion, Malcolm did the best he could. Even the parts that would evoke disapproval or anger, the parts that had gotten him in such bad trouble—the drinking, the gun. Through all that she said nothing, showed as little as she could.

Not until he said that the dead man had mentioned her name did her expression change. Leaning forward, she said intently, "So he knew who you were."

"And you. He called you some names. I'm sure he was looking for me."

For a moment, her eyes closed. In the same quiet tone, she said, "Tell me about the shooting."

Haltingly, Malcolm recited the horrors he could barely believe, saw the sickening image of the dead man's shattered forehead, his eyes staring at nothing.

When he finished, she was quiet. But what Malcolm saw shook him to his core—tears running down her face that she made no effort to stop. Though he was sure there were times she had cried alone, his mother never permitted herself to cry anywhere he could see her. Not even on the night his grandfather died.

"I'm sorry, Mama. I'm just so sorry."

She shook her head. "My fault, baby. This thing is on me, not you." For an instant, her voice caught, and then she seemed to recover a semblance of herself. "I've got you a good lawyer, the best. You tell Jabari everything, like you did me. Then just hang on until we can get you free again."

7

As Kara slipped into the shower, Chase went downstairs to make breakfast.

He passed through the living room, modern in its carefully spaced furniture and glass tables, as well as its art—a Kandinsky, a Klee. Like his love of sailing, collecting art was an enthusiasm he seldom mentioned in public, aware that his lifetime passion for the Boston Red Sox better evinced a common touch. But this morning, as often, he stopped to admire his favorite piece: a remarkable triptych by his friend Peter Sacks, which combined paint with pieces of cloth, metal, and paper to form a sinuous collage of images so mysterious and evocative that, from whatever distance, Chase discovered new recesses of his subconscious whenever he studied it.

His kitchen, too, was bright. Through its glass doors to the outside he could see the covered slate patio from which he would contemplate the garden, often while sipping a martini on those rare nights of solitude when he got home early enough to enjoy it. At times like that, he was especially grateful for the unearned good fortune that had spared him from having to share an apartment with other congressmen who, having left home and family back in their districts, were compelled to save money by living in collegiate semisqualor with other middle-aged men in return for the privilege of serving their all-too-restive constituents.

The truth, Chase had long since come to appreciate, was that many of his colleagues were far better than the system that compelled them to work like dogs on top of courting lobbyists and countenancing the pompous pronouncements of the wealthy contributors they needed to finance their next campaign. The irony of his particular situation was that his piratical great-grandfather, Charles Bancroft, who had viewed politicians as contemptible pawns to be purchased at will, had left Chase wealthy enough to afford him the occasional pleasure of telling the old man's contemporary equivalents to go fuck themselves.

Smiling at the thought, Chase went to the kitchen and brewed a pot of the dark coffee he and Kara preferred. As he was covering a slice of toasted wheat bread with English marmalade, another favorite of hers, she materialized at the kitchen table already dressed for work. Sitting, she asked, "So when *did* you decide to run for the Senate?"

"Have I?"

"Of course," she said airily. "Last year you hired Jack Raskin, probably the best political consultant in Massachusetts, then added a whip-smart Black woman to run your communications shop, and after that a finance director with experience in fundraising at the presidential level. You don't need all that talent to win reelection in a district you'll carry this November by thirty percent. You're looking to scare Lucy Battle out of running two-plus years down the road."

Pouring her coffee, Chase asked, "So how do you like my chances?"

Kara took a bite of toast, considering the question. "Pretty good. Two years is a long time from now, but you're starting out way ahead. The speaker of the House, the most powerful female in American political history, likes you even more than she dislikes Lucy. So she gives you high-profile committee assignments that help in Massachusetts and make you a regular on CNN and MSNBC. You're strong on issues that appeal to progressives, like the environment and gun control, and you're as out front on voting rights for minorities as any member of Congress..."

"All that may be true," Chase objected mildly, "but it helps that I actually believe what I'm saying. That way I don't have to constantly remind myself what I think."

"It also helps," Kara continued, unfazed, "that you don't seem to make mistakes. Like ever. Then Lucy comes along and embraces 'defund the police.' Give her this much: It takes real conviction to embrace a slogan so dumb that it alienates both conservatives and whole chunks of the Black community. But it's one big reason you're likely to beat her."

Chase grimaced. "Lucky me, I suppose—like always. But as I suggested last night, I can't say I'm thrilled to know how many whites will vote for me because Lucy isn't one. Too many white people are all tangled up about race—they're angry about feeling subliminal guilt without knowing enough about our history to understand why. Instead they feel resentful and, in an odd way, victimized. A classic case of projection."

"No news to me. I didn't grow up in Boston for nothing. Try telling half the people in my parish what you just said to me."

"Try telling my mother. I've begun thinking that the only cure is remedial history combined with intensive group therapy, and primary voters would hate that. Way too woke."

Kara regarded him curiously. "So when did you start thinking about all this?"

"Not until Harvard really, the last part of my senior year. It's funny what you learn if you actually start listening. A good thing for a politician to remember."

At this, Kara leaned across the table and kissed him.

"What was that for?" Chase asked. "Not that I'm complaining."

"Maybe for last night. Maybe just for being a pretty good guy." She smiled. "So cheer up, Congressman. If someone made me bet my imaginary firstborn, a beautiful daughter who looks charmingly like me, I'd take you over Lucy in a heartbeat."

"You're pretty good yourself, Kara McGuire. As for me, to quote Ernest Hemingway, 'Isn't it pretty to think so?'"

"*You* can quote him," Kara rejoined. "What I learned in college is, that man couldn't write women to save his life. Once you navigate America's racial divide, maybe you can figure out why so many men are so completely obtuse. It's one problem I can think of that totally transcends race."

As occasionally with Kara, Chase suspected that the remark might be directed at one particular man, and he decided to seek asylum with MSNBC. Inclining his head toward the small TV on the kitchen counter, he inquired, "Want to turn on *Morning Joe?*

Her eyes hinted at a knowing amusement. "Sure. I don't think about politics nearly often enough."

As the picture came on, Mika Brzezinski began reading the news. It was, for Chase, a depressing summary of problems left unaddressed—a mass shooting in Illinois, a wildfire in California, the collapse of a high-rise in Orlando. "In a late-breaking story," Brzezinski went on, "the son of Georgia voting rights activist Allie Hill is in custody pending investigation of the shooting death of a sheriff's deputy in rural Georgia."

Chase's hand froze on the remote. In a film clip, a slender Black woman spoke to a packed church with passionate intensity.

"I met her once," Kara said. "When she was up here raising money."

Chase kept watching the screen. "What did you think of her?" he heard himself ask.

"She was amazing. You could just feel this absolute commitment, like she's one of those semisaints whose cause was her life."

The clip vanished, replaced by what appeared to be the yearbook photograph of a smiling young Black man. "Eighteen-year-old Malcolm Hill," Brzezinski continued, "will appear tomorrow morning before a court in Cade County, Georgia."

Kara, Chase saw, was regarding the photograph with a faintly puzzled expression. But Chase remained silent. All at once there was far too much for him to assimilate, let alone explain.

8

Allie sat with Jabari Ford in the car he had parked near the Cade County courthouse.

The skies had cleared, and the early-morning sun augured stifling heat and humidity. The scrum of media and equipment had already clustered by the front steps—reporters with handheld microphones; photographers; television cameras; sound trucks—a warning of worse to come. "Don't give them anything," Ford admonished. "Malcolm's innocent, simple as that. I need to see him before we say more."

However weary and heartsick, Allie felt better for his presence; she had worked with Jabari Ford for almost a decade now. He looked like what he had become: an exceedingly smart and mediagenic lawyer with close-cropped hair, piercing brown eyes, a smooth and handsome face more watchful than expressive, a slender frame swathed in a tailored gray suit. He understood the politics of Cade County and its neighbors, a legacy of having been born into them: He had no rough edges, and had long since adopted the guise of unwavering professionalism that he deemed best suited to wringing justice for Blacks from mixed-race juries. He was experienced in homicide cases, and while he had lost far more than he'd won—the fate of a defense lawyer in a relentlessly punitive jurisdiction—thus far he had warded off the death penalty for his clients. No doubt it helped, Allie knew, that until now all of them had killed other Blacks.

The realization jarred her yet again. Quietly, she said, "I'm so grateful you're here, Jabari."

"Sorry I have to be. But seeing how I do, there's nowhere else I want to be." He touched her wrist. "Let's get this done with, sister."

They got out and crossed the street to the courthouse, the county's pride, a modern three-story redbrick structure with a black slate roof from which jutted an octagonal clock tower. Its stately progression of steps climbed sloping landscaped grounds that reflected the preferred social history of long-dead whites: a statue of General Augustus Cade, the notably sanguinary commander who had helped drive out the Creek Indians who once lived here; a heavy brass bell preserved from the old courthouse where justice had been rendered during the days of Jim Crow; a black plaque with raised gold letters commemorating the founding of the county, as well as its principal contribution to the Confederacy—a prison camp for Union soldiers that, despite an extraordinary mortality rate caused by dysentery and disease, the lettering described as "unjustly criticized." In Cade County, Allie had learned as a child, denial had its own history.

As she and Ford reached the steps, reporters thrusting microphones like weapons called out dueling questions: "What happened, Ms. Hill?" "Did Malcolm murder Deputy Bullock?" "How will this shooting impact the Blue Georgia Movement?" Allie stared straight ahead, fighting back a seething anger at their indifference to the only person who mattered in this moment—her son.

Passing through the heavy glass doors of the courthouse, they went through security as a grim-faced sheriff's deputy sifted the contents of her purse with exaggerated care. Then they climbed two flights of stairs to a long marble corridor that ended at the oaken double doors of Judge Tilly's courtroom.

It was clean and modern, its walls bereft of ornamentation save for several oil paintings of white judges in black robes. The judge's bench loomed over two tables for the prosecution and defense, a jury box, and a sitting area for spectators. A courtroom deputy stood near the bench, and Al Garrett had stationed armed sheriff's deputies along the walls. As Ford took his place at the defense table, Allie sat behind him hearing a low expectant murmur fill the room.

Already at the prosecution's table was District Attorney Dalton Harris, a slender, unremarkably pleasant-looking man on the cusp of middle age, whose blue eyes, sandy brown hair, and languidly gracious manners betrayed his descent from one of the county's founding families, their wealth inherited at a comfortable distance from its genesis in cotton fields and slavery that the people of his class deemed too embarrassing to mention, but whose fruits endured. He was not a hater, Allie knew. But

Harris was nonetheless a danger to her son: The local aristocracy and its allies in business had survived over time by managing, and as necessary accommodating, the hardscrabble whites whose votes they needed to preserve the social order as they preferred it. Amidst the racial vortex she already felt consuming Malcolm, Allie feared where such instincts might take him.

As if summoned by her forebodings, Malcolm appeared at the back of the courtroom between two more sheriff's deputies, a white man and a Black woman. He was wearing the same orange jumpsuit as before, and he walked like a somnambulist, suspended between nightmare and the shock of awakening. But when he managed to find his mother among the spectators who stared at him with expressions of curiosity or disdain, she responded with a brief but affirming nod she hoped would fortify him for what was about to come. As Malcolm sat down beside his lawyer, Ford clasped his shoulder in reassurance—they had never met before, but Allie hoped that her friend could help Malcolm maintain the confidence he needed to endure the caged solitude of protective custody for however long it lasted.

"All rise," the courtroom deputy intoned through the babble, and Judge Albert Tilly ascended the bench in an abrupt and suffocating silence.

Settling in, the judge surveyed the courtroom with a somber, faintly proprietary expression. He was well past sixty, tall, thin, and pale, with an air of patrician weariness that, to Allie's embittered mind, evoked the daguerreotype of some desiccated Confederate pseudo statesman. However hard she had worked, Allie thought, the presence of Tilly and Harris symbolized how little her efforts had changed the justice system that would pass judgment on her son. There were no Black judges in Cade County, and Al Garrett had no power in Albert Tilly's courtroom.

"Good morning," the judge said crisply. "As a preliminary matter, I note the presence of print and broadcast media, as well as a substantial crowd outside the courthouse. It is reasonable to anticipate that public interest in this matter, and perhaps the emotions surrounding it, will increase. Accordingly, I've directed Sheriff Garrett to position deputies at the entrances to this courthouse and inside the courtroom itself. I've also sought and received his assurances that he is taking all necessary measures to protect Mr. Hill as long as he remains in custody of the county."

As if the sheriff needed your benign intervention, Allie thought—the pronouncement seemed only to deepen the tension focused on her son. Scrutinizing Malcolm, the judge said, "Please step forward, Mr. Hill."

Malcolm did so, squaring his shoulders. Unable to see his face, Allie tried to imagine her son as Tilly would perceive him. He was tall, well-muscled, and often assumed an expression of prideful defiance. She thought of the bigoted white kid he had punched out in school—with good reason, for sure, but Malcolm had grown up too ready to fight. Yet beneath that surface was the boy she knew better than anyone, grown from the sweet-smelling newborn with a full head of black hair, lying on her chest in his first moments of living as her heart swelled with gratitude that he had survived. He'd been vulnerable then—they'd both been—and so often had seemed vulnerable since. Beneath his good looks and air of studied confidence, she could feel the doubt and insecurity as he'd tried out different roles on the way stations of adolescence and the teen years that followed.

There was so much good in him, so much promise, wedded to a fundamentally gentle soul. But perhaps knowing that scared him—he seemed equally wary of enemies and the idea that he might give way. Already she was torn, wondering whether buying a gun had saved him or doomed him to imprisonment—or worse. Especially after his grandfather died, she had hurt for Malcolm, and feared for him as a young Black man coming of age in a county with a scarifying racial history, in a country that daily found ways, some deadly, to remind boys like her son that their very existence could too swiftly become tenuous.

And now, in a few fateful moments, it had happened.

The judge scanned some papers with a perfunctory eye, as though verifying what he had already seen. "Mr. Hill," he said gravely, "I have before me three warrants executed by Special Agent Walter March of the Georgia Bureau of Investigation and signed by this court. They set forth charges of malice murder, felony murder based on aggravated assault with a deadly weapon, and aggravated assault of a law enforcement officer, Deputy Sheriff George Bullock, resulting in his death."

Tilly paused, as though allowing Malcolm to absorb the full import of his words, which echoed in Allie's mind like some biblical judgment. Then Tilly asked, "Do you have counsel here this morning, Mr. Hill?"

Ford stepped forward. "He does, Your Honor," the lawyer responded with equal formality. "Jabari Ford, Cade County."

"Thank you, Mr. Ford. Please step forward so the court can give you copies of the warrants."

Ford approached the bench, taking the warrants from Tilly's hand before pausing to read them. When he looked up, Tilly asked, "Does your client understand the charges against him?"

Briefly, Ford glanced back at Malcolm. "He does, Your Honor."

To Allie, the ritual felt all the more menacing for its perfunctory bloodlessness, the preliminary grinding of the slow but relentless legal machinery set in motion to ensnare her son.

For the first time, Dalton Harris spoke up. "For the record, Your Honor, there is a significant possibility that the state will seek the death penalty against Mr. Hill. Among other factors, this matter involves the killing of a law enforcement officer in the lawful discharge of his duties."

Though Ford had prepared her for this, Allie felt herself buckle beneath the weight of Malcolm's entrapment, her own inability to protest the chasm between what her son had told her and the charges of murder that now could extinguish his life. "Deputy Bullock," Harris continued, "was killed with the defendant's own gun during a routine traffic stop. There is ample basis for believing that Mr. Hill is not only a flight risk, but a danger to this community. For that reason, he should remain in custody pending further proceedings."

The judge nodded curtly. "Very well, Mr. Harris. As you know, the state has ninety days to notify this court as to whether it will seek the death penalty and, if so, on what grounds. Otherwise, the defendant is entitled to seek bail."

"Thank you, Your Honor. On behalf of my office, I also want to assure every member of this community that we will investigate this matter fully, fairly, and impartially in order to determine what justice requires."

Allie believed not a word of these pieties. Nor, she was certain, did Malcolm's lawyer. "Do you have anything to add?" the judge asked Ford.

"Not at this time, Your Honor."

"Very well," the judge responded promptly. "That concludes today's proceedings."

"All rise," his deputy said again, and the courtroom stirred to cacophonous life.

In the tumult, Malcolm turned to face his mother. She desperately wanted to hug him, to will away all that was happening. But she could not. Instead she forced a smile that surely looked as artificial as it felt.

Once more Ford placed his hand on Malcolm's shoulder, murmuring something before the two deputies escorted him from the courtroom. Just before he disappeared, her son glanced back at his mother. *In moments,* Allie thought, *he will be staring at the walls of his windowless cell.*

She sat again, awaiting Ford. After a moment she scanned her cell phone, a reflex from the normal life that had vanished so abruptly.

There was a text from her assistant: "A Congressman Brevard wants to speak with you. What should I tell him?"

9

Like his home in Georgetown, Chase's office in the Rayburn Building reflected aspects of his life.

The bookshelf was filled with volumes he had actually read: Jill Lepore's revisionist history of America, *These Truths*; Jack Newfield's memoir of Robert Kennedy; *Stony the Road*, by Henry Louis Gates Jr.; Robert Caro's books on Lyndon Johnson; David Blight's biography of Frederick Douglass; *Caste* and the *Warmth of Other* Suns, by Isabel Wilkerson; *On Tyranny*, by Timothy Snyder; *Between the World and Me*, by Ta-Nehisi Coates; poetry by Jorie Graham and Tracy K. Smith; *Matterhorn*, a searing novel of Vietnam; and the collected works of Flaubert, a present to the fourteen-year-old Chase from his somewhat ethnocentric father. On his desk was a baseball signed by members of the 2004 Boston Red Sox, who had broken the World Series drought that had frustrated Chase from childhood through college. Though he was not above displaying photographs that evoked his proximity to power, those on his wall captured favorite moments with people he genuinely liked and admired: being sworn in by Nancy Pelosi for his first term in Congress; playing basketball with Barack Obama; laughing with Joe Biden at the Democratic convention; and, his favorite, a photograph with Ted Kennedy taken shortly after Chase became an assistant district attorney.

For Chase, contemplating these mementos helped to leaven long days spent in the increasingly embittered environment on the floor of the House, his memories of the stricken hours when an insurrectionist mob had overrun the Capitol. On entering politics, he had not quite anticipated that it would become a zero-sum game, a cage match without rules that could consume its practitioners, if not democracy itself. But this morning, Jack Raskin had come to remind him.

"This is insane," Raskin protested. "You don't cancel a speech to the Service Employees International Union one day before you're supposed to give it. A lot of the members already love Lucy, and I'm sure she'd be thrilled to step in."

Impassive, Chase gazed across the desk at the shrewd and seasoned consultant he trusted as much as the calculating subculture of Washington allowed. Generally, their meetings featured an amiable professionalism rooted in Raskin's assessment that Chase was a good horse to ride. At fifty-five, Raskin had spent three decades in politics, developing sharp elbows, keen judgment, and a deep understanding of the Darwinian media environment that menaced any politician who hoped to survive. "I despise Facebook and Twitter," Chase had told Raskin on first meeting. "They're crack cocaine for the reptile brain."

"Doesn't matter," Raskin had responded. "In the Commonwealth of Massachusetts, reptiles vote. I can help manage your social media accounts."

By the end of the meeting, Chase had decided to hire him. In the two years since, this marked their first real conflict.

"I wouldn't call it insane," Chase parried mildly "But I might go for nonoptimal. Anyhow, there's no help for it. She's a close friend from college."

"So why have I never heard about that?"

"Why would you? That was nearly twenty years ago. There are still a few corners of my life I get to keep to myself."

Raskin gave him a long, probing look. "Nothing important, I hope. By the time we'd taken inventory of your personal life, I was less titillated than exhausted. Why don't you just get married?"

Chase shrugged. "It's like I told you before. Much to my sorrow, no one has asked me."

"At last I understand why." The consultant's words crackled with frustration. "I can't count the reasons that involving yourself in this case would be criminally stupid. No matter why this kid killed a cop, depending on people's politics he'll become a predator or a victim. Either way, you'd be an interloper from Massachusetts pandering to Blacks and progressives by insinuating yourself into a politically charged case to swipe a few votes from Lucy."

"I'm not pandering to anyone, Jack, and this isn't about Lucy. It's a private matter."

"Private?" Raskin paused, as if to replenish his own store of patience. "Granted, most congressmen aren't visible outside their district—nobody else knows who they are or cares what they do. But we've spent the last two years fixing that, all so you can run for the Senate. How many times in the last six months have you been on MSNBC or CNN?"

"Often enough," Chase acknowledged. "But I think I can get in and out of Georgia without being noticed. It's not like anyone's expecting me."

Raskin shook his head in dismay. "I don't get this at all. For somebody in a business full of narcissists, you've always shown the judgment and self-discipline of an almost-normal human being. Until now. I don't know how many formerly promising politicians have ruined their lives by imagining they can make themselves invisible. You get spotted in Georgia hanging out with Mom, and the fun is just beginning."

This was too apt to quarrel with, Chase knew. Quiet, he considered what to tell a man who spent long hours nurturing his career because, at bottom, he believed that Chase Brevard had more to offer than most. "She's not just a friend, Jack. She saved my life once—literally. It's too long a story, and I've no time to tell it. Just take my word that it's so."

Raskin considered him. "All right," he said at length. "Let's stipulate that Allie Hill is not just a voting rights activist, but Florence Nightingale. She's also a smart and capable Black woman with a nationwide constituency. So what does that make you? A rich white congressman from Boston rocketing into Georgia as her personal savior by exploiting a family tragedy. If I didn't know you better, I'd say the whole thing reeks of grandiosity and condescension." His voice slowed. "Instead, other people are going to say it for me. So how do you know young Malcolm isn't a murderer?"

"How do you know that he is?" Chase shot back. "One thing I learned as a prosecutor is how easy it is for the wrong kind of cop to go off the rails."

"Not nearly as many as all the good cops who do a hard job well. That's why we've been working overtime to help people in law enforcement forget that you prosecuted one of their own." Raskin paused again, as if struggling to address something he could not quite comprehend. "I've always seen you as a classic WASP, a guy who'd rather die than emote. Clearly, this touches something pretty deep. But you know as well as I do that every right-wing demagogue who hates Black Lives Matter and nonwhites voting in droves will be trashing Allie Hill and her son on Fox and all over the internet. She'll be a radical who hates America; he'll be a cop-killing Black man. The truth won't matter.

"As much as you may want to help her, you can't—it would be like sticking your thumb in the dike. So consider your own interests, and steer clear of Georgia. Call her every day, if you want to. Issue a statement saying that Malcolm deserves a fair trial. But for Chrissake don't go down there."

It was the best advice Raskin could give, Chase knew—in terms of pure politics, close to unassailable. All at once he felt too tired to argue.

Abruptly, he stood. "Sorry, Jack. I've got a plane to catch tomorrow, and a lot to do in between." Circling the desk, Chase placed a hand on Raskin's shoulder. "Honestly, I wish I could explain this better. But I can't." Conjuring a facsimile of his usual persona, he added, "As you so often remind me, I've always been lucky. I'm going to Georgia, and then I'm going to the Senate. I'll call the president of the service employees myself."

PART TWO

Harvard

10

From the first moments that Chase Brevard encountered Allie Hill, he thought her remarkable.

It was March 2003, the day after America invaded Iraq. Perhaps five hundred Harvard students had gathered in front of the Science Center, a sprawling modernist structure that, for Chase, evoked the soulless modern architecture he had encountered on a trip with his parents to post-Soviet Moscow. The afternoon was cool and gray, and the protesters who had gathered on the plaza to hear professors and students opposed to the war wore jackets or woolen caps for warmth. Chosen by the Young Democrats to represent them, Chase came next to last.

Standing on the speakers' platform, he scanned the faces in front of him, more white than not but sprinkled with minority and foreign students. Though by now he had spoken in public often enough, this was his biggest audience by far, and the occasion made him edgy enough that he had stayed up distilling his remarks into a few hopefully persuasive paragraphs that arraigned the arrogance of America's foreign policy establishment.

But as was his tendency on such occasions, Chase could not avoid stepping outside himself to perceive an unseasoned twenty-one-year-old suspended between the seriousness of his own convictions, his need to stir an audience, and a subversive sense of his own vanity and unimportance. Even as the crowd passed around petitions and chanted slogans like "They say go, we say no, endless war has got to go," Chase felt certain that nothing that he or anyone said here would dent the consciousness of the men who had authored this war. But silence was worse, he knew, and no amount of self-awareness would diminish his desire to speak memorably and well.

At last, the professor who had organized the event called his name.

Walking to the microphone, Chase scanned the audience in silence, a device he had learned to use to command attention. Then he began with a sentence crafted to hold that attention.

"This war," he called out, "will be as murderous as it is pretextual."

"There aren't any WMDs in Iraq. We have no strategic interest there. Instead a claque of neocons in Washington think they can use this war to rearrange a region they don't remotely understand.

"Their besetting delusion," Chase continued in a contemptuous tone, "is that Iraq is the first in a series of dominoes that will produce a Middle

East full of Jeffersonian democracies who'll ship their oil from America out of gratitude for our beneficent intervention."

The scattered laughter and applause this provoked spurred Chase forward. He forced himself to speak more slowly, picking out faces in the crowd to establish a sense of intimacy.

"But Iraq isn't a domino," he told them. "It's an actual country, fragmented by religion and ethnicity. This invasion will break it up into warring factions who kill Americans and each other, destabilizing its neighbors while spawning dozens of would-be Osama bin Ladens.

"This war is not simply immoral—it's delusional. The smug and insular men who planned it sat around a conference room in Washington making up a Middle East of their imagination. They won't have to die for their fantasies of an American imperium. Others will." Chase paused, then concluded in a low voice that resonated through the microphone. "It's our job to stop them. Our obligation as Americans. We must remember the tragedy of Vietnam and say on behalf of our generation, 'Never again.'"

It was the speech he had wanted to give, as he wanted to give it. But the applause that followed, while strong enough, left Chase wondering what else he might have said.

★ ★ ★

The next speaker enlightened him.

The young Black woman was slender, almost wiry, with dark brown eyes; a mop of tight, curly hair; fine features; and a look of intense seriousness leavened, Chase soon observed, by surprising dimples that accented the sardonic smile she flashed while mocking America's leaders. Her voice, though light, carried to the edge of the crowd.

"On the day I arrived here from Georgia," she began, "the freshman class gathered in Harvard Yard. One of the first things I saw were the words engraved on Memorial Church: 'In grateful memory of the Harvard men who died in the world war we have built this church.'"

At once her voice lowered. "There is so much irony in that inscription. Since it was chiseled, too many more have died—men, women, and children—in too many wars across far more of the world than the Europe that birthed what we now know as World War I."

She stopped abruptly, gaze fixed on the crowd. "But in 2003, that toll of death is unlikely to include *any* of you.

"In announcing this latest war, our president told us: 'We will carry on the work of peace. We will defend our freedom. We will bring freedom to others. And we will prevail.'" She stood straighter, her body seeming to vibrate with passion. "How will America 'carry on the work of peace'? By bombing, incinerating, shooting, killing, and maiming thousands of Iraqi soldiers and civilians.

"How will America 'bring freedom to others'? By sending too many people to Iraq who too many in his own party try to deny the freedom to vote in America.

"How will America 'prevail'? By exporting the injustices far too many of us ignore."

Feeling this woman capture her audience, Chase wondered how far she would take them. She seemed to him utterly fearless.

"The Americans our government will send to die," she continued, "too often poor or nonwhite, the spare parts of a country that by and large won't give a damn about their deaths, or the lives of those who survive. 'Thank you for your service,' we'll as good as tell them. 'Now we don't have to think about you anymore. Even when you come back traumatized or disabled or in coffins draped with an American flag.'

"Most of you don't know them. Instead of coming to Harvard, their pathway to a better life was joining the army. So now our leaders will send them to kill or be killed for no good reason. Just like so many Black men in America get killed by police—for no good reason."

As the applause kept building, her voice cut through it, as if only telling her truth mattered. "Our soldiers aren't going to build a democracy in Iraq. We don't even have a democracy over here. Surely not in Georgia, where too many white people want to keep power all to themselves. But for sure some of my Black high school classmates will die in Iraq." Her tone, while still quiet, had the edge of bitter prophecy. "And when this war is over, their bodies will rest in a segregated cemetery, and the powers that be will put up a plaque near the courthouse with the names of the dead and forgotten.

"Until people with the power, people like those who go to school here, actually imagine the lives of people different from them, nothing's going to change. It will just get worse. Racial injustice will get worse, and politicians will keep frightening ordinary white people into being scared of people like me so they can help their rich donors keep all of us down."

Whatever envy Chase felt for this woman was overcome by admiration. Then she surprised him again—her timbre became softer, imploring. "When I came here that first day, I was in awe of what I found. So much opportunity, so much wealth, so many smart people poised for a life of success. Together, I thought, we can do so much. But first we have to share the path of opportunity with those who have yet to find it.

"Trying to stop this war is a start. But that's all it is—a beginning. We have to leave this place imagining a different America. Then, and only then, will we deserve all that good fortune has given us."

In the profound quiet that followed, she finished simply, "Thank you for listening."

She walked away, head down, ignoring the waves of applause that followed her. To Chase, she seemed to have entered a world of her own.

★ ★ ★

To Allie's surprise, the guy who'd spoken before caught her leaving the speaker's platform.

"You were great," he said. "I just wanted to tell you that."

"Thanks," she said briskly, and then decided to respect his compliment enough to be honest. "I thought you were OK too, as far as it went."

Instead of being nettled, he laughed with a marked lack of rancor. "Mind defining 'OK'? Maybe I'll learn something."

She stopped to consider him. He had brown-blonde hair, blue eyes, and symmetrical features saved from conventional good looks by a ridged nose that struck her as somehow European, offset by a movie star smile so annoyingly perfect that she resolved to ignore it. All in all, she concluded, a portrait of the privilege and ease that permeated their environment. Still, he seemed interested enough in what she had to say that she resolved to say it.

"'OK,' she answered bluntly, "means 'Americentric.' You made it sound like the biggest problem with this war is geopolitical misjudgment. It's like reading all those histories of Vietnam focused on Lyndon Johnson, this great suffering white man who spoiled his place in history. No one stops to count the dead Vietnamese."

He flashed that smile again. "So what's new?" he retorted. "The Swedes gave Kissinger the Nobel Peace Prize for being a semisuccessful war criminal. Anyhow, military intervention can be both racist and brain-dead geopolitics. So can not intervening when you should.

"Why did we let Black people get slaughtered in Rwanda? OK, maybe that's racist. But it also says that our priorities about military intervention are hopelessly warped. Instead of saving lives in Africa, we're going to get a lot of people killed by screwing up Iraq. This isn't just about who our soldiers are, but how and why we choose to use them. Unless we stop using them at all."

At this, Allie upgraded him to quick-thinking and reasonably smart. "That's fair," she conceded before turning to leave. "Next time you might throw that in."

★ ★ ★

Though she had given him little encouragement, Chase quickly decided that he liked her enough to risk embarrassing himself before he lost his chance. "Can I buy you a cup of coffee?" he hastily interjected. "I'd enjoy talking about this for a while more."

Pausing, Allie pinned him with a cynical look, as if concluding that their conversation had been a subterfuge for something else. "Thanks anyhow. But I've got a job to go to. It's this thing I do to pay for books."

At once, Chase felt chagrined and more than a little defensive. "Really, I think maybe you're misreading me."

This time a mild amusement surfaced in her eyes. More lightly, she said, "I certainly hope you get over it. I'd hate to think some random Black woman has scarred you for life. So good luck with whatever you're doing next."

Turning swiftly, Allie walked away.

11

That Saturday night, Allie resolved, would be spent like so many others—keeping ahead.

She had a term paper to write, a lead role to master for an upcoming play, and much of her Sunday would be spent working at the local bookstore, the Coop. She did not much believe in unplanned time; it was a sin, her mother had told her as a kid, to lose track of your own life, and Allie steered clear of drugs, drinking, or the pointless partying she considered the social equivalent of empty calories. Allie Hill chose her own course.

As she glanced up from her desk, her roommate, Diana, was applying makeup in the mirror. Contemplating her friend's form-fitting black dress, Allie wondered with a touch of envy what life would be like if she had the striking face and tall, sculpted body of a supermodel. But she was as she was, she reproved herself, and no doubt better off for it. The downside of being Diana was too much distraction.

"So what's up tonight?" Allie asked.

Finishing her lipstick, Diana took a last look in the mirror. "A party at the Sophocles Club. I met a guy at the library, and he asked me to come."

Allie rolled her eyes. The fraternity culture of the finals clubs put her off—the drinking that descended into license and stupidity, the ingrained sense of entitlement and freedom from consequence. "Of course he did,"

Allie responded with a trace of asperity. "He saw a woman of color who looks like a magazine cover and figured you'd improve the environment. You do realize the only Blacks will be there will be women, except maybe for some guy tending bar."

"Yeah, I get it. But it's a party, and the clubs are pretty much the only place you can find one."

"They're also the best place to find the predator of your dreams," Allie rejoined. "Maybe the Sophocles Club isn't as rapey as some, but I expect it'll do."

Tugging her dress into place, Diana adopted a tone of muted impatience. "I went to Deerfield, remember? I've known boys like this for years, and I know how to take care of myself. There's a lot of territory between not drinking, like you do, and me passing out on somebody's couch."

Quiet, Allie considered the differences between her roommate, the product of a prosperous family from Chicago, and a churchgoing Black girl from the rural South. No doubt the far more sophisticated Diana was entitled to the tolerant amusement with which she sometimes viewed Allie, but she had a restless quality that, in Allie's mind, verged on impulsivity. "OK," Allie said. "So here's what Mama Hill would tell me. Never drink from a punch bowl. Never pick up a drink you've put down somewhere and forgotten about. Don't drink too much, period. It's all a matter of avoiding the downside."

"Oh come on, Allie. God knows I love you. But you are way overthinking this. It's the last semester of our senior year, and all I'm looking for is a few hours of fun."

Allie felt herself standing. "All right, then," she announced. "I'm going with you."

Turning, Diana gave her a look of satirical alarm. "As a chaperone? Lord help me—you following me around with eyes like lasers and the look of an avenging angel? Now there's a *real* downside."

"Too bad," Allie said. "I haven't been to a finals club since sophomore year, and this may be my last chance. For a country girl from Georgia, I'm sure the exposure will be life-changing."

★ ★ ★

The Sophocles Club was an unremarkable redbrick pile a block down from Kirkland House, where they lived. Greeting them at the door with an appreciative smile, a somewhat wasted-looking guy said, "Welcome, ladies," and waved them into a dark and somewhat cavernous room with a muted crimson-and-brown-leather palette that, to Allie's eye, evoked decades of inherited entitlement.

The atmosphere, too, was pretty much what she expected: loud music, the acrid smell of marijuana, a cacophony of voices from white guys and women with a few Black females thrown in and, sure enough, a Black guy and a white woman tending bar in dress shirts and bow ties. Some celebrants were showing the first signs of alcohol- or drug-induced abandonment, and in a corner near the bar two couples hovered over a pool table as one of the guys thrust his cue at the ball like a rapier. Knowing no one in sight, Allie and Diana edged through the press of bodies in search of an open place to stand.

Suddenly a tall guy with horn-rimmed glasses; thick, wavy brown hair; and an amiable, somewhat soft-edged face materialized in front of them, his smile trained on Diana. "Hey," he said cheerfully. "Diana, right? I wasn't sure you were coming."

"Well, you invited me," Diana rejoined. "Didn't want you to feel all let down."

"Me neither. Can I get you a drink?"

To Allie, the guy acted as if she weren't even there. "Why don't we follow you?" she interposed. "See what you have."

The guy gave her a swift appraising look. "Hi. I'm Scott Warren."

"Allie Hill." Angling her head toward Diana, she added pointedly, "Diana's my roommate."

"That's great," Scott replied with minimal enthusiasm. "What can I get you two? We have to fetch the drinks—house rules."

Ignoring Allie's swift glance of admonition, Diana responded, "I'll take a margarita."

"I'm fine for now," Allie added coolly.

This time, Allie thought, Scott's quick look toward her hinted at displeasure. "Be right back," he told Diana.

Alone with Diana, Allie watched him forge his way toward the bar. "Can't remember becoming so invisible this quickly."

Diana laughed. "Maybe it's the way you looked at him. Like he'd just spilled wine on your dress."

"Don't like him, that's all."

"You don't even know him."

"Somehow it feels like I do."

She didn't need to say anything more, Allie knew. Her instinctive distrust had distanced her from Diana, and made Allie wonder whether she was too guarded, the self-appointed keeper projecting her own apprehension on a friend who didn't need or want it.

When Scott came back with a drink for Diana, offering to show them around, Allie decided to let her go.

★ ★ ★

She would stay for an hour or so, Allie told herself, looking for Diana every now and then. Then she could return to her room.

Time passed as it often did for her in a place she didn't want to be—making small talk with a couple of guys in which her own efforts came back to her from some uncomfortable space between awkward and banal, increasing her own sense of aloneness. But the next guy looked somehow familiar.

"Hello, Allie Hill."

She gave him a brief look of puzzlement. "I'm Chase Brevard," he added helpfully. "The guy you blew off at the speakers' platform before blowing me off in person."

Of course he's a member, Allie thought at once. He's an attractive guy, probably well-off, who had probably entered Harvard with an easy entrée to a club that no doubt included people he'd known before college, affording him a preordained landing spot that offered a social life spent among his peers, some with a bent toward politics, the undergraduate milieu of Roosevelts and Kennedys. But, as before, Chase Brevard seemed nice enough.

"Was I really that bad?" she inquired with minimal remorse.

"No worse than the average near-death experience. But after a week, I could smile again. That was when my roommates knew that I'd live."

She mustered a smile of her own, glancing around in an unsuccessful search for Diana. "Speaking of roommates, I've mislaid mine. Have you seen a tall Black woman who looks kind of like Iman? I want to tell her I'm taking off."

"Nope. But she shouldn't be hard to spot in this crowd. Why don't we look around?"

Together, they worked their way through the crush, discovering among partygoers just having fun those exhibiting various states of inebriation—a chubby guy who stumbled into Chase without seeming to notice, another guy in an overstuffed armchair staring up at the ceiling in a seemingly profound state of rapture, still another hitting piano keys at random with a look of moronic concentration, a man and woman whose eye contact was so intense, it verged on the comedic. "Ever feel like an anthropologist?" Chase asked. "Why go to New Guinea?"

Allie kept surveying the room. "I don't think she's here."

Chase gave her a curious look. "Was she with anyone?"

"A guy named Scott. Horn-rimmed glasses, thick brown hair with these kind of flying wings on each side. I can't see him either."

Chase's eyes seemed to narrow a bit. After a moment, he said, "No harm in looking upstairs."

Something in his tone was different, Allie thought. "All right," she agreed, and they began working their way through the crush toward the bottom of a spiral staircase.

★ ★ ★

On the way up the stairs, they encountered a somewhat disheveled-looking couple leaning on the banister, staring down at the room as if they had just discovered there was a party going on. Looking back from the head of the stairs, Allie still saw no trace of Diana. The hallway they entered had several closed doors.

At once, Allie sensed trouble. "Help me find her," she demanded.

Chase hesitated, then went to the second door and knocked.

"Go away," a thick voice called out. To Allie, it sounded like Scott.

Chase opened the door. Inside was a couch and a bed. Half-conscious, Diana lay in the bed, her dress pulled up. She was naked below the waist, her legs spread open as Scott took pictures with his cell phone. He wheeled toward Chase. "What the fuck…"

Crossing the room, Chase seized him by the throat with both hands, using his weight to slam Scott's head against the wall. It struck with a hollow thud, knocking Scott's glasses askew as his phone hit the floor. Chase stared into Scott's dazed eyes, their faces inches apart. Then he loosened his grip on Scott's throat, pressing one hand against his chest, the other beneath his chin, wrenching his neck at an angle that caused Scott to yelp.

Allie rushed to Diana. Her friend's eyes fluttered, and she seemed to comprehend nothing. Glancing at the floor, Allie found Diana's underwear and shiny black dress shoes.

She heard a second thud, the sound of Scott's head against the wall. She dressed Diana, then gently lifted her by the waist so that her friend sat up, her head resting on Allie's chest. Over her shoulder, she snapped at Chase, "Help me, all right? She needs to get on her feet."

Turning, she saw Chase grip a dazed-looking Scott by the shirt, wrenching him sideways before dropping him to the floor. Scott stared up at him, seemingly caught between incomprehension and fear. In a hoarse undertone, Chase told him, "Don't fucking move."

Allie could hear the sound of his breathing. Chase shattered the cell phone with his boot, then sat beside Allie on the side of the bed. Neither looked at the other.

After a moment, Diana's eyes focused on Allie. "Can you help us get you home?" Allie asked.

Mute, Diana nodded. Hands around Diana's waist, Chase lifted her up, and then he and Allie each put an arm around her shoulders. "Easy," Allie instructed. "Just take a step."

Diana took one, then took another, a little steadier than the first. It was like teaching someone to walk, Allie thought. "Help me get her out of here," she told Chase. It was not a request.

★ ★ ★

They guided her down the stairway, then through the main room. Some of the people closest stopped to stare; several men or women offered to help. As a path cleared, Allie and Chase steered Diana to the door and out onto the sidewalk. They stopped for an instant, and then began laboring in the crisp night air, Diana between them, to the door of Kirkland House.

"Our room is upstairs," Allie said tersely.

Silent, Chase helped her get Diana through the door, up the stairs, and into her room. Together they laid her on the bed. As Allie went to the bathroom to dampen a washcloth with cold water, Chase sat with Diana, watching the shallow rhythm of her breaths.

Returning, Allie ran the cloth across Diana's forehead. Closing her eyes for a moment, Diana murmured feebly, "Thank you."

Bending, Allie kissed the top of her head. "*De nada.*"

Another roommate had come in, Chase saw, a short, roundish woman who studied Diana with large, worried eyes. "What happened?" she asked Allie.

Glancing up at her, Allie turned back to look at Diana, their eyes meeting in silent communication. "One margarita too many," Allie said over her shoulder. "It just snuck up on her."

"Is there anything I can do?"

"Maybe look after her for a minute."

For the first time in a while, Allie turned to Chase. "Let's go downstairs."

Silent, he followed her to the alcove.

They faced each other beneath a dim overhead light. "You knew," Allie said angrily.

Shamed, Chase forced himself to continue meeting her eyes. "Enough to guess. I think we need to talk about this."

"Why? Because you're embarrassed?"

"Because we both saw what happened."

After a moment, Allie nodded. "All right," she answered. "For Diana's sake."

12

For a time they silently walked in the light and shadow that illuminated the campus at night, coats buttoned against the chill, sorting through their separate thoughts. After a few minutes they reached the grassy expanse of Harvard Yard, so shrouded in trees that even the afternoon sun brightened only a few asymmetrical swaths of grass. Now it was as dark as Allie's mood.

Absorbing how angry yet shaken she was, she glumly recalled her more impressionable eighteen-year-old self, arriving for her first day on a campus she had never before seen. With its shaded lawns, meandering walks, and redbrick structures aged by time, Harvard Yard had seemed lifted from some college in a movie. On one side was the white-spired grace of Memorial Church, whose inscription became a passage in the speech she had given the day she met the stranger walking beside her; on the other was the steep rise of steps and stone pillars fronting the Widener Library, the formerly awe-inspiring repository of learning turned pickup spot where Diana had encountered Scott Warren only hours before. Without speaking, Allie walked toward the library and sat on the steps until Chase sat beside her.

Staring straight ahead, she said, "What was it you wanted to say?"

"First? That I'm sorry."

"Why? Because someone finally put a face to what you'd known all along?"

He hunched forward, hands folded, considering his answer. "I suppose, if you want to put it that way. I could see how worried you were for your friend."

She angled her head to look at him. "Too bad that didn't bother you before."

He turned to her, as though in search of understanding. "It's more like you know something, but you don't. Does that make any sense?"

Allie felt outrage give way to weary impatience. "To you, probably. That's pretty much how a lot of white people think about what Blacks deal with their whole life. They kind of know something but don't want to. Why inconvenience yourself?"

"Is that what I did? Inconvenience myself?" Pausing, Chase seemed to curb his own emotions. "As to Scott, all I'd heard was rumors about his so-called interest in photography. I didn't like him and wasn't interested in the particulars.

"Maybe I should've been—he seemed pervy enough to try spiking drinks. But when you told me about him and Diana, and we couldn't find either of them, the pieces started coming together. I didn't want to just assume that she was OK." His voice lowered, striking a note of fatalism. "That's the simple truth. You can make of me whatever you like."

Allie pondered this. It probably was the truth, she thought—at least as honest an accounting as he knew how to give. "About tonight," she finally told him, "as bad as it was, it could have been worse. I wouldn't have known where to go."

"I'm not looking for a medal," he answered. "If Diana decides to go to the dean of students, I'll go with you. When it comes to this kind of thing, two witnesses really are better than one."

"You'd do that."

"Yeah, I'd do that."

"What about all your friends?"

"At the club, you mean? I doubt I'm going back there, except to tell the guys who run it about Scott." His tone assumed the faintest trace of irony, directed at himself. "After tonight, the Sophocles Club just isn't feeling like a place where a good Young Democrat should want to hang out."

To Allie, the last phrase contained layers of complexity, a fusion of self-interest and self-awareness that suggested he was more clear-eyed about himself—for better or worse—than she had credited. "You don't believe Diana will go to the dean, do you?"

"No," he acknowledged. "Not really. But you're the one who knows her."

Allie shook her head dismissively. "All three of us know all that matters. This place looks after itself, not its students. It's like *Lord of the Flies* with better landscaping. How many suicides have there been since we got here?"

Chase cocked his head. "Five or six?"

"I'd guess more. How about sexual assaults?"

"Until tonight? I know a couple of women who say there were assaulted but never reported it."

"No big surprise," Allie said with muted disgust. "I know a lot more than a couple, and they didn't turn in the guy because they already knew the school would dance around it. How many guys have you heard about getting thrown out of Harvard for rape?"

"None."

"Diana knows that too. By tomorrow she'll be saying that her memory is foggy, and that she's only six weeks from graduation. All she'll want is to grab her diploma without any more embarrassment than what she's already blaming herself for." Allie paused to study him. "But you already knew *that*, too. Just like you already knew that this whole conversation was pointless."

"Not unless you want it to be," Chase retorted sharply. "Because you and I are having it. Would it be better if we never talked about this? Not for me, and not for you unless you want to go deeper into your shell." He regarded her intently. "So tell me something. You came to that party pretty sure that Diana was heading for trouble. You turned out to be right, but to me it felt more personal than that."

Surprised, Allie suddenly felt off-balance. "Was that a question?"

"If you let it be. I certainly wouldn't want to presume on our friendship."

Beneath the deflective remark, Allie detected something more. "It is personal," she finally answered. "Part, anyhow. But Lord knows why you and I need to talk about that."

"Maybe because you need to talk to someone, and whatever I think doesn't matter enough to keep it bottled up. But you should know this much—when it comes to other people's stories, I don't go around repeating them. Because they're not mine to tell." Pausing, Chase looked into her eyes. "I know I'm not on your list of great human beings. Fair enough. But I respect you enough to listen."

"Makes all the difference," she replied with a sardonic edge, and turned to gaze through the trees at the roofline of Memorial Church. "OK," she finally said. "If it matters that much to you."

He was smart enough to remain silent, Allie realized as she contemplated whatever she might choose to say.

"It was freshman year," she finally told him, "a few weeks after I got here. I went to a final club with a bunch of girls, mostly Black, wearing short, kind of skimpy dresses so they'd let us through the door. I wanted to be more like the others, not some girl from nowhere Georgia who'd never been anywhere else." Her voice turned brittle. "So I let myself get pressured into drinking too much wine despite all of Mama's teachings, and ended up trapped in the bathroom with some guy who wouldn't let me out until I gave him what he wanted. He didn't even know my name."

She felt, rather than saw, Chase restrain himself from asking the obvious question. "I was lucky," she continued without inflection. "Instead of giving in, I started screaming. When he finally let me out, I ran all the way to the dorm and sat on the edge of the bed, just shaking. I felt so stupid, and so alone.

"Ever since then I've barely touched alcohol. I still haven't used drugs or even smoked weed. I try never to go places where I don't have some control over what happens to me." Finally, she faced him again. "I learned that you can pay for trusting people you don't know, no matter how they seem. Diana didn't really get that until tonight."

Chase gave her a look that seemed to combine empathy and curiosity. "Did you ever tell her that story?"

"No."

They fell back into silence. After a moment, Allie recalled why they were talking in the first place. Standing, she said, "I need to check on Diana."

"Sure." Briefly, Chase touched her arm. "Just give me a few seconds more than you did on the speakers' platform."

Impatient, she squinted at her watch. "Go. I'm counting."

"I'd like to see you again." Hastily, he added, "Look, I know my timing couldn't be worse. But the last time it was no good either. If I don't try now, it feels like I'll regret that."

Despite herself, Allie felt the faintest pulse of interest in whatever he might say next. "For how long?"

"Decades, at least. Buying you dinner would give me a chance to do better. You like Chinese?"

"I do. But it's an acquired taste. We've got no Chinese restaurants in Cade County, Georgia."

"So why not extend your field research?"

She hesitated, unable to sort out her feelings. "OK," she finally responded. "The first prize for unwarranted persistence in totally inappropriate circumstances is one dinner with Alexandria Hill."

"Alexandria? Really?"

"Really. My mom thought it sounded elegant enough for her daughter." Allie looked at her watch again. "Time's up. Walk me back to Kirkland, OK?"

13

The Hong Kong was an unpretentious place with a brightly illuminated yellow sign and a banner that read "Chinese Restaurant." "Truth in advertising," Chase remarked to Allie. "In case there's any doubt."

There wasn't. The dining room had nondescript leather chairs and brown wooden tables, and its walls featured Chinese characters and depictions of classically dressed Chinese men and women in contemplative poses. Chase and Allie sat by the window, occasionally glancing at the street traffic on Massachusetts Avenue.

"How's Diana?" he asked.

Allie frowned. "OK, I guess. Quieter, though she doesn't really talk about it." Meeting his eyes, she added, "I told her about what happened to me."

"Did it help?"

"Maybe. Afterwards, she just hugged me. I just kept thinking about all the women who don't feel like they can say what happened to them, even to each other. It makes me sad, and it makes me angry."

Absently, Chase rearranged his chopsticks. "For whatever it's worth, I've been thinking about that night a lot, and everything that went into it. It makes me angry at myself."

The young Chinese waitress brought menus. "Anything look good to you?" he asked.

"For sure the soy sauce chicken," she answered. "How about shrimp with lobster sauce?"

Chase ordered both and, after Allie made a dubious face, ordered calamari with scallions. Pointing out a list of exotic cocktails, he asked, "Something to drink?"

"I don't drink much, remember?"

"Of course I do. But this is a special occasion."

"What would that be?"

"We're having dinner. So what about having a Pineapple Passion?"

Allie rolled her eyes. "You can't be serious. What do they put in that?"

"Rum, whiskey, and juice from nectars. No extra ingredients, promise."

"Not funny."

"No, it wasn't. Sorry."

Mollified, she hesitated. "All right, I'll take a sip, and you drink the rest. You can be impassioned all by yourself."

"Not very rewarding." He looked at her. "Seriously, thanks for coming out with me. I was worried you'd change your mind."

"You had good reason. It must've occurred to you that we're as different as two people can be."

"In some obvious ways, sure. Still, we're both here. That gives us four years in common."

She shook her head in demurral. "Your Harvard and mine are not the same place. Start with root causes—parents and family. You get to go first. Except you can skip all those bankers. I already know about them."

Seeing Chase register that she had been curious enough to research his background, Allie regretted her last remark. But he responded easily enough. "My dad, then. A true rags-to-riches story. When he met my mother, he was a beginning professor of literature at the Sorbonne, hanging on to the bottom rungs of academia in what sounds like semi-genteel poverty. She was living in the Latin Quarter, pretending to be a free spirit on the family dime."

"How did that work out?"

"OK, I guess. When my father isn't being arrogant in the distinctively supercilious manner of French intellectuals, he can be outright charming, and from what I can put together she was busy acting more liberal and less entitled than she was." He smiled at this. "A mutual case of mistaken identity. You're having dinner with the result."

They sounded so different from her parents, Allie thought—not simply the privilege but the texture of the relationship. By comparison, her mother and father were grounded in the same place, and knew each other to the marrow. "Are they happy?" Allie asked.

Chase shrugged. "I'm not sure I can tell you. They're not very demonstrative or big on self-revelation. But they're both smart and sophisticated, with cultural interests in common, so it seems to have worked out well enough. He's a tenured professor at Boston College, and she runs a couple of art galleries when she's not raising money for Democratic politicians. Plus she's close to the Clintons, and I'm pretty sure she's angling to become ambassador to France in the Hillary administration. A long way from the Latin Quarter."

The waitress brought their Pineapple Passion. Sipping it, Allie thought once again that he was more self-reflective then she might have expected. But she also detected that for all of his ease, there was something withheld about him, perhaps reflecting what struck her as his family's arid emotional life. "So tell me about your parents," he requested. "My own research came up short."

How to explain, she wondered, when what seemed so obvious to everyone who knew Wilson and Janie Hill would be so foreign to him.

But his curiosity made her decide to try. "It would help," she began, "to understand where they came from."

★ ★ ★

Listening, Chase watched her from across the table. She had jet-black curly hair; tawny skin; small, sharp features; and the dimples that made her infrequent smiles all the more surprising. A range of movements and expressions animated her speech—head tilted in inquiry; shrugs that could imply amusement, resignation, or indifference; eyebrows raised to signal doubt or disbelief. Some of this, he supposed, was culture—whereas his French father was given to emphatic gestures and grimaces that suggested disgust or dismissal, his mother's affect, like his own, was more languid and cool. But much of Allie's energy seemed personal to her, betraying a coiled intensity more pronounced than in anyone else he knew.

But what held him most were her eyes: They could flash anger, amusement, skepticism, interest, or curiosity, all in split seconds, accented by a widening or narrowing that could signal annoyance, attentiveness, or incipient laughter. He found every facet arresting.

As if registering this, she said, "OK, start with how I look. I'm no Diana, but there's a whole history there. Back a couple of generations, one of my grandfathers was what they call a Redbone, a mix of Black and Chehaw Indian that came out a little in me. Some Black folks said Grandpa wasn't a true Black, but what else would he be for white people but that? Even the ones named Hill a few counties over, the white part of our family tree left over from slave days."

This piqued his curiosity. "What do you know about them?"

"Enough," she answered with marked indifference. "Seems like some of the white Hills rebounded from the Civil War to become lawyers, bankers, doctors, and local politicians scattered across South Georgia. I've got no interest in them, any more than most would have about me if they even knew I existed. The idea of some DNA-inspired family communion spent with oblivious or well-intentioned white people just seems tiresome to me. As far as I'm concerned, enslavement and nonconsensual sex don't inspire a whole lot of family feeling."

To Chase, her matter-of-fact bluntness carried the edge of sardonic humor. "Can't imagine why."

"I don't think you can, actually. Down home, some sharp-tongued Black people call my complexion 'rape color.' But that's just a part of it. After the Civil War, three generations of us went through peonage, Jim Crow laws, segregation, enforced illiteracy, and the constant fear of lynching. In our family annals *that* was a real thing, a story passed down about someone's great-uncle who white people lynched after church one Sunday for something he supposedly did that no one can remember. Then they photographed him hanging from a moss-covered tree before they doused his body in kerosene and lit him with a torch. Growing up, I always wondered whether some white Hill or another was part of the mob."

There was nothing, Chase found, he could say to that. "So how did your family get from there to Harvard?"

To his surprise, her eyes glinted with humor. "Dead people sent me."

"You inherited money?"

The dimples flashed again. "And you say we're not different. Your family got rich helping other white people get richer by investing or buying and selling big companies. Know who made my family the nearest thing to Black aristocracy Cade County allows? Dead Black folks."

Belatedly, Chase got it. "They're in the funeral business."

"Great-grandfather Hill," she answered, "became the John D. Rockefeller of the deceased, owner of the biggest Black funeral home in South Georgia. The only way Blacks could build wealth was embalming other Black people before laying them out in the nicest casket their family could afford. I still remember my grandfather saying, 'No matter what else these racists try do to us, death is an equal opportunity activity, and there is no way on earth to stop Black folks from dying.'

"Funeral directors became the people Blacks in rural Georgia looked up to, the ones who helped preachers ease the pain of death. That gave them influence, a network of friends, superficial deference from white politicians who wanted to use them to keep lesser Blacks in line." Allie took another sip of their cocktail. "Anyhow, sometime in the 1950s my family stopped playing their game. Especially my grandmother, then my mother—they were the first women in the family anyone could afford to educate, and to some people's surprise they got educated right out of docility. To borrow a phrase, you're having dinner with the result."

As if on cue, their waitress brought heaping plates of Chinese food. "I'm still not sure about the calamari," Allie remarked once the young woman had departed. "Some might call that squid."

"By whatever name, it tastes good—honestly. The least you can do is give it a try."

"You keep saying that. Seems like that's how you got me here."

Chase gave her an exaggerated version of his very best smile. "Yeah, I'm clever that way. Just take one bite of the apple, little girl."

She shot him a look. Then she picked up her chopsticks and took her first bite of calamari. "It'll do," she told him. "I'm hungrier than I thought."

★ ★ ★

Toward the end of dinner, Allie let him order a second Pineapple Passion, conditioned on his promise to drink most of it himself. "So tell me more about your parents," he prodded.

Allie took a last piece of calamari. "They're good, and as far as I know always have been. On the surface, Dad and Mom are pretty different—he's a big Black man, kind of quiet, and she's where the Redbone comes from, this small quick-moving woman who sometimes has too much to say. But people always told me they were destined for each other. Their families were close, and they were around each other before either of them had learned to walk. The only time they were apart was when my dad went to Vietnam. Mom prayed for him every day, she remembers, knowing all the other boys from the county who never came back."

Chase thought about her speech again. "Does he ever talk about the war?"

"Not a lot. But he came back a whole lot more political, my mom says. She's the activist—the one who registers voters and got a street renamed after Martin Luther King by organizing a boycott until the city council gave in. But there's nothing she does that he doesn't support, and there's no couple in the world I respect more than them."

Her words, though matter-of-fact, were immutable. He wondered how it felt to be so bonded to parents. "What were they like growing up?"

Allie paused to reflect on some memory. "I didn't grow up in any Montessori school. They had rules, and that was that—no hats on inside the house, mind your manners, do your homework, keep your room neat, respect your elders. But at the dinner table my parents encouraged me to say what I thought, and expected me to defend my opinions." She took another sip. "Both of my folks had a lot of them, especially my mother about the rights due Black people and women and what we had to accomplish. We weren't just a family off on our own. We were part of a community, including the folks in our church and a core group of friends they'd come up with. What happened to any one of them happened to us all."

Chase took another sip of their drink. "That kind of cohesion is pretty hard for me to imagine. It's not that my parents didn't have friends; it's more like they saw them by appointment, at a restaurant or dinner parties."

"Did they know *your* friends?"

"A few, especially the ones I'd bring home from prep school. They'd take us out to dinner at some nice place and find out something about whoever it was. Beyond that I don't remember them asking much about friends."

She tilted her head, thoughtful. "I don't know why, but that sounds kind of sad."

"Actually, I thought it was pretty convenient. I liked living in a space of my own."

Allie pondered this. "All that solitude just seems funny to me. When I was in junior high, my mom took a special interest in a friend of mine whose mom had to work two jobs. Susanna was with us for more dinners than not. Not just her. I remember people always coming in and out of the house."

"Any white people?"

"At our table? I don't remember any. My parents' friends were Black, my friends were Black, and their friends were Black. That was the way of Cade County." Allie leaned forward a little. "I don't want you to misunderstand me. I've made some white friends here who I like a lot. But when you're from a place where the people who run things want to exclude you, maybe even hate you, you take care of each other, do business with each other, go to church with each other. You try to lift each other up. There's no way you can understand that, and I don't expect you to."

Chase found himself bridling at this. "You make it sound impossible."

"Not impossible, just hard. Every Black guy I know has had encounters with police, including some bad ones. But someone like you can go through life believing that cops are your friend, and that the justice system is fair. Because as far as you know, it is."

Briefly, she touched his wrist. "I'm not trying to put you down. I'm just stating the obvious. The world around you has never been threatening, or hated you for who you were born to be. That's not my reality. Caring about my community in Georgia is part of who I am, because my community always cared about me. I've never felt like I had no obligations to anyone but me."

For a moment, Chase looked at the pedestrians passing by the window, unknown people heading for unknown places. "I've always felt like a free agent," he acknowledged. "At least in terms of what to do with my life."

"Not surprising, and that's great for you—seriously. So what *will* you do?"

Though Chase had considered the question many times before, for the first time he appreciated his blessed lack of urgency, his inherent confidence that things would turn out as he ultimately chose. "I guess I've always taken for granted that I'd stay in Massachusetts, maybe go into politics. My mother is wired into the Democratic Party, and whatever you make of them, my roots are right here." Pausing, he laughed at himself. "Here I've been thinking that where you come from sounds incredibly insular, a place without a single Chinese restaurant. But I was raised in Boston, chose a prep school just outside town, went to college all the way across the Charles River, and next fall I'm going to law school a ten-minute walk from where we are now. I guess that makes me the walking definition of provincial."

"I'd call that the walking definition of comfortable. So don't let me spoil it for you."

Abruptly, Chase realized that for the last hour or so he had felt a heightened appreciation of being alive, and in the company of this particular woman. "I'll try not to. What about you?"

"No confusion there. I'm going back to Cade County, to work with a group that does voting rights and criminal justice reform. The general idea is making Georgia a better place for Black people to live. I expect that will keep me busy for a while—like, the whole rest of my life."

Despite himself, Chase felt a disappointment he had no basis for feeling. "I guess we don't have a whole lot of time."

She gave him a quizzical look. "Time for what?"

How to answer? he wondered. "Maybe we can start with a walk after dinner."

14

The night was balmy, the breeze light and pleasant. "So?" he inquired. Briefly, Allie sorted through her shifting perceptions of Chase Brevard. On one level, it was easy enough to see him as a type—careless, self-confident, amused by a world in which little had ever shaken his serenity. He clearly expected people to like him and, in spite of that, Allie was finding that she did. For a moment, she had the odd, quasi-maternal hope that nothing would happen to permanently erode his pleasure in life.

But there was more to him than that, she divined. He clearly got himself well enough, and seemed to grasp at least some of the advantages that set him apart. Unlike other privileged guys she had encountered at Harvard, he seemed curious about lives different than his, and dwelt on himself relatively little. But what surprised her was realizing that she did not want their evening to stop quite yet.

"I have to go pretty soon," she told him. "I've got a play coming up, and I need to go over my lines."

"I didn't even know you acted."

"Why would you?" she answered lightly. "You don't know me, though you seem pretty set on fixing that in a single night. But OK, maybe a half hour."

Crossing Massachusetts Avenue, they walked toward Harvard Yard. "What's the play?" Chase asked.

"*Romeo and Juliet*." She looked askance at him. "Believe it or not, I'm Juliet."

"Why wouldn't I believe it? Worked well enough in *Othello*." He flashed her that smile again. "Though, come to think of it, it's easier to imagine some guy throttling you out of sheer irritation than you expiring out of love for a guy."

"That's why they call it acting."

Reaching Harvard Yard, Allie pointed out a tree. "Why don't we go over there? Kind of reminds me of sitting under the big oak tree near our farmhouse after the dishes were done, just listening to the crickets and looking up at the stars."

"Sounds nice."

"It was. But some nights I'd also imagine the ghosts of slaves who'd worked those same fields. Where I come from is still haunted by history."

They sat beside each other with their backs against the tree. She was certainly loquacious tonight, Allie reproved herself. Maybe it was the Pineapple Passion.

In the light and shadow, Chase looked around them. "This place seems to have made an impression, too. You mentioned coming here our first day at school."

"Yeah, that was a pretty big deal—being with kids from all over the world, picking out your classes and activities. But I didn't mention what rubbed the glitter off that for me."

"You had to take economics?"

"I wished. Remember that they gave everyone a folder with a bunch of information? Mine had a red dot on the cover, telling me there was some problem with my financial aid package. Instead of choosing my classes, I had to run over to the finance office." She leaned back against the tree, gazing across the lawn at the illuminated stone pillars of Widener Library. "It was a computer error. But I still remember that red dot—I'm eighteen years old, already feeling out of place, and it's like somebody assigned you a scarlet letter." She laughed at herself. "My first day in New England, and I'm already Hester Prynne. Now it's just funny to me, but right then I was downright mortified. It wasn't a good day to feel singled out."

★ ★ ★

In a quicksilver change of mood, her face clouded, as though reexperiencing how tentative she had felt, and felt with him now. Watching her, Chase concluded that Allie Hill was a complicated woman—and for him, perhaps, a special one. It was the strangest feeling—at once stimulating and disconcerting.

"A while ago," he ventured, "you said that your Harvard is different than mine. I'm curious about how."

She gazed up at the sky, collecting her thoughts. "Pretty much from the start, I realized that most of my classmates hadn't been around that many Black folks. They lived in their own segregated world, and never thought of it that way. Instead they made me even more aware of being Black. It seemed like some were intimidated just because I was Black, and that others thought I'd never have gotten into Harvard except for *being* Black. I even got used to other girls touching my hair to see how it felt…"

"Here? You have to be kidding."

"Trust me, I'm not. It got pretty annoying."

He held up his hands in mock surrender. "OK, Allie Hill. I promise never to touch your hair without asking."

"Good idea," she rejoined. "Anyhow, as a Black woman you get used to a lot of things. You stop counting the people who think they're a friend to Black people without ever stopping to listen to an actual Black person. You learn not to argue with rich whites who think they got born on third base because America's this great meritocracy. You learn which whites are flat-out racists, and which are just so blind they're not worth bothering with. Most of all you learn there are some people for whom you'll never be real."

"Who wound up being your friends?"

"I really liked one of my roommates, an Asian girl from San Francisco. But starting the next year, all my roommates were Black. That's just how things worked out here."

Chase contemplated the truth of this. "Still, it's too bad. College is where we're supposed to branch out."

"Really?" She gave him a quick, sardonic smile. "How're you doing with that? Going back after this to hang out with all your Black roommates?"

"Never had one," Chase conceded.

"Didn't think so. It always amazes me when whites wonder why Blacks hang together, and never stop to think that's exactly what *they* do. But then white people don't need to think about race at all. Blacks do." Pausing, she stretched her legs in front of her. "Once I entered this majority-white world, I felt this need to reclaim my own Blackness, the familiarity of being with other people like me.

"Even that wasn't simple. Most of the other Blacks I met came from private or boarding school, some level of comfort. I remember calling my mom just to tell her I was in English class with a genuine Nigerian prince."

"What did she say?"

"'Bring that boy home for supper.'"

"Think you could run me in as a ringer? I'm pretty good with mothers."

"Wouldn't work. I guess you're some kind of prince. But you could never pass for Nigerian."

"Sure I could. That's why they call it acting."

She mustered a look of mild reproof. "We're losing the thread of my story. Point is, I wasn't a lot of things that other Black students were. Still, being among Black women I had less to explain and, to be fair, less to understand that was foreign to me. Not just about race but class."

"Sounds like there's a class system in Cade County, Georgia."

"Sure. But Harvard is way different. The wealth among some of the white students just shocked me—classmates getting two thousand dollars a month from their parents, or ordering takeout instead of going to the cafeteria, flying to Europe for the weekend on a whim." Her voice filled with remembered bemusement. "I was so stunned, it seems almost comical. One of the girls down the hall had her own Mercedes. It's like they were all so oblivious to how crazy rich they were. No offense meant."

"None taken. My parents kept the Mercedes for themselves."

Briefly, he saw the trace of a smile. "You're not on trial here, so don't worry. The People's Committee is saving the guillotine for later. But to me that's the root cause of so many of our problems—this kind of radical self-involvement in too many people who come here, the sense that their personal wants, plans, and desires are more important than anything around them. That they can be whoever they want to be, and not bother with anyone else."

Her voice, turning softer, had the faintest touch of melancholy. "That's what I was trying to say at the end of the speech you liked.

Nothing will change until people with the power really try to imagine the lives of other folks beyond their own direct experience. I can't tell you how many times over the last four years I've imagined spending the rest of my life just trying to get people like our classmates to care a little more—and failing."

"Still, you must have chosen this place for a reason."

"I had a lot of reasons. To start, it seems like this school breeds half the people who wind up running this country, or at least big pieces of it." She gave a fractional shrug. "Can't say I'm as impressed as I thought I'd be—seems like the most successful affirmative action program in America is the one for white folks with money. No offense meant."

"None taken yet again. Though sooner or later you'll score a direct hit. Seriously, though, it's kind of dawned on me that we come from different places. I'm remarkably quick that way."

"Quick enough." She paused, as if deciding what to say next. "Still, I guess I've been dancing around the reason we're sitting here."

"Which is?"

"I'm not a fool, Chase Brevard. Your interest in me runs to the boy-girl thing. I figured out that much the first time we met."

Narrowing his eyes, Chase feigned a struggle to retrieve something from his distant past. "Now that I think about it, that's coming back to me, too. I seem to remember considering self-immolation."

She tried repressing a smile, and failed. "Poor baby."

Chase hesitated, then decided to take a chance. "I'm hardly poor, as you keep pointing out. But while we're being candid, another reason we're sitting here is that you also like me. At least enough to tolerate my hereditary flaws."

Her eyes crinkled. "You mean the insular smugness of an affluent white male, combined with a sense of entitlement so strong that you think everything will turn out the way you want it? Or was there something else?"

Gently, he placed a finger to her lips. "You're spoiling the moment."

Her eyes widened a little. "What moment?"

"This one." Leaning forward, Chase gave her a brief and decorous kiss.

She neither resisted nor returned it. He drew back, looking at her. "Tell me what you're thinking."

She hesitated. "OK, I kind of like you. At least more than I thought. I'm sure you're not all that surprised."

"Try grateful."

She shook her head in apparent dismay. "Seems like I'm the only one who knows this makes no sense at all. You just happened to stumble into me at the end of a time none of us will ever have again, and you don't want to spend it alone."

Chase rested his hands on her shoulders. "Stumble?" Chase repeated. "You underrate how hard you make it. So try this on for size. True enough, I barely know you. But I like what I know more than I've ever liked anyone. You're super smart, you're driven, and you come with a heart and a trace of poetry. Even your porcupine side is kind of appealing. For sure, you're by far the most uniquely individual woman I've ever met."

She gave him a long, skeptical once-over. "I'm not all that special. Meet my mother, and you'll figure out quick enough where I came from."

"Does she look like you?" Chase inquired. "Because if it makes you any more comfortable that you've got me pegged, I'll be as much of a guy as you like. For openers, I think you're way more attractive than your supposedly beautiful roommate on the best day she ever lived. Right now I don't even want to tell you the rest of what I'm thinking. Any better?"

She laughed softly. "Not hardly. But at least the last part's credible." To his surprise, she raised her face to his and then kissed him, a brief but firm pressure of lips. "Now walk me home, and I'll think about it. Though probably not the same way you are."

15

After that night, by unspoken agreement, Allie and Chase began spending time together. With nothing left to worry about, he could take his last semester lightly. Far more driven by nature, Allie had to juggle taking classes, working at the Coop, and rehearsing for *Romeo and Juliet*. Though it was Chase who made himself available, he sensed her setting aside time for them as she could.

Sometimes he met her at the library when she had finished her studies, and they would walk together to Kirkland House. Once he took her to a Red Sox game, and was surprised by the knowledge she had gained from hanging out with her father as they watched his beloved Atlanta Braves. On a few sunny afternoons they sat against the oak tree in Harvard Yard that he came to think of as their spot. In its shade, they would read together in companionable silence, or Chase would listen as she ran her lines.

"When did you decide you liked this?" he asked one afternoon.

She put down her paperback *Romeo and Juliet.* "I did some acting in high school and surprised myself. When I came here, I began taking acting lessons at the ART. So now I'm Black Juliet in a racially conscious Shakespeare." She gave him a wry look. "Don't know that I believe any of it, but you might like it. A bunch of Black and white folks killing each other in dress clothes so they can realize the futility of racism."

"Yeah, that appeals to my sentimental side. Like the last fifteen minutes of *Schindler's List.* Still, you seem to enjoy doing it."

Allie paused to consider that. "'Enjoy' isn't quite right. It's more like a complete escape—you forget yourself and become somebody else. At the end I feel lighter, somehow, with this kind of exhilaration."

"That goes away pretty quick. But what stays with you is feeling more confident about putting yourself out there."

"You weren't already? At that rally you were as good as anyone I've seen in person—totally in command."

"That's why they call it acting," she answered with a smile, and then her expression became serious. "That was a performance, too, just covering up how scared I was. I was speaking my own lines, things I really believe. But the whole time I felt like this alternate Allie Hill—the person I need to become in public to accomplish the things I want to."

"You'll get there, Allie. Believe it."

To his surprise, she kissed him. "Nice that you do, anyhow."

Afterward, he thought about the moment. The kiss meant something, he felt sure, and so did the conversation that had led to it. But all Chase could do, as best he could, was that which in Allie's mind made a person whole—try to imagine someone else's life.

★ ★ ★

Settling into his seat at the ART, Chase wondered what to expect.

He had never liked the play. He thought the premise too contrived, the central characters unbelievable, their romance too precipitous and insipid to inspire sympathy. He preferred the darker, more nuanced Shakespeare rooted in the psychology of its central figures: Othello, Macbeth and, to a lesser extent, Hamlet. Though he enjoyed the comedies, it was these tragedies that, for him, defined the genius of a man interested in the darker recesses of the mind long before such reflections became the stuff of seminars and cocktail parties.

Nor was the idea of racializing the feuding parties original or, in his mind, particularly persuasive or devoid of stereotyping. His mother had compelled their family to watch a tape of *West Side Story,* her favorite musical—an experience that Jean Marc Brevard, the quintessentially severe

French intellectual, had found particularly excruciating. But watching this production unfold, Chase allowed that the concept, though it struck him as overdetermined, at times enlivened Shakespeare's warhorse.

That the Capulets were Black, the Montagues white, at least helped lend the otherwise rote feud the edge of deep-dyed conflict, and some of the characterizations came with a twist that served the director's conceit. Romeo's kinsman Mercutio was a self-satisfied lout, and Juliet's cousin Tybalt had a hair-trigger pride seemingly rooted in deeper grievances. The presumptively benign white friar who dispensed the fatal potion seemed somehow untrustworthy, and a sense of societal doom hung over the proceedings, subsuming the supposed sweetness of the lovers' innocent passion for each other. Race would become their undoing.

Still, Chase had come to watch Allie and, increasingly, he felt the audience around him perking up at her appearance. After the first love scene, the severe-looking woman next to Chase whispered to her husband, "She's really exceptional."

She was.

To Chase's eye, the rest of the cast was adequate to fine. But Allie Hill was a revelation: passionate, steely in her willfulness, almost fierce in her reckless resolve to break free of the suffocating quasi apartheid grafted onto the play. Whether Allie herself believed in it had ceased to matter: As an actress, she had committed to this production, and summoned a Juliet whose attraction to Romeo seemed less an act of love than rebellion. In one sense, her portrayal altered the balance of the play: At times she made Romeo seem callow and undeserving—which, Chase acknowledged, sometimes matched his feeling in her presence.

For him, her death scene came far too quickly.

It was this dénouement, in particular, that Chase had always found unsatisfying: With jarring abruptness, Juliet discovers Romeo dead, then kills herself—a passage of about ten lines. But in roughly a minute, Allie summoned shuddering grief before stabbing herself with the ferocious conviction of a martyr to hatred and incomprehension. As she fell to the floor, staring upward at something beyond reach, the rapt quiet all around him was like a single caught breath. The sense of loss Chase felt astonished him.

The actors took their bows. Allie came last—at once a part, then all, of the audience stood applauding, whistles and bravos cutting through their collective sound. Then Allie did something surprising: Instead of simulating actressy appreciation, she grinned, dimples framing an expression of joyful surprise, at herself and at the audience. In that instant, she looked to Chase like the girl she must have been when she first came to Harvard, but whom he had heretofore only imagined. The moment moved him more than anything that had gone before.

God, he wondered to himself, *am I falling in love with this woman?*

★ ★ ★

Afterward, he waited outside the theater in the cool night air. When Allie appeared, he kissed her, for once letting it linger.

She responded in kind before, stepping back, she gave him a somewhat puzzled look. "What was that about?"

"You've already forgotten the play? I fell in love with Juliet."

"Just as long as you don't get us confused. So where are we going?"

"My place, I thought. My roommates have taken off for the weekend, and I was hoping we could celebrate with champagne and pizza."

She hesitated, just long enough to signal her misgivings. "As far as I know, I don't drink champagne. But I guess pizza's OK."

The rambling two-story house he lived in, a worn artifact of early-twentieth-century elegance, featured wood paneling, overstuffed furniture, and a long dining room table bespeaking a formality alien to four disorderly college guys. Chase ordered a pizza split between pepperoni and sausage, his preference, and tomato, mushrooms, and red peppers for Allie. Then he dimmed the lights, lit two candles, and opened a bottle of Pol Roger—his father's favorite, he explained to Allie, even though it was also the favorite of Winston Churchill, who Jean Marc Brevard insisted was a dangerous egomaniac dragooned into greatness by Adolf Hitler. "One Christmas," Chase concluded, "I suggested to him that the total collapse of the French army must have figured in there somewhere. As they say, he was not amused."

"What does amuse him?"

"My mother. Sometimes intentionally."

When the pizza arrived, Chase filled two water glasses with champagne and placed them on the dining room table. "Just for a toast."

"OK. I guess one sip won't hurt."

Gazing at Allie across the table in candlelight and shadow, Chase touched his glass to hers. "To you, Allie. For being so good, it's hard to describe."

She tasted the champagne on her tongue. "Sort of fizzy, but not sweet. I actually like it."

"My dad would be thrilled." He paused to look at her intently. "Seriously, do you have any idea what you did tonight? You had a theater full of people watching you like they were hypnotized. You must have felt that by the end. It sure looked like you did."

"Yeah," she acknowledged. "I kind of did." She took another sip of champagne, and then her tone hovered between rueful and confessional. "I loved it, all right? I had this feeling of complete elation, like translating Juliet through my own experience was this special kind of magic. Then I found myself wondering who they were seeing—an actress, or a Black woman they wanted to like for doing something different."

His own impatience surprised him, not least because he had always treated her with a certain studied caution. "Jesus Christ, Allie. Does it always have to be about that? Can't you just let people appreciate you for being fucking amazing?"

Her eyes glinted. "Easy for you to say," she snapped back. "You haven't spent the last four years walking into a room and wondering what people are thinking, and who they're seeing." Abruptly, she stopped herself. "I'm sorry. But you and I can only be who we are, and that means we've spent our lives navigating different spaces. It's unfair of me to expect you to get it, and unfair of you to expect me to forget it. So why not just say we're two pretty OK people who both do the best we can."

Finishing his glass, Chase tried to organize his thoughts. "I'm sorry, too," he said at length. "But to me that feels like surrendering to a world neither of us made. So let me try again.

"I don't know if anything about me is really OK with you—what I am, who I am, or where I come from. Maybe you think that I'm hopelessly oblivious to your experiences as a Black woman, whether from Georgia or anywhere else, and that I can never get inside you enough to be the company you need. From what little I know you may well be right, and for sure I can never tell you otherwise." He leaned forward, watching her face. "Because of that, I always feel off-balance with you, no matter how confident I may seem on the surface. But to me you're not just an OK person; you're a terrifically interesting and talented woman with a whole lot of stuff going on inside you. I feel lucky to hang out with you. As best I can manage I want to know you, really know you. But I don't know if I'll ever get the chance, and that's started making me sort of sad."

Even as he spoke, Chase realized that he was revealing things to her that he had barely realized himself. But he no longer cared. "About tonight," he hurried on, "you were completely astonishing. I felt proud of you, even though I have no right to, and I was hoping like hell that you felt proud of yourself. You looked happy, and I wanted you to have that so much it took me by surprise. I felt a whole bunch of things I can't put a name to. But here's the point—all that's about you. For sure you're a Black woman, which for whatever little it's worth to you is more than fine with me. But you're also Allie Hill. And that makes you way more special than any woman I've ever known."

In the candlelight, he could not quite read her expression. What he felt most acutely was her unwonted silence.

By instinct, he came around the table and gently lifted Allie from her chair to face him. The look in her eyes, he realized, was somehow different.

When he kissed her, her answering kiss went deep. Then she drew back, resting her face on his chest. "I guess we can reheat the pizza," she said softly.

★ ★ ★

They climbed the stairs to his bedroom.

Silent, he unbuttoned her blouse, removed her bra. The slender perfection he uncovered only made him want more, as though he would never get enough of her.

"Are you sure about this?" he asked.

"Yes."

Peeling off his sweater, Chase held her against him, kissing her neck, both of them swaying a little as they pressed closer. For all that this was the first time, for all that she so often put him on edge, he felt no anxiety or rush. To him it felt like they both knew something no one wanted to say.

Finally, he knelt, unbuckling her belt and sliding down her jeans. Stepping out of them, she did the rest herself.

He did not stand. Instead, he kissed the soft place between her legs, felt her stroke his hair as she murmured something indistinct.

Standing, he undressed, then took her hand as they walked toward his bed. In the faint glow of a nightlight, he saw she was lean yet muscled, a ballerina who moved with a dancer's grace.

He lay beside her, kissing her mouth, her nipples, her stomach before rediscovering the softest part of her with his tongue. He stayed there, the fingertips of both hands on her nipples, as he slowly drew the faintest of sounds from within her. He felt her tighten, pressing against him until, all at once, she bucked and then shivered in waves of release that, diminishing, subsided into stillness accompanied by a wordless sigh of contentment.

He raised himself, placing his torso between her legs. "OK?" he asked.

After a moment of mute hesitance, she nodded. As he slid inside her, they looked into each other's eyes as if to seek out what this meant. Then he felt her arms encircle him, and they began to move together. Chase had never felt this lost, or this much at home.

★ ★ ★

Afterward, they lay beside each other, languorous, gazing into each other's faces. Then, to her own surprise, Allie laughed aloud, a happy sound that seemed to come from deep inside her. But what struck her next was how vulnerable he looked, how different than the face he presented to the world. "Chase Brevard," she said softly. "Who knew? For sure not this girl."

"Really?"

"Really. My mom always said that it's foolish to be surprised by your own life. But tonight wasn't in any plan I knew about."

"That's because I've always been the one who sought you out. So maybe it's less of a surprise to me."

"Hard to be surprised by what's been on your mind since the first time we said a word to each other. Can't say you exactly sneaked up on me—it's more like I sneaked up on myself. So now I guess I have to give up and go on the pill."

He gave her a somewhat tentative smile. "Am I imagining things? Or are you actually suggesting some kind of commitment?"

"Some kind." She summoned a deep mock sigh. "All this time, I've been telling myself that what you wanted from us made no sense. It still doesn't. But in spite of all that, there's so much about you I really do like. I even like how careless you are, and that sometimes you make me feel that, too. Like tonight—for better or worse."

"For better. Can't you feel it?"

Suddenly Allie experienced a kind of wistfulness, as though she needed to console him for something only she knew. "Wish I could," she answered gently. "But here we are. So I guess I'm going to ride with this until we run out of time. At least I'll have something sweet to remember on those hot, muggy nights in Cade County, Georgia."

It was strange, Allie realized, to hear how sad that sounded, and how true.

16

"Martha's Vineyard?" Allie asked. "That's not exactly next door."

They were sitting with their backs against the tree in Harvard Yard, studying together on an unseasonably warm day in late April. "It's not in the Aleutians, either," Chase answered." My parents have a place there. It's beautiful, and with luck the weather in early May will be OK." Seeing her skeptical expression, he added, "You said it yourself: We don't have a lot of time. I was hoping you'd get someone to cover for you at the Coop, take a long weekend."

She raised her eyebrows. "So let me get this straight. Your parents just let you bring stray women to their summer place for a long weekend doing whatever, whenever you choose and whoever she is. If *my* mom and dad had a second home—which is ridiculous even to think about—I'd be no more welcome to take some guy there than to sleep with him on the living room couch. And if you ever ran into Janie Hill coming out of my bedroom, her first look would terrorize you so much you'd never have sex again."

Chase laughed. "When it comes to the details of my relationships, my parents have a driving lack of curiosity. Anyhow, the Vineyard is a special place to me. I've spent my summers there since I was a kid, and I'd like you to see it."

This time her expression suggested fond exasperation. "A long weekend on Fantasy Island, or any kind of weekend, won't change anything come graduation. But I guess I'd rather be with you than straightening shelves." Briefly, her eyes softened. "I should know better, and so should you. But we just keep right on doing this, don't we?"

★ ★ ★

The ferry to Martha's Vineyard was a large double-decker boat that labored across the channel between Woods Hole and the island. So that Allie could see the panorama of water and land, she and Chase sat in the outside chairs atop the ferry, wearing sweaters to cut the breeze.

The surface of the water was blue in the noonday sun, the waves glinting a silver white. Allie saw Chase's look of pleasure at leaving the "normal" world of Harvard—which to her wasn't normal in the first place—as they entered a wrinkle in time. She discovered that her cell phone didn't work.

"Welcome to the land that technology forgot," Chase told her.

They landed in Vineyard Haven, a working harbor dotted with small boats, and took a taxi to Edgartown. Entering Main Street, they passed uniformly white wooden homes with manicured gardens, some with picket fences; the Old Whaling Church, an imposing building with large pillars and a tapering white spire on top; a redbrick courthouse; and then rows of shops with modest signage.

"Where's the McDonald's?" Allie asked.

"Not allowed. You have now entered Theme Park, New England."

They ended up at a large three-story home from the nineteenth century, with a rear porch overlooking a harbor graced by sailboats, dinghies, boat tenders, and yachts of various sizes. Inside, Allie discovered, the Brevards' summer home featured a first floor with high ceilings, a formal dining room, and a commodious living room that faced the rear porch. Allie put down her roller bag to look around.

The decor was perfect, she decided—too much so. Every piece of furniture—the off-white couch and chairs, the wooden end table with Chinese vases, the glass coffee table, the white curtains that Chase drew aside to admit sunlight, the paintings of seascapes and landscapes—made the space feel more like a photograph from a magazine than a place where people lived. "I know," Chase observed. "My mother turned the whole place over to a decorator. It's like an expensive museum to someone else's taste."

Allie kept looking. "I mean, it's pretty. But it kind of makes you afraid of sitting down."

"Can't say I spend too much time in this room. Neither will we, I hope. Places to go, things to do."

"Like what?"

He kissed her. "It's like that Andrew Marvell poem. If you can't stop time, make it vanish."

★ ★ ★

In late afternoon they made leisurely love in Chase's bedroom upstairs, sunlight through the window grazing their skin. She liked feeling him get lost in her, liked his lean, athletic body, the appreciation in his green-flecked blue eyes as he looked into her face. "You really are beautiful," he told her.

"You're the beautiful one. At first it annoyed me, but now I've gotten used to it."

"Thanks for your tolerance."

She scanned the room, registering clues to the boy he had been: a trophy from sailing camp, a signed baseball, Winston Churchill's *History of the English-Speaking Peoples*, a history of the Boston Red Sox, a group photograph of his soccer team at Middlesex, a group of grinning teenagers who looked like overgrown adolescents.

"When you were a kid," she asked, "what were you like?"

"At first? I was a big daydreamer, perpetually lost in my own head. It made them both crazy, especially my dad. For a literature professor, he's unsentimental in his ruthless pursuit of reality. I don't know that he ever had a daydream in his life." He lay back, gazing at the ceiling as if at whom he once had been. "Anyhow, they'd send me upstairs to get dressed in the morning, and forty-five minutes later they'd find me staring out the window in my underwear, living in God knows what imaginary world. Even then I read a lot, and that was my King Arthur phase."

"Which knight were you?"

"Lancelot, of course. I wanted Guinevere to pine for me hopelessly. In desperation, my parents sent me to sailing camp, where the choice was between paying attention and falling overboard. It worked. Not only did I learn to love sailing, but I became insanely competitive when something matters to me. If I ever become a trial lawyer, that'll probably help."

It made sense to her, Allie thought—the romantic subordinated to the concealed drive she had begun to perceive in him, ready to call on when he decided that he needed it. She felt a kind of tenderness for the boy he no longer was, innocent of purpose or entitlement. "Sort of wish I'd known the daydreamer," she remarked. "But I guess in some ways you still are. You sure want to make things turn out the way you imagine them." She kissed him. "Tell you what. You be Lancelot, and I'll be Black Guinevere. It's been nearly an hour, and I'm tired of pining."

★ ★ ★

That evening they walked a few blocks for dinner at the Charlotte Inn, a converted home on a tree-shaded street. Entering, Allie found herself in a large anteroom with burgundy wallpaper; ornate carpets; antiques of all varieties; walls covered with paintings of landscapes, birds, or horses in gold-filigreed frames; elaborately designed curtains; and overstuffed chairs. The side dining room, where Chase had reserved a quiet table, featured burnished wood paneling, another painting of someone who looked like a nineteenth-century captain of industry, and yet more depictions of horses doing the various things horses do—racing, jumping, or just standing around.

"Is this where you come to commune with your ancestors?" she asked.

"Not unless they were horses."

"Not necessarily. There's a painting of a white guy on a horse right in my line of vision."

Chase grinned. "The Bancrofts," he informed her, "preferred dogs. Less poop, and you don't need a barn."

To start, they ordered a bottle of chardonnay. Though Allie retained her wariness of alcohol, she had taken to sharing wine with Chase—perhaps, she admitted to herself, to dull the increasingly unhappy knowledge that they were running out of time.

He raised his glass, touching it to hers. "To us, Allie Hill."

At that moment, like others, she sensed that he had grasped her thoughts. "To our weekend," she amended. "I'm enjoying it so far."

He put down the wineglass, absently touching the rim as he continued reading her face. "Why do you always qualify things, or talk like we're about to turn back into pumpkins?"

"Because we're going to turn back into the people we actually are."

"As people," he retorted, "we have free will. You've heard of that concept, I guess."

"Amazingly, yes. What does it mean to you? That I get to choose what you want me to choose?"

With a tentative air, their waitress approached, formal in a crisp white blouse and black bow tie. "Do you have any questions about the menu?"

Allie saw Chase stifle his irritation at having their conversation interrupted. "Ever had escargot?" he asked her.

She smiled a little. "You mean snails?"

"If you prefer. My dad likes them here, and as a native Parisian he's annoyingly particular."

"Speaking as a native of Cade County, Georgia," she rejoined, "snails stayed in the garden until Mama tossed them in the garbage can. She never thought they were food."

Out of the corner of her eye, Allie noticed the waitress suppressing a smile. "So consider her surprise," Chase responded, "when you tell her you ate a half-dozen. It will open up a whole new world beneath the daffodils, or whatever grows in all that heat and humidity."

Allie turned to the waitress. "I'm so lucky," she said lightly, "to have someone like this for a kind of boyfriend. It's like junior year abroad, and I never have to leave home. Please just kill them before I eat them, promise?"

They completed their order: steak for Allie, salmon for Chase. When the waitress was gone, Allie said, "Seems like we were working up to a fight. We've never really had one, so maybe we should see how it goes."

Briefly, Chase glanced around them. The restaurant was beginning to fill with men dressed like Chase, in sport coats and slacks, and women in expensive-looking dresses. "All right," he began. "You're a superstar at Harvard. You can go anywhere, be anything you want. Why go to the trouble of killing yourself to get in here if you won't even consider anything else but going back?"

At once Allie felt genuine anger. "Like Georgia doesn't deserve an overachieving Black girl like me? Or maybe it's that any overachieving Black girl who's got her priorities straight comes to Harvard so she can make it in Washington or New York."

Chase held up a hand. "I'm just saying that you have choices."

"I know that. You still don't get me—at least in this way. So let me spell it out for you. I don't want to be some fungible Black woman, making my way in the white world of law or finance, maybe being the first this or the first that. I don't deny that might do some other Black people coming up behind me some good. But there's a whole community where I come from that needs all the rights you've never had to think about, and never will. Not just voting rights, but the right to be treated like human beings by a justice system that treats them like a separate race." Her voice turned sarcastic. "Funny how that still happens.

"If I stay up north, part of me will feel like a deserter. I'm sure that doesn't make any sense to you. But that's the problem with us, and I won't make it my problem. If you don't like that, it's your problem."

He frowned. "That's not a very pleasant way to look at what I'm saying."

"'Pleasant'?" Her brief laugh combined exasperation with amusement. "What kind of word is *that*? We're having a *fight*, Chase Bancroft Brevard. It's not supposed to be pleasant."

Despite himself, he laughed somewhat ruefully. "OK. I get that. And I apologize. So let's call a truce in the hopes we can do it again. Even if I have to come to Georgia and sleep on your parents' front porch."

The escargot arrived. "Wait until you taste them," Chase assured her. "Butter and garlic put your garden-variety mollusk in a new and more attractive light."

"Chase?" a baritone voice interrupted.

Standing beside the table was a tall, broad-shouldered man with thick auburn hair and an air of importance. Rising, Chase shook his hand. "Nice to see you, Senator. Aren't you here early? My parents won't be along for a month."

"The Senate's in recess. I'm getting our boat out on the water, and Elizabeth wanted to inspect our eternal remodel. So we decided to come for the weekend."

From an adjacent table, a slender, well-maintained blonde waved to Chase before regarding Allie with pleasant curiosity. "This is Allie Hill," Chase informed the senator. "My sort-of girlfriend from Harvard."

"You clearly need to work harder." As Allie stood, the senator extended his hand. "I'm Dennis Burke."

Returning his smile, she responded, "I know. I applied for an internship in your office last summer. Nice to finally meet you."

"What happened with your application?"

"Never heard back. I never really expected to. I know you're swamped with applications."

"Still, we should do much better than that." He turned to Chase. "If you can, do me a favor. Elizabeth and I are having a dinner party tomorrow. I'd like for you both to come."

Reflexively, Chase started to answer, then glanced at Allie. "I'd be honored," she told the senator.

"Terrific." Putting an avuncular hand on Chase's shoulder, he said, "Please give our love to Caroline and Jean Marc. And tell them for me that you seem to have outrun your traumatic upbringing."

"Will do, Senator. I'm sure they'll be relieved."

"Seven o'clock then. And 'Dennis' is fine for you both. I like to remember that was my name before the citizens of New Jersey gave me a lease on a title." Turning back to Allie, Burke said, "Nice to finally meet you, Allie."

He walked off, waving over his shoulder. As they sat back down, she said, "'Chase' and 'Dennis.' And, for an evening, there's even an 'Allie.'"

"Consider it an opening. You're no longer a résumé buried in a pile of them."

She gave Chase an inquiring look. "I guess the Burkes and Brevards are good friends."

He considered the question. "I've known the senator and his wife for years. The Burkes come to our place; we go to theirs. Sometimes we sail together. As I got older and began to understand politics, I realized that my parents had raised a lot of money for his campaigns.

"The senator is an operator by trade and so, in her way, is my mother. More often than not, donors think they're a politician's friend, and maybe they are. But only the politician knows for sure."

Quiet, Allie gazed at the white tablecloth, the silver dish with circular indentations for six shells. "What is it?" Chase asked.

After a moment, she looked up at him. "Sorry. I'm just processing all the access you have to a life most people don't know exists, and the casual way you accept it. I mean, Harvard is one thing, but just now is another thing yet. So just let me take it in."

17

In the morning, Chase and Allie ventured out in sweaters and blue jeans and took coffee and bagels to the sweeping campgrounds in Oak Bluffs, a grassy field surrounded by a semicircle of brightly painted gingerbread houses oriented toward the water. Along the sunlit waterfront, Allie saw a procession of couples and joggers and parents with kids or mothers or fathers pushing strollers. Noting a woman walking beside a tall man with a toddler in cornrows squirming on his shoulder, Allie observed, "Actual Black people. First I've seen since we got here."

"Oak Bluffs has its own history," Chase answered. "The first Blacks who came here were slaves from West Africa brought here as farmworkers or to crew on whalers. Generations later, runaway slaves from the South started showing up. A hundred years or so after that, a Black would-be entrepreneur turned one of these houses into an inn for other Black people. A lot of artists and writers followed, and eventually OB became a Black bourgeois vacation spot.

"Now, like everywhere on the island, rich people are driving up the price of housing so high that cops and nurses and teachers can't afford to live here—not to mention artists and writers. It's the American way."

Allie gave him a wordless sideways look. "I get the irony," he told her. "But when the Bancrofts came in the 1950s, no one thought about that. The question is what people like us are going to do about it now. If anything."

Quiet, Allie looked out at the water. "Sometimes I can't quite place you," she said at length. "I catch myself putting you in some political box, and then you surprise me in some way or another."

"Just trying to be agreeable. I'm very pleasant that way."

Allie laughed in self-recognition. "I'm pretty hard on you, aren't I?"

"Occasionally. But I really don't mind that much. Pretty often you're just reminding me of what I try to remind myself."

"Like what?"

"That I was born lucky, and that I'm perfectly happy with that. But when it comes to politics, I don't want to be like my parents."

"I thought your mom was pretty liberal."

"When it comes to rights for nonwhites, gays, or women, I guess that's true enough. But turn to income inequality, and how things are is just the natural order for her. As for my dad, he's one of those champions of ordinary people who doesn't particularly like ordinary people. Because of my mother, I've got a way into politics—you got a sense of that last night at dinner. Again, fine with me. But I don't want to forget that I'm insulated from things most people worry about every day of their lives.

"That's part of what I like about you—you never let me forget." He turned to face her. "I don't want you to misunderstand me—you're not some great experiment in consciousness-raising. But I'm not with you just to try and fuck your brains out, even if I could. I like trying because

I like everything about you. I even think that it's started mattering to you that I become the person you think I should be."

The look he was giving her, Allie thought, was way too serious, his remarks too pointed for comfort. With a mixture of regret and trepidation, she understood how important she was becoming to him. "That's why I haven't wanted us to get too tangled up, even if I've done a pretty poor job at that. If it's any help, which it probably isn't, you've made going back to Cade County a little harder than I ever wanted it to be."

He regarded her with an expression that, to Allie, combined hope and curiosity. "Have you told your parents anything about us?"

She shook her head. "I can talk to my mother about most things. But not you. Less because you're white than because you'd seem so alien to her, someone who could hurt me without knowing or caring. But the worst is that I'm sleeping with you.

"That's not what our church says I should do, no matter how the people filling all those pews carry on six days a week. I said we're a community, and that's true. But close communities come with gossip and judgment. My mother wouldn't want that coming down on me. As for my dad, forget it. In this kind of sweet, patriarchal way, he thinks I should marry someone like him, or at least someone familiar enough that it doesn't stretch his imagination too far."

"But what about your imagination?"

For a time, Allie fell silent. "I'm finding out mine is better. Sometimes I wish it weren't."

★ ★ ★

In the early evening, Chase and Allie turned down a bumpy gravel road outside of Edgartown, passing stands of bare trees and fields of grass, stunted by winter, now barely coming into newly green life. Then he turned again, and she realized they were on a private drive winding through a large piece of grassland toward a distant house, obviously new but built in a sprawling New England style.

Scanning the property, Allie remarked, "Strange to think this is a senator's summer home."

"Not really. Dennis started a software company before he went into politics. Money makes it easier, as half his fellow senators could tell you. And no, if you're curious, I don't think that's the way it should be. But that's the way it is."

Within moments, Allie found herself sitting somewhat stiffly beside Chase, sipping mineral water in a large living room with high windows and a view across the meadow to a distant pond, its decor strangely similar in style and warmth to that in the Brevards' home. "Same decorator," Chase murmured under his breath.

But the strangest part was that she recognized, on sight or by name, most of the six strangers to whom she had been graciously introduced by Dennis and Elizabeth Burke, and who now sat around her in identical couches and chairs.

There was a well-known novelist, Warren Sparks, a robust Southerner noted most recently for a controversial first-person novel from the point of view of no less than Malcolm X, and his wife, Phylicia, a tall and somewhat grand professor of literature at Yale. Sir Philip Stern, she realized, was the scion of a prominent British banking family; his wife, Sidney Randolph, was a barrister noted for human rights work, as forbidding and opinionated as her cherubic but shrewd-looking husband was amiable.

Finally, the Barbie-doll beautiful but suspiciously unwrinkled Jessica Wright had been the innocent blonde in an ensemble situation comedy formerly popular among young people, which had left her so wealthy that she never needed to work again. The one person Allie had never heard of was Wright's equally beautiful but somewhat younger companion, Slade Horton, who apparently also was some sort of actor—assuming that he ever had to be.

Feeling awkward, Allie adopted the role of quiet observer. The characteristic the others most had in common, she concluded—including Chase—was the supreme confidence of people for whom, seemingly, the laws of economic gravity had been suspended. That could not be true, she reminded himself—it was simply that their anxieties were more rarified, and therefore less visible, than those of more earthbound humans.

The conversation turned to Warren Sparks' novel, which came with a title Allie found pretty astonishing: *I, Malcolm X.* From where she sat, this was a leap of imagination so grandiose as to verge on comedic. Beset by Sidney Randolph, who apparently felt much the same, Sparks adopted an air of magisterial patience. "The purpose of literature, Sidney, is to transcend one's own experience. How else can fiction serve as a bridge to the imagination and empathy essential to human understanding?"

The smile Randolph gave him was edged with skepticism, and her accent became so sharp that it could have cut glass. "Isn't that a bit grand for a literary parlor trick? I'm not saying you should write sixteen books about precocious white boys from Alabama, who grow up to craft novels with the uncanny propensity for becoming movies and making them rich. I'm merely suggesting that the daring of this particular concept, while brilliantly calculated to arouse controversy and sell books, way overruns your capacity to actually understand it. How in the world can you inhabit Malcolm X?"

Allie found herself suppressing her own smile at the woman's withering exactitude. Unruffled, Sparks turned from Randolph to her. "With all due respect, Sydney, you're not exactly an expert witness. I'm curious about what Allie thinks."

Taken by surprise, Allie found herself on edge, both about being called on and about becoming the designated spokeswoman by default for African Americans at large. Cornered, she said, "Wish I could be some universal Black person, sum this up in a sentence or two. But I've got my own limitations.

"So, on behalf of Allie Hill, a couple of thoughts. I know some folks get all wrapped up around 'cultural appropriation'—in this case, the idea that only Black people can write about other Black people, and that Warren should have his computer destroyed and his book turned to pulp. I just don't find him all that threatening to my sense of identity."

She looked around her, catching expressions that reflected various degrees of interest, curiosity, and, in Chase, an amusement rooted in knowing her. "No offense, Warren," she continued. "As far as I'm concerned, you can write about anything you want. But I don't much care what you write about Malcolm X. It's not relevant to anything, as far as I can see. The real man is what I care about, and I've already read his own version of *I, Malcolm X*. His autobiography."

Cutting through the undercurrent of surprise, Sidney Randolph laughed aloud. Turning to Sparks, she said, "You should have stuck with me, and quit while you were merely losing."

It was time for dinner, Elizabeth Burke announced brightly.

★ ★ ★

Somewhat abashed by her candor, Allie retreated to the role of onlooker. The animated table conversation ranged from the Iraq War—which Dennis Burke supported with reservations in the face of skepticism from everyone except Slade Horton, who said almost nothing but smiled a lot at pretty much everything—the lack of affordable housing on Martha's Vineyard, whether Dick Cheney was America's de facto president, the best methods for avoiding Lyme disease, whether future wars would be fought over water instead of oil and, finally, whether reparations were a necessary redress for racial grievances or a divisive political dead end.

"About reparations," the senator was saying. "The danger is that it becomes another political football. Democrats tiptoe around it, and Republicans use it to badger us with charges of reverse racism."

"What I can never quite get," Chase interposed, "is why so many whites feel so victimized. It's like Allie says about Harvard—look at who goes there, and you realize that the most comprehensive affirmative action program in America is still the one for white kids from prep school."

Immediately, Allie wished that he had not implicated her in this discussion. But Burke was already asking, "Care to elaborate, Allie?"

Allie summoned a smile. "Not sure. Seeing how I'm hanging out with a rich white boy from prep school."

The senator chuckled. "Seriously, though," Phylicia Sparks prodded. "Surely you have some thoughts about reparations."

Looking at the expectant faces around her, Allie resigned herself to performing. "A few. Like, it makes me crazy when people say that slavery was over 140 years ago, then turn around and wonder why Blacks aren't more like this or that group of supposedly high-achieving immigrants. How about the fact that we were America's only draftees, at least if you don't count Native Americans. We didn't have a cluster of relatives waiting in New York or Boston to give us a hand. We had auctioneers selling us off to this or that white man, who'd keep us from reading and break up our families by reselling Mom, Dad, or the kids to some other white man. We weren't like everyone else because America didn't let us be."

"I understand," Jessica Wright responded with theatrical sincerity. "But what can you do to compensate people for something that happened so long ago, or even know who to compensate? What do you do for Colin Powell?"

"Not much," Allie responded with more asperity than she intended. "He's Jamaican. But let's get off who's writing checks to whom. What about the pathology of racism running through the fabric of this entire country?" Looking around her, she felt passion overwhelm her reserves of reticence. "Ever wonder why you can drive through suburb after suburb in the north and never see a single Black face? Last semester I wrote a long term paper about that.

"The federal government practiced redlining—disqualifying Black neighborhoods for mortgages backed by the government. It would only ensure property covered by restrictive covenants. It cut off Black areas by building highways around them, which made it easier for white people to run away to the suburbs. The neighborhoods left behind have a fraction of white wealth and an oversupply of substandard housing, ill health, infant mortality, and lousy schools.

"I'm from Cade County, Georgia. I make no excuses for the South. But what people up here don't get is, there's always been different ways of killing people than hanging them from a tree, and all sorts of ways of killing their hope in the cradle. And too much of white America just zips by all that on the highway to somewhere nicer."

Finishing, she noticed Dennis Burke grinning at Chase. "I'll tell you this much, young Mr. Brevard. I don't quite understand why Ms. Hill hangs out with you. But I sure understand why you hang out with her. You might actually learn something, like I just did."

Fondly, Chase placed his hand on Allie's. "No mystery why I like her, Dennis. I can never escape being edified."

Later, Allie promised herself, she would tell him how much this annoyed her. It was never too late to be edified.

★ ★ ★

After dessert, Senator Burke asked Chase and Allie to stay for a while. As the others peeled off into the night, all but Warren Sparks told Allie how much they'd enjoyed meeting her. *You don't have to like me,* she thought, *and I don't have to read your dumb book. That's what makes America great.*

Burke ushered them to a comfortable family room with pictures of his grown kids arranged on a bookshelf filled with biographies and books on politics and policy that also held a flat-screen TV. "This is where I watch the Yankees torture the Red Sox," he told Chase. "Year after year. Sorry, but in my lifetime Goliath always wins."

"Wait until next year," Chase responded. "That's what I've been living for since elementary school."

The senator poured snifters of brandy for Chase and himself, more mineral water for Allie. Then he settled back in a comfortable leather chair, clearly his favorite, as they took their places on a couch. After some desultory conversation about Harvard, of which Burke was an alumnus, he told Allie, "My office really screwed up."

"How's that?" she responded, though she knew at once what was coming.

"We should've offered you a job last summer. It's downright embarrassing."

"It's fine, Senator. I was a needle in a stack of résumés. I'm sure you hired someone great."

"Frankly, I wouldn't know. I don't get to spend much time with summer interns." He leaned forward. "But I do spend quite a lot of time with the smart people I'm lucky to have on staff. I'd like you to be one of them."

Allie bit her lip. "Thank you," she said. "Really, I'm way beyond flattered. But I'm planning to do social justice work in Georgia."

Burke glanced at Chase. "I understand. I admire that. But Washington is where policy gets made. I'd like you to work in the part of my shop that deals with urban policy and racial equity. You can make a difference, and help *me* make a difference."

Disconcerted, Allie gathered her thoughts. "I don't know what to say. But I do know that people would kill for a job like that. I never expected this kind of offer."

"Then just say you'll consider it. You don't have to tell me tomorrow. Let's say in a month. I'll spend that time hoping you sign on."

Allie felt Chase watching her intently. "I'll consider it," she responded at last. "It's a wonderful opportunity, after all."

18

On the drive back, Allie was unusually quiet. Chase wondered if he had done something to offend her, or whether she feared the seduction of easy access, the temptation to stray from her mission in Georgia.

Arriving, they sat on the porch overlooking Edgartown Harbor, the lights from the yacht club shimmering on the dark, inky waters. Chase waited for her to say something.

Finally, she asked in tones of wonder, "Is this how it works? Is this *really* how it works?"

"What, exactly?"

She faced him in the semidarkness. "I just show up to dinner in the Magic Kingdom as your girlfriend, string a few sentences together, and job offers from senators start falling from trees. I don't know whether I'm just stunned, or maybe even angry. I know I shouldn't be, and the senator seems like a nice man. They were all pretty nice, even the guy who thinks he's Malcolm X. Why wouldn't they be? But it reminds me of how hard it is for ordinary people, let alone ordinary Black people, to get anywhere—and why. I wonder if it will ever be any different."

Against his better judgment, Chase took a stab at humor. "They weren't all billionaires, Allie—at least Warren isn't. It's good of Dennis to remember that the bottom one percent of the top one percent are people, too. Even if they're all his donors."

She turned away from him to gaze at the harbor, her face in shadows. "Oh, I'll remember. Believe me, I learned something for myself tonight, and I'll remember." She spoke more softly. "It's just that the concentration of money, credentials, and access was kind of overwhelming. You accept this is normal, but it feels totally dissociated from how I grew up and what I care about most. And yet I'm going to need these people, aren't I? At least if I mean to accomplish everything I want to.

"You're going to be one of those people. I just wish it weren't another thing about us that makes me sad."

★ ★ ★

Later on, in bed, neither could sleep. Finally, Chase said, "Talk to me, Allie."

She rolled over on her back, and Chase heard her draw a breath. "It's all a jumble."

"Try me."

She was quiet for a moment. "It's just so hard to explain. At Harvard, Black women are two kinds of 'other.' We learn how to stand up for who we are, how not to look vulnerable. So there's this whole strong-Black-woman trope, another way we become a stereotype. I never cry in front of other people, no matter what happens and how they may have hurt me. I only let myself cry when I'm alone.

"Tonight, for most of those people, I was a representative Black woman. I wasn't their daughter, or one of their daughters' friends. I wasn't even sure whether you were my boyfriend or one of them. Sometimes it makes me so tired."

Chase felt at sea, a failure. "How can I tell you how important you are to me? Not who I might want you to be, but who you are."

"It's not your fault, really." Allie paused, continuing with what Chase heard as muted anguish. "There's a kind of glamour to the way you live, the sense of escaping so much of what I deal with in the world, and inside myself. I don't know whether caring for you is good for me or not, no matter how good you are or want us to be.

"What I got offered tonight is another way to work on things I care about. But it's not the way I ever imagined. I know you'd like me to take it. I can even hear some Black woman friends telling me I'd be crazy not to. 'Who's going to be company for you in backwoods Georgia? Why not take the world Harvard gives you?' I feel myself listening and suddenly losing who I've always been."

Unsure of what to do, Chase restrained himself from reaching across the bed, doing or saying anything that might feel wrong to her. "I'm not sure of what to say."

It was Allie who took his hand. "You listened," she said after a time. "Right now that's enough. Let's try to get some sleep."

19

After sleeping late, Allie and Chase sat on the porch, drinking coffee and gazing at the sunlight spreading across the harbor below. It was already ten o'clock, and the morning was bright and unseasonably warm. Though the residue of their discord lingered, Allie sensed that neither wanted to explore it.

"Any interest in sailing?" Chase asked.

"Never tried it."

"There's always a first time. My parents have this wonderful nineteen-foot daysailer, and it's just been launched. If you like, we can take it out on a shakedown cruise for a couple of hours. I always did that when we got here for the summer."

Sipping more coffee, Allie catalogued her reservations. "Where I come from," she informed him, "the boats have outboard motors, and we use them for fishing. My dad would take me out on the lake, and then Mom cooked up whatever we caught. Don't know I'd be that much use on a sailboat."

"You wouldn't need to. I've been out on the water since my parents dropped me off at sailing camp like a bag of dead cats. When I was thirteen I started crewing for a family friend in races off Long Island, and by the time I turned fifteen I'd started taking the *Caroline* out by myself. So I have seven prime years as Captain Brevard."

Allie considered this. "I'm a strong enough swimmer," she allowed. "But isn't that water pretty cold?"

"You could say that. It's still near fifty degrees, and if you got pitched overboard you'd die of hypothermia in less time than it takes to boil a pot of water. But it's a beautiful day for sailing, with not much breeze." Abruptly he stopped himself. "In weather like this we can do anything you want, including hike up a hill where you can see for miles. Just tell me what sounds good to you, and we'll do it."

Though he was feigning indifference, Allie could tell how deeply this sail connected with his memories of summer. "I can already put one foot in front of the other," she answered. "Might as well learn something about sailing."

★ ★ ★

When they got to the mooring below his parents' house, the temperature had dropped, and Chase calculated that the wind had stiffened to thirteen knots. "Even when the land gets warmer," he told her, "the water's still cool. So you can get more wind and maybe some fog."

"When do you start to worry?"

Chase glanced at her. "Over twenty knots of wind gets your attention. I've seen that plenty of times before, and it was always fine. But I don't want to take you out if you're uncomfortable."

She already was, Allie acknowledged to herself. But Chase surely knew what he was doing, and it somehow felt important not to be disagreeable. "If you're OK," she answered, "I'm sure I'll like it once we're out."

They clambered into the *Caroline*, a trim wooden boat that, while beautiful, struck Allie as none too big. When Chase started explaining its various parts, she observed and listened closely.

The tiller, which to Allie resembled a large wooden stick shift instead of the wheel she'd expected, steered the boat. The largest sheet of canvas was the mainsail; the forward sail was called the jib. Chase showed her the halyard, a cable he would use to raise the mainsail; the jib was controlled by the furler, a metal drum with cable wrapped around it that was attached to the deck. How much sail he let out, Chase concluded, would depend on the force and direction of the wind.

"Do you ever sail at night?" Allie asked.

"Not me, though I've been out after dark with some really experienced sailors. You can get incredibly disoriented—at least I did. You can't see the land very easily, or figure out distances. It's hard even to know whether a light is coming toward you or away from you. Fog makes it that much worse. But we'll be back on the porch with a glass of wine long before the sun goes down. Want to start us off?"

At least, Allie thought, she'd seen an outboard motor before—even if you started this one by pushing a button. When she did that, the engine purred instantly to life. As they began moving away from the mooring, Allie felt a childish satisfaction, like she had actually accomplished something.

"The adventure begins," Chase told her.

They motored out from the harbor past the Edgartown lighthouse, white and stubby, and out onto blue-green waters beneath a slowly graying sky that had begun to dim the sunlight. "Mind taking the tiller?" Chase asked. "Just hold it steady while I get the sails up."

Feeling like an actor in someone else's make-believe, Allie held the tiller as Chase pulled on the halyard, hoisting the mainsail aloft. He moved with grace and confidence, and Allie gave herself up to accepting that the water was his dominion.

Enjoying the mild breeze on her face, Allie noticed the first translucent mist of fog descending; though Chappaquiddick Island was quite near, it felt to her as if she were viewing it through smeared sunglasses. Then Chase hoisted the jib by uncleating the furling line, and the *Caroline* began cutting more swiftly through the water. "We're heading into the wind," he called over his shoulder. "That fills the sails so we can get going."

Rising from the deck, Chase reclaimed the tiller. As they sliced through the water with the harbor behind them, Allie felt a sense of escape and adventure, and understood why Chase found sailing so appealing. "Where are we going?" she asked.

"I don't know if I can make sense of this. But our first reference point is Cape Poge, off in the distance to our right. At the moment you can barely see the lighthouse."

Peering across the water, Allie spotted what looked like a tiny spike on a spit of land vanishing in the mist. "We're heading out toward a red channel marker at the head of the harbor," Chase continued. "It's called R-2. When we get closer you'll begin to hear its bell ringing, and feel us going faster as the wind picks up."

They continued pushing forward through choppier waters, the wind quickening, the sailboat accelerating. Allie heard a bell clanging in the distance. "That's R-2," he told her. "We'll reach open water, sail past Oak Bluffs, turn around, and head home. We should be back by four o'clock."

Sitting near him, Allie heard the metallic ringing becoming louder, and saw the red metal marker bobbing in the water. Then Chase pulled on a line, and the mainsail came flying above Allie's head. The *Caroline* changed direction and, for Allie, their experience changed with it.

★ ★ ★

The wind became much stiffer. Through the deepening fog, Allie saw whitecaps all around them. Spray hit her face, and it seemed like the edge of the sailboat as it tilted steeply toward the water might touch its surface.

They sailed like that for what, to Allie, seemed like endless minutes. Fighting gravity and the first traces of nausea, she hunkered down into what she thought of as the cockpit, and saw Chase smiling into the elements.

"How strong is this wind?" she asked.

Turning to look at her, he seemed to realize how conditions he took for granted might affect her. "Maybe twenty knots now—it's picking up a little more than I thought, and the fog is thicker. We'll be fine, but I'm wondering how you are."

"A little sick," she acknowledged.

"Sorry," he said at once. "I'll shorten sail and turn us back. It's no fun for me if it isn't for you."

"Are you sure?"

"Absolutely. First thing to do is furl the jib sheet so we're not catching so much wind. Can you hold the tiller for a moment?"

She looked around them into a world of gray, no longer afraid to seem afraid. "How will we know where we're going?"

"I've done this a lot," Chase assured her. "We'll tack toward Cape Poge. That orients us toward R-2 and the mouth of the harbor. Once we get closer to shore, we can putt-putt to dry land."

Knees bent for balance, Allie gripped the tiller. Amidst the roiling waters, she felt small, helpless but for Chase.

Swiftly moving to the furler, Chase began pulling on the furling line. Flapping in the wind, the jib made sharp cracking sounds as it eased. To her relief, Allie could feel the *Caroline* slowing. "It'll be down in a moment," Chase shouted over his shoulder.

Abruptly, the jib stopped descending.

The crackling and flapping became wilder, louder. The boat kept heeling. "What's happening?" Allie called out.

"Furler's stuck," Chase snapped between gritted teeth as he strained against the handle. "Never happened before."

Rising in a half crouch for more leverage, Chase tried to free the furling line, grunting at the effort. The furler did not move. Then the boat was jolted by a precipitous wave that frightened Allie beyond anything that had gone before. Blinded by sea spray, she clutched the tiller.

When she looked back toward Chase, he was gone.

She stared around her in disbelief, and then saw his head bobbing in the untamed water, calling out something she could not hear. For an awful moment she thought of the painting called *The Scream*. Then he vanished in the fog.

She bent forward, throwing up, water stinging her eyes. When she righted itself, she realized that the boat was moving away from where she had seen him. These could be the last moments of his life, she understood with sickening suddenness, spent losing consciousness before he died of hypothermia.

Desperate, she tried to remember something—anything—he had told her about the boat. The flapping jib increased her panic.

She willed herself to take a deep, shuddering breath, slowing down her thoughts.

What came to her was to push the button on the motor. It sputtered to life, giving her a spurt of hope that she could still find him in the fathomless waters.

Trying to steer the boat, she began fighting the mainsail. It was as though she were alone on a watery treadmill, suspended in her own horror.

Taut, she tried to think of what else to do.

When they got to the harbor, he had told her, he would release the halyard and take the mainsail down. Letting go of the tiller, she scrambled forward, jerking the halyard.

With a terrible flapping sound, the mainsail crashed to the deck. The boat buckled in the water.

Suddenly the fuller came unstuck. All at once the jib collapsed, the edge of its canvas hitting the water.

The *Caroline* righted itself.

Allie felt the boat straining forward, driven by the directionless churn of the motor. But now she could steer. She felt a tenuous calm come over her and, with it, purpose.

Seizing the tiller, she pointed the foundering craft toward where she guessed she'd last seen Chase. She began calling for him in the fog and spray.

She saw nothing, heard nothing.

Please God, she prayed, *don't let him die.* In that moment she loved Chase Brevard without reservation, could not bear the thought of his losing the future that life had granted him.

Through the dampness and mist, she saw his face above the water.

It was unnaturally white, almost bloodless, and his eyes were shut. "Chase!" she cried out.

His eyes seemed to open, and then he made a few feeble paddling motions. Allie turned the tiller as she thought she should, and the boat began heading toward him.

For agonizing moments, it tossed and veered in the roiling waters, until Chase was a few feet away. She saw his eyes close again.

Abruptly, the boat lurched forward, the hull nearly striking his head. Releasing the tiller, she scrambled to the side of the boat. "Just reach out for me!"

Slowly, his right arm stretched from the water. Bracing her knees against the side of the boat, she reached out to grasp it, struggling against the deadweight of a half-conscious man in waterlogged clothing.

"Help me," she demanded. "I can't do this by myself."

Both hands reached out for hers. Gripping them, she strained to pull him closer. His eyes, filled with shock, met hers.

With the last reserves of strength they possessed, she got him over the side and onto the deck.

He was trembling uncontrollably, and his breathing was shallow. Looking into his stricken face, Allie knew that he might still die.

20

Chase was in shock, Allie knew—trembling uncontrollably, barely conscious. She struggled to strip off the waterlogged clothing that swathed him in the lethal chill of hypothermia until, at last, he was naked. So recently his body had aroused her. Now he was pale, vulnerable, seemingly incapable of movement save for tremors she could not stop. She held him tightly, trying to transmit her warmth to him.

Behind her, she smelled the noxious emissions of the motor as it churned the waters. Rising, she started to turn it off, then perceived that its labors were heating the spaces nearby. Struggling, she dragged Chase closer to the gasoline-powered warmth.

Abruptly, Allie grasped her dilemma—that they could run out of fuel where no one could see or save them. All around her, the lowering fog admitted only patches of light through which she saw churning gray waters. She felt the onset of a mental and emotional paralysis, caught between a fear of inaction and the terror of making a fatal mistake.

Toward the front of the boat, she saw a covered storage area that held down jackets, a blanket, and an overstuffed duffel bag. Scrambling forward, she grabbed the jackets and blanket and spread them across Chase's body. As she looked down at his face, porcelain white, she summoned the prayers of childhood. For another moment, she hugged him fiercely. Then she forced herself to start thinking about how to preserve them both.

It was better, she decided, to keep the motor running.

Alone, she took the tiller. Muscles straining, she battled against headwinds and a tide pulling them out into open water, from time to time bending over Chase to determine that he was still breathing, and that his skin felt warmer. She could see no lights, hear nothing but the wind and water that jolted the *Caroline* up, down, and sideways. Glancing at her watch, she saw that it was five o'clock, and feared the coming darkness.

At her feet, she heard a long tremorous breath, then a muffled groan. Eyes opening, Chase stared up at her, and she saw the dawn of comprehension steal into his gaze. She felt a surge of gratitude, stifled by the fearful exigencies of survival. "You have to get us back," she snapped at him. "I can't do this anymore."

After a moment, he raised his head, resting on his elbows to examine himself. "The duffel bag," he told her in a faltering voice. "There's clothes inside."

She stumbled forward to get the bag, then laid out its contents beside him—a wool sweater, jeans, and socks. Pushing the blanket aside, he strained to wrestle on the fresh clothing, and then held up his arms so that Allie could slip on a down jacket.

He sat up, wordless, scanning the fog and water. Gripping the tiller, he pulled himself upright.

For more than an hour, Allie watched him steer the boat in restive, unmarked waters. The occasional light vanishing in some indeterminate distance seemed to have no meaning for him. She feared to ask questions, ask anything at all.

Suddenly Chase became still, peering intently into the enveloping darkness. Following his gaze, she saw what seemed like a speck of light. "The Cape Poge lighthouse," he murmured. "Thank God."

Changing course, they fought their way into the teeth of the wind, the engine making the nerve-racking sounds of a machine straining to the edge of capacity. Any moment now, Allie imagined, they would run out of fuel. Then she heard a sound that made her heart leap: the distant clanging of R-2.

★ ★ ★

When at last they arrived at the mooring, night had fallen, and the only light came from a few houses above the harbor. Silent, they climbed the steps to the Brevards' porch and then stood facing each other. "You nearly killed us," she told him.

She meant this to have a redemptive trace of humor, distancing the horror she felt deep in her soul, the lingering disbelief that they had escaped the chill grip of the ocean. But it came out as what she knew it was—a statement of fact.

His eyes brimmed with shame. "I know."

She could think of nothing else to say or do. Then he placed his hands on her shoulders, looking so intently into her face that he seemed to be memorizing each feature. "You saved my life, Allie."

"I had to," she answered.

By unspoken consent, they walked upstairs to his bedroom.

Without speaking, they peeled off their clothes and held each other as if to reaffirm that they were still alive, to somehow banish a fear of mortality that, having come too soon, would now occupy some corner of her soul and, perhaps, his.

After a while, they lay beside each other, at once together yet solitary. *We could have died out there together*, she thought, *disappeared in water that erased everything about us—our past, our future, the people we love or could love.* Then she felt him touch her face.

"I can't lose you," he said. "Not now."

★ ★ ★

For a long time, Allie was silent. "Please," she murmured. "I'm too tired for this."

But it seemed that Chase could no longer listen. "I can't believe you don't feel it."

Tears sprang to her eyes, unbidden. "Don't *you* know how unfair you're being? Today I realized how much I care for you. If you'd died out there and somehow I'd lived, I don't know what I would've done."

"But doesn't that mean we should give ourselves a chance?"

She gripped his arm. "What about *my* life? I've had these plans since high school. I'm not going to throw them overboard because we nearly drowned and now we're suffering from PTSD. Once that passes, we'll be the same as before."

"Will we?" he demanded. "Tell me you really believe that, and I'll shut up."

"You really are relentless," Allie shot back. "Talk about bad timing." She stopped herself, speaking more calmly. "You make going back to Georgia sound like a death sentence. But today we found out what actually dying would be. Nothingness."

He softened his voice. "Sorry, yet again. But being with me means doesn't mean giving up what you want. Or who you are."

"Of course it does."

"It doesn't need to." He paused, as if coming to a decision. "I love you, Allie. That means loving all of you. So I want you to hear me out."

Allie hesitated, caught between exhaustion and her instinctive sense that whatever he said, and whatever she thought of it, could change both their lives—and that, despite herself, she wanted to hear it. "Go ahead."

"Senator Burke has made you a great offer. If you don't like working on the Hill, it's not forever. You can go back to Georgia with some unique experience behind you…"

"This isn't new," she cut in. "You want to buy us some time while you're in law school, then talk me into staying if we're still together."

"No," he answered simply. "I don't."

"What, then?"

"If you want to stay up north, great. But if you choose to go back to Georgia once I graduate, I'll go with you. I'm pretty good at second languages."

Allie stifled her surprise. "That's crazy talk, Chase Brevard. Your whole future is in Massachusetts—law, politics, whatever you decide. You've never been to Cade County, Georgia. But I can tell you right now it could never be home to you…"

"*You* feel like home to me."

"I'm not, and believing it isn't fair to either of us. Think of the pressure you'd put on me by coming to Georgia. You'd be miserable, and I'd be the only reason you were there. I can't be anyone's whole life, and I don't want to try."

"I'm not asking you to," Chase retorted with the first edge of anger. "You're turning me into a rich guy from Boston who can only survive in my own personal greenhouse. With all due respect, I've got a whole lot more in me than that. I can decide what's best for me."

"And what if that changes?"

"I don't think it will." His voice softened again. "OK, it's only been a few months. But I know we could have a good life, wherever it is, and that both of us would be better for being together. Down the road, we could have a family of our own. Even now, I look at you and can't imagine giving my kids a better mom."

Allie felt her throat catch. "You really *are* a romantic, aren't you?"

"If that means knowing I'll never find anyone like you, I guess I am. Maybe it's not the same for you. But if it is, or could be, I'm asking you to think about it."

However she answered, Allie realized, she had the awful sense that anguish might follow—that giving in might damage them both, but that to lose him might feel irreparable in ways she could not yet define. "All right," she finally heard herself say, and perhaps even mean. "I'll think about it."

21

They enjoyed a peaceful drive back to Cambridge, Chase at the wheel. Respectful of her uncertainties and her reasons for having them, he ventured nothing more about the future.

But there was so much he wanted to say, if she were ever ready to hear it. *I understand what you're afraid of,* he imagined telling her. *I know this feels like too much too soon, and that we need a lot more time together. But if we're as good as I think we can be someday, I want to marry you.*

But that was far ahead, he knew, and he'd already said more than she could absorb and believe. All he wanted was the time and space to say what he knew in his heart when it made more sense, and then find out if they could live it together.

★ ★ ★

As they neared campus, Allie lapsed into silence, seemingly pensive and preoccupied. After a while he said, "Penny for your thoughts. Or whatever the going rate is."

She waited a moment. "I was thinking about you, actually. When you were lying there in the boat, half dead, I prayed for you to live the life you were destined for. Now I look over at you, and it's like my prayers were answered."

Touched, Chase glanced at her. "Do you believe that?"

"I used to believe pretty much everything my parents did—including that God answers our prayers. Now I'm not sure. Freshman year I'd go to religion class and feel kind of old-fashioned. It was like everyone else was saying, 'Who believes in this stuff anymore?' and I wanted to say that *I* did. At least parts of it."

"Which parts?"

For another moment, she considered her answer. "For one example," she told him, "my church doesn't believe in abortion, and neither do my parents. As for me, I believe in it for others. But I don't think I could ever abort my own child.

"I'm still trying to explain my religion to myself—where I've grown away from it, where I'm still the same, and how to reconcile all that with what I choose to do and what I should expect from others. All I know for sure is that the answers are important."

Listening, Chase wondered if this was a metaphor for other confusions, perhaps concerning their future. "I'm sure you'll find the right ones," he contented himself with saying.

★ ★ ★

Soon exam week was upon them, their days at Harvard swiftly vanishing. In their fleeting times together, Chase sensed Allie's appreciation that he was leaving her to reflect on her own. But he also felt that something was troubling her, and feared for what it might be.

The morning after finals ended, Allie came to his house unannounced and found Chase sleeping in.

She sat on the bed beside him. Stirring awake, he saw at once that she was tense, her face drawn as though she were coming down with something. He waited for her to bend over and kiss him, but she did not.

Covering his anxiety, he said, "I was talking to my parents about graduation. They're hoping you can go out to dinner with us. Your parents, too, if you can manage that without inflicting too big a shock."

She looked down. "I'm not staying for graduation," she said in a near monotone. "I'm going back home tomorrow."

He sat bolt upright. "Good God, Allie. Why?"

Meeting his eyes, she seemed to steel herself. "Because what's happened between us has gotten too hard. It's asking too much from us both."

He placed his hands on her shoulders. "Maybe you. Not me."

Suddenly, her voice began shaking. "Please, Chase. I have to leave now. I can't do it any other way—it's too painful." She stood, tearing herself from his grasp. "Please, I have to go."

Before he could answer, she hurried toward the door, then stopped to look at him once more, tears running down her face. "Please, baby," she whispered. "Forgive me."

Turning, she rushed through the door and down the stairs, out of his life.

★ ★ ★

Seven months later, Allie found herself in a delivery room at Cade County Hospital—afraid, once again, for her own life and that of another person she already imagined loving more than anyone she had loved before.

She was alone except for a nurse and her mother, Janie. Her ob-gyn, Dr. Wells, a capable Black woman in her thirties, was delivering another baby. Wells' substitute, a white male doctor Allie didn't know, had given her an epidural and, for some reason, antibiotics.

Almost immediately, she had been assaulted by blurred vision, shortness of breath, a headache so savage that her skull pounded. Straining to look at the monitors, she saw that her blood pressure was rising, her baby's heartbeat slowing.

Janie gripped her hand fiercely, as though willing them both to survive. "Please God," Allie whispered, "don't let him die." Then she remembered saying this prayer for the baby's father, and was seized by the scarifying fear that in some cruel cosmic bargain, she had traded one precious life for another.

"Should I call Mr. whoever he is?" her mother asked urgently. "Wouldn't he want to know?"

For a moment, Allie imagined him beside her, his face filled with love and concern. "It's too late, Mama. I didn't want to tell him, and now it's too late."

Rushing into the room, the white doctor ordered Janie to leave. Glancing at the monitors, he said hurriedly, "There's no time. We're going to have to do an emergency C-section."

Suddenly Dr. Wells rushed in. "No time for *that*," she snapped at her colleague, then turned to the nurse. "Get me epinephrine this minute."

Looking wildly around her, Allie fixed on the picture of her son's failing heart. "He's dying," she rasped. Panicky, she struggled for breath. "*He's dying.*"

"Not on my watch," Dr. Wells said. "I'm going to fix this right quick." Holding an oxygen mask to Allie's face, she instructed, "Just breathe…"

"We need to do a C-section," Allie heard the white doctor protest. "Right now."

Wells did not turn. "Just get out of my delivery room," she said over her shoulder, and jabbed a needle into Allie's arm.

"I'm going to report you!"

"Beats letting you kill two people at once," Wells said between her teeth, then spoke softly to Allie. "Just keep breathing, and in a few moments you'll be fine. That comes before everything else."

Feeling her headache diminish, Allie began to breathe more easily. "What happened to me?"

"You had a bad reaction to an antibiotic. All I did was give you a shot of epinephrine. It's not rocket science, at least for most people."

Allie grasped the doctor's hand. "But what about my baby?"

Swiftly, Wells looked at the fetal heart monitor. "He's doing better already. But we need you to stabilize first. You're earth station now, like you will be for the rest of his life." She touched Allie's face with curled fingers. "Just rest up for a minute more. Then we'll give you a general anesthetic, and I'll do that C-section my colleague was so keen to hurry. Soon enough you'll be holding your baby, I promise."

After a few minutes they gave her the anesthesia. Breathing deeply at last, Allie felt herself falling asleep.

★ ★ ★

When Allie awakened, Dr. Wells was still there.

"Where's my baby?" she asked.

The doctor angled her head. "Right there in that bassinet."

Allie tried to sit up. "Is he all right?"

"Why don't you check him out?" Wells replied, and placed the newborn on her chest.

Filled with wonder, she kissed his head of black hair, smelled his light brown skin. "My name's Allie," she told him, her voice trembling with love and the residue of fear. "Your name is Malcolm, and I'm your mama. It's just you and me, so I hope that's OK."

PART THREE

Cade County

22

Entering Cade County, Congressman Chase Brevard took Highway 19 through spacious rolling country filled with oaks, pines, and pecan trees, periodically disfigured by strip malls, chain stores, fast-food outlets, gun shops, and snack stands. There was a church, it seemed, every mile or so. Religion was clearly a thing here, Chase concluded sourly, but zoning was not.

The land itself, green in the hot noonday sun, appeared fertile and benign. But over generations, he well knew, it had served as host to slavery, peonage, and the systematic oppression of Blacks too often reinforced by terror and violence. Now the county, like the state, was riven by a bitter struggle for power between whites and Blacks, Republicans and Democrats. More than any man or woman in Georgia, Allie Hill had become its symbol and its fulcrum, a magnet for hatred or adoration.

Suddenly her son was caught in a racial maelstrom, the work of centuries, from which there might be no escape. And so Chase had come here, filled with a bitter disbelief he could still not assimilate yet, inexorably drawn here by the life-and-death dilemma of a boy he did not know, the consequences of a decision in which he had played no part, but that might alter the course of his life in ways he could not anticipate. Nor did he know how, if at all, he could affect the onrush of events in this alien place. All that Chase understood was that he could not stay away.

The county seat, Freedom, featured a main street of two- and three-story brick buildings, streetlamps, and flowering trees. At first glance it looked orderly and prosperous enough. But politics had given Chase an eye for economic erosion; within a block or two, a few boarded-up buildings and light pedestrian traffic had told him that this was a town in decline. That, too, unsettled him—in the feral America of 2022, let alone Georgia, racial anxieties and economic distress could prove a toxic brew, a petri dish for scapegoating symbolic enemies. Like a young Black man accused of murdering a white cop.

Amidst the modest scale of its surroundings, the orange brick Winthrop Hotel stood out for its mass and height. After parking in front, Chase entered a commodious main room whose ceilings rose past four floors of railings and open hallways. Standing on a vast Oriental carpet, he took in the well-chosen antiques, plush couches and chairs, heavy chandeliers hanging from the ceiling on long brass chains, a fireplace whose mantel featured porcelain plates and vases, and walls covered with paintings of birds and landscapes. For a moment Chase thought of the Charlotte Inn, where he had once taken Allie for dinner. But the much larger Winthrop felt like a museum to lost prosperity, the last vestiges of a fading grandeur that had peaked a century before.

At the burnished wood front desk, a pleasant brunette took his credit card and pointed him to an elevator. "Mind checking my luggage?" Chase asked. "I'm meeting a friend, and I'd like to be on time."

★ ★ ★

After starting his rental car, Chase headed for their meeting place.

After a few miles of rural countryside, he turned into a quiet state park. About a quarter mile down the road, he parked near a large pond amid a sloping, grassy field encircled by oaks and pines and flowering rose-colored bushes. Allie's directions had been very precise, as was her reason for meeting in this place—on a school day in early afternoon, there would be few parents or kids here, and teenagers seeking out drugs or sex would not come until after dark. The chances were pretty good that no one would see them or, at least at a distance, recognize a congressman from Massachusetts.

Wearing a white blouse and blue jeans, she sat beneath an oak tree on a bench facing the pond. She did not turn until he was standing near, hands in his pockets, looking down at her.

Quiet, she examined him closely, as though to verify that he was real. Though Chase saw at once the smudges of sleeplessness, her face was unlined save for the first etchings at the corner of her eyes. She was much as he had imagined her, the woman he had known at Harvard— seasoned, but treated kindly, by the indefinable look of maturity that time brings. What jarred him was a feeling of betrayal so deep that at first he could not speak.

"You look good," she told him. "Just like you do on television. I'll flip on MSNBC while I'm eating dinner, and there you are."

"Is that all you have to say?"

"No." Deep sadness surfaced in her eyes. "How you learned about Malcolm wasn't fair."

"That's a way of putting it. Imagine waking up one morning to discover you have a Black eighteen-year-old son facing capital murder charges in a racially poisonous backwater that, as far as I'm concerned, is the last place he should be. This may surprise you, but it kind of spoiled my day."

She shook her head as if to clear it, then slid to the end of the bench. "Sit down with me. Please."

After a moment, he sat at the other end. "Now what? Am I going to find out we have twins?"

She drew a breath. "Do I really have to explain why I didn't tell you?"

"Seeing how I'm here, you might as well. Newly minted fatherhood seems to have swollen my sense of entitlement."

She drew herself straighter. "You already know the answer—it ran through everything we said to each other. We were too young, too new to be sure of anything. I didn't believe in abortion, and I didn't want to change your life. Your future was in Massachusetts, not Georgia. I was already committed to the place where I had roots, and I needed my parents' help in raising Malcolm. However hard it was to leave like that, I believed it was best for both of us.

"Maybe I had no right to do it the way I did. But until that deputy died, more often than not I could tell myself it turned out for the best. You became a congressman, and I helped make Georgia a better place and gave my son a loving family. What I never imagined is that we'd be sitting here."

"But we are. What did you expect me to do?"

"Exactly what you did once you found out—come to Georgia. But what you do next is what matters."

"I'm still playing catch-up. What do you suggest?"

For a moment, Allie hesitated. "Go home," she answered succinctly, "back to the life you've made. For everyone's sake—especially yours. There is nothing you can do here."

"In other words, I pretend that Malcolm never existed."

Her voice thickened. "If I had forever, I could never tell you how sorry I am. I've put you in a terrible place, with no way out that doesn't hurt. But at least the decision I made nineteen years ago freed you to become what I thought you could be—a politician who cares about the things I do, with no ceiling on how far you could go. Don't tell me you haven't thought about that."

★ ★ ★

She watched his face change in subtle acknowledgment, anger replaced by fatalism. "When I run out of daydreams," he answered. "But I can't base the rest of my life on abandoning my own son. It doesn't matter if no one else knows—including Malcolm. *I'd* know."

All at once, Allie felt the tension on her nerve ends, the bone-deep fatigue of sleepless nights. "He's *my* son, the boy I raised, and now I may lose him. He can never be to you what he is to me." Abruptly, she caught herself. "I know you want to help him. But you don't know the first thing about Cade County. What you *do* know is how fast anyone who wants to destroy your career would use you to bring down even more hate on our son. That I'm his mother is bad enough."

He shook his head. "I can't leave. Not without meeting him."

At once she imagined Malcolm pacing his cell, bereft of sleep and appetite. "What would you say?" she demanded "'Hi, I'm your dad the congressman'? Could you leave then? And if you don't tell him, how do you explain yourself? He's twisted up in knots already."

"What exactly does he know about me? If anything."

"Almost nothing. Only that we were involved, and that I broke it off."

"In other words," Chase said with cutting softness, "you let him believe that I abandoned him. That must have been terrific for a young boy to live with."

Allie felt hurt and defensive, though she knew she deserved to feel none of this. "I told him you didn't know."

"Just how did *that* go over?"

She thought of the younger Malcolm, seeking scraps of information before he sealed himself off from hurt. "Not well. For years after he was born, I turned it over and over in my head, wondering if I should reach out to you. But then you became a public figure, and I became a lightning rod. So I thought it best to leave things be."

Silent, she watched him gaze across the pond, watching a mother follow a very young son tottering across the grass as he tested his obviously newfound ability to walk. At length, Chase said, "Before this, has he ever been in trouble?"

"Not with the law," she answered soberly. "A year ago he got suspended from high school for hitting a white boy, the son of a town cop who'd stopped him for driving while Black. As Malcolm tells it, they had words about racist cops, and the Palmer kid called him a nigger. No one else heard what was said, but Malcolm threw the only punch."

"Was the other kid hurt?"

"Hurt enough. Malcolm broke his nose."

★ ★ ★

Absorbing this, the ex-prosecutor in Chase realized how easily this incident could be used to make a jury see Malcolm as a hot-tempered Black man who had assaulted the son of a white police officer, then bought a gun and murdered a white deputy sheriff. But instead of saying this, he asked, "How's he doing now?"

Allie looked at her hands, curled together in her lap, then seemed to slump with weariness. "He's a teenage boy afraid that he'll never see freedom again, that he'll die of lethal injection or live to old age in some Georgia state prison. He tries to be tough and stoic, for my sake and to buck himself up. But I can see him trying to take care of me, make me feel better by being the man he thinks he should be. Her voice softened with despair. "Maybe the worst part is that he's the only one alive that knows what happened. It's like he's all alone with a truth no one else can see, with so many people wanting to disbelieve him. It's already wearing down his soul."

Feeling her anguish, Chase forced himself to function as a lawyer. "Is there any reason you can think of to doubt his story?"

He saw her stiffen, instantly alienated. "You don't know him…"

"Not my fault," he cut in. "I'm the dad who's only seen a yearbook picture with my smile grafted on. You're the expert by default, and it would help to hear your answer."

She felt quiet, as if compelling herself to see the justice in his request. "Malcolm's got a temper, for sure. Always has. But there's no way he's a murderer. His lawyer doesn't believe it, either."

Or so he says, Chase thought. "What's *he* like, by the way?"

"Jabari? He's smart, and he's fearless. Whatever that prosecutor tries to do, Jabari won't back down."

Restless, Chase stood. "I need to see him, Allie."

She looked up at him, the wariness returning to her eyes. "Jabari? Or Malcolm?"

"I'll start with the lawyer," Chase answered.

23

Wearing a polo shirt and khakis in the sweltering heat, Chase walked the few blocks from his hotel to a park near the Cade County courthouse, where Jabari Ford had asked him to meet. The scene outside the courthouse made him understand why.

Separated by a line of sheriff's deputies, roughly a hundred protesters—some white but mostly Black—faced off against a smaller number of hostile whites distinguished by "MAGA" caps or T-shirts with white lightning bolts. Some of the protesters held hand-lettered signs saying, "Justice for Malcolm"; the whites carried semiautomatic weapons and placards proclaiming "George Bullock Died for America" or "Death for Cop Killers." Their leaders seemed to be a man in his thirties with the beard of an Old Testament prophet, and a full-figured woman of roughly the same age who appeared to be shouting imprecations at a cluster of young Blacks.

From the opposite sidewalk, Chase paused to survey the confrontation—prevented from exploding, it seemed to him, by an imposing Black man in uniform who directed the deputies stationed between the antagonists. The motorists passing on Main Street tended to stare straight ahead, as if willing the confrontation out of existence. But a few whites leaned out of the driver's side window to glare at the protesters. Most startling to Chase was the young mother driving two kids in the back seat of an SUV who, braking abruptly, extended a graceful arm toward the protesters before jabbing the air with her middle finger.

To Chase, the scene crackled with the volatility he had experienced just before the insurrection of January 6, when Capitol Hill police in D.C. had saved him and his colleagues from dangers far worse, perhaps, than the terror some had experienced. For months thereafter, entering the Capitol, Chase had an instant of hyperalertness, the residue of a day that had transformed his understanding of America. But even harder to comprehend was that these dangers were now directed at his own son.

Separated from the courthouse by a cross street lined with squad cars, the park sat on a modest slope shaded by oak trees. A trim Black man in a tailored suit surveyed the antagonists from a wooden bench, his face a study in impassivity. As Chase approached him, he glanced up and said casually, "Afternoon, Congressman. Welcome to Cade County."

Chase sat beside him. "'Chase' will do fine. I get why you wanted me to see this."

"Yeah, I thought it might capture the spirit of the thing. If they could, at least a few of those whites would hang Malcolm Hill from the tree we're sitting under. His mother, too."

Chase felt a fresh wave of disbelief that this boy he did not know, the target of hatred, had sprung from the night that he and Allie had made love after her performance as Black Juliet. "I've seen these people before," he responded. "But never with military-grade weapons."

"No help for that," Ford answered laconically. "Georgia's an open-carry state. These patriots are exercising their Second Amendment rights."

"Who's the one with the beard?"

In profile, Ford's lips compressed. "Charles Parnell. He and his sister Molly head up the local white nationalists. Right after the 2020 election, Parnell helped organize an armed protest outside Allie's office a few blocks down, claiming she'd helped Blacks and Democrats steal the White House. It was dangerous enough that sheriff's deputies had to clear a path to get Allie and her people out safe.

"Problem now is that about eighty percent of the whites in Cade County still believe that Trump should be president, and that Allie Hill is the Black Antichrist. It's the wrong moment for her son to be charged with killing a white sheriff's deputy after a hard day's work helping Black folks to vote." His eyes narrowed. "Well now, look who we have here."

Turning, Chase realized that Charles Parnell had peeled away from his followers and was crossing the street. As the man approached the park bench carrying a semiautomatic rifle at his side, Chase stared back at him to conceal his apprehension, the ways in which January 6 had changed him.

Perhaps ten feet away, Parnell stopped, fixing Chase with an implacable stare clearly meant to signal that he would remember his face. Instinctively, Chase started to rise, and felt Ford's hand on his arm. "Busy day, Charles?" he said conversationally. "So many niggers, so little time."

At once, Chase understood that Ford had meant this to distract Parnell's attention from his white companion. Then he saw the Black leader of the deputies sauntering into the park, standing at an angle where Parnell could see him. With a faint derisive smile, Parnell gave Chase a final once-over before turning away.

Despite himself, Chase was shaken—something in the man's spectral gaze had conveyed not only hatred but instability. "He's like something out of *Deliverance*," he murmured to Ford.

"This is no movie," Ford responded curtly. "That man figures out who you are, he may want to kill you sure enough. Just not in a public park, with Al Garrett watching."

"The Black guy in uniform?"

"Yup. Otherwise known as the first elected Black sheriff in this county's history. He's another reason people like Parnell hate Allie. No way Al gets elected in 2020 without her registering all those new voters."

Chase absorbed this—everything Allie had done to make change, he was realizing, posed a danger to their son. "What kind of department does Garrett run?" he asked.

"A better one. Enforces the law straight, and so do the new deputies he's brought in. But there's not much you can do about the older whites used to doing things their way."

Chase turned to him. "Like George Bullock?"

Ford shrugged. "Depends on who you talk to and what color they are. Ask most white folks, and George Bullock was a paragon of law enforcement and the scourge of drug dealers who target our youth, and his death is a tragic loss to the community."

"What about for you?"

"Not so much," the lawyer answered coolly. "But there's also some bad history here. Four years ago, two white city cops went to arrest a Black guy who was beating on his wife. The guy killed them both with a handgun and then took off. The Georgia State Patrol descended on Freedom with sirens screaming, locked down the stores, found the shooter hiding in the park, and air-conditioned him with bullets.

"Anti-Black feelings among most whites ran high. But two things kept the situation from getting worse. First, the Black community thought the shooter was a no-account, and extended a lot of sympathy to the families of those dead cops. Second, the Georgia state police had effectively executed the killer pretty much on the spot, so for white folk at least justice had been done." Ford turned to Chase, adding pointedly, "But Malcolm Hill is very much alive. His trial, if it comes, could release all the demons we'd kind of bottled up before 2020.

"The most dangerous people in this county are angry whites who think Black and brown people are stealing their country. They're the ones who hate Allie most, and think that lethal injection is the second-best punishment for her son. But the ones who'll decide whether to prosecute Malcolm, and whether to seek the death penalty, are the prosperous white folks who can only keep their place on top of the social pyramid if the haters don't start hating on them."

Silent, Chase contemplated the dangers facing the son he didn't know and the woman he had never forgotten. Abruptly, Ford stood. "Let's go for a ride, Congressman. A sociopolitical tour of Cade County should tell you even more than your meeting with Charles Parnell."

As they got into Ford's Toyota, Chase saw a baseball glove in the back seat. "How many kids?" he asked conversationally.

"Two." Instead of elaborating, Ford turned on the ignition.

Passing the demonstrators, a tableau of violence in suspension, Ford began pointing out landmarks with the impersonal manner of a somewhat jaded tour guide. They passed a movie theater that looked like an artifact from the fifties, with its current feature spelled out in letters stuck by hand on a stained fiberglass marquee. Slowing to look at it, Ford said, "Have Allie tell you about when her mother, Janie, tried to integrate that theater as a sixth grader. It pretty much captures why the Hill family is so important to Blacks in this county, and why so many white people look on them as a multigenerational curse.

"This may sound strange to you, coming from Massachusetts, but down here the Hills became the nearest thing we had to the Kennedys. Folks looked up to them. So things were expected of Allie, by her own parents and a lot of others. That's why she went to Harvard, people knew—to learn more about where the power was, then bring those lessons home. I was two years behind her in high school, and I remember what a big deal they made over that at graduation—more than her being valedictorian. That put even more pressure on her to achieve."

"What about when she came back?"

Ford looked at him askance. "Pregnant, you mean?"

"Among other things. In college, I kind of got the impression that the downside of community was collective judgment."

"It can be," Ford acknowledged. "Out of jealousy or envy, some mean-minded people seemed to enjoy judging her poorly. But she had that boy, raised him right, and went on to fulfill all the expectations anyone ever had of her—and more. Not only did she make this county a whole lot better, but by changing who votes in Georgia she became one of the most influential women in the country." Ford's voice flattened out. "Now, her enemies will try to use Malcolm to destroy her. Almost makes you wish she'd never come back."

There was no way, Chase knew, for Ford to comprehend the impact of those last words—not least because the same thought must have riven Allie throughout their recent conversation, their first in nineteen years, whose bitterness Chase was already coming to regret.

"I suppose it does," he responded. "But who could have known?"

★ ★ ★

Pulling over, Ford parked beside a Romanesque three-story stone building whose deeply-chiseled engraving announced the presence of Cade County Bank. Leaving the car, they stood on the sidewalk.

"On top of that building," Ford explained, "is the conference room where the board of the Winthrop Foundation meets to dispense the bounty Alexander Winthrop created to benefit the county over a century ago. These days the board includes the bank president, a Winthrop granddaughter, some landowners, a few leading businessmen, and Orval Prescott, one of the judges who sits on the bench with Judge Tilly."

"Where did the money come from?" Chase inquired. "Commerce or property?"

"Land, mostly. If you hear the phrase 'They have land,' it means that some of our leading white families still accumulate wealth by farming or renting out land from the old plantations, built on cotton and slavery generations back. It's nothing like hedge fund money, but it carries great weight here." Ford gazed up at the sunlight reflected from the opaque windows of the boardroom. "That board is like the Illuminati. No one knows exactly what goes on there. But whatever they talk about has a lot of influence over what happens in this county."

"Including with Malcolm?"

"It could. For sure Judge Prescott will pass on to Judge Tilly whatever his colleagues are thinking. Or worried about."

Chase took inventory of his initial impressions. "Seems like they've got more to worry about than pacifying racists. From the looks of downtown, this place is on the economic downslide. You can't keep people happy, white or Black, if they don't have jobs. So they're caught in a bind."

Ford gave him a keen look. "Good guess."

"It's hardly a guess. Boarded-up windows tell their own story, and being on the wrong end of a white nationalist's AR-15 concentrates the mind." Chase paused, then continued in a calm, even tone. "You've already told me that your Illuminati are riding the white tiger Trump unleashed in 2016. If the locals who hate and fear Allie don't get Malcolm's head on a platter, they may just rise and replace the establishment with their own mini-Trumps. So the inner circle that you describe resembles the Republican establishment before Trump ran them over. If you gave them truth serum, you'd find they probably don't give a damn about lower-class whites, or even George Bullock. But they can't fight off Allie's Black hordes without the help of whites they wouldn't want dating their daughters.

"Still, I imagine that's only half the equation." For a moment, Chase looked at the area around them. "Since we've been standing here, no one has passed us, and I've barely seen anyone enter a store. So what the town fathers *don't* need is bad national publicity that makes Cade County look like a racist backwater, especially at a time when they're trying to court new businesses to relocate here, and every other corporate TV ad features multiracial families eating cereal or bundling into SUVs."

For the first time, a look of amusement crept into Ford's eyes. "She told me you were smart. So I guess we can stop toying with each other."

Chase nodded. "Saves time, and I really don't have it to spare. I assume you've started thinking about a media strategy."

"I surely have, Congressman, and so has Allie. But the question becomes who and what scares our civic leaders most." Ford's tone became conversational, a tour guide dispensing information to a visitor from far away. "Take our district attorney, Dalton Harris. By the standards of inherited power, he's a decent man. But his family has been here for six generations, back to when his ancestors held slaves. Folks like that still tend to prefer things as they are. The people he'll look to for guidance are essentially the same as those who've held power since the 1920s—they've just changed faces and clothes and shucked off the worst of Jim Crow without giving up on paternalism.

"The civil rights movement forced them to adapt. But they still know what's best. If they decide Malcolm needs to be sacrificed to keep them in power, chances are good that he will be. They'll worry about jobs and publicity later, because the voters they're afraid of don't watch CNN or MSNBC. Especially fanatics like Parnell who might put a bullet through their head for selling out white America."

Alone on the sidewalk, the two men faced each other. "Understood," Chase said at length. "I guess you've got more to show me."

"Much more," Ford responded. "There's a whole road map that shows all that Malcolm is up against. So let's get going before it turns dark."

24

On the way to Freedom's largest Black neighborhood, they passed a four-story tan brick building with two ambulances in front. "That's Cade County Hospital," Ford explained, "the best option in miles for Black and poor people and middle-class whites. But Allie's still trying to get the funding it needs, and the richer folks around here treat it like they're living in the third world. They have their surgeries and babies in Atlanta."

"Where was Malcolm born?" Chase asked.

"Here. So was Allie, and so was I. Not like our parents. They were delivered in segregated hospitals with lousy facilities and substandard care. This hospital is a big step up, but we still have trouble attracting doctors."

"Any Black doctors?"

"Hardly any," Ford answered. "There's a story that goes with that. Allie nearly died on the delivery table, and so did Malcolm. A Black ob-gyn saved them both. But one of her colleagues, an old-school white, complained that she wasn't "collegial," and a lot of white women didn't want her delivering their babies or even examining their vaginas. The last straw was when a local service club of upper-crust white ladies rejected her for membership. All that silent disapproval wore on her, and she left."

Chase contemplated this doctor's professional suffocation based on race, and then another thought struck him. "How many white clients do you have?" he asked.

"Now, or ever?" Ford showed a brief, mirthless smile. "Either way, the answer's the same. None."

★ ★ ★

They crossed some railroad tracks after waiting for a parade of worn boxcars to pass. "Welcome to the other side of the tracks," Ford observed. "Literally."

Almost at once, Chase began seeing beauty shops, barbershops, and churches amidst streets of shotgun houses, some run-down, others set in pristine yards that reflected a deep pride in ownership. A few Blacks tended their gardens or came in and out of shops, and a couple of kids on a patch of asphalt shot basketballs at a hoop with no net.

"How do these people make a living?" Chase inquired.

"Various ways. Some own these businesses; some work in paper mills or peanut-shelling facilities, others as domestics or yard workers. Their problem is that white folks pay them under the table, so they don't build up Social Security." Turning a corner, Ford added, "More and more people don't have enough work—or any. When our big tire factory closed down, there was nothing to take its place."

"What's here for kids? I'm not seeing any playgrounds."

"Glad you noticed," Ford responded sardonically. "You won't find a Boys &Girls Club or YMCA, either. Growing up in this neighborhood, young people don't see a lot they can aspire to, or how to get out. They don't have much in the way of educational opportunity, so too many end up like their parents." Ford's tone became weary. "You can lay a share of blame on family structure, dads who go missing. I've been known to myself. But it's also about moms who have to work two jobs, leaving their kids with grandparents too old and unsophisticated to keep up with adolescents—let alone teenagers.

"So there's gangs. That's about selling drugs, which for some of these kids seems like the only way to get ahead. That jacks up the homicide rate, along with domestic abuse by guys high on drugs or drink. But that's Black-on-Black crime. White people can live with it." Pausing, Ford pulled over to the side of the street. "What upsets the natural order of things is when a Black man is accused of killing a white, especially when the dead man is a cop."

Once again, Chase was consumed by the simple, stunning fact that Malcolm was also *his* son. "Look around you," Ford prodded. "This was the last neighborhood Malcolm canvassed before George Bullock stopped him."

The street, Chase saw, was a portrait of squalor—scrofulous patches of yard, unpainted houses. In front of one deteriorating hovel, a rotund grandmotherly-looking woman sat in a metal chair beneath a dead tree. "For a lot of white people, folks like that lady are too worthless to vote, and getting them to the polls undermines everything white America should be. For them, putting absentee ballot applications in their hands makes Malcolm a criminal."

Chase turned to him. "Do you believe George Bullock was waiting for him?"

"Malcolm knows he was. Let me show you one more thing."

After a couple of blocks, Ford stopped by a small wooden home with a shaded front porch and some chairs. "Some of Malcolm's coworkers are renting that place. They were sitting on the porch that night, drinking beer, when a truck or car drove by real slow. Like the driver was checking out who was there."

The porch, Chase calculated, was only ten yards from the street. "Could whoever it was have recognized Malcolm?"

"He believes so. The porch light was on, and Malcolm's car was parked right in front. From here, there's only one route back to Allie's place in the country—several miles of backroad without any lights. I think Bullock knew he was coming."

"Could the vehicle that drove by have been a squad car?"

"There aren't any streetlights here, so except for the porch it was pretty dark. But it didn't look like one to Malcolm."

"I guess he couldn't see whether the driver was Black or white."

"No way of telling." Ford turned to look at Chase. "Not many whites drive through this neighborhood. But then why would a Black person slow down to stare at some Black kids sitting on that porch? Doesn't feel right to me."

For Chase, nothing did.

★ ★ ★

Freedom High School was a one-story tan brick building with small windows, a couple of them broken, and sterile architecture from the Eisenhower years. The basketball court outside was marbled with cracks through which grass sprouted. Nothing looked new, Chase noted, except a separate building for Junior ROTC.

"For a lot of Black kids here," Ford told him, "the army is their best ticket out. That's what Al Garrett did, and he wound up in the military police."

Chase reflected on this. "When I first met Allie at Harvard, she was giving an antiwar speech. She said something about the county putting up a plaque for kids who died in wars, then forgetting all about them."

"That plaque is right inside," Ford responded at once. "Only back in our day it stopped with Vietnam. Now there's names from Iraq and Afghanistan, mostly Black."

"What are the demographics these days?"

"Around eighty percent nonwhite. That's been building since desegregation, when any white family who could scrape together tuition or get a 'scholarship' sent their kids to our so-called private school, Southern Academy. Ever since then the county and the school board have starved this place of funding." Ford's tone became caustic. "Now there's just enough whites in this school for one to pick a fight with Malcolm when no one was looking."

"From what Allie tells me," Chase interjected, "the kid was the son of a town cop who'd hassled Malcolm, and Malcolm broke his nose. Sounds like a problem to me."

"Oh, it is," Ford answered, "and the district attorney is bound to make the most of it."

For an instant Chase hesitated. "What's your impression of Malcolm?"

Ford gave him a veiled look, then shrugged. "Easy enough to see that he struggles with being a young Black man with a strong mother and no father to model himself after. Losing his grandfather so sudden-like didn't help. But he's pretty much everything people expected Allie's son to be, and more—a top student wrapped in a three-sport athlete.

"No Hill before him was much when it came to sports. Allie and Janie are small, and Wilson was a big, slow-moving man best suited to lifting heavy objects. But Malcolm was different." Ford pointed to a football field flanked by wooden stands. "I used to take my family out here Friday nights to watch that young man play. He's rangy, six feet tall, and could run past you, or over you, or do whatever got him closest to the goal line." His voice softened. "Watching Malcolm Hill dancing in the end zone, I never imagined trying to keep him alive."

Lost in thought, Chase said nothing.

★ ★ ★

A few moments later, they entered a tree-shaded street running through an affluent neighborhood of large houses in the Old South architectural style, many with wide and comfortably shady front porches, set along a profusion of oaks, pines, green foliage and multicolored flowering trees that had exploded into the violence of beauty Chase associated with photographs of former plantations in springtime.

"We're on Davis Street," Ford informed him. "Named after the Confederacy's one and only president. This is where the white establishment lives, the folks who hold the key to Malcolm's future. What you see all around us captures how it thinks of itself—a polite and orderly society tucked within the magnolias and manicured lawns.

"The town calls this an historic district, but Blacks have no history here except as servants. I can think of one African American who lives on this street, a doctor. But that's it. Their country club is all white, and you'd think from all the quiet on the subject that it happened by accident without anybody noticing." Ford slowed down the car in front of a gracious old home with a pillared front porch that, like its neighbors, was freshly painted white. "That's where the district attorney resides. His family built this house generations back with money from the land they've owned since before the Civil War.

"Same with Judge Tilly. It's like Faulkner said—the past isn't dead; it's not even past."

On the edge of the neighborhood, they stopped in front of a large brick church with a white spire set on a sweeping and neatly mowed lawn edged with daffodils and roses. "That's the First Baptist Church," Ford told Chase. "All white. That's where the judge and district attorney attend church. Along with the late George Bullock and his family."

This surprised Chase. "This seems like a pretty class-conscious place. Judges and cops are from different strata."

"Yes and no. Belonging to a church like this one creates a bond of respectability all its own, part of the cultural glue that holds white people together in a community where there are barely more of them than us." Once again, Ford adopted the neutral manner of a docent. "For the local aristocrats like Tilly and Harris, Bullock was a trusted overseer, someone they counted on to drive off the drug dealers and keep things in line. Chatting with him after services gave them a benign democratic feeling.

"Now his wife and kids will be looking to them for justice. The God of this church loves the people who go here best, and expects them to take care of each other. On a conscious level, the judge and district attorney may not think of it this way, but they'll go about their duties with that lodged in their subconscious. George Bullock was one of theirs, and the young Black man who killed him is not."

No, he's only my son, Chase thought. *And I don't know him, or this place, or how to help protect him from the strangers who run it.*

★ ★ ★

After a few blocks of declining grandeur, they entered a modest neighborhood of ranch-style houses on cramped lots. At once, Chase began noticing a spate of yard signs proclaiming "Back the Blue."

"This is another all-white neighborhood," Ford told him, "but way more hostile than Davis Street. I don't know how many times I've been stopped here driving to the cemetery where my people are buried. Once by Woody Palmer, the peanut-brained cop who harassed Malcolm on the way to visiting his grandfather's grave.

"What goes around comes around, as they say—maybe this time more than once. Woody's kid Billy is the one Malcolm punched out. But if there's a trial, he'll have another shot at Malcolm."

A potentially lethal one, Chase knew. "What was Billy doing in a majority-Black school? Why not Southern Academy?"

Ford chuckled perfunctorily. "Because he's dumb as a plant, for one thing, and comes from rednecks. The Board of Education provided a safety valve so people like that wouldn't try to get into Southern—a public K–12 'charter school' barely better than the high school, but with no bus services from Black neighborhoods. Problem is, Billy imagined some college giving him a baseball scholarship, so he went to the only school where the level of competition is good enough for anyone to notice. Now he blames Malcolm for ruining his chances."

"How so?"

"Billy was scheduled to pitch the afternoon Malcolm decked him. I guess there was a scout from some college there to watch him pitch."

Chase found himself imagining Malcolm's aggrieved classmate on the witness stand. Scanning the street, he saw that the "Back the Blue" placards had multiplied. "What are those about?" he asked.

"For one thing, a lot of white cops and deputies live here. After Black Lives Matter started popping up on TV screens, so did these signs. Instead of being racists, these folks could be righteous supporters of law enforcement. One thing for sure, I'd want as few of these people on Malcolm's jury as I could manage." Abruptly, Ford braked, stopping at the side of the street. "Here we are."

About a half block down, Chase saw a one-story house with a flowering tree beside a white picket fence. Against the fence, a profusion of flowers had been arranged in a makeshift memorial that included a deputy's wide-brimmed brown hat. Through its open gate, a thirtyish man and woman went bearing a casserole dish.

Chase felt an involuntary frisson. "Bullock's house."

"Uh-huh," Ford answered softly. "I do believe that young man's Nick Spinetta, the arresting officer. The way I hear it, some people think he was a saint for not shooting Malcolm on the spot, and others think he should have."

"What do you know about him?"

"Next to nothing. But unless I miss my bet, if there's a trial you're looking at the prosecution's first witness. He'll be the one Harris uses to identify the crime scene pictures of George Bullock with a gaping hole in his forehead. Don't want to make the jurors wait for that."

★ ★ ★

The Black cemetery, Planting Field, was set in a sprawling, sunbaked expanse whose grass was turning brown in asymmetrical patches. As Ford drove deeper, Chase saw that it was largely ill-tended, the markers modest. But for a few spires and tablets, they were inlaid in the earth, their worn engravings filigreed with moss.

"Any whites here?" Chase asked.

"None I've heard of. This is where they laid my grandparents to rest, and all of Allie's people. Including her father."

"Know where he's buried?"

"Of course. Want to pay our respects?"

"Please."

Leaving the car, they climbed a gentle slope to the shelter of a single oak tree. Unlike those surrounding them, the gravesite for the Hill family was newly weeded, and someone had rested fresh flowers at the base of the newest monument. On its granite face was engraved: "Wilson Hall, 1948–2020. Beloved husband of Jane, father of Alexandria, grandfather of Malcolm."

"Those were Wilson's instructions," Ford observed. "He didn't want his grandson left out."

"He sounds like a good man."

Ford nodded. "He was. Of all that's besetting Malcolm, among the worst is that he can't come here every week, like Janie and Allie do. I'm sure those flowers are theirs."

Looking around them, Chase tried to absorb that his son's ancestors through Allie were interred here. His own ancestors and, he reminded himself, Malcolm's, rested in the hushed and shady parkland of Mount Auburn Cemetery in Cambridge, with places reserved for his mother and father and, though Chase preferred cremation to burial, his own notional remains. Here, too, there were plots reserved for family still living. With startling suddenness, Chase realized that his son might someday lie here among the only family he knew, and far too soon.

Ford was regarding him, Chase noticed, with open curiosity. "You all right?"

"Just reflecting," Chase answered. "To me, death has always been something awesome and enormous, even when it's expected. I was wondering about how it felt for Malcolm to lose his grandfather."

For a moment, Ford let him be.

"Let's go," he finally said.

Circling the cemetery in silence back in the car, they slowed beside a section of unusually small tablets, some with toys or stuffed animals beside them. "We call that Babyland," Ford explained. "It's for Black kids who died as children. They're another of Allie's causes."

"Mind if we get out?"

Stopping, the two men stood in front of the miniature gravesites. Some, Chase saw, were disturbingly recent. He found himself fixated on a marker with a red plastic fire truck beside it: "Benjamin Page, 2013–2019."

"A true monument to infant mortality and rotten childcare," Ford remarked.

It was pointless to tell him, Chase reflected, that as a congressman he had sponsored legislation to expand Medicaid and rural healthcare—the site before them memorialized failures beyond redemption. Quiet, he wondered what had taken Benjamin Page from whoever had loved him enough to bring his favorite toy.

★ ★ ★

The seemingly endless grounds of Oak Hill Cemetery, Chase discovered, were dedicated to a monumentalism unknown to those who rested in Planting Field. Beneath the canopy of oaks and pines, it was divided into section upon section of obelisks and spires, traversed by smooth asphalt paths, among which even the relatively modest gravestones were more elaborate than most he had seen for Blacks.

The history, too, was different. Among the first sections Ford drove them through were gravesites for the gallant soldiers of the Army of Tennessee, who had been tended, their plaque said, by the gentlewomen of Cade County before dying of wounds or illness. Amidst them a tall flagpole flew the stars and bars of slavery and secession.

Almost directly beneath it was an enormous piece of flat stone. Pointing it out, Ford said, "As the story goes, there lies a Confederate general who insisted on interment with his favorite horse."

After everything else, this struck Chase as comedic. "Sure hope they had an open-casket funeral."

To his surprise, Ford cracked a smile. "Now that would've been something to see, wouldn't it? Especially if they sat both widows in the front pew."

But this moment came and went. As they drove deeper into the cemetery, Chase felt enveloped by the hush, the lengthening shadows, the sense of generation upon generation of white people who had maintained their primacy of place by excluding Blacks, even in death. "I assume we're passing the gravesites of Tillys and Harrises back to the Civil War."

"Yup. In Cade County even the dead keep to their own."

They drove to the top of a hillock, shrouded in a shadowy stand of pine trees that admitted slanting shards of late-afternoon sunlight. "Let's get out for a minute," Ford suggested.

Leaving the car, they together stood on a swath of dense grass, gazing from the shadows at two tapering marble spires whose pointed tips loomed above them. To Chase, the site felt sepulchral, immersed in gloom. Engraved on the marble were the names James Dixon and Bobby Spann. Their dates of death were identical: July 17, 2019.

"The two murdered cops," he said.

Ford nodded. "The Winthrop Foundation put up these monuments, a tribute to all those who sacrifice to keep Cade County safe. I expect they'll do the same for Bullock."

The last statement had a caustic undertone. "It's not the same thing," Chase said. "They'd be making Bullock a martyr without knowing he is one. And Malcolm a murderer."

"Oh, there'll be no end of white people doing that. But standing here I'm wondering about Dorothy Bullock."

"The widow?"

"Uh-huh. There's two models she can choose from. James Dixon's widow got food from all over the community, and shared some of it with the widow of the Black spousal abuser who'd killed her husband. It was her way of saying that hatred was wrong. But Bobby Spann's mother, Fay, started spewing racist venom every way she could." Ford's tone became harsher. "After those killings, a well-meaning white lady started a Facebook page to promote racial understanding among people in Cade County. But Fay Spann polluted the page with so much hate, the woman had to take it down. She's also the walking definition of white trash, an attention seeker who turned her son's murder into a racket for soliciting money to buy herself a nicer house.

"She'll be all over Malcolm, for sure. But what worries me more is which way Dorothy Bullock is going—dignified mourning, or avenging angel." Ford turned to Chase, arms crossed. "The funeral's tomorrow, and I hear rumors that the governor of Georgia is showing up to give a eulogy. I'm sure you know better than most that he's deadly afraid that Allie will turn out enough voters to beat him this November. If he wants to take her down by going after Malcolm, canonizing Bullock is a good place to start."

That could well be right, Chase knew, the first among the converging pressures that could make Ford's defense of Malcolm excruciatingly difficult, even dangerous. No matter how able, Ford might swiftly find himself and Malcolm caught in a vicious game of four-dimensional chess that involved the legal system, the media, white nationalists, and politicians whose ambitions far outran any concern of fairness to a Black voting rights worker accused of killing a white cop.

A motor sounded, and they turned to see a truck stop beside an open space near the twin marble spires. Two Black men with shovels got out and began digging a hole in the earth. Softly, Ford said, "That's for Bullock, I expect. Monument to follow."

★ ★ ★

As they reached the edge of town, they encountered a line of motor-cyclists heading in the opposite direction, motors snarling, their drivers variously featuring beards, caps, a few sleeveless T-shirts with a bolt of white lightning across the front, and what appeared to be gun cases attached to their cycles.

"Locals?" Chase asked.

Eyes narrowing, Ford scanned the procession. "Too many for that, I believe. I'm guessing these fine patriots came all the way from North Georgia, to help Charles and Molly Parnell exercise their constitutional right to protest the continued existence of Malcolm Hill."

Chase felt a stab of alarm. "Think he'll be safe?"

Ford glanced at him. "These knuckle-draggers could never break into Al Garrett's jail. But them showing up will give the polite white people who still run this county something else to think about. They don't want armed racists on motorcycles taking root here—it's a bad look if you're wanting to attract more business. The best way to head that off might be prosecuting Malcolm to the limit."

Yet again, Ford's phlegmatic commentary had the disturbing ring of truth. "Mind if I buy you dinner?" Chase asked. "Feels like we've still got more to talk about."

"That we do, Congressman," Ford answered. "For Allie's sake, Malcolm's, and mine. Maybe even yours."

25

The hotel restaurant was another throwback from a resort in the late nineteenth century. Its burgundy ceilings were at least twenty feet high, with elaborate white wainscoting and alabaster pillars that descended past chocolate brown walls and tall windows, still admitting faint daylight, to an inlaid tile floor. Arrayed around the spacious room were Oriental screens, a grand piano, large porcelain planters with lush green ferns, and tables covered in white cloths and graced with comfortable leather chairs. Chase could still feel the pride of prosperity that had once favored the town before the modern economy had so decisively decamped.

Awaiting Ford, he was attended by a slight and pretty brunette waitress of twenty or so. As was his custom, and today for other reasons, he asked a little about her life. She was in college nearby, he learned, aiming for law school.

"I used to be one of those," Chase told her. "A lawyer. But then I got offered another job, and now all that seems like a long time ago."

"Are you here on business?"

"No. Just visiting a friend."

Her brow knit. "Plan to be here long?"

"I don't think so. Perhaps a couple more days."

"Sure hope you don't get the wrong impression," she said firmly. "You probably know we've had a tragedy here. A deputy sheriff was murdered, someone a lot of us looked up to. Now there are outsiders come to stir up trouble nobody needs. But if you can stay long enough, you'll find that Cade County is a friendly place. Very hospitable."

Not so much for my son, Chase imagined saying. "I'm sure it is," he assured the young white woman. "It's already been more interesting than I could have imagined."

★ ★ ★

When Ford arrived, they both ordered drinks—Maker's Mark and ginger ale for Ford, a dry gin martini for Chase. Taking their order, the waitress gave the two men a brief, puzzled look, and her formerly pleasant face became a blank. As she retreated, Ford remarked, "Feels like she knows who I am. Sure can't be you. When I walked in here, she was eyeing you up like you'd just hung the moon."

Glancing around them at the sparsely occupied tables, Chase saw several couples, what appeared to be a family, a commercial traveler eating alone, and one Black man and woman on what looked to be a date. "We're the only interracial couple in the place," he responded. "There's bound to be talk."

Ford barely smiled, setting the template for what Chase expected to be, at best, an evening of mutual wariness. Though Chase felt quite certain that Ford was different around familiar locals and Black friends like Allie, he clearly saw the visiting congressman as an unwelcome and puzzling phenomenon he had been compelled to deal until—hopefully sooner than later—he was not.

Fishing for a change of subject, Chase ventured, "Allie tells me you're looking at going into politics. If not now, down the road."

Ford gave him the same cool look. "A long road, feels like. Near as I can tell, Congressman, you were born into so much money that you've never had to worry, and the district you grew up in is filled with comfortable white liberals you fit like a glove. But my way forward is harder. I don't come from wealth, and too many whites around here won't vote for a Black man. Without Allie Hill, I couldn't even think about it. But she makes me possible, the way she made Al Garrett possible. Like we all do, I owe her.

"Now they'll use Malcolm to batter her politically and emotionally, trash her reputation, dry up her funding until she's finished as a force in the state. Assuming someone like Charles Parnell doesn't murder her first."

The shattering truth of this made Chase wince inside. "I know all that," he responded succinctly. "Why do you suppose I came here?"

Ford's eyes flashed with impatience. "I've got no earthly idea, Congressman. What do *you* suppose you'll accomplish?"

"That's what I'm trying to figure out," Chase responded. "What's puzzling me is why you seem to resent it."

Ford fixed him with a gelid stare. "Resentment's not what I'm about. Granted, I don't need some hotshot ex-prosecutor from Massachusetts coming in here like the Second Coming of Christ. It's bad enough dealing with all the crackers down here who think that Jesus was white and spoke English. There's nothing you can tell me about defending Malcolm Hill on a potential charge of capital murder in Cade County, Georgia.

"Living in this place, I've figured out how to talk with whites and Blacks of various classes. It's like mastering multiple languages. You can never be here long enough to learn even one." Ford paused for emphasis. "But that's not it. The reason I want you gone goes to your current profession. Politics."

"With all due respect," Chase retorted, "there's nothing much you can tell me about that I don't already know." His voice became conversational. "Long ago, I got used to condescension from people who don't know me. It's a class thing, mostly. Generally, they learn better."

Ford smiled without humor. "Oh, I can see beneath all the polish well enough. I expect you can be a pretty hard man when it matters, and I've been watching you taking things in while pretending you're not. And there's at least one or two things, whatever they are, you're choosing to hold back." He leaned forward. "Problem is, you seem to think Massachusetts prepares you for the worst, and that the House of Representatives is as bad as it gets. It's not. After the 2020 election, white people with military-grade weapons came pouring in from North Georgia to join the Parnells in massing outside Allie's office brandishing AR-15s. But for Al Garrett, I think they might've gone in to get her.

"This year it's worse. There's a Black preacher trying to get reelected to the Senate, a Black woman running for governor, and every Republican candidate in sight will be racializing the election by demanding the death penalty for Malcolm. Stick around, and sooner or later someone or another is going to recognize you." Ford softened his voice. "This case is a racist tar baby, and you'll end up with tar all over you."

With some difficulty, Chase maintained the same air of calm. "So what do you advise?"

Ford stared at him. "I can't speak for Allie," he said at length. "I don't know what you were to each other at Harvard, or what's driving either of you today. But none of us needs the extra trouble and publicity you may bring down on all of us if you stick around." He paused, then finished quietly. "Save yourself now, Congressman, and leave before evil catches you out here. Just go."

★ ★ ★

Afterward, Chase sat alone in his room.

They had given him what they called the presidential suite, once graced by Jimmy and Rosalynn Carter, featuring a ceiling fan, a carved wooden bed with an intricate headboard, and an antique wardrobe. *Why not?* he had thought—it seemed as close to the presidency as he was likely to get.

Gazing out the window, Chase considered anew all that he could not tell Jabari Ford, and could barely believe himself: that an eighteen-year-old he didn't know, his son with the woman he had loved most in his life, was facing the prospect of death, caught up in the force fields of history and race in such a strange and labyrinthine byway.

He thought of calling Kara, but could not.

Through the window, the sunset over Cade County smeared the clouds a violent orange. Chase had never felt so far from home.

PART FOUR

The Decision

26

On the day of George Bullock's funeral, Chase awakened from a fitful sleep.

Through his window, dawn had broken clear and bright. He made himself coffee and, with reluctant curiosity, switched on Fox News. The bland face of Georgia's governor filled the screen.

He was addressing a press conference in Atlanta. "As you know," Jackson Trask intoned, "I have directed the Georgia Bureau of Investigation to dedicate all resources necessary to thoroughly investigate the fatal shooting of Cade County sheriff's deputy George Bullock, and the culpability of the activist arrested in connection with his death."

My son, Chase thought again. He wondered how it felt for Malcolm to be locked in the county jail, perhaps watching his fate unfold on the television screen of a windowless cell. "To maintain public safety," the governor continued, "I've ordered Georgia state troopers to guard the courthouse, Deputy Bullock's home, the church where his funeral will occur, and the cemetery where his family and friends will lay him to rest…"

It was starting, Chase understood at once—Trask was not protecting public safety, but stoking mass anxiety for his own political benefit. Driven by anger and disgust, he turned off the screen and walked the three blocks from his hotel to the courthouse.

As Trask had promised, it was surrounded by uniformed state troopers whose squad cars blocked Main Street, enhancing the sense of incipient danger. A few Black demonstrators with signs stood behind wooden barriers, and a cadre of white militia occupied the park adjacent to the courthouse. From the bench where Chase and Ford had sat the afternoon before, Charles Parnell surveyed the scene, a semiautomatic assault weapon cradled in his lap. As the governor had no doubt hoped, reporters and television cameras were clustered among a group of curious onlookers, broadcasting his gratuitous but ominous mini-drama.

Checking his watch, Chase headed back to the hotel. It was barely nine o'clock, and the first waves of heat were already rising from the asphalt street whose sidewalks, it seemed to him, had been largely emptied of pedestrians by anxieties to which some could not put a name, but that were woven by time and history into the fabric of Cade County, and increasingly, America.

★ ★ ★

At nine thirty, Chase hit the Zoom link on his laptop.

After a moment, the alert visage of Alister Stott appeared. British by birth and not yet forty, Stott had become a leading expert on America's domestic terrorism, and after January 6 had testified before a House subcommittee of which Chase was a member. Though Chase trusted him implicitly, he chose not to mention where he was.

"Good morning, Congressman," Stott said cheerfully. "How have you been?"

"Never better. And you?"

"The same," Stott replied with a shade less good humor. "How could I not be? January 6 was a righteous demonstration, they're rigging election laws all over America to fix the Electoral College in 2024, and white people are exercising their God-given rights to carry weapons and keep nonwhites from voting. I'm grateful you lovely people gave me a green card." Glancing at some notes on his desk, he added, "So you want to know about White Lightning. Seems like you're taking an interest in current events in the sovereign state of Georgia."

"I am." Chase paused to consider how best to explain his inquiry. "I'm thinking about speaking with the Justice Department. The last thing we need after this shooting is more violence."

"You're right to worry. There are a lot of maniacs in this country to choose from. But the people in our shop think White Lightning could turn out to be a bad one."

"What do you guys know about them?"

Briefly, Stott glanced at his notes. "They're centered in North Georgia but looking to branch out across the state. They already have a foothold in Southwest Georgia, including where that deputy got shot. They're also tied into extreme right-wing politicians like your colleague Dorothy Turner Dark, and they enjoy showing up in public to intimidate whoever they don't like—which means anyone who's not a gun-toting white Christian extremist."

Chase scribbled some notes. "Do they have a specific ideology?"

"The basic ugly. Black people stole the election. They're trying to replace whites. Armed revolution may be America's last hope. And so on down the rabbit hole."

"Nice. Any idea of their numbers?"

"Hard to say. Groups like that don't collect dues or pass out membership cards. There's also a multiplier effect—just by spreading hatred, they can inspire lone wolves to commit acts of violence on their own. Those types are just as dangerous, and perhaps more deadly. You may never know who they are until they've already done their worst."

Chase looked up. "As I understand it, after November 2020 armed members of White Lightning gathered outside Allie Hill's office in Cade County loaded down with weapons."

Stott's expression turned sober. "To White Lightning, she's a promiscuous Black woman who's facilitating the nonwhite takeover of America. I hope to God she has enough security."

"So do I. What do you know about a Charles Parnell, or his sister Molly?"

"More about him than her. He clearly wants to make White Lightning more of a presence in Cade County, something that elected officials are afraid of crossing. Fear of getting killed by crazies can make for interesting public policy. If I were the judge or prosecutor stuck with this case, I might feel their crosshairs on the back of my neck."

Facing the computer screen, Chase pretended that he had been struck by a new thought. "Do you think White Lightning has any reach into law enforcement?"

"We don't know. But that possibility is one of the things we worry about with all these groups. People in law enforcement have the authority and skills that extremists hope they can turn on America's supposed enemies. You'll remember from that hearing last year that over ten percent of the people arrested for overrunning the Capitol had a military or law enforcement background."

"Yeah, that kind of stuck in my mind. What about connections in Georgia?"

"There's only one instance we know about, and it's not specifically connected to White Lightning. A couple of years ago, the FBI arrested a sheriff's deputy in rural Georgia who was texting the leader of another extremist group. The subject was killing or intimidating voting rights workers. It never happened, so maybe it's just talk. But it's the kind of thing that *could* happen." Stott gave him a querying look. "Any chance you're thinking about the deputy who stopped Hill's son?"

"Let's say it's occurred to me."

Stott considered this. "If I were the young man's lawyer, I'd certainly give it some thought. Still, it's a long shot. And even if it weren't, generally you only figure out the connection if some cop goes completely off the rails, or you get a tip from a colleague. A cop who gets caught playing footsie with extremists is too likely to lose his job."

Chase contemplated how to pursue this, and then felt caution rein him in. "I really appreciate this, Alister. Especially on such short notice."

"No worries at all, Congressman, and don't hesitate to check back. Before it's done, this thing in Georgia could leave more people dead. Did you see the governor calling out the troops this morning? A nice piece of fascist theater, I thought."

"So did I," Chase answered. "But I'm afraid that was only Act One. Too many politicians in Georgia may want a stage of their own."

27

Alone in his hotel room, Chase watched Fox News cover Deputy Sheriff George Bullock's televised funeral.

The tableau was much as he had expected, but worse. The church Ford had shown him was now ringed by state troopers, and inside it was airy but unadorned, a portrait of pristine Protestant religiosity invaded by tragedy. Draped in the state flag of Georgia, Bullock's casket lay before the altar. From the first pew, Dorothy Bullock gazed at it fixedly, her thin face drawn and pale, her eyes swollen half shut with grief.

At her sides were two children, both blonde, a fresh-faced daughter of college years who clutched her mother's hand, and a gangly teenage boy who looked utterly lost. Chase could too easily imagine the viewership contrasting this devastated boy, stripped of a father, with the frightening Black specter of Malcolm Hill. That there *was* a viewership, he well knew, had required the widow's permission. This was not simply a funeral—it was an event designed to arouse an audience of millions, and to draw presumptive mourners with designs of their own.

As the camera panned the pews behind the dead man's family, yet another blonde, a Fox News commentator, pointed out the notables: Governor Trask, his right-wing rival in the Republican gubernatorial primary, a Republican senatorial candidate, and the perfectly groomed daughter-in-law of the man many of George Bullock's mourners no doubt still considered America's rightful president. Sitting beside the district attorney of Cade County, one of the few Blacks Chase could find, the sheriff, had assumed an expression of fathomless impassivity that suggested, at least to Chase, that his sense of duty exceeded whatever he felt about his deceased subordinate. Not for the first time, Chase pondered the heartless calculation of public figures enacting public grief.

Which of these, he wondered, would try to claim this moment for himself?

At the event, to Chase's unsurprise, it proved to be Governor Trask.

Rising to speak, he implicitly answered the question Jabari Ford had posed to Chase at the gravesite of the two murdered police: Dorothy Bullock had chosen to lend her late husband to the higher cause of the governor's political survival—the better, perhaps, to strengthen him as an ally in exacting her own vengeance against Malcolm Hill.

Trask stood before the congregation in a somber gray suit and tie, his voice striking the carefully modulated organ notes of remembrance, sadness, and muted moral indignation.

"This is not a day for politics," he solemnly averred. "It is a day for honoring a man who gave his life for the safety, and for the good, of an entire community regardless of race or station. The kind of man who looks out for our families and our homes. The breed of man of whom we can never have enough: a devoted husband, a deeply attentive father, a dedicated member of this church, and a brave and resolute law enforcement officer who made Cade County more secure.

"More than that, George Bullock was a person who made everyone whose lives he touched that much better. He was a pillar for his devoted friends, a Little League coach of boundless enthusiasm, the caring neighbor we all want. His wife, Dorothy, is a nurse at Cade County Hospital. They fell in love in seventh grade, married after high school, raised a fine young woman and man, Martha and George Junior, and brought joy to others throughout thirty-one wonderful years together. Those who know them best say that no one, and they mean no one, ever came to George and Dorothy Bullock for help without receiving it." Pausing, Trask nodded to Dorothy, who responded with a slight and tremulous smile. "The Bullocks are loving people," the governor continued, "and George Bullock was a deeply loving man."

Considering each brushstroke, Chase contrasted the governor's artful portrait of a model Christian with Malcolm's account to Ford and his mother of a frightening bigot who abused his powers under the cover of darkness. This mythical Bullock, if left untarnished, could destroy Allie, her cause, and their son.

Abruptly, Trask raised his voice in a stern and steely recitation of George Bullock's public virtues. "As a law enforcement officer, George Bullock was a servant leader who practiced love in action. The kind of love that knows that law, not license, keeps us from descending into savagery and sin. He had a nose for illegality, and a passion for protecting this county from the scourge of drug addiction. For George, traffic stops were about more than speeding tickets. There were about spotting dangerous criminals who would callously line their pockets by stealing the future from our youth.

"The money he seized by stopping drug dealers—which the department got to keep—helped pay for more deputies and better equipment. He was not only doing the department's work; he was doing God's work by keeping our children safe. Knowing, as all law enforcement officers know, how risky traffic stops can be, and how often they lead to tragedy."

The calculated cynicism of this infuriated Chase; implied, though not stated, was that Malcolm Hill was the moral equivalent of a drug dealer, and had murdered Bullock for the deputy's righteous act in stopping him. "When we lose a man like George Bullock," the governor concluded, "we lose a piece of ourselves. Not just our sense of security, but a good and decent man who helped make the people he served better and more decent.

"We can honor him best by rededicating ourselves to seeking justice, as he did.

"By fighting the forces of violence, as he did.

"And by protecting the brave men and women who serve by rigorously enforcing our laws, as George Bullock did to the end of his days."

Pausing one last time, Trask gazed solemnly at Bullock's casket. "To preserve the safety of all law-abiding citizens, we can do no less. Bless you, George, for showing us the way. May we prove by our actions to be worthy of your sacrifice."

For Chase, this was more than enough. But he knew too well that the ritual of mourning, and its undertone of reprisal, was far from done, and with it the damage to Malcolm.

★ ★ ★

When the service was over, uniformed pallbearers carefully bore the casket down the stone steps of the church. Watching them, Chase thought he recognized Deputy Nick Spinetta, the arresting officer, and realized that Spinetta and his wife had been seated beside Dorothy Bullock and her children. Hastily he scrawled a note: "Bullock/Spinetta?"

On both sides of the walkway to the church, a line of deputies and police, Black and white, watched the casket move toward the hearse awaiting Bullock's body. In front and behind it was a long motorcade of squad cars from across Georgia. Gravely, the pallbearers slid the casket inside the hearse, and Spinetta and another deputy closed the double doors behind it, the muffled echo sounding in Chase's room.

In seeming unison, those driving the squad cars turned on their engines. As the lead cars crept forward, beginning the slow procession to Oak Hill Cemetery, the voices on Fox News provided a soundtrack of white grievance. "Ask yourself this," the network's prime-time anchorman asked the brittle blonde whose program preceded his. "Why can't Democrats bring themselves to defend the police instead of defunding them?"

"That's a given," the woman responded flatly. "To radical Democrats, white lives don't matter. Blue lives don't matter. Only the lives of Black criminals matter. They're turning the race card into a hunting license."

On the screen, the procession glided forward, evoking for Chase the funeral of a beloved statesman. "Then ask yourself *this*," the anchorman countered. "Will this country allow the mother of Malcolm Hill—the killer of George Bullock—to continue abetting the rampant voter fraud that helped Democrats seize control of the White House and the United States Senate?"

Unable to listen, Chase muted the television.

For a while he sat lost in thought, heedless of time. At last he took his cell phone and hit the number he had entered only days before. "Can I see you?" he asked. "I think we need to talk about our son."

28

An hour before dusk, Chase drove to the home Malcolm had shared with Allie.

Deliberately, he chose the route Malcolm had taken the night of George Bullock's death. There were no streetlights, no houses close to the long stretch of road on which Bullock had stopped Chase's son. Even now it was lightly trafficked; past midnight, it would have been dark and untraveled. Nearing the spot where he guessed the shooting had occurred, Chase pulled over to a stop and got out.

There were fields on both sides, nothing else. Looking around, Chase felt his son's helplessness—then and now—and, once again, his own. The fatal moments were a black hole created by a dead man: only Malcolm knew what had happened.

Chase got back in the car.

A gravel road bisected acres of grassland, studded with oak trees; on that road rested Allie's one-story house and, a hundred or so yards beyond it, the larger farmhouse where her mother still lived. For Chase, it was strange to enter this place: He remembered from college Allie's descriptions of her life here, of sitting against a tree listening to the crickets and looking up with wonder at the stars and moon, yet envisioning the specter of the slaves who had once worked these fields.

Whatever Chase had wanted for Allie and himself, this place and its history had possessed her.

But what unsettled him now was how isolated it was, yet how easily found. Allie was no longer safe here.

Getting out, Chase saw a basketball hoop on a cement rectangle beside the driveway, then a horseshoe pit near a tire swing still hanging on a frayed rope from the thick branch of an oak tree—Wilson Hill's gifts to his grandson, he imagined. The still-humid air carried a faint perfume from a flower bed beside the screened porch.

Framed in the doorway, she awaited him. It was a trick of the mind, he knew, but in her blouse and blue jeans, she looked as she had that last morning at Harvard, before she turned and ran through the door of his bedroom knowing, as he had not, that she was bearing their child. For a moment, it felt as though the nineteen years since had vanished.

★ ★ ★

Approaching, Chase looked to Allie more like he sometimes had in college—vulnerable, a little uncertain about what to do with her—than the tempered man that time and ambition had made him, driven here by what he so keenly felt as her betrayal. But that somehow intensified her sense of the space she had created between them by bringing their son here to raise on her own.

She opened the door to let him inside.

Quiet, he slowly looked around the living room—nondescript, in Allie's mind, except for its photographs of Black people, some family, some not, none known to him. To her his presence here felt impossible, and then sad. "You wanted to talk about Malcolm," she said.

"I do. But first maybe you could show me his room."

For a stray, poignant moment, Allie remembered lying with Chase in his bedroom on Martha's Vineyard, divining clues to the boy he had been. "Of course."

They stood in the doorway to Malcolm's bedroom, Allie at his shoulder. He seemed reluctant to step inside, as though this were a place he did not belong. She wondered whether Chase was thinking, as she had since the shooting, that their son might never set foot here again.

Briefly touching his arm, she led him inside.

He stood there, hands in his pockets. Looking first at the photographs, he stopped to consider the picture of Malcolm with his grandfather outside the Atlanta stadium. "I guess that's your dad."

"Yes." For a moment Allie considered whether it would be hurtful for Chase to hear about Malcolm's grandfather as surrogate father, then decided not to censor the truth of their son's life. "They were very close. They'd watch sports together, go fishing, play horseshoes or catch after dinner. My dad went to all his games, never missed a one."

Chase's voice was tinged with regret. "That must have been nice. For both of them."

"It was." But Allie could not bring herself to say that Wilson Hill was the man Malcolm sat next to every Sunday dinner, the man who pretended that Malcolm could outrun him until, soon enough, he could. Nor could she mention the moments when Malcolm was little and she had imagined that it was Chase, rather than her father, playing in the yard with their son.

Chase was looking at another picture, of three-year-old Malcolm on his grandfather's shoulders. "Was it hard for him when your dad died?"

At once, Allie remembered the stricken look on Malcolm's face when he'd run inside to find her. "More than hard. They were outside playing horseshoes, and Dad just dropped to his knees and was gone. By the time we got back to him, there were already tears streaming down Malcolm's face.

"In his own way, Malcolm took it worse than my mom or me. At least Mom has her faith, and I still have some. But I think Malcolm is still trying to find a God he can entrust his grandfather to."

For a moment, Chase was silent. Then he resumed contemplating the artifacts of Malcolm's life—his certificate as class president, his trophy for Athlete of the Year. "I hear he was an incredible football player."

You should have seen him, Allie almost said, and then stopped herself. "For me, it was always more about leadership and how he did in school. But hand that boy a football, and he was something to see."

Quiet, Chase kept looking around for clues—Malcolm's books, mostly concerning the present or past of Black Americans; his acceptance letter to Morehouse; the barbells he lifted; the full-length mirror in which Allie would find him studying the man he was swiftly becoming. Finally he turned to face her. "I guess you know how strange this is for me. I have a son who existed in a parallel universe, and I missed everything about him. Everything he ever did or thought or felt."

It was less that he was blaming her, Allie realized, than that she was the only person to whom he could say this. In that moment she felt the full weight of his disorientation, caught between the life he had made for himself and the son he had never known existed, and whose plight he had done nothing to create.

Chase turned back to the photograph of Malcolm as a child. "What was he like growing up?"

To Allie, the inquiry felt unspeakably poignant. But despite her terrible fears for his future, Allie found that remembering Malcolm's childhood still gave her pleasure. "He was like lots of things," she told his father. "He was curious. He was active and liked to do new activities. He loved anything you could do with a ball of any shape or size. But he was also a reader." She hesitated, then smiled a little. "When he was small, he used to daydream a lot. I don't think he got that from me."

"Did he ever ask about me?"

Where to start? Allie wondered. "Quite a lot, until he just stopped. More than once, he asked if you were white. I never said. But he's lighter skinned than my parents or me, a reminder of the great unanswered question running through his life." She paused, remembering her misgivings about the path she had chosen. "Sometimes I'd catch him just staring into that mirror, and imagine that he was trying to see through the glass to find you. Maybe it was actually me, looking into the mirror of my own guilt. Because I could see you clearly enough."

"Would *he*, I wonder?"

"If he met you?" She crossed her arms, pondering the question. "I don't know. He's a Hill from Cade County, for sure. But then there's that smile, the way he moves, and certain angles when his face looks kind of, I don't know, maybe European, and suddenly I remember that his other grandfather was French." She looked up again. "So maybe he would, if he wanted to. But that's something else I need to explain.

"He grew up in a world where his family is Black, our friends are Black, our causes are Black. Maybe most important, *his* friends and classmates are Black. That's who he wanted to be, maybe needed to be to claim his own place in a society that would always treat him as Black." For a moment Allie stopped to reabsorb her own anger. "He grew up hearing about one Black person after another being shot dead by cops or self-appointed vigilantes—starting with Trayvon Martin. There are whole studies about what that does to the psychology of young Black men—to grow up in a world that threatens them just for existing.

"When that tape of George Floyd came out, Malcolm couldn't sleep. He never said it, but I knew in my soul that the last thing he wanted to be was half white."

Chase fell quiet again. Watching him, Allie imagined him absorbing that the son he had never met harbored these fears and resentments, and then pondering the implications of that—for Malcolm and for him. "Did that change how Malcolm acted toward white people, or what he said about cops?"

She looked at him directly. "I know Malcolm consumed a lot of social media about police misconduct toward Blacks, and he got much more vocal in class. Getting hassled by that cop driving to his grandfather's grave was very personal to him." Her voice held a note of resistance. "I told you about punching the cop's kid. But that's a long way from deliberately killing a deputy."

Once more, she could follow Chase's thoughts, because she lived with them hour upon sleepless hour—that the bullet in George Bullock's brain came from the gun Malcolm had purchased a mere two weeks before. Finally, he said, "I need to see him, Allie."

She inhaled, quelling her own emotions. "You can visit tomorrow," she finally said. "If Malcolm's OK with it. Just do me one favor and let me tell him you're a friend. Anything more would be too much for him, and you haven't sorted out what you want."

She watched Chase consider this and then shrug. "All right," he said with the barest trace of irony. "Given everything, after eighteen years I suppose there's no rush. Father's Day was only three weeks ago, after all, and I neglected to call my own."

29

The Cade County jail was a grim-looking rectangle, surrounded by a high fence and then an open field that would afford escapees no cover, conveniently located across the road from a bail bondsman in a converted ranch house whose sign advertised that he took credit cards. For Chase, realizing that this facility housed his son was another landmark in his stations of disbelief.

Within moments, a female deputy had taken him to Sheriff Garrett's office. As Garrett greeted him, his manner was pleasant but phlegmatic, as if the advent of a congressman from Massachusetts was entirely unremarkable—the product of a considerable discipline, Chase suspected, that the Sheriff had cultivated over time to conceal his thoughts at will. In their first moment of acquaintanceship, Garrett struck him as a formidable man.

"Allie Hill tells me you're a friend from college," the sheriff said. "Guess you've never met her son."

"No. I'm hoping to see how he's doing, and if there's any way I can help him."

Garrett ignored the tacit question. "How he's doing is about how you'd expect. He's an active young man of eighteen with a big future ahead, who suddenly found himself living in an eight-by-ten box. Now he's realizing that his life will be some version of that until he goes free or dies—whatever year that is. He's accused of murdering a sheriff's deputy, and he's got no more chance of bail than if he'd shot the president. Maybe less. What he's got is an abundance of time to think about all that. So visitors are welcome."

Beneath the sheriff's flat baritone, Chase caught a hint of deep frustration, perhaps because Garrett had become a cog in the justice system of Cade County who, having been supplanted by the Georgia Bureau of Investigation and subordinated to the district attorney's prosecutorial authority, had no formal discretion to act beyond keeping Malcolm safe. The other instinct Chase felt was that Garret had a profound disinclination to utter niceties about the late George Bullock.

"I'm sure it's hard," he ventured. "Especially with what Malcolm says happened that night."

Garrett gave him a penetrant look. "I guess you know that's out of my hands."

"I do. But I can't help wondering whether Malcolm's story sounds plausible to you. From what little else I know, it feels like Bullock may have become his own law."

Crossing his arms, Garrett said in brisk reproof, "The only conversations I can have about this case are with the DA and GBI. I'm sure you understand that, Congressman." He paused, then added in a more even tone, "Let's just say that I understand your concerns."

Chase tried to think of how to keep the conversation alive. "If I crossed the line, Sheriff, I apologize. But after the problem with crowd control we had on Capitol Hill, I've taken an interest in white nationalism invading law enforcement. Malcolm's description of what Bullock said and did that night is pretty striking."

"Like I say," Garrett responded firmly, "I can't talk about that. Even if I could, I don't know what happened out there any more than you do. But I can tell you this much. If I *knew* George Bullock had the problem you're implying, he'd still be alive. Because I'd have taken this badge and gun and told him to find another line of work."

Swiftly, Chase took inventory of what Garrett was not quite saying. That he didn't know for sure if Bullock was dirty or a practicing racist. That the thought was not a novelty. And that, perhaps, he felt some measure of personal responsibility for what had happened that night.

"Let's get you to Malcolm," Garrett said. "He's waiting for you."

★ ★ ★

Opening the door, Garrett ushered Chase into the visiting room and closed the door behind him.

Malcolm Hill sat at a laminated table, looking up at him with mild curiosity. But though Chase had prepared himself for this moment, it jarred him beyond expectations.

It was not simply that this stranger was his son. It was how he looked. Unlike his mother, Malcolm was tall—standing, he stood eye to eye with Chase, and seemed to move with the same ease. He was as handsome and appealing as his yearbook picture, with Allie's large, expressive eyes and, most startling, the ridged nose and high cheekbones of Jean Marc Brevard. To Chase, it was as though in some curious transmigration, his father had become part of the stream of humanity that America called Black.

The young man's handshake was firm, Chase discovered. But there were hollows beneath his eyes inapposite with youth, and his face showed a closeness of skin to bone that suggested a loss of appetite. With a calm that surprised him, Chase said, "I'm Chase Brevard. I guess your mom told you about me."

Malcolm nodded, seeming to regard him more closely. "She says you're a friend of hers from Harvard, who turned out to be a congressman."

Chase had another moment of foolish surprise: Though he should have anticipated this, his son spoke, as did Allie, in the soft intonations of a Black from the rural South. "I was also a lawyer," Chase responded. "But you've got the basics. Anyhow, I was hoping we could visit for a while."

Like the host in an anteroom to purgatory, Malcolm gestured at a chair across the table. As they sat, he said, "I was asking Mom why I hadn't heard of you before."

What to say, Chase wondered, when all he wanted to do was word-lessly absorb his son's reality. Casually, he answered, "The last time I saw her was before you were born. But you know your mother. For a small person, she makes a big impression."

Despite his circumstances, Malcolm flashed a fleeting grin—rueful, but Chase's own. "Every day of my life, for the last eighteen years." Then the smile vanished, and Chase sensed Malcolm falling back into the chasm that separated past from future.

★ ★ ★

There was something familiar about this man, Malcolm thought, that he could not place. Despite the aura of comfort that Malcolm had seen in other powerful men and women who gravitated to his mother, on first meeting this one had seemed momentarily rattled. Then he had a harsh reflection—congressmen probably didn't spend much time visiting Black men accused of killing white police.

"I was thinking I'd met you somewhere," Malcolm told him.

"Believe me," the man responded, his manner easy now, "I'd remember. For one thing, you'd be one of two friends I had in Cade County, Georgia. I guess you're wondering why I flew down."

"Actually, I kind of was. Except I figured it was for my mom."

"Not just for her," the congressman said firmly. "I came because I believe you. Not kind of believe you, or want to believe you. I absolutely believe that what you've told your mom and your lawyer is the truth. And that you're no more a murderer than I am."

Suddenly, Malcolm found himself torn between disbelief and a surge of gratitude born of fear and desperation. "You don't even know me."

"That's not quite right. I know how your mom describes you. I know about your grandfather, your grandmother, and your life until now. I know you were class president and Athlete of the Year. I know about Woody Palmer hassling you, and poor Billy's blighted baseball career." The congressman leaned across the table. "Before I entered politics, I used to be a prosecutor. Like your mother and Jabari Ford, I've seen people like George Bullock before. I had the privilege of putting one in jail for killing a Black man. To me, the way you describe Bullock makes perfect sense.

"You didn't buy a gun because you wanted to ambush somebody— you bought one because racists posted your and your mom's pictures on the internet. You weren't drinking beer with friends hoping some random cop would stop you. You weren't out on that road trolling for trouble. You were driving home hoping your mom wouldn't be too pissed off to keep you from crawling in bed. Does that about cover it?"

Bending forward, Malcolm parsed his feelings. "Yeah. It does."

"That's why I'm sitting here," the man replied. "What I haven't quite worked out yet is how I can help you. Still, I *am* a congressman now, and that has to be good for something."

Malcolm tried to sort through the jumble of his emotions. He had lost control of his life, even the ability to speak for himself. He didn't know how to make the hours pass without reliving Bullock's death over and over again while he desperately wished he could turn back time. They were trying to kill him for being Black, for being stupid on a single night, and he kept being whipsawed between helplessness and rage, including at the white racist he had killed by accident. Sometimes he thought he needed to break out of here before he went crazy. He wished his grandfather could come to see him, missed his grandmother Janie as soon as that door closed behind her. Most of all he missed his mother and home so bad it hurt.

Now here was this congressman just showing up out of nowhere. He was used to powerful white people who thought they were liberal, and maybe were, deferring to his mother and treating him with respect. But this felt different somehow, and he desperately needed help from anyone who could do anything to give him back his life.

"How long can you stay here?" Malcolm asked.

★ ★ ★

Reading the hopefulness on Malcolm's face, Chase felt caught between the inexorable demands of his public duties, the gravitational pull of ambition, and the instinctive imperatives of the heart that warred against abandoning his and Allie's son. "I'm not sure yet," he heard himself temporize. "Maybe a couple more days."

Across the table, Chase felt Malcolm shutting down, the exhaustion of an overtaxed boy feeling another hope evanesce. "A couple days," he repeated. "I'm likely to be here a little longer. But thanks for coming, Congressman."

My name is Chase, he wanted to tell him. Pointlessly.

A sheriff's deputy opened the door to announce that their time was up. "I'll be back," Chase promised, for lack of anything else to say.

After a brief silence, Malcolm shrugged. "I'm not going anywhere," he said, and Chase felt his indifference as a last defense against despair.

★ ★ ★

Outside, Chase sat in the car, with the air conditioning running to combat the suffocating heat. Time passed. Again and again, he replayed his half hour with Malcolm. He could not remember feeling so drained since the day Allie Hill had walked out of his life.

At last he took out his cell phone and called her.

★ ★ ★

Without preface, Allie told Jabari Ford, "Chase Brevard wants to sit in on your meeting with the district attorney."

Instantly, she could hear his exasperation. "Sure he does. The man was born walking on water."

"Dog-paddling, maybe. I know him better than you do, and he's not here out of ego. More to the point, he lives on MSNBC and knows the attorney general. Maybe it's not the worst thing for Dalton Harris to think somebody in D.C. is watching what he does."

On the other end, Allie heard the silence of thought. Finally, Ford said, "Mind telling me exactly what this congressman is to you?"

So many things, she thought. *Including a father who has just met our son.* "A lifeline," she answered. "You know better than I do the cases like this aren't always decided in a courtroom. Thing is, Chase knows that, too, and so does Dalton Harris."

30

To Chase, the district attorney's office befit a mainstream member of the local establishment: photographs of a refined-looking, perfectly groomed wife and three pretty daughters who ranged from adolescence to the cusp of adulthood; framed awards and certificates from legal or civic organizations; college and law school diplomas from Emory and the University of Virginia. Though Chase had learned from Ford that Dalton Harris was a Republican, he detected no overt sign of his political leanings.

Harris himself matched Ford's description of a Southern aristocrat. He had clear blue eyes and carefully barbered sandy brown hair, and his tall, rangy frame rested comfortably in a battered leather chair he could have inherited from his father. His manner was gracious, his expression pleasant and attentive, and he spoke with the clear, softly accented enunciation of a Southerner who came from generations of educated men and, Chase posited, women. He would have bet that, like Chase himself, Harris had attended an elite boarding school, had Ford not spoken of Southern Academy.

"Good to see you," Harris told Ford. "As always." Turning to Chase, he added, "Welcome, Congressman. I don't think John F. Kennedy ever visited Cade County. So you may well be the first future senator from Massachusetts ever to grace this office."

The underlying message was clear: Dalton Harris was no backwater prosecutor, but a political sophisticate who understood the stakes for Chase Brevard in the larger world. "But not the last," Chase responded amiably. "Lucy Battle will be dropping by later."

Smiling, Harris waved a dismissive hand. "You're going to beat her, the handicappers say."

At the corner of his vision, Chase noted, Ford seemed to be weighing the unstated implications of this exchange. "So I'm told," Chase rejoined. "But I'm not visiting in my capacity as a congressman, and for these purposes Mr. Ford is the only lawyer on this side of the desk. I'm merely a quiet but interested observer. Allie Hill is a close friend from Harvard."

Harris gave him a look that combined curiosity with polite skepticism. "Whatever the case, you *are* here, so I should state a few principles. Or, if you're inclined to cynicism, prosecutorial platitudes."

"Oh," Chase said pleasantly. "I'm not here in my capacity as a cynic, either. In a potentially inflammatory case like this, principles are important. Particularly the ones that separate prosecutorial discretion from political pressure."

Harris drained the humor from his face. "All right, then. We can start with what I always say to civic groups. I didn't run for this office to be a politician. Law is what holds our community together and makes civilization civil. I believe that to my core." As though seeking trust, he looked from Chase to Ford and back again. "Speaking personally, this case is the acid test of those principles, and it's already weighing on my conscience. I imagine that both of you watched the service for George Bullock. So it won't surprise you that more than a few people used that solemn occasion to ask what I was going to do about Malcolm Hill. Or that the death penalty came up…"

"No surprise to me," Ford interjected softly.

Harris faced him. "Nor to me. One lady had tears in her eyes, and more than one man lectured me on my duty to protect police officers. Including people who hold high office in the state, and other people who may want that very same office." He paused, then adopted a tone of intense sincerity. "All three of us know what this case could become. So I want to assure you that I'm concerned with the health of this entire community, whites and Blacks. If that makes me unpopular somewhere or another—and it will—at least I'll have done my job as I conceive it."

By his lights, Chase judged, Harris believed this. But the man had the fate of Chase's son in his hands, and Chase knew too well how easy it was to recast political calculation as higher principals. "I'm sure the politics are challenging," he observed. "I used to have your job, or something like it."

"But not in Cade County," Harris countered. "In a small community like this one, weighed down with history, the permutations of race become harder to follow. As Jabari can tell you, it's a complicated thing."

"You could say that," Ford observed trenchantly. "By your own admission, you belong to an all-white congregation where some of the members have already decided that Malcolm should die by lethal injection. I'm not trying to be contentious, mind you, just stating facts. One of which is that people here still tend to stick to their kind, and wind up believing whatever their kind believes. Doesn't seem all that complicated to me."

Harris held up a hand in a gesture of mollification. "All I'm saying is that our past isn't a straitjacket." Once more, he turned to Chase. "I truly believe that here in Cade County we're partway to better. Our sheriff's Black, and Black people have started voting in record numbers..."

"You've got Allie Hill to thank for that," Ford cut in sharply. "Funny how so many whites don't seem all that grateful. Suppose that has anything to do with their less-than-tender feelings about Malcolm?"

"I expect so," the district attorney acknowledged. "But the divisions in this county aren't just about Blacks and whites. The people I'm personally closest to—the town's traditional leaders, I suppose you could say—don't have much to do with the people who think Allie Hill stole the presidency in 2020. Even the ones who keep their guns at home instead of brandishing them in public.

"It's no secret that my tenure in office depends on keeping a slice of their goodwill. But I won't dishonor this office to keep it. Within the Black community there are people who'll listen to reason, and others who'll believe that any prosecution of Malcolm Hill for killing George Bullock amounts to a de facto lynching, albeit conducted with palliative ceremony. I can't listen to those voices either. Even when they try to make me a symbol of Davis Street."

Ford smiled faintly. "It's not all that hard, Dalton. You *do* live there, after all. In a house I believe you inherited from you grandfather."

"True enough," Harris acknowledged. "But my grandfather Harris saw himself as a custodian of our past. I'd like to become the custodian of a future where Blacks and whites feel they belong. So if Jabari will indulge me, Congressman, I'd like to tell you two stories from the past that may illuminate the present."

"Fine by me," Ford responded dryly. "I've been introducing Congressman Brevard to some of the more colorful aspects of our history, as it were. But I may have omitted a lynching or two."

Harris chose to ignore this last comment. "Congressman?"

Abruptly, Chase had a swift, telling perception. For Harris, Ford was an adversary and a Black man, to be treated with courtesy and caution. But Chase was not just a congressman, whose power in Washington augured potentially unknown consequences, but a Bancroft and therefore, despite their regional and philosophical differences, a peer by inheritance and social position. What the district attorney would find inconceivable was that Chase was Malcolm Hill's father.

In the former role, Chase answered, "I'd appreciate hearing anything you think I should."

"All right, then," the prosecutor responded. "The first story my grandfather told me; the second I experienced after I took office. Together they form the narrative of evolution, however painful.

"Back in 1919, a Black man was arrested for robbery. The chief of police in Freedom, a man folks looked up to, was taking him to the county jail. But somehow the robber took away Chief Jackson's gun and shot him through the head.

"Before he could escape, some white men wrestled him to the ground. A crowd gathered to call for his lynching. The minister from the First Baptist Church, my church, begged them to stop. But they strung him up from a flagpole sticking out over the sidewalk from the Winthrop Hotel, and left him hanging there with the American flag covering his face..."

"Believe it was the Fourth of July," Ford helpfully informed Chase. "That explains the flag part."

"It was," Harris affirmed grimly. "But the second story better illuminates the present.

"As you probably know, two years ago a Black man who was resisting arrest for domestic violence killed two rookie cops. Because he was dead within hours, there was no need for a trial." Harris paused for emphasis. "But here's the important thing: Both Blacks and whites saw that man as the killer he was, rather than as a symbol of race. Both Blacks and whites supported the families of the dead police officers. When the murderer's sister started wearing a T-shirt with his picture on the front, like he was some sort of martyr, other Blacks talked her down."

"With respect," Ford said evenly, "what may have saved the situation is that the shooter was dead. Malcolm isn't." Nodding toward Chase, he continued, "During the demonstration outside the courthouse, Charles Parnell introduced himself to the congressman by standing in front of us and fondling his weapon. I don't imagine you missed him and his friends."

"I didn't miss any part of it," Harris retorted. "Not the two hundred or so demonstrators who showed up to support Malcolm Hill without knowing the facts, or the handful of white militia they drew like iron filings to a magnet." His tone became precatory. "You know me, Jabari. So I hope you believe I'll handle this case without bowing to prejudice. For my part, I know you've got your own responsibilities. But in one way I'm sorry you were drawn to this case. Because we desperately need responsible Black leaders like you to make common cause with responsible white leaders in keeping this community on a more constructive path."

It was instructive, Chase thought, to watch this seemingly well-intentioned man implicitly offer Jabari Ford a seat at the table of power in exchange for representing Malcolm "responsibly"—or, not at all. He had been in Congress long enough to know how its leaders squashed or co-opted the young and ambitious. But Ford's expression showed nothing—in fact, was so blank that it seemed to betray considerable practice.

"My biggest responsibility," Ford rejoined coolly, "is keeping Malcolm alive and off the seemingly endless roster of wrongfully convicted Black men. So on this trip through the minefield of race, my friend, you'll have to find other 'responsible' Black folks to help keep the lid on. Because providing a full-on defense, which is what I'll do if you make me, just might get some people overly excited. For me to worry about that would amount to a conflict of interest. You understand, I'm sure."

In Harris' silence, Ford added pointedly, "As a Black man with aspirations of my own, I'm a student of funerals. Watching Bullock's told me something important about his widow. My guess is she'll be visiting your office soon enough."

Harris pursed his lips. "Actually, she already has, along with her kids. They believe that only the death penalty is commensurate with what they're sure was a deliberate act of murder. She may not refrain from saying that to their friends, or even in public."

"In public, I'd say," Ford responded laconically. "The governor is facing a primary challenge, and it looks to me like he's decided that Malcolm Hill is his ticket to ride. That may well suit Mrs. Bullock just fine."

"Or maybe not," Harris countered softly. "Over time she may find what I've seen others in her sad situation discover—that living for revenge pollutes the soul. But I don't control any of that, Jabari. All I can do is pray for the wisdom to follow the facts wherever they lead."

"Amen, brother," Ford responded with commensurate gravity. "So let's explore what that actually means."

31

"Let's start with the investigation," Harris began. "In case you're wondering, Congressman, the Georgia Bureau of Investigation is as good as it gets, and they have a field office in Freedom. I heard about the shooting in minutes and asked them to take over the investigation. I didn't want any implication that the sheriff's department was railroading Malcolm Hill for killing one of their own.

"Within two hours, the GBI had combed over every inch of the crime scene; photographed the location of the stop, the position of the two vehicles, the inside of Malcolm's car, and George Bullock's face, head, and torso; found Malcolm's weapon and the cartridge expended by the fatal bullet; taken Malcolm's blood sample; bagged his hands for gunshot residue; and seized his electronic devices pursuant to a lawfully issued search warrant. Everything by the book." Addressing Ford, he added, "You know our policy, Jabari. We don't try to hide the ball from defense counsel. We'll share with you whatever we know, whichever side it hurts or helps."

"Appreciate that," Ford said equably. "There was only the one bullet, right?"

"That's right," Harris responded, adding pointedly, "George never pulled his weapon."

Chase saw Ford assimilate this. "Would you call this an execution, Dalton? Or do all those forensics suggest a struggle for the weapon?"

Harris' eyes narrowed slightly. "For example?"

"For example, you bagged Malcolm's hands for GSR. What about Bullock's hands?"

"Of course."

"Find GSR on them as well?"

"We did."

Ford regarded him with a look of curious interest. "So both men touched the gun."

Harris shook his head. "Not necessarily. It does suggest that the bullet was fired at close range. But we already knew that from the autopsy." Glancing at Chase, Harris added, "Another thing is that Malcolm was legally intoxicated, as in way over the blood alcohol limit for anyone under twenty-one. George had ample reason to stop him."

"Good to know," Ford said briskly. "So naturally he turned on his body camera before pulling Malcolm over."

Briefly, Harris hesitated. "Actually, no."

"Really? What about his dashboard camera?"

"No to that, too."

Ford leaned back in his chair, hands behind his head, looking up at the ceiling in exaggerated puzzlement. "In other words, this model law enforcement officer violated two separate department policies before stopping a Black kid who'd been passing out absentee ballot applications. Think all that's a coincidence?"

Silent, Chase found himself absorbing how sharp Ford was. Harris parried, "Deputies sometimes forget about their cameras."

Ford smiled without humor. "Seems like a shame, though. Seeing how a video of the moments before and during the shooting would pretty much clear things up. Sure would save you from having to guess about whether to bring a murder prosecution." He cocked his head, as if another thought had just occurred to him. "By the way, did Bullock call in the stop to the sheriff's department?"

Harris adopted an expression of fatalism. "He did not."

"My, my, Dalton. Your friend George Bullock really *did* have an off night. Must have been all that excitement. Of course, that could easily happen to any law enforcement officer with only thirty years' experience."

Harris conjured a sour smile of his own. "I imagine you're suggesting an alternative."

"You mean like racially induced amnesia? Yeah, that might've crossed my mind. Ever cross yours?"

"Lots of things cross my mind," the district attorney retorted. "That's why our investigation is ongoing."

Ford nodded his approval. "A good thing, I'd say. Thanks to Deputy Bullock, you've got no idea what happened past midnight on the darkest strip of Old County Road."

"Not *no* idea. For instance, both of us already know that an experienced law enforcement officer who never drew his weapon got killed with Malcolm's own gun. So here's a question you might want to ask him—just how do you feel about cops?" Harris' voice took on an edge. "For that matter, you might want to ask Billy Palmer. That surgeon did such a great job on his nose, you'd hardly know Malcolm left him lying in the hallway of Cade County High School with even more blood running down his face than George had when Malcolm shot him."

Ford's face hardened. "Yeah, that can happen when you call a Black man 'nigger.' So I wouldn't want to premise a prosecution on Billy Palmer's claims of victimization. A while back I understood you to suggest to Congressman Brevard that the moral arc of Cade County has started bending towards justice. But even if you believe that, you damn well know that a lot of white folks are nostalgic for the old days when the local bigots in and out of law enforcement would rough up voting rights workers.

"Back in the sixties, I understand, one just disappeared. For all anyone knows, that Black man's bones are rotting in a swamp somewhere." Ford's tone became cutting. "How do you know, Dalton, that George Bullock didn't decide to turn off his camera so he could turn back the clock? Because I'm convinced that's exactly what he did with Allie's son."

"Show me the evidence," Harris shot back. "One person's version of George Bullock as a racist cop can be another person's slander of a good and decent man who was murdered for going about his job."

Watching Harris, Chase understood what he had sensed from the beginning: that beneath his politesse, Harris was a prosecutor by temperament, and bent on keeping his job. Whatever his stated principles, he would bring any case his constituents wanted if he could come up with reasonable grounds, and as a matter of survival and sheer competitiveness needed to win the cases he brought. Especially this one.

The perception caused Chase to break his silence. "I don't know Georgia," he told Harris, "but when I was a prosecutor in Boston, some of the most lawless and corrupt cops I encountered were narcs. They got around all that drug money, and temptation went to their head. So they wound up becoming a law unto themselves.

"Bullock made his reputation busting drug dealers. To me, all the rules he broke with Malcolm suggest a cop who had a practice of making up his own. Throw in racism and a hatred of voting rights, and you've got some powerful intoxicants. Were I in your very uncomfortable shoes, I'd take a hard look at that."

Harris faced him. "As you can tell, Congressman, once I knew you were coming in I did my homework. I know all about the Kerrigan case. But every case is different.

"I'm not saying George Bullock was color-blind. Few people are. But he had good reason to stop Malcolm Hill. Until Jabari can show me something more than whatever Malcolm's uncorroborated story may be, that's where we are."

For an instant Chase considered what else to say—if anything—and then came to a decision. "Whatever you decide about Malcolm Hill," he began, "it's a matter of prosecutorial discretion. In an incendiary situation like this one, that gets all mixed up with politics.

"From where I sit, it looks like they're two ways you can lose this office. You get beaten by a Black Democrat in a general election, maybe a smart lawyer like Jabari Ford who exposes all the flaws in a racially charged prosecution. Or you get primaried by a white Republican who claims you're soft on Black radicals like Allie and cop killers like Malcolm. One way or the other, your survival in this office becomes all about race.

"There's no way of telling which way that could go. That leaves you alone with your conscience, wondering how whatever you decide impacts what this county will become. I've only known you for a couple of hours. But I'm already sure you'll sleep better if you do your damnedest to figure out who George Bullock was on the night he died."

"That's part of the job," Harris said calmly. "Anything else, Jabari?"

Briefly, Ford glanced at Chase. "Not for now," he told the prosecutor. "Appreciate your time."

"Always a pleasure." Standing, he extended his hand to Chase. "It was an honor to meet you, Congressman. I wish you a safe trip back to Massachusetts, and a bright future in the United States Senate."

★ ★ ★

Walking with Ford down the steps of the courthouse, Chase observed, "Wasn't very subtle, was he? Seems like everyone I meet here wants me to leave."

Ford gave him a brief sideways look. "Must feel like a landslide."

"A lousy day for both of us, then. I'm a carpetbagger, and you're busy blowing your big chance to become a 'responsible' Black leader."

"Yeah, that was nice of him to offer. Barely noticed how conde-scending it was."

Despite this brief moment of humor, Chase felt glum. "Anyhow, sorry to break in at the end. I meant to keep quiet."

Ford shrugged. "For the most part, you stayed out of my way, and having you there seems to have worried Harris some. Anyhow, you were right about one thing. If Harris doesn't go after Malcolm, he's looking at a primary challenge."

"From whom?"

"This creepy right-wing evangelical whose personal God wants him to become the district attorney. That's what happens when you're crazy enough to confuse your own ambitions with the call of the Almighty." Ford stopped at the bottom of the steps. "To look at him, he resembles the farmer in *American Gothic* without the overalls or sense of humor. His biggest thing is that Allie Hill stole Georgia out from under Donald Trump and the only true Americans, the white Christian kind. No way Harris doesn't hear his footsteps in the middle of the night."

Chase felt leaden. "What was your read on him?"

"Worried, I'd say. He's caught in a vise and hasn't found his case yet. I don't think he's happy with the physical evidence. So what he's looking at is having to convince a jury that Malcolm hated cops so much that he deliberately killed one pretty much at random. That's what Billy Palmer's about, and I'm guessing he thinks that's not enough."

"What do you think?"

"The same. He needs something more on Malcolm than he's got. And I need more to dirty George Bullock, or I'm stuck with defending this case by arguing reasonable doubt." He looked up at Chase. "Your take on Bullock makes sense. What he did with Malcolm that night sounds like he'd gotten used to making his own rules."

"Heard any rumors about that?"

"Nothing concrete. I make him out as a shrewd motherfucker more than smart enough to cover his own tracks, and he wouldn't be the first deputy in rural Georgia who supplemented his income by stopping drug dealers, taking their suitcases full of cash, and sending them on their way without telling anyone. But now he's become this white folks' martyr on the altar of law enforcement. You sure won't see any dealers coming forward to complain that St. George ripped them off."

"Have any sense about what Garrett thought of him?" Chase inquired. "When I visited Malcolm, Garrett wouldn't say. But he left me with the impression he didn't like the man."

Ford gave him an incredulous look. "You didn't think he'd tell you, did you? He paused, "For whatever reason, it's pretty clear to me that you care about Allie, and worry about what you see happening to her son in this benighted county. But that last part's a problem only I can deal with.

"Granted, you did a nice job of reminding Harris about the risks in prosecuting Malcolm for something he didn't do. But outing yourself to an ambitious Republican exponentially increased the risks to your own career. Maybe Dalton's too honorable, or simply class-bound, to rat you out on Fox News. Maybe you intimidated him a little. But you need to leave before someone tougher and meaner tries using Malcolm to destroy you."

Silent, Chase thought again of what he could not tell Jabari Ford. But Ford's ignorance of one truth allowed Chase to speak another. "I think about that often enough," he answered. "But you know that what I'm saying is true. The truth is out there somewhere, and we may never know it."

32

In the fading light of early evening, Allie sat with Ford on her screened front porch. "Look," he said in a tone of strained patience. "I accept that you and the congressman are friends. But every day he spends here complicates our lives."

Cornered, Allie debated telling Jabari the truth—dissembling exhausted her more, and she was already too weighed down with sleeplessness and worry to parse her own conflicted feelings about Chase's presence, a compound of sympathy, remorse, resentment, and the odd sense of consolation that came from sharing her burdens with the one person bound to Malcolm, as she was, by the connection of parenthood. Malcolm was no longer her son, but theirs.

For a time she merely gazed at her son's lawyer, her friend, before saying quietly, "Don't make me try to explain this, Jabari. Right now I'm way too tired for that."

★ ★ ★

As dusk fell, crickets began chirring in the grass. Ford and Chase occupied lawn chairs facing each other, with Allie sitting on a couch between them. Ignoring Chase, Ford spoke to Allie. "Based on our meeting with Harris, here's how I see his case shaping up. No time to be mincing words, so I hope you're OK with that."

"What's real is real. Just tell it."

"All right. First of all, Malcolm was legally intoxicated. That justified Bullock in stopping him and compromised his impulse control. He already hated cops, and a couple of weeks before, he'd bought a deadly handgun and hidden it in the glove compartment. Once Bullock pulled him over, he took out the Glock and hid it under the absentee ballot applications on the passenger seat..."

"He was scared," Allie countered.

"So goes his story. But the only weapon in play was his own, and in the prosecutor's version your boy has a very bad temper. Harris' problem is that Billy Palmer is the only basis to argue that Malcolm was predisposed to violence. Why else would they have come here with a subpoena for his laptop and iPad?"

Allie grew pensive. "Do you think there's a problem? Social media was one place I decided to give him some privacy."

For a moment, she could feel concern behind Ford's querying expression. "Not to worry, mama; I'll ask him about it myself. Realize I should've done that before."

Malcolm's lawyer looked around him, to signal that he was including Chase in what would come next. "We need to talk about the defense team, Allie. Starting with whether you and Malcolm still want me to lead it."

She paused, aware that this case was a burden that, but for her, Ford did not want—the pressure would be suffocating, his lost family time irretrievable, the pace exhausting, and the hatred surrounding her and Malcolm dangerous to any lawyer who defended him. But she believed deeply in Ford's intelligence and skill, and loved her son far too much to put anyone before him. Carefully, she said, "Can you think of any reason I shouldn't?"

He hesitated as if feeling the temptations of escape. "Can't think of one, gifted as I am. Watching me stand up to a white judge and white DA would get Black jurors a sense of empowerment. Instinctively, they won't want either one of us to go down." Glancing at Chase, he inquired, "Make sense to you?"

"Especially to me," Chase responded. "When I prosecuted a white cop for killing a Black man in Boston, my boss went through all sorts of calculations. He wound up deciding it was better for a white guy to prosecute a white police officer."

"Can't please everyone," Ford remarked. "Was the second chair Black?"

"Yup, and a woman. Don't imagine I have to elaborate on the calculation there. Am I right in guessing you want a white co-counsel?"

"Sure do. All I need is someone with talent, experience, guts, a passion for social justice, a total indifference to disapproval, and a home-grown Southern accent who can disarm white jurors, help keep Harris off-balance, and doesn't mind playing second fiddle to a Black guy. His tone became ironic. "No problem, of course."

"What about experts? Started looking?"

"Not yet. But I'll need a pathologist, a toxicologist, a ballistics expert, a forensics expert who can talk about things like blood spatter, gunshot residue, and DNA. Then we can argue that the physical evidence is as consistent with accident as murder."

Watching the two men together, Allie thought, yielded some interesting perceptions. It seemed clear that Chase respected Jabari as a lawyer, and that they communicated well enough in areas of common experience, though Chase's experience was a decade old. "What about investigators?" Chase asked. "Someone who can start digging into Bullock's background, along with Woody and Billy Palmer."

"I'm looking. You need someone with local law enforcement experience, a white guy who can circulate among Bullock's friends and colleagues. I'm not imagining Bullock shared his intimate feelings about race with all his Black friends."

"Seems reasonable." Turning to Allie, Chase asked, "So who's paying for all this?"

It was a point of anxiety for Ford as well. "I've got resources," Allie said stiffly. "Not my own. But I've got fundraising sources across the country."

"I know you do," Chase responded. "But if this goes on much longer, you'll be torn between raising money for Blue Georgia in an election year and getting the cash you'll need to finance Malcolm's defense. At some point your enemies will say you've got a conflict of interest, and that you've put Malcolm's interests over the minorities you claim to represent. They'll say that Blue Georgia has always been a racket. They'll try to ruin your reputation, make your biggest donors uncomfortable with you. They'll try to use Malcolm to torch everything you've worked for since the day you left Harvard."

"I know," Allie cut in with asperity. "So what are you saying?"

"That I refuse to stand by and let that happen, Allie. My great-grand-father Bancroft worked too hard."

Ford stood, looking from one to the other. "Would somebody mind saying what's going on here? Whatever it is has started filling up this place."

Allie faced him. "Among other things, Congressman Brevard just offered to finance Malcolm's defense. At least if it gets too much for me to do on my own."

"So what's that's about?" Ford asked. "I need to know who pays the bills, and why."

"I'm not trying to buy a seat at the table," Chase responded with a fair show of calm, "if that's what you're thinking."

Allie stepped between them. "Please," she implored Jabari. "This is personal, and it's got nothing to do with you."

Ford was quiet. Evenly, Chase told him, "I'm asking you to take it on faith that what happens to Malcolm matters to me. I certainly didn't come here to jump-start my race for the Senate, or because I'm starved for undesirable public attention, or need to waste your time and mine second-guessing your defense of Malcolm.

"But there are things I can do if you want. I can help relieve financial pressures, get the attention of the Justice Department. Just tell me what you need from me—or not."

Watching Ford, Allie saw him trying to make sense of what he was hearing and seeing.

Turning to Allie, Chase asked, "Would you mind calling Al Garrett? Before I go, I'd like to see Malcolm again. I bought some books for him to read."

"Sure," she said, and felt the constriction in her throat. "I know he'll appreciate that."

33

Driving to the county jail, Chase was once again riven by the convolutions of his relationship to Malcolm.

Their profusion far outran his ability to reconcile them: the debt Chase owed this young man for the accident of his existence. The knowledge that Malcolm might be extinguished by the hatred enveloping his mother. The cost to Chase himself of leaving Malcolm to his own fate. The burden of concealing from Malcolm that Chase was the missing father he had sought. The shame of hiding that from the world as he pursued his own ambitions. The confusion of being neither father nor lawyer, but a bystander without standing in his own son's life. And, perhaps most painful, the ineradicable reality that Malcolm was the embodiment of his love for Allie, only three years younger than they had been on the night that they conceived him—the night that Chase had fallen in love with her so deeply that the pain of losing her, he realized now, had left its own indelible mark.

It wasn't fair, he told himself, and then dismissed this complaint as contemptible. Life had given him so much else, and its emotional deficits were his own doing; what was unfair was that it might give his son so little. For that he could blame Allie, but at this point it barely mattered. All that mattered was what happened to Malcolm now.

Once again, Chase thought of his relationship to his own father, so different than this shadow relationship with Malcolm. Chase had always been a given in Jean Marc's life, the child he expected to have and, for that, unremarkable. Through the predictable passages of Chase's life, his father had paid attention as he thought was needed. But nothing about Chase had been essential to him and, for Chase, their detachment became a given, even a convenience.

Such dispassion was not Allie's way, nor the way of her family, least of all the loving Black grandfather who had done his best to fill the void in Malcolm's life. But Wilson Hall was gone, and in terms of a man who cared for him as a matter of blood, all Malcolm had now was Chase—or, as he believed, no one. Taken by surprise, Chase would have to find his own way in a maze of unfathomable emotional complexity, with little in his own life to guide him.

What can I be to you? he imagined asking Malcolm. *For both our sakes, what should I be?*

★ ★ ★

Malcolm looked even thinner and more tired, Chase thought, as though every day of imprisonment stole a piece of who he had been the day before. As the door closed behind him, Malcolm stayed in his chair before remembering his manners and standing to shake Chase's hand. Chase found this decorum strangely sad, a measure of the gulf he alone understood. Seeing yet again the traces of his father's features in Malcolm, and therefore his own, he pondered the cognitive dissonance of race, the common inability to see through our own categorizations to the particulars of a singular person. Would he have seen himself in Malcolm, he wondered, had he not known to look?

Sitting across from him, Chase reached into the bag he had taken through security. "Your mom says you like reading about our history, as long as it's real. So do I. So I bought you a couple books I have in my office in D.C."

Silent, Malcolm watched him lay two books on the table: *These Truths*, by Jill Lepore, and James Baldwin's *The Fire Next Time*.

"I know James Baldwin" Malcolm said. "What's the other book about?"

"*These Truths* is an American history that doesn't skip the shameful parts. In the fifties and sixties, your mom told me back in college, Baldwin was one of our leading Black writers." Chase smiled a little. "She got me to read him. She figured I needed some consciousness-raising."

"Sounds like her." Malcolm gave him a curious look. "What was she like then?"

Chase considered the complications of answering. It was more than that whatever he said could implicate the nature of his relationship to Allie but, Malcolm might reason, whether Chase knew her well enough to have met his father—or, though Malcolm appeared not to have considered this, to be his father. "A lot like now," he said easily, "but not so weighed down with worry, and funnier if you didn't mind being the joke. The first time I met her, she completely blew me off. But we met again at a party, and it turned out we actually liked talking to each other. So we wound up being friends."

To Chase's surprise, the antiseptic response induced in Malcolm struck him as a look of rueful nostalgia. "That's sort of like me and Ella, the girl I took to the prom. We could talk about pretty much anything."

Chase wondered whether this was ingenuous or, however subconscious, a probe. Choosing to avoid the subject, he ventured, "Your mom says your friends visit a lot."

Malcolm nodded. "Ella does when she's not too busy working, and some of the guys I played sports with have come by. It's like they want me to know I didn't just disappear. But they'll tell me what they're doing, and I've got nothing to say." His tone filled with muted sorrow at the strangeness of his new life. "No one asks me what happened, and Jabari says I can't explain."

Already, Chase understood, Malcolm's separation from friends wasn't just physical, but a mixture of their ongoing immersion in a future to which he might never return, and the strictures of speech imposed on a prisoner whose life was at stake. "Jabari's right," Chase said. "They don't understand the legal system. They can't keep whatever you tell them a secret if the wrong people ask."

Malcolm stood with his palms on the table, as though rebelling at his constrictions. "Maybe so. But I can see them wondering how I wound up killing this cop, and I can't tell them anything about how it happened. It's like this dead racist cut off my tongue."

Chase could feel the weight of Malcolm's solitude, his helpless sense of paralysis. "I understand. But if there's a trial, and you and Jabari decide you should testify, it's better if the prosecutor's hearing your story for the first time. After you've had a chance to prepare."

Malcolm stared down at him. "Of course I'm going to testify. They can't be trying to kill me, and shut me up forever."

It was not his job, Chase reminded himself, to tell Malcolm how easily a skilled prosecutor could turn the truth in the mouth of an anxious and inexperienced witness into a sequence of damning improbabilities. Especially when Malcolm feared so acutely that a legal system rooted in racism could steal his future while claiming the right to dictate the time and manner of his death in reprisal for accidentally shooting a bigoted cop.

"I'm sorry," Chase responded quietly. "I understand that no one else can know how you feel. But I'll do whatever I can to help."

Malcolm sat again. "I thought you were going back to Washington."

Once more, Chase felt the depth of his own artificiality. "I can stay for a couple more days. After that I've got hearings to attend, bills to vote on, my constituents' problems to look after. But I can be helpful from there." Hearing how inadequate that sounded, he added, "What happens to you won't stop mattering to me. If you or your mom want me to come back, I will."

What was he promising, Chase wondered, and where would it lead? But all he knew at that moment was that silence would have felt worse.

★ ★ ★

The man seemed like he meant it, Malcolm thought. Yet his mother had never once mentioned him, let alone, as near as Malcolm could tell, seen him since college. Now this important stranger from up north was professing concern about the fate of a Black kid he had never met in the eighteen years of Malcolm's existence—the entire lifetime before his gun put that sickening hole in another white man's forehead.

But he had no idea how to probe this. For lack of anything else to say, he asked, "What's it like, being a congressman?"

The man's eyes narrowed, Malcolm saw, as if he were giving his question the thought he believed it deserved. "It's something like your mom's life," he answered. "People expect a lot, and you give up any real hope of privacy. These days that comes with more and more people who want to destroy you, in or out of the media. I have to raise money, like she does, and sometimes that means listening to rich donors who know too little and go on too long. There's always a crisis somewhere, something or someone who needs your attention when all you want is a moment's peace.

"It's not that they necessarily like you. More people than not think every other politician is a hypocrite, a liar, a crook, or just hungry for power. Too many of my colleagues are some or all of those things, or so pathologically narcissistic that they run for office just to feed their own egos."

"So why do it?" Malcolm interjected.

"Unless I'm one of them?" the congressman responded with the briefest of smiles. "The only good reason is if you honestly think you can change people's lives for the better, maybe make the country a little bit better. Most of my colleagues believe that we're in a crisis right now, and that if we don't pull together we'll lose our democracy. I didn't think those were the stakes when I first arrived in Congress, but I sure as hell do now."

He leaned forward, looking at Malcolm intently. "That brings me to your mom, and what's happening to you both. I don't have to worry about my personal safety like she does, or like you had to on the night George Bullock came looking for you." Pausing, Chase spoke quietly but emphatically. "No one should be punished like that for trying to make this country the place it should be. Not Allie as your mother, or you as her son. So when I say that what happens to you matters to me, maybe that starts with knowing her at Harvard. But my reasons for caring don't end there."

It made a kind of sense, Malcolm supposed, that the congressman's connection to his mother, and therefore to him, had some larger meaning than a friendship in college. "I've been wondering about something," Malcolm said. "What else do you know about my mother from Harvard?"

The congressman smiled a little. "Whatever it is, she's probably the one to ask. She's pretty keen on her privacy, and I do my best to stay in her good graces."

Malcolm felt years of banked emotion break through the barriers of unfamiliarity. "I *have* asked," he retorted, "over and over, until I finally gave up. But I've had hours locked up here just thinking about that. My mother comes here every day. So does my grandmother. My grandfather would if he hadn't died. But what about my father?"

The congressman steepled his fingers, looking at Malcolm with a look of mild perplexity. "Do you know anything about him?"

"Nothing," Malcolm said tightly. "She wouldn't even tell my grand-parents who he is. All I can guess is that he was tall, maybe some sort of athlete. No one in our family comes close to six feet, and the nearest anyone came to being Athlete of the Year was winning a spelling bee. That has to come from him." His voice rose in hurt and frustration. "So now I just keep wondering. Does he know that I'm here? Does he even know I exist? If he does, why doesn't he give a damn about whether I live or die?"

The man across the table considered him in silence. But unlike Malcolm's mother, or anyone else in her family—all of whom had a complete inability to disguise their emotions—the congressman seemed as difficult to read as he chose. "All good questions," he said at length. "Maybe now's the time to try your mom again."

In Malcolm's silence, Chase fell quiet. "You've got me thinking," he finally continued, "about my own dad. He wasn't very involved with me, not nearly as much as your grandfather was with you. But at least I knew who he was, and as I got older I understood more or less why.

"Turned out my father was to me pretty much what my French grandfather was to him. Mystery solved, and I had the consolation of knowing it wasn't about some big defect in me. But I've never had the chance to do any better."

There was a knock on the door. Leaning through the doorway, a Black female deputy said, "Time's up, Malcolm. Sorry, but your visitor has to go."

★ ★ ★

Standing outside, Chase marinated in the sweltering heat and his own queasy evasions. What else might he have said, he wondered, had they been together five minutes more? But he needed time to consider the impact on Malcolm, and to talk with the woman who had raised him alone. He could not declare himself a father without at least trying to become one—whatever else that meant in his son's life, and his own.

His cell phone buzzed again. "Time to leave Cade County ASAP," Jack Raskin had texted, "before it turns radioactive. Dorothy Turner Dark is coming for Malcolm, and you don't want to be anywhere near."

34

Congresswoman Dorothy Turner Dark embodied everything Chase feared and despised about the right-wing extremism that had infiltrated the House of Representatives.

From the time she arrived in Congress from North Georgia four years prior, Dark had stood out for her racism, nihilism, and fanaticism. She was obsessed with weaponry, and had tried to bring a handgun to the floor of the House. She had threatened a Hispanic congresswoman with physical violence. She defended the insurrectionists of January 6 as patriots who had bravely protested the supposed theft of the presidency by minorities, perverts, atheists, and socialists. She had links to white nationalists and demented conspiratorialists who believed that the Democratic Party was harboring a ring of child sex traffickers. She flirted with Holocaust denial and had a strange fascination with the symbols of fascism. She relentlessly promoted voter suppression laws targeting Blacks, and explicitly loathed Allie Hill with an unreasoning passion. Her political platform, such as it was, seethed with nativist hatred divorced from any comprehension of public policy other than as an expression of her own pathology.

That was the worst part, Chase thought—in his considered view, Dark was incurably psychotic. Her political career, however long it lasted, would be an obsessive and dangerous quest to destroy anyone or anything she deemed inimical to the authoritarian white Christian America she would summon from the ashes of an effete pluralist democracy that—through her psychologically distorted lens—empowered the racial minorities she deemed subhuman. In the fever swamp of her inflamed and disordered mind, Chase Brevard was a traitor to his race who in turn, with a casual contempt that cut her to the quick, had referred to her on CNN as "an evolutionary cul-de-sac."

Now, however unwittingly, Dorothy Turner Dark was coming for his son.

She had scheduled a rally for noon on a Saturday, proceeded by her arrival in an open convertible flanked by armed members of White Lightning on motorcycles. Chase watched from the window of his hotel as Dark proceeded down Main Street like a warrior queen spearheading some Visigoth invasion, her expression a disturbing mixture of rapture and vengeance.

Dressed in blue jeans and a T-shirt, he went to a store on Main Street, purchased an Atlanta Braves baseball cap, and walked toward the site of Dark's speech.

The park by the courthouse was already full of whites, from old people to parents with children. Some held aloft Christian symbols, Trump or QAnon flags, "Back the Blue" placards, and, most unsettling to Chase, a large blow-up of George Bullock in uniform. At the base of the platform, Charles and Molly Parnell led an armed deputation in White Lightning T-shirts ostentatiously stationed as Dark's bodyguards.

Above them, Dark was flanked by a man and a woman. The woman was middle-aged, with a hatchet face and hair dyed a monochromatic jet black; the man, who looked barely thirty, had gold wire-rimmed glasses through which, even at this distance, Chase perceived the hard gleam of God-bit ambition. Though he had never seen them before, Chase had been in Cade County long enough to guess who they were.

Pulling down the brim of his baseball cap, he stood at the edge of the crowd. Al Garrett, he noticed, had stationed deputies around the park. But there would be little trouble today, Chase felt certain: There were no Blacks in sight, and perhaps by Allie's fiat Malcolm's supporters had stayed away, denying Dark the chance to provoke the televised confrontations in which she openly delighted. But there were television cameras peering up at the platform, mirrors for the intoxicating attention that animated Dorothy Taylor Dark's rhetoric of anger and revenge like a current of electricity.

As she stepped to the microphone in hunting boots, jeans, and a camouflage jacket, the crowd cheered and whistled its anticipation. She stood there, a tight-lipped smile twisting her mouth, bathing in the visceral emotions that affirmed her reason for being. To Chase, she looked as unstable as she was: a bleach-blonde, hard-faced woman with orange makeup coating coarse skin from which glowed her most unsettling feature—emerald green eyes alight with volatility yet as soul-less as a snake's.

"I've come to Cade County," she began without preface, "to stand up for justice. To stand up for a righteous America with patriotism in its veins, steel in its spine, and Christianity in its soul. To remember a champion of the traditional law enforcement that once separated America from the savagery of rapists and murderers, savage predators who would turn our streets to a jungle…"

The first cries from the crowd split the air. In less than a minute, Chase thought, Dark had conjured the witchcraft of culture and race. Standing beneath her, Charles Parnell had the thousand-yard stare of a man fixated by his inner vision of white domination.

Raising her unnaturally deep voice above the crowd's cries, Dark continued, "A man who in life deserved our veneration, and who in death deserves our righteous call for justice."

Abruptly, her voice quickened in a litany of rage. "I'm sick to death of the forces that are sickening America unto death." She drew herself up in a pantomime of righteous anger. "I'm sick of groups like the Blue Georgia Movement who stole the White House from our rightful president."

The woman standing in front of Chase hissed an attenuated "yes-s-s" beneath the raucous catcalls of rage and approbation that seemed to act on Dark like a drug. "And today," she shouted, "here in Cade County, I'm especially sick of any public official who acts like our sacred commitment to the unborn means that those who murder a police officer have the same right to life as an innocent baby…"

All around Chase, voices rose in a deafening crescendo. He forced himself to remain there, silent, fists clenched in impotent fury. "But if you think *I'm* sick," Dark cried above the din, "imagine the sickness in heart of a mother who is watching history repeat itself." Turning, she touched the shoulder of the woman glowering beside her. "You all know Fay Spann. So you all know how deeply she has suffered from the loss of her only son, Bobby, and how hard it is for her to share that suffering aloud…"

Not according to Jabari Ford, Chase distinctly recalled. "But that terrible murder," Dark continued, "imposed on our sister in Christ a mother's duty to bear witness."

Dark reached for the woman, as if to coax her forward. But Spann had already seized the microphone. "To me," she said in a tight, angry voice, "the execution of George Bullock by another vicious lawbreaker is like spitting on my son Bobby's grave. The only way to protect the lives of our police officers is to take the lives of those who kill them. That means the swift and sure justice of capital punishment."

With this, Spann beckoned to the clean-cut young man in wire-rimmed glasses, saying, "Not only is Matthew Bell an able young attorney, but a man who is one hundred percent loyal to America's rightful president, a man who believes in using the law to prosecute the perpetrators of voting fraud." She gave a malicious smile. "Or maybe I should say the perpetrator—we all know who she is, and who her son is."

Amidst the boos and bellowing, Spann's voice rose to a screech. "Matthew's looking at running for district attorney. And if Dalton Harris doesn't do right by George Bullock and his family, Matthew is going to stop *looking* and start *running*..."

Amidst more cheers and applause, Matthew Bell gave Fay Spann a kiss that struck Chase as an act of quasi-religious veneration. Gripping the microphone, he intoned, "Thank you, Fay, for your bravery and, equally, for your patriotism."

He turned to the crowd, waiting out their respectful applause for the bravery of an aggrieved mother. "Faced with the murder of a good man like Deputy Bullock, we stay the hand of vengeance in exchange for imposing lethal injection after due process of law. Should I run for district attorney, I will stand for the principle of equal justice in demanding punishment equal to the crime. And I will do everything in my power to ensure that the next Malcolm Hill doesn't murder the next George Bullock."

Righteous cheers rose from beneath the oak trees. On the platform, Dorothy Taylor Dark stood between Bell and Spann, holding their hands like celebrants in a church, head bowed, before she started scanning the crowd with an expression of triumph so naked that it moved Chase to despair. These people would use Malcolm as a human sacrifice to their own demons and call it righteous. Only after a moment did he think to look toward Charles Parnell and perceive, or perhaps imagine, that Parnell was staring back at him.

Walking to an empty space on the sidewalk, Chase called Jabari Ford. "Yeah," Ford answered at once. "I watched. I'm at my office, talking to an investigator. You seem to be interested in who we're hiring, so maybe you should come on down."

35

Jabari Ford had a neatly appointed suite of offices on the second floor of a pharmacy where, he briefly told Chase, his father as a young man had been forced to seek prescriptions for his mother by waiting at a side door. "We can talk about Dark's speech," Ford told him. "But the investigator I've got waiting is a former special agent for the local office of the GBI. He knows the county, and he's got a whole network of friends. One of the subjects is Bullock. No harm in you listening in."

Joe Briggs was sitting in a small conference room decorated with lawbooks superannuated by the internet—a man of late middle age with shrewd eyes, a thinning gray-brown comb-over, and a slightly upturned mouth that suggested some secret that amused him. Introducing Chase, Ford explained, "Congressman Brevard is a friend of Allie Hill's. Once you leave, feel free to forget he was here."

"No worries," Briggs responded wryly. "I can even forget that I recognized him on sight. Welcome to the epicenter of Southern hospitality, Congressman. Happen to bring your camouflage jacket?"

Chase sat across from him. "I guess you saw that speech."

"Sure did. Are all of your colleagues batshit insane?"

"No. Dorothy's special."

Briggs' look of amusement vanished. "That's how she struck me. The woman sure wanted to make life for your friend and her son as hard as can be. Seems like the kind of lady who watches executions for fun." Turning to Ford, he asked, "So what can I do you for, Counselor? Sounds like you want a workup on George Bullock."

"More like a colonoscopy," Ford answered. "Personal life, money problems, racial attitudes, women on the sly. Whether he ever crossed the line as a deputy."

The investigator's look of veiled humor returned. "You mean like, to pick a wild example, whether now and then George relieved drug dealers of their ill-gotten gains and forgot to mention it to anyone else?"

Ford gave him a sharp look. "Not so wild, seems like."

Briggs shrugged. "I heard such a story once, second- or third-hand. Never knew, and back then I had no brief to investigate."

"Still," Chase prodded, "did that seem plausible to you?"

Briggs inclined his head, considering the question. "His role as righteous drug buster came with a pretty serious ego. People like that can get spoiled by the power of a badge, until they think it's their personal property to use as they please. That could have been George, but I don't know that it was. All I can do is try to learn more."

"Please do," Ford responded. "What about political beliefs?"

"Same thing. If I had to wager my firstborn, I'd bet that George was a Trumpite. I mean, Bullock was a churchgoing white guy from the rural South with a career in law enforcement. What odds would you give on him being a member of the NAACP or ACLU?" Briggs glanced at Chase, his demeanor now sober. "What you're really asking is whether the man was a stone-cold racist, enough of one to go hunting for Malcolm Hill. And that I don't know—at least without digging deeper, and maybe not even then.

"George was no college professor. But a guy in law enforcement who's smart, like he certainly was, develops a keen sense of his environment and first-rate survival instincts. Maybe like the governor said, he was a charitable, churchgoing man who loved helping others and took after drug dealers for the sake of our youth. But that works equally well as protective coloration for somebody with an agenda of his own. Who but a very few people besides George Bullock himself—if any—would ever discover the difference?"

That was right, Chase thought in frustration. "Malcolm did."

"But that's exactly my point. It happened in the dark, with no witnesses. Just like it would have if George had decided to burglarize a drug dealer in the middle of the night. Out on patrol, he was on his own, free to turn hunter when the moment was right. If he showed himself to Malcolm, it was because no one else could see or hear him."

Ford nodded. "What do you know about Nick Spinetta? I keep wondering why he got there so quickly, and why he sensed there was trouble."

Briggs pondered this. "No idea. Offhand, he seems like a decent enough young guy who takes the job seriously. But I'll go deeper if you want."

"We want." Turning to Chase, Ford asked, "Anything occur to you, Congressman?"

"It does," he told Briggs. "Every time I replay Malcolm's description of Bullock, I think of a subcommittee hearing I chaired on white nationalism in law enforcement. Specifically, about whether he knew Charles Parnell."

Briggs raised his eyebrows. "Here in Cade County, every white person knows a good chunk of the others. But with Al Garrett in charge, any sheriff's deputy smarter than a rutabaga would steer clear of deep philosophical conversations with Charles Parnell. At least when anyone could overhear them."

"Put me down as compulsively curious," Ford said. "Deconstructing George Bullock is the key to Malcolm's defense. On that basis, you're hired."

★ ★ ★

Afterward, Ford and Chase sat in his office, Chase facing a bookshelf holding Ford's law school diploma and photographs of a pretty wife, daughter, and son. "I know," Ford told him. "That speech was terrible for Malcolm and Allie. But the not-so-secondary message was to Dalton Harris: Seek the death penalty, or else.

"Allie heard it, too. Right now, she's already decided to counteract Dorothy Turner Dark by giving a speech of her own—tomorrow night on the courthouse steps, hopefully on national television. She's already reached out to MSNBC."

Chase tingled with alarm. "Out in the open, in a town full of white racists with AK-47s?" Swiftly, he thought of what he had learned from the Secret Service on two presidential campaigns. "They could shoot her from anywhere. From bushes, from darkness, from a passing car, from an open window in a building across the street. It takes the Secret Service days to scrub an outdoor site like that. What kind of security does she have?"

"Al Garrett and the sheriff's department, along with the town police. We can try the governor, but I already know what he'll say: 'Cancel the speech.'" Ford softened his voice. "Don't try to stop her, Congressman. I already have, and it was no use."

"I can't let her do this," Chase rejoined, "at least without seeing her myself."

Ford regarded Chase with a puzzlement tinged, it seemed, with a veiled sympathy. "Maybe you're something to her that I'm not. But Malcolm's her son, and there's nothing you or I or anyone can do."

"Only this," Chase said after a time. "I'm staying in Cade County until she finishes her speech and walks down the steps of the courthouse. There's nothing she, you, or anyone can do about *that*."

36

At eight o'clock, Allie Hill stood on the plaza atop the steps to the courthouse, bathed in a circle of light.

It was dusk. The air was warm but pleasant, and the many thousands—Black and white, young and old—who had come to hear her covered the steps, the lawn, and the street below. Some were from Cade County; others had come from as far as Atlanta in buses chartered by Blue Georgia. Arranged just behind her were leaders of the voting rights movement; prominent entertainers who had flown in from New York, Nashville, and Los Angeles; her friend and lawyer Jabari Ford; and sheriff's deputies assigned by Al Garrett. But some Black officeholders and politicians with statewide ambitions had stayed away—moved, she suspected, by realistic concerns for their own political and personal safety. If, as some clearly feared, the evidence went against Malcolm, the spotlight Allie had drawn to this place at this moment might prove too hot.

Directly in front of the podium, the blank eyes of television cameras from two cable news channels stared back at her. Sound trucks lined the sidewalks, and to her side was a section cordoned off for reporters. But what caught her eye in the descending darkness was the shadowy figures of the snipers whom the sheriff had placed on the roofs of the two-story buildings facing the courthouse—one part of his hastily devised plan to thwart or intimidate would-be assassins. On his orders, other deputies had closed access to the buildings, fenced off the park to her left so that no one could shoot her from the dark, and penned Parnell and his armed followers in a constricted section of Main Street. But there was no time or equipment to herd the crowd through magnetometers, and nothing Garrett could do to keep a lone shooter indifferent to his own fate from getting close enough to kill her.

Somewhere below, Allie knew, Chase Brevard was watching.

She could not convince him to leave for his own sake; he could not dissuade her from speaking. With a vehemence born of the determination to overcome fear, she had told him, "It's not just that they're trying to disenfranchise Black people; they're using my son to do it—if necessary, by killing him. If you were me, could you do anything different?"

"He's also *my* son," Chase shot back. "So, no, I wouldn't do anything different. The difference between us is that as far as Malcolm knows, you're the only parent he's got. If anything happens to you, I could never take your place."

The simple truth of this, and the complexities beneath it, gave her pause. Finally, she said, "I'm scared, all right?"

For a long moment, he simply looked into her face. "OK," he answered. "See you after the speech."

In a flash of perception, she grasped how difficult it would be for him to watch her, yet how much harder he would find it to walk away. She chose not to tell him that her offices had been flooded with a record number of death threats, or about the message she had received on her cell phone moments before: "Try to give that speech, and I'll blow a bigger hole in your head than your boy did to George Bullock."

Now, about to speak, she could not help but think of her son, and his father. For an odd moment, she remembered speaking at Harvard on the day she and Chase had first met, fearful that she would fail to stir a modest crowd of student protesters. But those misgivings were about the potential for embarrassment, nothing worse—unlike now. That was why, tonight, she had rejected Jabari's offer to introduce her, and her mother's to stand at her side. The risk was hers to take.

Stepping to the podium, she felt jittery. Looking out, she saw the snipers on the roof. Then she forced herself to think of Malcolm.

"Bless you," she began simply, "for being here."

Her voice was steady, she found, and its resonance through the sound system as it echoed to the edges of the crowd gave her a fresh jolt of resolve. "You all know about my son, Malcolm," she continued. "He's in jail, awaiting trial for a crime he didn't commit—all because he was targeted by a racist deputy who didn't want Black people to vote. But now the powers that be want to take my son's freedom, and even his life.

"Sometimes he's all I can think about. But then I remember he's in jail because he stands for something bigger. Why else are the enemies of democracy demanding the death penalty for my son without knowing what happened to him in the dark of night?"

For an instant, captured by her own imagery, she reimagined her son's fear of the white deputy who had entrapped him. Then she pressed forward. "I have to live with that every day, thinking of Malcolm in jail. But I woke up this morning, like I do every morning, believing that we can seize the future for all of our children."

Suddenly Allie heard shouting beneath her, the sounds of a commotion. At the foot of the steps, she saw, a sheriff's deputy had wrestled a bearded white man to the ground. Giving herself up to fatalism, she forced herself to continue. "Like the deputy who stalked Malcolm," she called out, "too many people in Georgia never want us to vote. So they invented nonexistent voter fraud as a fig leaf and started passing laws to keep minorities from voting."

Waves of applause started rising, the voices of call and response crying out their encouragement above the din. Allie felt her voice gathering rhythm and power.

"The state legislature says we need even more ID laws to keep folks who don't have the right identification from voting—like, say, a driver's license. No big deal, right? All you have to do is go to the Department of Motor Vehicles."

Knowing laughter rose from the crowd. "Yeah," Allie told them, "those lines at the DMV feel kind of familiar. They're like the lines in a county filled with Black folks where they've shut down all but one polling place. You can get born, marry, have kids, and die in that line before you ever get to the end. It's like purgatory for Black people."

More laughter and applause. "OK," Allie continued, "but everyone has a birth certificate—right? All you have to do is get born.

"Funny thing, though, none of my grandparents ever had one. I can promise they were just as real as you and me. But back in the good old days of Jim Crow, the hospitals for Black people didn't bother giving them birth certificates. Why would you need one of those when the law doesn't treat you as a person?"

Her voice became cutting. "That's the problem. Too many of the same powers who are persecuting my son still don't see us as people. So there are a lot of seventy- or eighty-year-old Black men and women walking around who seemingly never got born. But they damn well don't want to die without ever casting a ballot…"

A crackle sounded—the percussive *pop-pop-pop* of gunfire.

Allie flinched, knees buckling. Two sheriff's deputies rushed to her side. Bracing herself on the podium, she swiftly looked around her, then forced herself to stand straighter.

At the foot of the steps, three Black men had wrenched the arms of a grinning white man behind him, his expression filled with triumph. "Firecrackers," someone called out.

For a moment, Allie had thought her life would end. As deputies dragged away her leering antagonist, she managed to say, "Bet that man has no trouble voting. But the enemies of voting rights are way more inventive than some moron barely smart enough to light a firecracker.

"One of their tricks is closing polling places where Black people live. That way you don't know where to vote, or you have to stand in one of those endless lines. If you have kids to look after or can't take hours off from work, or you're too sick or old to wait in line forever, you effectively can't vote." She hesitated, as if just remembering something else. "Oh, and in case all this trickery doesn't work, they try making it a crime to give food or water to people standing in line. They'd rather have Grandma drop dead from dehydration than vote."

She paused amidst the derisive laughter, fortifying herself to deliver the heart of her speech. "But that brings me back to my son. The young man I sent out that morning—filled, as always, with the worry of a Black mother for her son—was himself full of hope, not hatred. But what he encountered in darkness was just that: pure hatred." Her voice rang out.

"So I have to tell you right now that my son is innocent, and that he's in jail for defending himself."

Composing herself, she reined in her emotions. "In the coming days, I will have much more to say about that, and so will Malcolm's lawyers. But right now, I want to share a little relevant history about what got him in such terrible trouble.

"Right up to 2020, Republicans loved voting by mail. They wanted all the old white folks to support them to vote without ever leaving their rocking chairs. So they made sure to mail absentee ballot applications to every registered voter." Her voice turned ironic. "Any conservative Caucasian this side of the grave didn't even have to lick a postage stamp."

Murmurs of affirmation rose from the crowd. "Until 2020," Allie continued, "Republicans thought democracy was a beautiful thing. Problem for them was that the committed folks of Blue Georgia started encouraging the wrong kind of people to mail in their ballots." Beneath the sarcasm, Allie felt the molten anger she channeled into many of her speeches, but this one most of all. "We were using the master's tricks to dismantle the master's house, and boy did they ever hate *that*."

The murmurs of response became calls of derision. Pausing, Allie let them swell. The crowd was in her hands now.

★ ★ ★

Watching, Chase understood far more clearly how dangerous Allie Hill had become to the proponents of white minority rule. By attacking Malcolm, they had given her a platform far bigger than before, and the desperate resolve to use it at whatever risk to herself. Yet he could see and feel how slight she was, how vulnerable beneath the steely confidence she had trained herself to present. She was living on an emotional and psychological tightrope.

"Like that deputy who stalked Malcolm," she called out, "the enemies of democracy are determined to kill voting by mail any way they can. Why? Because it grants ordinary people with challenging lives the dignity they deserve. If you're a single parent or responsible for a family struggling to make ends meet, you don't have to worry about paying someone to watch the kids, or taking too much time off from work, or being too sick to stand in line."

Her tone became scathing. "Like that deputy who stalked Malcolm, the enemies of democracy can't have that. So they've banned election boards or groups like Blue Georgia from mailing absentee voter applications to registered voters." She drew herself up. "Know what Malcolm was doing the day he got arrested? Passing out applications by hand because that's all anyone can do. That's why they went after my son.

"Like the deputy who stalked Malcolm, *these* people aren't one bit different in spirit than the people who stopped our parents and grandparents from voting with guns and police dogs. They're exactly the same people. Except *these* people wear the pious masks of propriety instead of white hoods, and they're a whole lot more sophisticated."

Suspended between fear and admiration, Chase glanced around him for signs of trouble, perhaps a sudden movement in the crowd. Every word she spoke closed the distance between thought and action in the fevered minds of racists armed with semiautomatic weapons.

"*These* people," Allie said, "elected themselves a president who hates democracy as much as they do, and now they're killing democracy to get him back."

★ ★ ★

Pausing, she swept the audience with her gaze. "And if we don't do everything in our power to stop them, they will. Because in state after state, including this state, they're passing laws to rig the Electoral College so that voting won't matter."

Stopping, Allie reminded herself to strike a balance between anger and hope.

"Here in Cade County, and across Georgia, we hold the key to our own empowerment—voting. That's not the work of any one person or group of people.

"But together we can do so much. We can make Georgia a model for the America that can be but never was. A place where Malcolm—once he goes free, as he must—can breathe the air of *true* freedom with every Black or white son or daughter of this state."

Abruptly, she lowered her voice, as though commanding her audience to listen. "Then, at last, we will have redeemed our history by freeing our future from our past, and honored the souls of all those whose hardships still haunt this land. And yes, we will have honored my son."

Exhausted, she bowed her head, barely hearing the crescendo rising from the crowd, so sustained that, minutes later, she realized that it continued unabated.

★ ★ ★

Afterward, a phalanx of deputies headed by Al Garrett led her through the crowd to the caravan of squad cars that would escort her home.

At the bottom of the steps, she saw Chase Brevard waiting for her. Touching Al on the shoulder, she asked that her guardians make room for Chase.

Swiftly, he issued orders, and she and Chase stood alone in the space Al Garrett had made for them.

"You were great," he said. "I just wanted to tell you that."

Across the years, she remembered him speaking these words after her speech at Harvard. "Seems like I've heard that before."

"You have, actually. But I've never seen anyone do something so hard so well. I hope Malcolm hears it."

For a moment, Allie was silenced by their unspoken bond. "I was thinking about him the whole time," she answered quietly. "There are one or two times I wasn't sure I could finish."

He nodded. "I could feel that for you. But it never showed."

"That's why they call it acting." Briefly, she looked into his eyes. "I remember things, too."

Nodding to Al Garrett, she began moving again, toward whatever she had to do next. Perhaps, she hoped, even sleep a little.

37

The next morning, filled with misgivings, Congressman Chase Brevard began packing.

His office had booked a late-afternoon flight from Atlanta to Washington, D.C. In the next few days, there was much to do. His staff had sent a list of questions for a Tuesday-morning hearing on healthcare; there were two votes on subjects crucial to Massachusetts scheduled for later in the day, a meeting on Wednesday morning with representatives of the state's embattled lobstermen, another that afternoon with the finance director for his prospective Senate campaign, a reception in the evening to raise money for a handful of Democratic congressional candidates in winnable races, a speech on Thursday to the national convention of the firefighters' union. He had been in Georgia for less than a week, and the once-familiar routine felt surreal. It had been seven days since Chase had learned of a son facing murder charges in Cade County.

He tried to imagine circulating among people who knew nothing of this, perhaps deflecting idle chatter about the political implications of the Malcolm Hill murder case, or listening to the calculations of colleagues in swing districts about how to position themselves. He tried to envision deceiving Kara McGuire about where he had been and what he was feeling. Friends and colleagues would become strangers, separated from Chase by a secret none could imagine. He felt like a stranger to himself.

His cell phone rang.

"Hi," Allie said.

She sounded somber, reluctant. "Are you OK?" he asked. "Is Malcolm OK?"

"Seems like neither one of us is." She hesitated. "Until a few minutes ago, this call was going to be about trying to say what it meant to see you, and that I was sorry about why. For whatever it's worth, I was going to wish you a safe trip home and ask you to stay in touch with us both. But now there's something else."

"What is it?"

Allie hesitated. "Can you come to Jabari's office? Sounds like he's got a video we both need to see."

★ ★ ★

When he arrived, she was already there, regarding Chase with a grave expression as he sat down beside her. On Ford's desk was a laptop with an incongruous pink cover. Without preliminaries, he told Chase, "I borrowed this computer from a classmate of my daughter's who friended Malcolm on Facebook."

To Chase, Ford's dispassionate tone was that of a lawyer faced with a serious problem and, for that, more ominous than an alarm. Sitting to the side, Ford turned the computer screen so that Chase and Allie could see it, and began scrolling down Malcolm's Facebook page.

What Chase saw first was the expected—a dizzying array of communal self-promotion, gratuitous oversharing, advertising, emails, articles, snippets of something or another, old photographs, invitations to add new "friends," blandishments to join supposed affinity groups, curated news spewed by skewed algorithms, and buttons for adding more posts. As Chase well knew from congressional hearings, one could post pretty much anything: rapes, murders, child pornography, foreign propaganda, vicious slanders, incitements to body shaming, and videos or messages that were merely self-destructive. "Here we go," Ford said, and clicked again.

On the screen appeared a video recorded by a rap artist called Double-XX. His dress seemed chosen for attitude: He wore a woolen cap, a black turtleneck accented by a gold chain, camouflage pants, and high-laced boots. Dangling from the finger of his right hand was a black handgun.

"From the looks of it," Ford observed, "that would be a Glock 19."

On the screen, Double-XX begin declaiming in the propulsive cadences of a rapper: "Here's the real message of George Floyd, people. This white so-called justice system ain't nothin' but a killing field. The cop who killed George gets convicted, more cops keep killing Blacks. These motherfuckers won't stop till we start killing cops every time some cop kills a Black man." The rap artist flashed an icy smile. "Don't matter which cop, long as they're white. It's like white people say about the death penalty—it's a deterrent. So start deterring, brothers."

The screen went blank. In silence, Chase and Allie stared at Malcolm's Facebook page. "Yeah," Ford said mildly. "Nothing much to say. That video is a white person's nightmare."

Shaken, Chase collected his thoughts. "I guess Malcolm never told you about this."

"No," Allie answered. "If he had, no way I would've let those GBI agents inside the house."

"When did he post it?" Chase asked Ford.

"A couple months before the shooting."

For a moment, the two men marked this with more silence. "I assume Harris has already seen this," Chase said to Ford.

"Sure he has. Maybe not before we met with him, but by now. Wonder when he was going to get around to telling us."

Allie looked up. "Just how bad is this?" she asked Malcolm's lawyer.

"Bad enough, Allie. You know that yourself."

"I'm feeling pretty dazed right now. So spell it out for me."

Briefly, Ford looked at Chase. "There's two things. First is, it gives Harris a basis for arguing that Malcolm intended to kill Bullock. Second, it ratchets up the pressure on Harris to seek the death penalty, and gives him a stronger case for doing that. Is that how you see it, Congressman?"

Chase glanced at Allie. "Yeah," he said reluctantly. "That's how I see it. The other thing is what happens when the media gets ahold of this. Harris doesn't need to leak it to them—sooner or later they'll find it on their own. That's when the right-wing politicians will start feasting."

"I must have told him a thousand times," Allie murmured. "Don't post anything you can't live with having the world see. Say the wrong thing at the wrong time, and you'll never outrun it."

It seemed to Chase that she was talking to herself. After a moment, he asked, "Any idea what was on his mind?"

"No," Allie answered slowly. "He was outraged about cops killing Black men, like he should've been. But that rapper doesn't speak for Malcolm's heart. We talked about all that, how hate goes nowhere.

However tempting it is to believe, there's no way forward if we're all on our own. That's just reality."

Chase felt Ford watching them closely. "Your reality," he said to Allie.

After a time, Allie met his eyes. "For a lot of reasons, Malcolm needs more than most for people to know he identifies as Black. Some of that was about classmates, things they'd say to him that hurt. One boy told him to nigger up." Her voice hardened, "I don't believe for a second he wanted to kill a cop, or thought that was any way forward. He's eighteen years old, and for one moment in time he was trying that video on for size."

But that moment in time, Chase knew, could last the rest of Malcolm's life—or shorten it. Everything about the cast of Allie's face told him she understood that, and was already grieving her son and, perhaps, her failings as a mother. He chose to say nothing more.

★ ★ ★

Because they could not be seen together on the street, Chase and Allie parted in the conference room.

"I'm sorry I have to go," he told her. "Especially now."

Her face and eyes were opaque to him. Perhaps, Chase thought, it was the shock of seeing the damning videotape. At length she responded tonelessly, "You've got your own responsibilities. There's about a million people who expect you to fulfill them."

That was *his* reality, Chase knew. "Jabari's a smart lawyer," he finally said. "He'll work with Malcolm to find the best way to explain this."

"I know that, too."

There was nothing Chase could add to this. "Please say goodbye to Malcolm for me."

"I will," she answered, and went to visit their son.

★ ★ ★

Sitting beside Malcolm, Allie gazed at the bare walls of the visiting room.

Elbows on the laminated table, her son slumped with his face in his hands. "I couldn't tell you," he mumbled between his fingers. "Before that night, I'd half forgotten."

She believed him. In quiet anguish, she imagined him absorbing what he had done to himself with one twitch of a finger in a careless nanosecond that now reverberated in his life. "It's done," she said. "But you've got Jabari to help with this."

He raised his head, his eyes dark pools of misery. "Is that congressman still here?"

The question pierced her. "No. He had to go back to Washington. But he asked me to say goodbye."

38

On arriving in Washington, Chase proceeded to enact a passable imitation of himself.

He had long since become skilled at concealing his thoughts and feelings, Chase appreciated with new acuity, and the other-directed demands of politics—for worse or better—had distilled this predisposition into a form of performance art. For him the easiest parts were the hearings, votes, and speeches focused on issues he genuinely cared about—the core reason he had sought public office. Harder was the small talk at constituent meetings or political events, the rote inquiries about wives and kids and grandkids while thoughts of Allie and Malcolm crept through his consciousness unbidden and unspoken, creating a sense of alienation that the people with whom Chase interacted, he kept reminding himself, did not deserve. That too much of him had gone missing was no one's fault but his.

The apotheosis of difficulty came at a cocktail party Wednesday night. Chase had considerable empathy for novice congressional candidates who had chosen to enter the Darwinian gauntlet of national politics—less than a decade ago, he had been one of them, and he valued the chance to provide what insight or encouragement he could. But the compulsory chitchat with donors who thought that monetary success made them political savants, never easy for him, was on this occasion close to intolerable. Mingling in a large room at The Hay-Adams hotel, he found himself detaching from both sides of a conversation—his functional insincerities and whoever's overconfident oversimplifications—as if he were hovering fifteen feet above, wondering which of them sounded more inane. The gulf between these moments and the emotional urgency he had felt in Cade County—rooted in his discovery of a son who did not know him, and whose mother Chase had loved more than any woman before or since—defied even his well-honed gifts for compartmentalization.

Perhaps, he found himself thinking, it might have helped were Kara with him—at other times, they'd been able to repair to the bar for a solitary nightcap, comparing nuggets of insight or amusement from the hours preceding. But her firm had assigned her to help perform triage on a flagging senatorial campaign in Iowa; on closer inspection, the

Democratic candidate was close to hemorrhagic shock, suggesting that Kara's absence might prove indefinite. That she imparted all this matter-of-factly, on a cell phone call from an airport lounge, suggested that his abrupt and unexplained departure for Georgia had accelerated the dwindling of their relationship.

The sudden regret Chase felt at his own neglect brought Kara from the margins of his consciousness into sharp relief. No doubt, he told himself, that it was better she was gone. He could not tell her about Allie and Malcolm, and dissembling to a woman he cared for would have been far more difficult than dispensing counterfeit charm among people, however well-intentioned, with whom he had no personal connection. He kept thinking of that video, set to blight or shorten Malcolm's life, as a ticking bomb only he could hear.

But he was all right, at least on the surface, until the reception started winding to a close.

Preparing to leave, he was accosted by a wealthy businessman from Northern Virginia who considered himself a strategic investor in moderate Democrats. "Most of these candidates of yours," he announced to Chase, "look all right to me. But unless we stop swimming upstream, we'll lose our majority in the House. Without a new message, even promising guys like you will be singing castrato."

Mercifully, Chase thought, *you're about to give me one.* Calling on his reserves of political muscle memory, he manufactured a look of genuine interest. "Sounds painful, Jerry. I'd be grateful for your thoughts."

The man put a proprietary arm on Chase's shoulder, moving his paunch dangerously close. "We've got to get back to the basics—making people feel safe. I mean, this stuff about Black Lives Matter and reforming police departments is all well and good. But it can't be a license for looting and rioting."

"I grant you there's a balance to maintain," Chase responded mildly. "But as far as I can see, looting and rioting aren't part of our agenda."

Jerry grimaced in disgust. "You couldn't tell that by listening to Republicans. Just before I came here I was watching Fox News, performing reconnaissance. Did you see the stuff about that fucking kid in Georgia?"

Chase felt his expression freeze. "Which kid?"

"The Black who murdered that sheriff's deputy," Jerry said vehemently. "It's not enough that the victim made his career busting drug dealers, or that the shooter's mother is this voting rights activist progressives worship as an icon. Turns out he posted a video calling for Black people to execute cops. The sharks on Fox were having a field day."

So soon, Chase thought. "I can imagine," he responded. "But precisely what are Democrats supposed to do about that?"

"Make this killer an example of everything we're against. Decent people of all races want police protection—Blacks as much or more than anyone. The kid's going down anyhow, so why should we go down with him?"

Chase paused to ensure his composure. "Tell me this, Jerry. Have you considered the prospect that Malcolm Hill could be innocent? You might try it as a thought exercise."

"I'll leave that to his lawyers," the man said vehemently. "This is practical politics, Chase, and the Republicans are smart enough to play hardball. I'm disappointed you don't grasp that."

Chase removed the donor's arm from his shoulder. "I know how crushing disappointment can be. So let's not extend the moment. If not for your sake, for mine."

Turning, he walked out of the reception.

★ ★ ★

Returning to Georgetown, Chase went directly to his den and turned on Fox News.

It did not take long for Double-XX and his Glock 19 to make an appearance. Listening to the rapper's words, Chase tried to calculate their impact—not just on the bigoted, angry, or anxious, but on anyone who lacked a predisposition to sympathize with Malcolm, or even withhold judgment. But however bad the political optics in America at large, Chase kept returning to the effect on Dalton Harris, Judge Tilly, and prospective jurors in Cade County.

The female anchor provided a soundtrack for his anxiety. "So let's stuff all the liberal garbage about abolishing the death penalty in the trash compactor," she told her audience in a grating, metallic voice. "Malcolm Hill is not some impoverished and cognitively deficient Black man, railroaded by the justice system for something he didn't do. The mother of this arrogant murderer is a graduate of Harvard, with every advantage and all sorts of resources, who chose to have him out of wedlock. He's the ultimate combination of privilege and pathology, the product of our societal blessing of families without fathers."

As Malcolm's mug shot appeared on the screen, her voice rose in indignation. "And don't tell me about 'innocent.' Innocent? Malcolm Hill is a racist executioner who claimed the right to kill a heroic law enforcement officer with a traditional family and an exemplary life. That disgusting video is like a confession signed in Deputy Bullock's blood, and the heart's blood of his wife and children."

Switching off the television, Chase sat in the dim light of a standing lamp beside his chair, gazing at shelves filled with books from another life.

For a long while, he tried to reduce his thoughts to reason, balancing one consideration against another, and found that these powers of rationalization had been short-circuited by feeling. The window behind his rolltop desk framed the darkness outside, but in the windowless cell where Malcolm lived there was neither day nor night. All Chase could imagine was how solitary his son must feel—sensing fate closing in all around, ceaselessly replaying the shooting no one else living understood, the careless moment when he had sent a video that obliterated the truth of what had happened into a world that now would see it as the truth of who he was.

But there was one truth Malcolm had never known, and Chase held it in his heart.

Sitting at his desk, he scrolled through his schedule—two speeches and some appearances in Massachusetts over the weekend, a congressional recess after that. But he already knew what he would do, must do. It was simply a matter of when.

Taking out his cell phone, he called the only person who could understand. "I'm coming back," he told her. "I don't think there's anything much I can do. I just have to see him again."

★ ★ ★

As before, Chase and Malcolm sat across from each other. Beneath Malcolm's eyes, the bruises of sleeplessness were deeper; his oncefirm handshake was limp, his movements torpid. "No one believes me anymore," Malcolm said.

How to respond? Chase wondered. On the morning after he had given his last speech in Massachusetts—preserving the routine, or perhaps the façade, of a politician tending to his constituents and his own ambitions—he had flown from Boston to Atlanta and driven directly to the Cade County jail. But despite the time for reflection afforded by an eighthour journey, he had little idea of what to say in Malcolm's presence. There wasn't any script for this—the concealed father, the unknowing son afraid for his own life. Even in far better circumstances than these, Chase realized, he would have been hampered by his own deficiencies; Jean Marc Brevard was hardly a role model for parental engagement. But at least his father had witnessed Chase's growth from child to man and, from whatever emotional distance, had processed the stages in between.

Chase had none of this. It was as though Malcolm had been dropped into his life as an eighteen-year-old foundling, raised by a Black mother and grandparents, however loving, in a culture Chase barely understood. Malcolm and he had no memories between them, no reference points from which to extract conversation, no common understanding of who they were to each other. The central fact that bound them was Malcolm's imprisonment, and Malcolm could not even comprehend why that should matter to Chase.

"I know it can feel like everyone's against you," Chase answered. "There's a universe of people who understand the George Bullocks of the world, who want the truth regardless of race. If it comes to a trial, Jabari will make sure some wind up on the jury. All that will matter in the end are those twelve people."

Hearing himself, Chase hoped that he sounded more convinced than he felt. But Malcolm's face relaxed, a sign of how desperately he sought out hope. "I just keep wishing my grandad were here. I could use his company about now."

It keeps coming back to that, Chase thought sadly—*the absence of a male figure in Malcolm's life.* But this was a chance to understand more about his son's growing up. "Your mom says he was pretty important to you."

Malcolm looked off at some middle distance, as if gathering memories. "It's funny—I remember him almost as far back as I remember her. He was just always there."

For a moment, Chase felt envious of this man he didn't know—Malcolm could never say this about Chase himself. "I guess you did a lot of stuff together."

"Yeah," Malcolm said softly. "Like everything. He taught me how to play checkers until I could beat him. So we moved on to chess, and soon enough I could whip him all the time. Sometimes he got so irked, it was kind of funny."

"Maybe you should have given him a participation award."

Malcolm smiled a little. "I think that was mostly for show. He always liked me getting better at things. He was the one who showed me how to hold a baseball bat, put up a hoop near the house so I could shoot baskets. There wasn't a game of mine, not one, he didn't come to until the day he died." His voice softened again. "He never had a boy of his own, he told me. So I was the best thing that ever happened to him."

Though this touched him, for fear of throwing Malcolm off-balance Chase chose not to show it. "Not your mother?" he asked lightly. "I thought she was the best thing that ever happened to everyone."

The humor surfaced in Malcolm's eyes again. "'No offense to your mother or grandmother,' Granddad told me. 'But you and me got our own club. Before you came along, I'd gotten pretty weary of being the only member.'"

Watching his son, Chase could feel the warmth and kindness of this man, Allie's father, who had known how to touch the heart of a boy with no father of his own. "Sounds like a two-man club was more than enough," Chase observed. "As far as I can see, his only disservice was making you watch the Atlanta Braves."

Malcolm looked askance at him. "Don't see that's a problem. Last year they were world champions."

Chase held up a hand. "Wait a minute. You were born in 2004, right?"

"Right."

"So how many World Series had they won before 2021? Please don't knock yourself out here—it's pretty easy to count to zero."

Malcolm sat straighter. "Six division titles, two wildcard appearances..."

"Doesn't matter," Chase interjected. "You and your granddad played horseshoes, right? As in the only game where 'nearly' counts. There are no participation awards in baseball, only world champions. Or not. 'Not' pretty much defines the Atlanta Braves since the day you were born."

"So who's your team?" Malcolm asked. "Oh, wait a minute, has to be the fucking Red Sox."

Chase smiled again. "Otherwise known as the world champions in 2004, 2007, 2013, and 2018. You can be forgiven for blanking on 2004—you were barely out of the womb. But four championships in your lifetime ought to start sinking in. After all, you're an honors graduate of Cade County High School, otherwise known as the Harvard of Southwest Georgia." He skipped a beat. "No offense, by the way. I used to tease your mother like this. She showed that same high level of good sportsmanship I can read on your face."

Malcolm shot him a challenging look. "Maybe that was because it took three years of watching Bill Russell turn the Celtics into an NBA trophy machine before the Red Sox called up a Black baseball player. Last team in the majors to do it."

"Yup," Chase responded crisply. "Elijah 'Pumpsie' Green, 1959. I've got his baseball card in my collection of old Red Sox players I was hoping to pass on to my son." He raised a hand again. "Look, I learned the hard way never to spar with your mother about race. So you won't catch me arguing that Boston's some garden spot for Blacks. Never has been; isn't now."

For a moment, Malcolm fell quiet. "My mom told me some more about that case you prosecuted. Sounds like you pissed off some white people."

Chase shrugged. "No big surprise—where I come from this stuff runs pretty deep. But the verdict turned out right, which is all that mattered."

"Guess you were a good lawyer."

Why, Chase wondered, had Allie told their son about the Kerrigan case—to elevate Chase for some reason or another, or to give Malcolm more hope for the justice system than she herself felt? "Good enough," he responded. "But not as good as Jabari."

There was a knock on the door, and their visit was done.

Suddenly Chase wished it were not. For fifteen minutes or so, he seemed to have almost succeeded in diverting Malcolm from the dangers that encased him, exceeding his own best hopes and, he had thought, his capacities. But now Malcolm appeared deflated, restored to misery by a knock on the door. "I'll be back," Chase heard himself promise. "Your reeducation has a ways to go."

Malcolm said nothing until Chase reached the door. "I've been reading that history you gave me," he called after him.

Surprised, Chase turned back. "What do you think?"

"It's pretty good." Malcolm hesitated. "If you bring something else you've read, that's fine with me."

Chase lingered in the doorway, grateful for this fragile connection. "Maybe a novel," he answered.

★ ★ ★

Once in the rental car, Chase sat behind the wheel, replaying the last half hour with his son. So much of what went on between them was subterranean, a matter of inference and guessing. He could lose the thread before he even knew it.

Reluctantly, he turned on his cell phone.

The numerous messages from his other life included an irritable text from Jack Raskin. "Sorry," Chase texted back, "I left my ankle bracelet at home. Call you tonight."

How much longer, Chase wondered, could he get away with this? He felt the time for this tenuous double life with Malcolm and Allie running out quickly. Too much media, too much malice, and far too little time to resolve his own debts and confusions.

He reflected a moment longer and then called Jabari Ford.

"I guess you know I came back to see Malcolm. Thought I'd call you while I was here."

"Praise the Lord," Ford said sardonically. "I've been experiencing separation anxiety."

Despite himself, Chase laughed. "Yeah, I do that to everyone. But there's only so much of me to go around."

There was a momentary silence. "If this is my moment," Ford answered, "your timing's pretty good. On the outside chance you're still interested, Joe Briggs is coming by with something on Bullock."

39

"For a few weeks in late 2020," Joe Briggs told Ford and Chase, "George Bullock was a standard-issue conspiracy theorist. At least on Facebook."

They were sitting at the end of Ford's conference table, looking at a screenshot on Briggs' computer. "Where did you get this?" Ford asked.

"Easy enough. George and Dorothy Bullock had a Facebook page—pretty benign, mostly, with pictures of kids, recipes, religious homilies, articles denouncing drugs, etc. The wife of one of the guys I play softball with friended them to swap stuff on cooking. But when I looked at this, I found three postings from Bullock after the 2020 election. Then he just stopped."

"What were the sources?"

"One pro-Trump website with a single theme: Democrats stole the election through massive voter fraud—rigging voting machines, casting phony mail-in ballots, and stuffing ballot boxes in minority precincts." He gave Ford a wry look. "Too bad you don't live in Philadelphia, Jabari. You could have voted every hour or so."

"Sounds perfect," Ford responded in an acidic tone. "Find anything specific about Allie or Georgia?"

"Nope. You can look for yourself. He didn't write anything himself, either. At least on Facebook."

"Going back before these postings, was there anything local? I'm thinking about those police shootings, maybe stuff from Fay Spann."

"*Nada.* George and Dorothy helped send food over to the widows and contributed to a scholarship fund for their kids. But so did a lot of people, and that was all through the First Baptist Church. It's the kind of thing folks remember him for."

Chase contemplated a rectangle of late-afternoon sunlight cast through a window onto the conference table. "Was there anything showing a predisposition toward white nationalism?" he asked. "Or the 'Great Replacement' theory?"

Briggs raised his eyebrows. "Like that Blacks are setting out to replace whites and transform America into Africa West? Maybe Bullock was looking over his shoulder, like some of the commentators on Fox, but there's no sign of it here. To get anything more, I'd have to see his personal computer and departmental and personal cell phones, and you'd need a court order for that."

"Unless Dalton Harris cooperates," Ford put in. "Our line of attack is no mystery, so I imagine he's checked out Bullock himself. Seems strange to me that Bullock started posting this crap right after the election, then stopped before New Year's. The people who believe that Democrats stole the election tend not to get over it. They just get worse."

A corner of Briggs' mouth turned up. "Meet my brother-in-law, and you'd realize that consuming disinformation eats the brain. Although in his case it's an afternoon snack." He looked from Ford to Chase and back again. "But you have to consider Bullock's personal situation. The same election made Al Garrett sheriff. When your new boss is a Black man and close to Allie Hill, best to put your political sentiments somewhere no one can see them."

"What do his friends say?" Ford asked.

"Pretty much what I thought they would. No one took George for a liberal, but no one ever heard him say 'nigger' either—at least that they'll admit." Briggs' mouth twitched again. "Of course, none of them ever use that word either."

Ford waved this away. "Did you get to Nick Spinetta?"

"No. As the arresting officer, he's a witness at any trial. Harris has him all buttoned up."

Ford nodded. "Any idea about his politics?"

"Naturally, I've been asking. But nothing I heard makes Nick out to be political, let alone a right-winger or a racist. There is not even a whisper of that in the sheriff's office as far as I can tell, including among Blacks."

Listening, Chase kept crossing off questions as Ford asked them himself. "What do you know about Spinetta's relationship to Bullock?" Ford queried. "Just before the shooting, they were exchanging texts."

Briggs sat back, hands folded across a modest potbelly. "The way I understand it, it was a little-brother, big-brother kind of thing. When Nick joined the department seven years back, Bullock helped train him. Over time the families got close. They'd have Sunday dinner together, and sometimes George and Dorothy would babysit Nick and Susan's two little girls so they could have a night out. All pretty wholesome."

"Was it just the families?" Ford asked. "Or did they do guy stuff together?"

"The latter. They'd go fishing or watch sports on the weekend, maybe have a beer after work. Out on the job, they kind of watched out for each other. George Bullock had a lot of guys who admired him. But outside of Dorothy, in the last few years probably nobody knew him better than Nick."

Pensive, Ford steepled his fingers. "What about Bullock's personal life?"

"You try rooting for dirt on a man two weeks dead," Briggs responded pointedly. "But so far I've heard nothing about conspicuous spending, and nothing more about sticking up a drug dealer than the rumor we've already heard. Nothing about the Parnells, either."

"What about women?"

Briggs gave a dubious frown. "A hero cop like George Bullock, with a big personality, is going to have women coming on to him while he pumps iron at the gym. So it wouldn't shock me if he fucked a badge bunny or two. But I haven't found anyone willing to say that he did. Can't say it matters, either, unless it somehow relates to what you're looking for—a racist cop stalking Malcolm."

"That's what I'm struggling with," Ford rejoined. "There's a big gap between the man Malcolm describes on the night of the shooting, and a guy who makes three postings about election theft in less than two months, then forgets all about it. Doesn't feel right."

"Not to me, either. But that's all there is on George's Facebook page. At the very least, he was a whole lot more discreet than Malcolm."

"Malcolm's a kid," Ford retorted. "He didn't know he'd be standing trial for murder. Strikes me like Bullock was the only one thinking ahead." Turning to Chase, he said, "Have anything for Joe?"

"Nothing concrete," Chase answered. "But I keep thinking about connections between white nationalist groups and law enforcement. The smarter the cop, the more careful." Facing Briggs, he asked. "Suppose Bullock wanted to use the internet in a way that couldn't be traced?"

Briggs nodded. "There's ways he could make tracing harder. For example, suppose he wanted to access a forum among right-wing extremists. He could invent a generic email address, use a password that gives no clue to his identity, and add on a privacy setting or web browser designed to hide who he is. Before you try to crack that, you'd need access to all his electronics—like the GBI got for Malcolm's devices. Wouldn't bet the outhouse on you getting that from Harris or the judge."

Chase thought for a moment. "What about ghost phones?"

Briggs gave him a curious look. "You mean where you go to some store, buy a prepaid smartphone, use a generic email address, and keep swapping out one phone for another? Where did you hear about that?"

"Before the congressman went big time," Ford told Briggs, "he was a prosecutor in Boston. Sounds like he prosecuted some drug dealers."

"I did, actually," Chase affirmed. "But you know who else uses ghost phones? Politicians who need a cell number for robocalls, and people who want to carry on affairs without their spouse checking their personal phone. No reason Bullock couldn't use the same trick, and from doing drug cases he'd know exactly how it worked."

"Yeah, he would," Briggs agreed. "When I worked narcotics cases, it always made me crazy. The bad guys buy prepaid minutes in bulk, and there's no billing process, so you don't even know the damn phone exists. Even if you get the cell phone number, you don't know who it belongs to.

"But that's just the problem here, isn't it? You don't even know where to begin. Unless you can find it somehow, then tie it to Bullock, the idea of him using a ghost phone is sheer speculation."

Ford nodded glumly. "Anything else?" asked Chase.

"Nothing."

Briggs stood. "I'm with you about Bullock," he told Ford. "If you believe Malcolm, there's got to be something more. But instinct is not evidence, and it may be hard to find anything more concrete."

"Just keep digging," Ford answered. "It would be good to have something more before Harris decides about the death penalty."

"Will do," Briggs assured him, and left.

Chase turned to Ford. "Guess you're going to see Harris."

"As soon as I can," Ford responded. "I don't want him making up his mind before we try to get more about Bullock, including through him. How long are you planning to grace us with your presence?"

Chase thought for a moment. "Maybe two or three more days. For all sorts of reasons, I need to get back. But we're in recess for the rest of the week, and I'd like to see Malcolm again. Allie, too, and she had to fly to New York to pacify donors."

Ford crossed his arms. "No help for it. With that video out, there's going to be more pressure for her to step down."

Chase tried to imagine the conflicts Allie was feeling. "Is it that bad already?"

"Getting there." Ford paused, "If you're still here, feel free to call on Harris with me. Right now I want him thinking about anything but that video. Like you calling up the Justice Department if he stonewalls about Bullock."

40

That evening, Allie met with Blue Georgia's major donors in New York. Her patrons had gathered at Patricia Farley's penthouse apartment on Central Park West, featuring a Matisse, a Rauschenberg, and two early Picassos. Dusk was falling, and through the floor-to-ceiling window she could see the light from streetlamps illuminating the pathways winding through the park. Allie could not help thinking of the darkness surrounding Malcolm on the night George Bullock had stopped him, and how strange it was to be in this opulent place with her son imprisoned in Cade County. But that was why she had needed to come.

Attempting to disguise her fatigue, she sat amidst a semicircle of people she had cultivated over the years: Patricia Farley, the widow of a philanthropist from one of the city's wealthiest families; Kenneth Ruben, a mergers-and-acquisitions lawyer from a prominent Wall Street firm; Patrick Moore, a hedge fund billionaire; Sheila Gray, a pioneering entrepreneur who had made a considerable fortune in the telecommunications business; and the only Black, Marshall Fox, a highly placed executive at Citicorp whom Allie had met through her late friend Vernon Jordan. Though she dearly wished to be elsewhere, Allie understood the concerns stemming from the charges against Malcolm, and badly needed these people to rally behind her. Without their support, and that of others like them, Blue Georgia could not continue the field operation that in 2020 had shifted the balance of power in Washington. As major donors often did, they took a certain proprietary credit while, as board members, they were entitled to a voice in crucial decisions. Though they had always given her ample space, this moment was very different, and Allie had sensed trouble going in.

Smoothing her dress, Patricia Farley began. "I know I speak for all of us, Allie, in saying that our heart goes out to you and Malcolm. I hope you can feel that."

How it felt, Allie thought, was somewhat ominous. "I do, Patricia," she said, looking around the group. "I appreciate all of you more than I can say. Especially now."

"How is Malcolm doing?" Sheila Gray inquired, with as much solicitude as she could about a young man she didn't know and about whose innocence, Allie already knew, she entertained considerable doubt.

"It's hard for him," Allie said simply. "He's innocent."

This induced a modest silence. Then Ken Ruben inquired politely, "Do you expect him to be exonerated? At least as soon as we all would hope?"

It had started, Allie knew. "Certainly not as soon as *I'd* hope." Looking around her, she decided to cut to the chase. "I know you've all seen that video."

Her donors looked at one another waiting for someone to speak. "We have," Patrick Moore affirmed. "We understand the problem it creates for Malcolm's defense. But that also creates problems for Blue Georgia."

He paused there, waiting for Allie to acknowledge this. But she decided not to help him. "How do you see them from your perspective, Patrick?"

Sitting back, Moore took a sip of his whiskey. "There are several, and all know what they are. So, with considerable regret, I'll go to the heart of all this: the fact that Blue Georgia is being conflated with a charge against the son of its leader for killing a policeman, a grievous problem that shows no signs of going away. Malcolm is heading for a murder trial at the very time that Blue Georgia is trying to win an election."

Steeling herself, Allie felt an emptiness in the pit of her stomach. "I understand."

"Of course you do, Allie," Sheila Gray interposed. "You're living with Malcolm's dilemma day and night, while simultaneously trying to run a turnout operation and a voting rights campaign. You're the nearest thing to Superwoman I've ever seen, but at some point won't that get to be too much?"

Allie met her eyes. "I've done a lot of hard things in my life. None of them yet have been too hard to bear. Trust me to tell you if this does."

Almost imperceptibly, Allie felt the tension in the room subtly rising. "It isn't just about what you can stand," Ken Ruben responded. "Before the shooting, Blue Georgia was the darling of progressives, and you were the charismatic face of a righteous cause—saving American democracy. Mention Allie Hill and Blue Georgia to anyone now, and their first thought bubble is—frankly—"Did her son murder that cop?" Everything gets tangled up with that video, and the fears of a whole bunch of Americans—again, I'm just being frank—about Black people and crime and attacking the police. Blue Georgia's brand is already getting dragged into the cesspool of national politics."

"I know," Allie said. "I saw the governor speaking at that funeral. I've watched Fox News. I heard that psychopath Dorothy Turner Dark. None of them were ever our friends. Are they what we're supposed to be afraid of?"

"Of course not," Ruben said with the first trace of impatience. "But when they start piling on, it bleeds into the public consciousness." He tried to look abashed, and failed. "I'm sorry, but by now you've heard all that stuff about Malcolm having no father, about him getting kicked out of school for punching out a white kid. I'm not saying he isn't a fine young man trapped in a terrible dilemma. But when he morphs into some rapper calling on Black men to kill cops, Blue Georgia suffers. It's just a matter of how much."

For a moment, Allie fell silent, buying time to subordinate her own feelings to what she must do. "Whether we succeed," she told the others, "comes down to two things. First, our people, and no one is quitting. Second, the money we need to support them. I'll let you know if donors begin running away. So far, none have." Looking around the room, she concluded evenly, "But seeing how we're all together, let's take a survey. Is anyone here thinking of withdrawing their support?"

The faces around her were a portrait of conflicting emotions—doubt, resolve, reflection, and, in Ruben, resentment at being cornered. But Marshall Fox, heretofore quiet, had a glint of arid humor in his eyes. "Before we go on," he said to the group, "something occurs to me. My own survey may seem a little off topic. But has anyone here been stopped by a cop for no good reason? Besides me and Allie, of course."

Patrick Moore smiled faintly. "We're not insensate, Marshall. You could have taken it on faith that none of us have."

Fox gave him a wry look. "Well, maybe it's my weakness to personalize this, Patrick. But a few things don't sit right with me. Maybe all that matters about Malcolm is perceptions—not reality. But when you start with suspecting that deputy in darkest Georgia was stalking Malcolm, which I do, you begin getting your back up about letting a bunch of right-wing bigots stampede us into running Allie out of Dodge."

"No one was talking about that," Ruben protested. "But I do find myself wondering whether Allie should take a leave of absence."

"Oh, I see," Fox rejoined amiably. "We're just sending her into exile, sort of like Napoleon on Elba. But on what grounds do you sideline the only leader we've ever had during an election campaign? Because that's what the people who hate us want?"

"Of course not," Ruben retorted. "But isn't there an inherent conflict of interest? Doesn't Allie have the problem of dividing her energies between leading Blue Georgia and defending her son? When is she forced to start approaching Blue Georgia's donors to help finance what could become a very expensive criminal defense?"

The two women, Allie noticed, were quietly watching. "Excuse me, Ken," she interjected, "but it's not like I've gone anywhere. So why don't I save Marshall the bother of answering for me?"

At the corner of her vision, Sheila Gray gave Ruben a keen look, confirming Allie's sense that the subterranean fissures of gender had begun intersecting with those of race. "About dividing my energies," Allie continued, "as a single mother, I've been doing it all my life. So this is more about managing my emotions. About taking a leave, for better or worse I'm the one with the national profile and donor base, the one who founded this organization and knows it inside and out, the one our people in the field look to for inspiration and support."

For an instant, Allie felt the tug of self-doubt—the question of whether ego was blinding her to reality. "If I feel all that going to hell to the detriment of Blue Georgia," she finished, "I hope I'll be honest enough to tell you. Until then, I'm staying. So I'd be grateful for any support that any of you continue to give us, and even more grateful if you chose to double it."

The room became quiet. But after a moment, Gray told Allie, "I will, for one. But I imagine all of us will, in the end. We invested in you years ago, and look at how far you've brought us since then. More to the point, brought the country."

"No one can doubt that," Ruben allowed. "But Allie passed over one question that I think is essential to the health of Blue Georgia: whether financing Malcolm's defense means tapping our donor base, potentially diverting the funds we need to sustain our field operation."

This was the crunch point Allie had been dreading—the choice between her cause and her son. "If it eases your mind," she answered coolly, "I can promise you that I won't approach our donors to help Malcolm. His lawyer and I will set up a defense fund for that, completely separate from the operations of Blue Georgia. Whoever wants to contribute can. Is that satisfactory, Ken?"

"For now," Ruben responded phlegmatically. "We'll have to see what happens next."

With that, at least for the moment, Allie had accomplished what she set out to do for Blue Georgia. But no one in this room, or anywhere, could know what it cost her.

★ ★ ★

Leaving, Allie made sure to share an elevator with Marshall Fox. As the doors closed behind him, Allie leaned back against the wall. "God, I'm tired."

"Sure you are, girl. But you handled it just perfect."

"Not me," Allie responded. "Us. Thanks for the warning."

Fox grinned. "Vernon would be proud of us both. Glad we had lunch to work it all out.

Might have forgotten my lines."

The elevator hissed to a stop. "I doubt that," Allie answered. "You ever get tired of being the smartest guy in the room?"

"'Guy' is the operative word, Alexandria. After all, you were up there." Lightly, he kissed her on the cheek. "Just let me know whenever I can help."

With that, Allie returned to her hotel. She needed to call Al Garrett to see how Malcolm was doing. The worst thing about rushing here was leaving him behind. But what made it harder was what had forced her to come here: that videotape.

41

At ten o'clock the next morning, Dalton Harris welcomed Ford and Chase to his office with the anticipated courtesy. But his manner was cooler, and it was apparent to Chase that Malcolm's video posting had changed the dynamics between the prosecution and the defense.

Handing Harris copies of Bullock's Facebook postings, Ford said, "Thought you should see these, sooner rather than later."

Harris read them over twice, as if fearful he had missed something the first time. Looking up, he inquired politely, "And the point is?"

"Obvious," Ford replied. "To both of us."

Harris seemed to stifle a sigh of indifference. "These postings," he responded, "are consistent with the beliefs among eighty percent of all Republicans in Georgia. Do you have anything more persuasive to show me? Or even more recent?"

"Not yet, no. But this case is barely two weeks old."

"Still, there are already things you do know, Jabari. For example, did Malcolm 'friend' George Bullock on Facebook?"

Chase grasped the point instantly as, he perceived, did Ford. With a look of synthetic bemusement, Ford said, "What does that have to do with anything?"

"Bear with me," Harris requested. "So when George Bullock stopped him, these postings hadn't put Malcolm in fear for his life? Am I off-base somehow?"

Ford did not answer. "The point is about Bullock's state of mind at the time of the stop. Not Malcolm's."

Briskly, Harris shook his head. "George Bullock stopped an intoxicated driver who could have been a fifty-year-old white guy. Show me more and maybe I'll be impressed. Though I'd be curious to know why you think he was stopping Malcolm in particular, as opposed to some drunk. About that, these postings don't tell me a thing."

"Not true," Ford insisted. "They tell you there's a basis for further investigating Bullock's political and racial beliefs. Including by looking at his social media, like you've already done with Malcolm."

Harris sat back. "I was wondering when we'd get to the elephant in this particular room. Assuming that's an appropriate metaphor for Mr. Double-XX. He does change things some, doesn't he? Including with respect to your client's state of mind."

"Only that?" Ford inquired. "To me, the elephant in the room is called equity. Whatever you make of that video, we want the same chance to explore Deputy Bullock's state of mind."

"As a matter of law," Harris rejoined in the same even manner, "I don't accept the principle. What is it that you and Congressman Brevard would like me to do?"

"It's pretty simple," Ford answered. "We want access to the deputy's electronic devices. You've already got Malcolm Hill's."

Harris' eyebrows shot up. "All of them? At least one part's easy enough. Well before the time of these postings, George gave up his personal cell phone."

Ford looked at him askance, "How can that be?"

"It's frowned on, officially. But once some deputies get comfortable in their job, they start using their departmental phones for personal communications. It's like a perk for being underpaid—why shell out for your own cell phone account when you've got one somebody else pays for?"

"And you're saying Bullock did that."

"Not just me—the GBI. They checked. Since 2017, George had no personal cell phone account—anywhere. End stop."

Ford's skeptical expression deepened. "In other words, every single personal cell phone communication George Bullock made for the last four years was on his departmental phone. Which, I assume, was taken off his body during the crime scene search shortly after he died."

"Exactly. Which means we know exactly what was on it. Not just his communications with Deputy Spinetta on that night he died, which we will be happy to show you. But every text, phone message, and email, including whether Dorothy wanted him to stop at the Piggly Wiggly for a quart of milk." Harris held up a hand. "No doubt you have a personal cell phone account, and so do I. But there's nothing on my personal cell I'd be ashamed to have the public see or hear, and I'm confident that's true of you and the congressman. But one thing I can tell you for sure— it was true of George Bullock. We've looked."

"What about his personal computer?"

"There's a lot of overlap with his departmental phone. Every email, for example."

"Even so," Ford persisted, "I'd like to see it. I'm curious about social media."

"On what grounds?" Harris' face closed. "You've got no idea, do you? The essence of your defense is making George Bullock look dirty, any way you can. If you've got some better reason, I'll listen. But I'll be damned if I'll go tormenting Dorothy Bullock just so you can drag her husband's corpse through the mud. You'll need Judge Tilly for that."

"Sorry, Dalton." Ford's voice was at once soft and unrepentant. "Seems to me like you're feeling the heat. Been getting phone calls at home in the middle of the night? Because I sure have, and so has Allie." His tone grew quieter yet. "We've got a problem here, don't we? You, me, Allie, and Malcolm. Even your friends on the county commission are getting a little weak in the knees."

Pausing, Ford glanced over at Chase. "I haven't had time to share this with Congressman Brevard. But just before coming over, I heard there's going to be a big rally tonight outside of town, for the right-wing whack job running against Governor Trask. Seems that commissioners gave the man a permit for the field right by where George Bullock got shot, and he's promising some special surprises. I'm guessing your prospective primary rival Matthew Bell will appear as a lesser attraction. Sort of sends chills down your spine, doesn't it?"

Abruptly, Harris looked queasy, though not as queasy as Chase felt. "I had nothing to do with that," he said stiffly.

"But it has something to do with you. And Malcolm." Ford paused, then continued in a ruminative tone. "Because I've got the funniest feeling you know or suspect more about St. George than you're saying."

At once, Chase understood what Ford was doing—counterbalancing the pressures on Ford with the possibility that outside forces, perhaps the

Justice Department or the media, would discover things about Bullock Harris he suspected might be true.

Gazing at Ford, Harris composed himself. "Bravely spoken, Jabari. At least for a lawyer whose client looks like a murderer. Get back to me when you come up with something that makes him look better."

He stood and, with perfunctory courtesy, ended the meeting.

★ ★ ★

Leaving, the two men were quiet until they found a private place on the lawn of the courthouse. "That rally's a nightmare," Chase said. "There'll be media descending like vultures to the site of Bullock's death, all to watch a political candidate call for revenge on Malcolm. I just hope to God he doesn't watch it."

"I'll ask Allie to call Al Garrett, make sure he doesn't. The young man's state of mind is already bad enough." Briefly, Ford looked over his shoulder. "In its own way, so is Dalton's. But I learned one other thing just now. For whatever good it does us, I'm guessing Bullock had a ghost phone."

42

In the early evening, Chase found that America's foremost right-wing news channel had unleashed a torrent of vituperation against Malcolm, a perverse pregame advertisement for the rally in Cade County.

Its most highly rated host—an Ivy League–educated heir to a fortune built on TV dinners who postured as a culture warrior—devoted a half hour to characterizing the Double-XX video as "irrefutable evidence that Malcolm Hill meant to fulfill a perverse racial quota by assassinating white police." Participating remotely from Cade County, Matthew Bell told his preening interrogator, "The eyes of America are once again on Georgia. If our district attorney does not seek the death penalty, it's open season on the thin blue line that is our last defense against barbarism."

Even the advertising, Chase discovered, provided little respite from the assault against Malcolm. In a close-up, Governor Trask declaimed: "We must ensure that those found guilty of killing our protectors receive the ultimate punishment. And I do not—repeat do not—mean a timorous justice system that makes the family of the victim suffer through endless and frivolous appeals."

The camera shot widened. Sitting beside the governor on a living room couch was Dorothy Bullock, her son, and her daughter. The widow's face was painfully drawn, and she spoke in a halting voice from what sounded like a script:

"Like so many of you, I'm a Christian wife and mother who put family at the center of my life. I never wanted the spotlight or paid much attention to politics. But when a vicious crime ripped out the hearts of the two children I hold dear, Governor Trask came to offer us comfort. And the greatest comfort of all was his promise to do everything in his power to ensure that another family would not lose a good man like my husband, Deputy Sheriff George Bullock." For a brief moment, her voice caught before she pleaded, "Please remember us in your prayers, and Governor Trask on Election Day."

With that, Chase switched off the television, went to his rental car, and began driving toward Old County Road.

★ ★ ★

Night had fallen. As Chase neared the site of the shooting, his headlights caught a long line of cars parked by the side of the road. He pulled up behind them, considering his own safety. But all others would see in the semidark of the rally, he concluded, was another white man in a baseball cap. They would not be expecting a congressman from Massachusetts come to witness the fever enveloping his son.

Leaving the car, he walked for twenty minutes toward the crowd already filling a field bathed in light, his footsteps crunching gravel. Near the entrance to the rally, he saw a makeshift memorial that marked the place of Bullock's death, bunches of flowers piling up beneath an easel that contained his photograph in laminated Styrofoam, gazing out with a look of resolute vigilance beneath his visored cap.

The field was surrounded by wooden barriers, with an opening manned by sheriff's deputies through which Chase passed. The last uniformed man, he realized, was Al Garrett. As Garrett marked faces, his eyes widened slightly in recognition of Chase.

Chase kept moving.

The scene resembled a rock concert in waiting. An ear-shattering sound system pulsed anthems to the patriotism and grit of white Christian America. Klieg lights split the night sky, illuminating a raised wooden platform. Edging through the crowd, Chase saw that the stage was surrounded by armed members of White Lightning who included Charles and Molly Parnell, and chose to stop where he was.

The throng pressing against him smelled of sweat and passion, antic-ipation and anger, with a fainter scent of beer, whiskey, and marijuana. One bearded man to his right, Chase guessed, was a crackhead or, more likely from the perspiration beaded on his forehead, gripped by opioids. Most of the men and women wore blue jeans and T-shirts, some embla-zoned with bolts of white lightning, and many sported red "MAGA" caps smudged and wilted with use.

Comingled among them were conventional-looking types—perhaps businesspeople or professionals—seized by the same passions as their more rough-hewn compatriots. No doubt many of those surrounding him were loving parents, good neighbors, loyal friends; now, as often, Chase wondered at the transformation of ordinary citizens by fear and hatred into people who loathed, at least in the abstract, others in whom had they known them they could have found the elements of their common humanity.

Except for a brown middle-aged couple he assumed were Hispanic, everyone he saw was white. Though they talked among themselves in an indistinct cacophony, their gazes were fixed on a massive movie screen at the rear of the stage. They had been promised a special surprise and, hoping against hope, longed for the ultimate rapture only one man could bring.

No wonder, Chase thought, that the ruling class of Cade County had come to fear them.

Suddenly, spotlights crisscrossed the stage and a lone figure appeared, his bland face and squinty eyes filling the screen behind him. At once Chase recognized the primary challenger to Governor Trask, an ordained minister–turned–firebrand legislator whose defining political brand was fealty to the man he repeatedly called "America's once and future presi-dent." The screams of recognition filling the air, Chase knew, were less for Larry Clapp the man than for him as a surrogate for their idol.

"You know me," he began. "I'm a pastor called to save America for the rightful children of a righteous God. I'm running for governor because a Judas who calls himself Trask betrayed His tribune, America's only true leader…"

At once, Clapp's biblical indictment was drowned in a confusion of sounds: boos and screams of outrage for Judas, a swelling chorus of longing for America's only true leader. When at last it had subsided, Clapp proclaimed in righteous contempt: "Like Judas, this traitor named Trask feigned devotion to the man God sent to save us. But two years ago our modern-day Judas betrayed all of us by allowing the enemies of America to steal the presidency…"

Abruptly, Clapp's visage disappeared. Stunned, Chase found himself deafened by a primal outcry of rage as a photograph of Allie Hill appeared on the screen, surrounded by her allies as she spoke from the steps of the courthouse. It did not escape Chase or anyone around him that the faces of America's supposed enemies were Black.

Reduced to a strutting pygmy beneath the massive image of Allie, Clapp launched his words through the sound system with reverberating contempt. "But *this* is the true face of Traitor Trask's Blue Georgia…"

Replacing his mother, Malcolm Hill's mug shot filled the screen.

To Chase, his son appeared dazed, his eyes filled with shock at a horror he could not quite believe. But the roar of bloodlust all around him was a call for revenge on a vicious Black killer who was not fully human. "Kill him," a man's preternaturally deep voice sounded above the crowd, and then a ragged chant rose from Chase's neighbors.

"*Kill him…kill him…kill him…*"

"But let us not despair," Clapp cried out. "Because *this* is the face of our once and future America…"

Instantly, Malcolm was erased by the tangerine apparition of their leader.

The crowd screamed in frenzy, fists raised to the sky. Then the leader's lips began moving, and his legions became still and silent so swiftly that this frightened Chase more than what had come before.

He was speaking, Chase realized, from the palm-rich grounds of the subtropical redoubt where courtiers came to pledge their obeisance. "Before the Great Betrayal," he said in a tone that fused nostalgia with anger, "we were returning America to what it should be: a proud nation that keeps good people safe from the enemies destroying our cities and overrunning our borders. But look at what's happened since Traitor Trask—and that's the perfect name for him—stabbed our country in the back by helping the radical socialist Democrats steal the White House on a wave of massive voter fraud…"

As howls of anger filled the skies, a knowing smile played on his lips.

"Before the Great Betrayal," he called out, "the radical Democrats and the vicious Black Lives Matter militants only wanted to defund your police. But now that I'm gone, they feel free to kill them."

He stopped, allowing those in the throng to state their need to cry out against Malcolm. Then he started again, punctuating the din with fresh incitements to hatred and fear.

"Right here in Cade County, a murderous militant who was harvesting illegal ballots killed a heroic deputy, a crusader against drugs who left behind a wife and two children." His voice rose in anger. "Has everyone seen that video…?"

The answering tumult, ripe with loathing, confirmed for Chase that Malcolm's moment of carelessness had metastasized from viral to lethal. "Back in the day," the leader said disdainfully, "we used to know what to do with people like that. But these days we're oh so polite. So your first line of defense is voting for the only man running for governor who will keep Georgia safe…

"Who will make the death penalty swift and sure…"

"*Kill him*," the chant rose again. "*Kill him…*"

"And who, above all, will stop the radical Democrats from defrauding the good people of Georgia in *this* election and—even more important—the presidential election of 2024."

At this promise, the apotheosis of rapturous longing for this man who personified his followers' unmoored cravings for restoration and revenge, they unleashed a sheet of thunderous noise that, in Chase's mind, encased them in their own insanity, linking those around him with the mob that had stormed the Capitol. The America they lusted for, so dangerous to Allie and Malcolm, had no place for him.

He was no safer here, Chase realized, than he'd been on January 6. The question was whether leaving or staying would endanger him more.

Surreptitiously, Chase looked around him at profiles illuminated by passions so consuming that perhaps they would not notice a single man edging away. "In 2024," their leader cried out, "we will stop America's enemies from running our government…

"Confiscating our guns…

"Toppling our monuments…

"Attacking our religion…

"Destroying our traditions…

"Defiling our schools…

"Corrupting our children…

"*And*"—here he paused for an emphasis pregnant with warning—"replacing our people, the real Americans, with rapists, murderers, subversives, and foreigners alien to our shores and contemptuous of our laws…"

Had Malcolm been with him, Chase thought, in a frenzy of recognition the people around him might have torn his son apart. It was this, running through him like an electric current, that jolted him into leaving before the rally was over.

Damp with sweat, Chase angled through the press of bodies with his head down, averting his eyes from the open mouths and angry faces, blocking out the cascade of noise summoned by the inflammatory rhetoric of their unstable and narcissistic leader from the safety of his self-obsessed cocoon. "Hey, man, why you leaving?" a man's voice demanded. "Where you going?"

Silent, Chase kept moving. It took him a half hour to reach an open space near the edge of the crowd and, when he did, the leader's demands for attention still reverberated through the sound system.

At the corner of his vision, a frazzled, middle-aged blonde woman in a White Lightning T-shirt was staring in apparent recognition. Suddenly, she ran up to him and tipped back his cap, peering into his face with glazed eyes. "Do I know you?" she asked thickly.

Chase tensed at once. "Don't think so," he answered, slurring his voice. "I'd remember."

She regarded him with nearsighted suspicion. Then, quite abruptly, she pressed her lips against his in a simulacrum of sexual hunger and tried to stick her tongue in his mouth, filling his nostrils with the smell of stale beer.

Instinctively, he recoiled. "That's OK," the woman told him vaguely. "I love you anyways." Shoulders slumped, she stumbled away in no particular direction.

Alone now, Chase walked quickly to his car, passing the sound trucks that beamed the rally to millions of American homes. Thinning in the air behind him, the leader's voice became the indistinct mumble of a grade B monster. In the rearview mirror, the smear of red lipstick on Chase's mouth looked like blood.

Wiping it off, he remembered accounts of spontaneous carnality after fundamentalist revivals in the 1920s, echoes from what he had thought of as a more primitive America.

Still shaken, Congressman Chase Brevard turned on the ignition and drove toward Allie's farmhouse.

★ ★ ★

When he arrived, Jabari Ford was already there, huddled in the dining room with Allie and her communications director, a tall Black woman, all three of them absorbed in a Zoom call with an anchorwoman from MSNBC. Only when the call was finished did Allie look up at Chase, her somber gaze resting on his face.

"I guess you saw the rally," she said.

"Actually, I was there."

"You're insane," Ford blurted in astonishment.

Chase kept looking at Allie. "Just white," he answered, "so I could get by with it. But *they* are."

For a moment no one spoke. Then Allie said, "I'm going on MSNBC tomorrow night. To tell Malcolm's story and ask anyone with information to come forward."

Chase looked from one expectant face to the other, then settled on Allie's again. "For whatever my opinion's worth, I don't think you've got any choice."

Only Allie understood his unspoken coda, the judgment of Malcolm's father about the dangers to their son he had witnessed in person. "I can see that you're busy," he said.

Slowly, Allie nodded. "I'll walk you out."

Outside, they faced each other in the darkness, crickets chirring around them. "Malcolm likes the books you brought him," she said.

"I'm glad."

She hesitated. "I'm just glad you're OK. You may be white, but you're not invisible."

He shrugged. "Maybe for now. I've always been lucky, right?"

Across the years, they both heard the echo of irony. "When we were at Harvard," she said, "who could have imagined this?"

"Which part?"

"Any of it. All of it." She hesitated. "If you're still around, maybe you can come back tomorrow. In the evening, after I'm done."

43

Preparing for her interview, Allie sat in her living room.

Around her the technicians from MSNBC were setting up the video feed with their studio in New York. In roughly twenty minutes, they would connect her with the network's leading anchor, Rebecca Marks. Though the subject was Malcolm, Allie understood how closely this interview was connected to the worries of Blue Georgia's donors.

But since the meeting, there had been a nationally televised rally calling for Malcolm's execution, and the district attorney had refused Jabari's efforts to investigate George Bullock. Now she was compelled to use the spotlight she had gained from building Blue Georgia to rally support for her son. There was no question of asking her board for permission, only whether the pressure would build for her to step aside.

Silent, she gazed into the camera. She had never liked speaking to a piece of glass instead of a person, and the pressure of conveying her humanity—and, more important, her son's—felt close to unbearable.

Crisp and professional, Rebecca Marks appeared on the screen, a lawyer-turned-commentator who was MSNBC's top-rated host. Swiftly and succinctly, Marks introduced Allie and thanked her for appearing. Then she asked her first question, setting the tone for what would follow.

★ ★ ★

Alone in his hotel room, Chase watched. "As a mother," Marks asked Allie, "how did you feel watching a former president effectively call for your son's execution?"

For an instant, Allie looked almost haunted. "Sick to my stomach," she answered. "Imagine watching a crowd of angry people howling at your son's face on a giant movie screen—'Kill him, kill him.' Imagine hearing a former president speak of him as some sort of animal..."

"I understand," Marks interjected. "But you must understand the impression some people have from watching the video Malcolm chose to post."

"Those *weren't* Malcolm's words," Allie rejoined "They're not Malcolm's real thoughts, either."

"You're suggesting that video said something about Malcolm's intentions that night. His lawyers have found postings on George Bullock's Facebook page, complaining that voting rights workers like Malcolm stole the last presidential election. So maybe we should ask whether those postings say anything about Deputy Bullock's intentions.

"But the district attorney won't help us explore Bullock's social media to see what else he may have said or thought, or why he so clearly seemed to have been stalking Malcolm that night."

Pausing, Allie gazed into the camera. "Unlike the district attorney, I have no power. So all I can do is try to reach anyone who knows something about George Bullock that Malcolm's lawyer should know, or knows someone who does. If you do, please contact me through Blue Georgia, or Malcolm's attorney in Freedom, Jabari Ford.

"I know what I'm asking may not be easy," she implored someone she could not know, and who perhaps did not exist. "But this is about more than fairness. It's about an eighteen-year-old on a dark road, at the wrong time, at the mercy of the wrong person. Please, help him..."

When it was done and a half hour had passed, Allie called him.

"Can you come out? Tonight, I mean."

"Especially tonight," Chase answered.

★ ★ ★

When Chase arrived, she was waiting, a slim figure in the light of her front porch. As he approached, she came forward to meet him, wordless.

After a moment, he gently clasped her shoulders. It was the first time he had touched her since college, and he felt again how slender she was. "How are you?" he asked. "Right now, I mean."

She shook her head slowly, less to dismiss the question than to acknowledge it. They stood there for a time in a cocoon of shared silence, his hand still resting on her shoulders. Then they went to the porch and sat beside each other, making a space between them. The sounds of night—crickets, a fitful wind stirring the leaves of an oak tree—came through the screen that filtered the light of the quarter moon.

"During the day," she murmured, "I just keep myself going. But I'm not sleeping much. All I can think of is Malcolm."

He touched her hand. "Tell me, then."

"The day he was born," she said after a time, "we both almost died. But he didn't. His life, our life, felt like a gift. Now people want to take it, and I don't know if I can protect him. I always understood some people would hate me, but I never imagined this." Turning, she looked him in the face. "How has all this been for you?"

"Everything it isn't for you. You've always been his mother, and this has always been your home. I don't understand this place. I don't know anything about being a father, and I have a Black son charged with murder who has no idea why I'm here." Chase paused, and found the essence of their differences. "You're the only parent he knows. You've got no choice but to be here for him, whatever happens and whatever the cost. I do have a choice between Malcolm and the life I lived before knowing he existed. Imagine trying to make it."

She looked down. "What's it like to visit him?"

"Hard. I never quite know what to say, or how he's reacting inside. Except yesterday when I asked about his grandfather." Chase's voice softened. "His expression—the best word I can find is 'desolate,' and I could see right through this smart, scared young man to the little boy sitting in your father's lap. In that moment, watching his face, I could feel my own absence. And he had no idea at all."

Still studying her lap, Allie absorbed this. "Is there anyone you can talk to?"

"About this? No one."

Glancing up again, Allie tilted her head in inquiry. "Not even your girlfriend?"

Thinking of Kara, Chase found, was painful, like a poignant memory of something lost in another life. "Sometimes I've wanted to. But I can't. He's not just my son, Allie—he's ours. How would I ask her to keep this kind of secret?"

"But would she?"

"I'm pretty sure. But it's not like she and I were married, or going to be. We just enjoy each other."

Even in the dim light, Chase could make out Allie's look of curiosity and skepticism. "Does she feel that way?"

For a moment, he remembered the night of Kara's birthday. "I think so," he answered. "That aside, I'm trying to imagine our theoretical conversation. Once I start talking about this, where do I stop? What do I say about us, and what do I leave out?"

"Oh, I don't know," Allie said somewhat tartly. "Whatever you say to all the girls. Seems like there's been a few."

"A few. And zero conversations about you."

For a beat, Allie was quiet. "Ever?"

All at once Chase felt cornered. "Ever," he responded. "As I said, once I started talking about us, what would I leave out? So maybe you can help me here. When you start reminiscing about old boyfriends, what do you say about us?"

"Nothing."

"Ever?"

"Ever." Suddenly Allie felt her own repressed emotions escaping control. "What would I say about us, and what would I leave out? The night we first made love, and I knew right away I couldn't just put you in a box. The day we nearly drowned, and I realized I loved you so much it hurt. Or the morning I walked out of your room, tears running down my face, using the last ounce of willpower I had not to tell you why. What man wants to hear about that, and why would I tell him?"

Chase stood, looking down at her. "Maybe because you cared for him enough to try? There must have been someone like that."

Still sitting, Allie remembered with piercing clarity what loving a privileged young man had told her about the foolish insubordination of her own heart—then, and perhaps still. But she had no time, and suddenly no desire, to consider the consequences of honesty. "There *was* someone, and I wanted to try. But that wasn't enough."

"What went wrong?"

"The things that do," she said impatiently. "At least for me. He resented how buried I got in my work, that I was gone a lot. That was one thing Robert and Malcolm had in common."

She felt Chase trying to read her face. "That was all? You worked too hard? That couldn't have come as a big surprise."

She looked away. "Not all. I couldn't be with a man who didn't love my son. Robert didn't, or couldn't."

"Why not? I've only met Malcolm three times, under the worst conditions possible. But he doesn't strike me as all that hard to love."

Abruptly Allie stood, facing him. "You can look at him and see yourself. So could Robert. Not you specifically, but someone he figured I'd loved—and, worse from his perspective, figured to be white. It didn't sit right with him."

"Enough to make a difference?"

She averted her face from the intensity in his. "There were ways in which we weren't that great, OK? Leave it be."

She felt him move closer. "Sorry, but I'm kind of curious. What was that about?"

She spun on him, angry. "Do you really need me to say it? OK, I will. No matter how little sense it made, I fell in love with you at Harvard, and never really stopped. How could I, when every time I looked at Malcolm he reminded me of you? Sometimes I'd imagine seeing you again in some made-up world that didn't exist, and for that minute I'd be happier than I was with anyone in real life.

"But it never stopped hurting, from the day I left until now. Now, especially." Allie's eyes welled up. "Is that enough for you, Chase Brevard? Because it's all I've got to give you."

Gently, he turned her face to his. In that instant, she saw that the searching boy-man she had loved despite herself, now the accomplished man she had imagined he could be and had wanted him to become, was still searching for something that he believed, even now, he had never found. Except with her.

"Not all," he said, and kissed her.

Kissing him back with an intensity that startled her, she understood that she had won, or lost, the war inside her. All Allie knew for sure was that she wanted him, that all she had to do was tell him without words.

Instead, she leaned her face against his chest, trying to imagine what this moment meant to the man who once had offered to follow her to Georgia, and now had come because of their son. "We can't do this," she said softly. "Not now.

"Malcolm deserves all I can give him, including a clear head." Looking up again, she touched his face. "It's not just me. You need to decide why you're still here, for him or for me, and what you want to be to him. I've made that confusing enough…"

There was a sudden hiss, then the sound of glass shattering. Instinctively, Chase pulled Allie to the wooden floor; a sharp pain tore through his elbow as he cradled her against the fall.

"Gunshot," she whispered. "Don't move."

Sitting up, she looked around them for some movement in the night, then listened for footsteps. Nothing. All she heard was the crickets; all she saw was a hole in the screen. "Get behind me," Chase said tightly.

Allie felt her nerves twitching. "Why?"

"You're his mother, for Chrissake."

Allie remained very still. "I'm guessing they're gone," she murmured. She took out her cell phone and called Al Garrett.

★ ★ ★

The sheriff and three deputies found them as they were, sitting on the wooden floor, Allie leaning back against Chase. She saw Al Garrett register the scene—the two of them, close together, the lateness of the hour. "You all right?" he asked her.

"Now I am. I'm thinking someone fired from the road, trying to scare me."

"Unless they took off your head. You only get to be scared because they didn't." Briefly, Garrett glanced around them. "I'm putting a deputy near the house, another where your driveway meets the road. I don't want anyone thinking they can just walk in here."

"Good idea," Chase said. "Allie goes on TV seeking information about your late deputy, and somebody takes a shot at her."

"Yeah, I noticed," Garrett responded brusquely. "But how do you know they weren't shooting at you? I don't know what you were doing at that rally the other night. But maybe it's time to be thinking about home."

The other deputies began searching the grounds. Sliding out of Chase's arms, Allie stood and walked over to Garrett. "Thanks, Al," she said in a quiet undertone. "I'm more grateful than I can tell you, for everything. But as best you can manage it, as a favor to me, Congressman Brevard was never here."

Garrett's eyes narrowed, as though registering what she chose not to say. "Don't know that you agree, but from where I sit that's something to hope for." Turning to Chase, he said, "Seeing as how you aren't here, I'll have a deputy follow you back to town."

44

The next morning, over toast and coffee in the ornate dining room of the Winthrop Hotel, Chase Brevard contemplated the crosscurrents overtaking his life.

They were impossible to reconcile: Allie. Malcolm. The conflict between the course he had charted since Harvard, a steady climb through law and politics driven by long hours, hard work, and dedication to issues he thought mattered, and an emotional reckoning that had awaited him in the ambush of time—the wholly unanticipated reopening of a chapter in his youth so compelling that the simple act of holding Allie Hill again had upended everything since.

Last night, someone had fired a bullet into her home. That moment, too, had changed something within him. He believed that she, not he, had been the target; he took no comfort in hoping that it was a warning shot. This place was awash in guns, including weapons of war in the hands of white nationalists like Charles and Molly Parnell. Chase understood that they might kill her—or anyone they decided was the enemy of the primitive white America whose unreasoning rage he had experienced at the rally. Intuitively, he sensed that these forces were connected to the events that had blighted Malcolm's life.

Compared to the dangers surrounding Malcolm and Allie, his own considerations were trivial. But whatever he decided would come at a cost that could not be undone. To walk away from Malcolm and his mother, concealing their connection to preserve his ambitions and perhaps his safety, would haunt him irretrievably; to do otherwise could mean that his life had been redefined by the existence of a son he had never known.

He had no illusions about his enemies in the media or politics; given the chance, they would use Malcolm and Allie to end his career, even as they were trying to destroy Allie by destroying her and Chase's son. Malcolm's trial in Cade County, should it come, could be defined by forces woven into the fabric of this place, and in this country, which had nothing to do with law or fairness.

Nor, realistically, was there anything Chase could do to change the outcome. The elements that would govern his son's fate were beyond his control. His central choices—who he was, what he could live with, what he feared, and who he cared about most—were matters of the heart not susceptible to reason or calculation. They went too deep.

In four days, Congress would be back in session. Chase tried to imagine himself restored to the company of his staff and his party colleagues—working, strategizing, and exchanging favors and quips—as if the discovery of a son, and the rediscovery of a lover, had happened in a dream. He remembered something Jack Raskin had said: Politics, like rust, never sleeps. Nor, it seemed, did the prosecution of Malcolm Hill.

★ ★ ★

Back in his room, Chase found several new emails—the first draft of a speech to an environmental group, a list of pending legislation, and a schedule of appearances across Massachusetts to raise his visibility for a prospective Senate race. Somewhat fitfully, he began scanning the speech, even as he found himself thinking of Malcolm and Allie. Perhaps he would call her.

His cell phone rang.

"Dalton Harris just called me," Ford told him. "He's appearing in court this afternoon to give formal notice that the sovereign state of Georgia is seeking the death penalty."

Though he was not surprised, the reality hit Chase hard. "Have you told Allie?"

"I have. I'm on the way to tell Malcolm."

Chase thought for a moment. "Will he be at the hearing?"

"Yeah," Ford answered grimly. "I'll do my best to prepare him. But nothing really prepares you for hearing a prosecutor tell a judge that the state wants to kill you by lethal injection. I've seen it before—that look on a defendant's face when they feel the machinery of death kicking in."

Chase found himself imagining the look on Malcolm's face, and the feelings beneath it. "For whatever it's worth," he said, "tell Malcolm I'm coming by to see him."

★ ★ ★

When Chase entered the visiting room, Malcolm did not stand.

Silent, he looked up at Chase with the dark, expressive eyes he had inherited from Allie. Sitting across from him, Chase put aside the books he had carefully chosen just a couple of days before: *Matterhorn*, a novel about the Vietnam War by Karl Marlantes, and *Harlem Shuffle*, in which Colson Whitehead applied his considerable gifts with a lighter touch that, Chase had hoped, might at least for a moment serve to distract Malcolm from the darkness of his circumstances.

"I know you heard," his son said in a monotone.

To Chase, his eyes looked wounded, as if exposed to too much light. He hesitated, searching for something helpful to say. "Jabari was prepared for this. Whatever happens, he'll give you a strong defense."

Malcolm said nothing; he seemed to have no impulse to sustain the rhythms of normal conversation. Then, almost absently, Malcolm said, "How can I explain what happened to strangers who don't know me?"

Chase already dreaded this. "Maybe you won't need to. The DA has to prove his case beyond a reasonable doubt in the mind of those jurors. I don't think he can."

"I have to," Malcolm insisted. "People think I meant to kill him."

Chase fell silent. Perhaps his simple presence was better, he thought, than whatever bromides he dredged up. Or at least better than nothing.

For long moments, Malcolm stared at the table. "I'm just waiting here," he murmured. "I can't eat. Can't sleep. I'm afraid to."

Chase inclined his head, miming inquiry in the hope that Malcolm could sense this and, if he wished, say more.

"I have nightmares." His son's voice thickened. "That deputy laughing at me in the darkness. Somebody closes the cell door, I hear a gunshot, see that man's face with blood all over it. When it's quiet, time stops. It's like I'm alone in a space capsule, floating somewhere, and the life I had before happened far away. Only this place is real."

Chase flinched inside. From his time as a lawyer, he understood the objective meaning of what he was hearing—a textbook description of acute distress disorder, which over time would harden into PTSD. But under the pitiless fluorescent light of a bare room, he was watching this happen to his son, and all he could do was try, somehow, to help him cling to hope for the world he had lost.

"I just want this over," Malcolm said dully. "Even if they kill me."

Over time, Chase feared, he would come to see death as not only a threat but an alternative. That this had begun happening was no doubt something Allie knew when she pulled back from Chase's embrace, choosing not to burden his conscience with their son's emotional deterioration. Now, seeing this for himself, Chase wanted to embrace not just Allie but Malcolm.

"I wish I could help you," he said.

But he could not, and his son did not answer. A glance at his watch revealed that their visit had three minutes left. Reaching into the book bag, Chase put the two novels on the table.

"I hope you'll like these," he told Malcolm. "I did."

★ ★ ★

Returning to his hotel room, Chase found that he, too, had little appetite. But there was sunlight through his window, and he was free to walk away.

It might be different, he supposed, if he thought the son he barely knew was guilty. But he did not. It was difficult to imagine the anger and anguish of an eighteen-year-old boy helpless to cry out his innocence beyond the walls of the cell that now bounded his world, and little easier at this moment to return Jack Raskin's phone call. But, like everyone save Allie, Jack did not know that Chase's past had claimed his present.

Picking up the phone, Chase called him. "Hi, Jack. From the tenor of your message, you miss me."

"Actually, I'm bereft. When are you coming back?"

His tone was new, Chase thought—polite, almost careful, as if talking to someone who, without explanation, had entered some psychological realm beyond his understanding. "In a couple days," Chase answered.

"Why not sooner?" Raskin inquired. "To my amazement, no reporter has called your communications director to ask why you're in Georgia. But once you get spotted, and you will, we're stuck with the truth."

"Which is that I'm supporting a friend. I hope that will do for our friends at the *Globe*."

"I meant the truth according to Fox. That you've been playing hooky—or nooky—with the mother of a cop killer who takes his cues from a rapper advocating the execution of blameless police. Won't matter what your truth is."

That was right, Chase knew, and likely far from the worst of it. "At the risk of quibbling, I don't think that deputy was blameless."

"Maybe not. But why concern yourself with the ills of some retrograde byway three thousand miles away from your district?" Raskin's voice became more emphatic. "It's one thing to hold your friend's hand for a couple days in private, or whatever it is you two are doing. It's another to stay there until you get caught. That's when the media takes out Occam's razor—when a male politician acts irrationally and there's a woman involved, look for the simplest explanation. Most often, they find it."

"Jack," Chase said slowly and coolly, "I want you to hear me. I haven't lost my mind, and there's nothing simple about this. What I'm doing here goes way beyond whatever you're thinking."

On the other end of the line, Raskin sighed audibly. "But it doesn't go beyond politics. Worst case, you'd not only blow your chances to become a senator; you'd put your House seat at risk. And for what?"

Chase paused "That's exactly the right question, Jack—'for what?'" If you don't mind, I need to spend the next couple of hours thinking about that."

But in his heart, he already knew. When he took out his cell phone again, perhaps an hour later, it was to call not Raskin but Allie. "There's something I need to ask you," he said. "It's about Malcolm. All of us, really."

★ ★ ★

Shortly before two o'clock, Chase Brevard and Allie Hill walked through the gauntlet of reporters lining the steps of the Cade County courthouse.

Allie had refused to enter surreptitiously—to show fear would have disheartened her friends, pleased her enemies, and demoralized the workers of Blue Georgia. Al Garrett had stationed snipers on the roof, cordoned off White Lightning, and assigned deputies to control the crowd and keep the media from stampeding Allie.

Their shouted questions were for her, not Chase; these were not the beat reporters from Capitol Hill who would know him on sight. But he saw the look of curiosity on their faces, and understood that it was only a matter of minutes, if that, before someone watching recognized a personage no one had expected to see—a rising congressman from Massachusetts transported to an already notorious murder case in Georgia.

Only when they were in the elevator, alone, did Allie dare to look at him.

"I know it's selfish," she said quietly, "but I'm glad you're here. I just hope you'll be OK with whatever winds up happening."

Looking into her face, he saw the play of her emotions: doubt, worry, guilt over the price he was paying, gratitude that she and Malcolm were not alone—even, perhaps, more.

Chase, too, felt his own uncertainty and confusion, the undertow of regret at chancing all he had worked for, a residue of bitterness that a decision in which he had played no part had come to this. But he had other emotions, for this woman and their son, and the prosecutor's call for this hearing had tipped the balance. Or, perhaps, the moment he had passed two books to Malcolm and known that could never be enough. So he mustered a facsimile of the smile he had given her on the day they first met at Harvard. "I was dying to come here, remember? I'm just nineteen years late."

★ ★ ★

Entering the courtroom to stares of anger, curiosity and, in a few cases, compassion, Allie and Chase sat in the first row of spectators. Harris was already at the prosecution table; Malcolm sat at the defense table beside Ford, wearing the charcoal-gray suit she had bought him for graduation. Turning to glance at her, Malcolm saw Chase. Watching her son's look of surprise, Allie stifled the instinct to touch Chase's hand.

"All rise," the courtroom deputy called out, and Judge Tilly ascended the bench.

Dalton Harris stood to address him. "As we informed the court and defense counsel this morning, we intend to seek the death penalty against Malcolm Hill for the murder of Deputy George Bullock. Accordingly, the State has filed papers formally charging the defendant with capital murder."

Though she had tried to steel herself for this, Allie felt a sickness in the pit of her stomach. Through the sheen in her eyes, she saw Malcolm square his shoulders.

The judge turned to Ford. "Under Georgia law, the defendant must be represented by lead counsel qualified by experience to appear in a death penalty case. Am I correct in understanding that you are, Mr. Ford?"

Ford stood, impassive. "Yes, Your Honor."

With this, Judge Tilly scanned the courtroom. "As before," he intoned, "the court notes that this case has attracted an unusual amount of national attention. Accordingly, it's our obligation to direct both the prosecution and defense to refrain from any further public statements about the substance of this case. Put bluntly, I don't want any lawyer before me tainting the jury pool should this case go to trial."

To Allie, this was at once superfluous, absurd, and wholly one-sided: Tilly was gagging Ford, the person best in position to speak for Malcolm in the public arena, and nothing the judge could do would offset the rally at the site of George Bullock's death—let alone stem the toxic effusions daily spewing at her son from cable news and the internet.

But suddenly, Tilly was looking toward her. "As to individuals not before the court, we cannot control their behavior. We only hope they will honor the spirit of our order."

Gazing back at him, Allie silently answered, *You're free to hope.*

Ford rose again. "May it please the court, the defense has filed a motion requesting that a subpoena be issued for Detective George

Bullock's computer, cell phone, and any other communications devices in the possession of his wife or family."

Lips compressed, the judge regarded him sternly. "On what grounds?"

"It's a question of intent," Ford answered. "We've submitted copies of screenshots from Facebook showing that the Deputy Bullock posted materials disparaging voting rights workers and asserting that Democrats and voting rights groups stole the presidential election of 2020. We're seeking to determine whether there are further such materials suggesting a hostility toward the defendant that, in turn, bears on the circumstances of his death."

"Do you have a response, Mr. Harris?"

"The state is opposed," Harris answered promptly. "Some two-year-old screenshots say nothing about his lawful stop of an intoxicated motorist three years short of the statutory age for drinking alcohol in Georgia."

"Your Honor," Ford rejoined, "before this so-called lawful stop, Deputy Bullock turned off his body and dashboard cameras in blatant violation of departmental policy. The evidence we're seeking may illuminate why."

Judge Tilly gave him a look of reproof. "You know the law in this state, Counselor. Without more evidence connecting the deputy's personal or political views to the defendant's state of mind at the time of the shooting, you have insufficient basis for seeking this subpoena. Until you can come up with that, motion denied." Looking from Ford to Harris and back again, the judge asked, "Is there any further business before the court? If not, this hearing is adjourned."

"All rise," the courtroom deputy called out again, and Allie saw Malcolm slump with the weight of all that had happened so swiftly. Then two deputies came forward to return him to jail. He was gone before she could speak, or even touch him.

★ ★ ★

Outside, Allie and Chase left as they had come, descending the courthouse steps. But the crowd had thickened, and more deputies had gathered. On the sidewalk below, Charles Parnell and his followers were calling out toward Allie and thrusting their weapons in the air. "Your boy's gonna die," someone jeered.

Face stony, Allie kept moving. At her side, Chase looked straight ahead, ignoring the media pressing toward them.

"Congressman Brevard," a female reporter called out, "why are you here?"

Stifling his own emotions, Chase considered how to respond. He could ignore her. He could say that this was a private matter, or that he was honoring the judge's request to refrain from comment. Or he could give the political and politic answer, that he was supporting a longtime friend.

But he was in no mood to do any of this. Instead, he stopped and turned toward the woman and the camera behind her, and gave the answer of a father.

"Because Malcolm Hill is innocent," he said, and began moving with Allie again.

PART FIVE

The Disclosure

45

That evening, to his surprise, Allie's mother invited Chase to dinner. Though the invitation was irresistible, Chase accepted with a certain trepidation. Among the many things that had complicated his relationship to Allie at Harvard was the prospect of her strong-minded mother's disapproval, and Chase was not certain of why Janie Hill wanted to meet him, or what would happen when they sat face-to-face. But he was also intensely curious to see for himself the woman who, as much as anyone, had shaped who Allie became. And so, at the appointed hour, Chase once again drove to the place where three generations of Hills, including his son, had made their home.

The softening sunlight of early evening turned the fields surrounding the two farmhouses a gentler green. At the head of the driveway, Chase waved to a sheriff's deputy leaning against his squad car, stationed as a warning to those who posed dangers to Allie. Passing her house, he saw the basketball hoop and horseshoe pit that Wilson Hill had provided for Malcolm, and thought again of the young man in prison, now facing a trial for capital murder.

The woman who greeted him at the door to the larger farmhouse was small and slender, like Allie, with gray-streaked black hair; dark, probing eyes; a handsome face whose age was betrayed less by lines than by an absence of softness; and a reddish-brown complexion that suggested the Native American ancestry Allie had mentioned at Harvard. Giving Chase an unabashed look of appraisal, she said, "Uh-huh, you're good-looking, all right, just like on television. Makes me wonder why you've never been married."

Despite his uneasiness, the complete absence of prefatory politeness made Chase smile. "People keep mentioning that."

Briskly, Janie Hill shooed him toward the kitchen. "Nice smile, too," she remarked over her shoulder. "Looks like some orthodontist did right by you."

This was not idle chatter, Chase sensed at once—there was a point to all this, and in due course he would learn what it was. "Nice to see where Allie grew up," he said. "Back in college, I could tell how important this place was to her."

Janie gave him a swift, sharp look. "Wilson's grandfather bought it with money made burying Black people. Allie grew up thinking these fields are haunted by other dead people—the slaves who worked from dawn to dusk. 'Only them?' I'd ask."

She turned to the serving dishes laid out by the stove. "Like all of Georgia, this land once belonged to Native Americans. But King George granted title to the dregs from English prisons, all so they could enslave the kings and queens of Africa to work the land they stole by terrorizing and killing the people who'd lived here. Pretty soon we had a holiday named after an Italian who couldn't sail straight. History for white people."

For Chase, this triggered a memory. "I remember Allie saying something like that."

She looked up at him so intently that, yet again, she reminded him of her daughter. Though the intonations of the rural South softened her speech more than Allie's, the two women were similar enough in appearance and manner that he could imagine Allie after the passage of years. "College again? Seems you two had a lot to say to each other."

He took his place at a white wooden table. With swift, darting movements that further evoked Allie, Janie covered his plate with the familiar meal her daughter had predicted to Chase she would serve—fried chicken, black-eyed peas, and collard greens—before serving side dishes of mashed potatoes and macaroni and cheese, accompanied by sweet tea that, he discovered, came flavored with sugar. No alcohol, Chase noticed—in the Hill family, unlike his own, cocktails before dinner were not part of the ritual.

"Looks delicious, Mrs. Hill. Though I can't help wondering how you and Allie stay thin."

"Simple. We worry." Janie paused for a moment. "I'm imagining you wonder why Allie came back."

The woman's directness, Chase found, no longer surprised him— what awaited discovery was why she had turned it on Chase. "I wondered back in college," he acknowledged. "But even more now."

Janie studied him again, quiet. "You've gone to a lot of trouble, Congressman, over the two people on earth I love most. I'd like to understand more about why. But maybe I should tell you some things about our family and Alexandria you may not be clear on."

Chase found himself intuitively grasping Janie's deeper purpose. "I'd appreciate that," he responded. "I've had easier assignments in life than understanding your daughter."

Janie smiled, almost imperceptibly. "Doesn't seem like life gave you a head start. So go ahead and eat, and I'll try to explain what Allie was born into, and why she couldn't leave it. Truth to tell, much of that comes from me, and what I passed on to her."

The chicken was moist and delicious, Chase thought, even if his cholesterol count was fated to shatter its previous high. "Wilson and I were born in segregated hospitals," Janie told him "We went to all-Black schools where the books were so old, the pages fell out. For a lot of our neighbors, that was just how things were." Her expression became ruminative, as if remembering why her life had changed. "But our parents were educated, and my mother took me to my first protest meeting when I was eight years old. That started me down the same road that Allie's following now."

"Jabari Ford told me something about your trying to integrate a movie theater when you were in grade school. If you don't mind, I'd like to hear about it."

For a moment, Janie's lips compressed. "That was a turning point for me, if you want to call it that. I was eleven years old. Me and some girlfriends from sixth grade got sick of climbing four flights of stairs to sit in the broken-down chairs they reserved for Blacks. So we decided to sit with the white folks." Her inflection became sardonic. "The lady at the ticket office called the town police. Next thing we knew, a bunch of town cops descended on us like they needed to control a riot, instead of some adolescent Black girls.

"There were sixteen of us. They threw us in a police wagon so close together, we had to stand up, but so dark inside we couldn't see each other's faces. We rode that way, stumbling into each other and scared to death, before they pushed us out beside an abandoned stockade one county over." Narrow-eyed, Janie picked up a fork and began rearranging the greens on her plate. "There was one toilet in that place, no running water, not enough to eat, a cement floor to sleep on. It got so hot, the cement was damp with our own sweat, and our school dresses started to rot…"

"My God, Mrs. Hill."

Briefly, Janie closed her eyes. "Soon enough that place was all the world I knew, my first experience away from home. We got light through a couple of windows with bars across them. When it got dark, I could hear the other girls crying for their mamas, like I was. But our families had no idea where we were, only that the police had taken us somewhere." Her tone grew harsh. "We were in that hellhole for forty-five days. Finally, a civil rights worker found out about the stockade. After that the police let us go."

Chase tried to imagine the trauma to an eleven-year-old girl, and the impact this story must have had on Allie. "How were you afterwards?" he asked.

For a moment, Janie Hill looked so abstracted that Chase sensed she was no longer at her kitchen table. "By then I'd left a piece of myself there. It was a long time before I could sleep right. I'd wake up in the dark and think I was back in that place. Now I imagine Malcolm, trapped in a cell with no windows and no future he can see, and feel like it's happening all over again."

Chase sat with her in unspoken communion. Finally, he said, "After what happened to you, most people would have given up."

Across the table, Janie met his eyes again. "You tend to remember who put you through something like that, and why. But the next lesson was one that I didn't volunteer for. Three years later, I was one of the first Blacks to integrate Cade County High School. No doubt it deepened my education—even after that stockade, I had more to learn.

"I'd always thought white people didn't like me because they didn't know me. I was raised up with manners; got almost straight As; my parents were good, educated, churchgoing, middle-class folks whose families had lived here for generations. Once they opened the doors, I thought, my friends and I could start opening hearts."

She shook her head at a Black girl's remembered innocence. "I was so wrong, so deeply, hurtfully wrong. That high school was a hotbed of hate—no circle of hell Dante ever invented could have been any worse. My girlfriends and I used to go to the bathroom together because we were afraid to go alone. We had no white friends, none, just people who thought we had no feelings or souls."

Her voice hardened with anger and the residue of sorrow. "That's when I truly understood what it meant to be Black in Cade County, Georgia, what it would always mean until we claimed the right to change that. By the time I went off to Spelman, I was determined that the next generation born here would grow up in better."

She did not need to add the rest—of the next two generations of Hills who had followed Janie's example, Allie lived with the risk of losing her life, and now Malcolm might lose his. "Is that why you took up voting rights?" Chase asked.

"You don't just 'take up' voting rights," Janie answered sharply. "Back in the eighties, when we started registering Black people in earnest, men in white robes came across the tracks separating the white and Black sections of Freedom carrying torches and guns. A line of Blacks with shotguns were waiting. So those men turned around, knowing their robes weren't bulletproof." Picking up her glass of tea, Janie circled the rim with a curled finger. "Allie was two years old then. But she could tell you the story herself. She could tell you *all* these stories, because

Wilson and I made sure she knew them. Generation after generation, we've had to remember how hard it has been to get the rights whites take for granted, how much we have to do for ourselves, how high the price could be."

But not this, Chase felt her saying. *Not my grandson.*

"It never stops," Janie continued. "Now they're saying that teaching about slavery will hurt white children's feelings and that talking about racism is racist." Her voice became freighted with bitterness and sorrow. "They don't throw Black girls in stockades for going to movies, and white people in this county found another way to have their own schools. But we still have racists with guns. It's still about voting, and in this family it's still about the work left undone."

Abruptly, Allie's mother pushed aside her plate. "I used to think that was peculiar to the South. But in the last election, the ugliness I've seen since I was a child has gone national, and now my grandson is the object of hatred all over America." The rhythm of her voice slowed. "Watching him grow up was a gift filled with misgivings. But long after I'm dead, Allie will be living with whatever happens to him, all because she came back home. I can't tell you how much that's been hurting my heart."

And mine, Chase thought. But he chose to remain silent, for there was nothing to say.

She was studying him intently, Chase realized, though her expression seemed subtly softer. After a time, she said, "Once you finish dinner, Congressman, let's sit out on the porch. Maybe we can catch an evening breeze, and I think the two of us have something more to talk about. Starting with Allie."

46

They sat in wooden rocking chairs on a screened porch similar to Allie's. In the dusk, Chase could see the light from her house, a shadowy outline, and thought again of the gunshots shattering her window. "Aren't you worried out here?" he asked.

"All the time. But not for me." Sipping from her glass of tea, Janie, too, gazed toward her daughter's home. "After the last election, she told me things to do, how to keep myself safe. I started looking under my car for wires that shouldn't be there, saying these little prayers before I turned on the ignition.

"That's when I truly understood what Allie lives with every day. That girl wakes up in the morning with no certainty about whether she'll see nightfall. Sometimes, except for being a mother, I think she's resigned herself to just being here for a season. But now she's sick with worry that Malcolm will die in her place."

So am I, Chase wanted to say. Instead, he responded simply, "That's too big a price for any human being to pay."

Janie turned to him. "I know you care about her, Congressman. I know you're wondering why she runs the risks she does. I'd like for you to understand that, too."

Beneath the words, Chase heard the plea of a mother for her daughter. Cradling the glass of tea, Janie seemed to organize her thoughts before she began speaking in the gentler inflections of reflection and, perhaps, regret. "From the moment Alexandria was born, already so pretty and alert and smart-looking, I wanted her to have more than I did. It was good she wasn't growing up under Jim Crow—she wouldn't know what it was like to buy barbecue at the back door of a diner. But the old attitudes were still there.

"By the time she was in elementary school, I could see how exceptional she was. So every opportunity there was in this county for a girl her age, I insisted she have, too." Her tone filled with remembered resolve. "So I was always on the alert for people wanting to slam doors in her face without making any noise. I never stood for her being deprived of anything, even if she was the one Black child participating—ballet, gymnastics, or whatever sport it was, I put her in.

"I never backed down or let her back down. I remember asking her once if she minded being the only Black girl in gymnastics. She just looked at me and said, 'I'm *always* the only Black girl, Mama.'"

That last sentence, Chase thought, was fraught with meaning for both mother and daughter. "Was that hard for you?" he asked.

"For both of us. But I couldn't let myself act like there was a choice." Janie paused reflectively. "I knew she wasn't invited to the parties the other girls had, just like I wasn't asked to have coffee with the white women in whatever carpool they'd organized. All we could do was claim what she deserved.

"I think that's what made her ready to go to Harvard. No one from our community had ever done that. But Alexandria Hill was going to take advantage of whatever the great world had to offer." Gazing out at the darkening fields, Janie softened her voice again. "It wasn't just about her. Allie's going off to Harvard meant so much to our community." To Chase, the sudden sideways glance she gave him hinted at defensiveness.

"Wilson and I never asked her to come home. But there was so much work to do here, and she'd grown up knowing that deep in her soul."

Silent, Chase found himself imagining how Allie must have felt, how different her passage into adulthood had been from his own, how freighted with obligations and expectations that she could not help but internalize and that, no doubt, had spurred her to success while defining her future. He had been a legacy at Harvard through two generations of Bancrofts, and his admission was neither a surprise nor a matter of particular pride. Nor did he have any communal imperatives to address, any sense of familial obligation deeper than sparing his parents gratuitous embarrassment. His future would become whatever he chose in his own good time.

To a considerable degree, Chase had always known these things about them both—even then. But only now, sitting with Allie's mother in the place where she'd grown up, did he feel what had shaped her with such a breadth of comprehension and, unavoidably, foreboding. Still, there was no way for him to say this, and to try would be gratuitous, even unkind. He was coming to understand why she had asked him here.

"When it came to the end of her senior year," Janie continued in a somber tone, "we were all planning to drive up for graduation—family and friends, even my mother in a wheelchair. Then Allie said she was coming home before the ceremony, and told us why, all the time crying over the telephone. So Wilson and I supported her in the way she most needed, whatever disappointment and embarrassment we had to swallow.

"But then Malcolm was born, the most precious thing to all three of us. For himself, and for the fact that whether or not she ever married, the Hill family was going on. You have no idea how much that means when you take so little for granted." Pausing, Janie turned to him with a newly keen expression. "Though maybe now you do."

Quiet, Chase chose to wait her out, buying time to compose his thoughts. Impatiently, Janie said, "So which one of you is going to tell me what goes on here?"

Despite the gravity of the moment, Chase could not help but smile. "Don't look at me, Mrs. Hill. You certainly know your own daughter."

"On occasion, to my sorrow. I left out the part where she came out of the womb so willful, there was no point in spanking her." She sat back, looking at him with piercing directness. "All right, Congressman. I'm thinking you're the daddy. That's why you came here, isn't it?"

Meeting her eyes, Chase felt a sense of relief so deep that it surprised him. "Yes," he acknowledged. "But I'm still working out why I stayed."

"Does Malcolm know about you?"

"I don't think so."

"Men," Janie said in maternal exasperation, "spend five minutes rooting around in the refrigerator for a quart of milk that's staring them in the face. About all I needed was a close-up of that smile, and Lord knows Malcolm spends enough time looking in the mirror to see where *that* came from. So exactly how did you and his mom think you could get by with this?"

"I'm not sure we did. But Allie was worried about telling him now, with him traumatized and in jail, and me not knowing what to do."

Janie sighed. "God knows he could use a father, especially with his grandfather gone. But it might be pretty hard for you to become one all at once." She gave him another probing look. "You didn't know, did you? Nineteen years ago, Allie just disappeared."

It wasn't a question. "All I can tell you," Chase answered, "is that she did what she thought was best."

"You think it was?"

"I don't think it was for me. Certainly not anymore."

Janie turned away to study nothing in particular. At last, she said, "The whole thing's just so terribly sad. Allie tries to be so tough and self-reliant, and mostly she is. But underneath, that girl's just aching for love. And so is Malcolm."

Chase felt a deep sadness of his own. After a moment, Janie turned back to face him. "I take some of that on me," she said quietly. "I just wish she could've told me about you back then. I know she must've felt guilty about your sleeping together, acting different than her father and I had been or raised her to be. But if she'd said she loved you, I'd have tried to understand." She shook her head. "Don't know that would've changed anything. But no good came to her from feeling she had no one to tell, or to me from knowing too late what it cost her.

"There is no more bitter regret for a mother than that. It's what Allie feels now about Malcolm—him buying a gun because he was scared and thinking he couldn't tell her."

"Posting that video was one thing," Chase responded. "That gun was worse."

Janie contemplated the weathered hands folded in her lap. "Maybe life would've continued on its way, Malcolm going off to Morehouse, you in Congress never knowing you had a son. Or maybe that deputy would've killed him—another unarmed Black man." She looked at Chase again. "That's the other thing I want you to understand. Not just how Malcolm came to feel about police, but how he grew up feeling about white people, and what he learned from watching them and us.

"Malcolm's like Allie, smart as they come. But the poorest, least educated, most miserable white person in this county still thinks to himself, 'Well, at least I'm not Black.' That rears its head in so many ways. You can feel it when you go in for a bank loan, or buy a car, or walk into some business and get ignored unless they think you're looking to steal something, even though you're there to put money in the cash register.

"So I don't have a lot of white friends. It's not like I hate all white people—I take them as they come, and we've got a cluster of white liberals who care about making this place different. But they're a minority." Gazing into his eyes, Janie spoke more slowly. "So you can't blame Malcolm for seeing white folks as he does, even before so many of them were howling for his head. It makes me sorry for you both."

"Why for me?" Chase asked, though he thought he knew.

"Because it makes it harder for him to accept you as a father, at least starting out. But you are one, and you're already learning what it means to have a Black son."

She paused, and her tone became at once sorrowful and fatalistic. "Every day I pray over my daughter and my grandson. My husband and I watched them grow up, knowing there was nothing we could do to ensure their safety, that they might die just for being Black. That's the same fear our parents and grandparents felt, and their parents, and every generation of Black mothers and fathers since the first of us were brought here in chains. We're connected over the generations by the inheritance of fear.

"Now you feel it, too, that fear you'd never have if your son were white. I'm sorry for that as well, Congressman."

Quiet, Chase considered the answer growing in his heart, and realized that Allie's mother had called it forth for him to examine and accept. "But he is my son, Mrs. Hill. I love his mother, always have. If I'd had the choice back then, he's the son I would've chosen. No matter how hard it is for both of us, I'm choosing him now."

After a moment, Janie nodded. "So when are you telling him?"

"We haven't talked about it. But once Allie decided I should come with her to court, I feel the media closing in on us, and I'm sure that she can, too."

Janie gave him a look of ineffable sadness. "There'll be no peace for the two of you, I know. All you've got left is deciding which way of finding out is best for Malcolm. Or worst."

47

Returning to town, Chase reflected deeply on his conversation with Allie's mother. But operating in tandem, a new hyperalertness sparked his nerves and sinews. The sheriff's deputy at the foot of the drive marked what, for him, had become a Twilight Zone from which racists on motorcycles who carried military-grade weapons fired gunshots into the home of the woman he still loved, his son's mother.

Turning onto Old County Road, he once more reimagined the night Malcolm had killed another deputy—who, Chase felt certain, had followed him until he reached the darkest stretch of asphalt. As on that night, the road was unlit, and lowering clouds had begun blocking the moon. Glancing repeatedly in the rearview mirror, Chase saw nothing.

He had chosen to return here, could not have done otherwise. But Janie Hill was right—he had lost control of his life. Drawn to helping a son who did not know him, he had begun making decisions with unknown consequences, to no certain end—for Malcolm, Allie, and himself. He had never felt less confident in his own judgments, more adrift, and in some ways, more alone.

He could find no ready answer. Certainly not in the fathomless dark of a sultry night hanging over rural Georgia.

He was driving deeper into the countryside, bereft of light, where Malcolm had encountered George Bullock. A pair of headlights coming the other way became, as it passed, a truck, before darkness enveloped him again. Then a sudden spatter of rain struck the windshield. This was followed, abruptly, by swirling sheets of windborne water making an arhythmic drumbeat that, fully reawakening his apprehensions, evoked a ragged fusillade of gunshots. The wipers cleared the moisture with a futile rubbery squeak.

The glass began smearing in front of him. Turning on the defroster, Chase perceived—or imagined—a single headlight in the distance, a shimmering Cyclops that disappeared, then reappeared, brighter, a little closer.

A second light flickered, a solitary speck in his rearview mirror, vanishing in the sweep of the wipers clearing the back windshield. Then it, too, became brighter.

Involuntarily, Chase flinched.

Motorcycles. One coming toward him, the other closing behind him.

Ahead, the single headlight grew larger, and he heard the first low thrum of an engine. Reflexively, he checked the gravel apron on the road. As he turned on the brights, their beams captured what might have been the stubby shadows of new pine trees planted in symmetrical rows.

He had little time to decide. Then a motorcycle and driver shot toward him from the darkness, and he slammed on the brakes.

His car spun sideways on the slick asphalt, tires squealing and spitting gravel. The motorcycle veered, then righted itself. As it passed him, his windshield shattered.

Shards of glass struck his face. In a reflex born of panic, Chase stomped the accelerator, heading for the field. As the second motorcycle passed him, he felt the car shimmy, then heard and felt the pounding thud of a flat tire.

The car lurched forward, suddenly stopping as it struck the first row of trees, jolting Chase backward as its spinning tires dug into the damp earth. Without looking behind him, he reeled from the car. Briefly, he stumbled, breaking his fall with the palms of his hand, feeling the downpour dampening his hair and clothing. Then he ran blindly into the shelter of the pines, their branches striking his face and arms as thunder broke from the skies.

Turning, he knelt, peering out above the trees. The motorcycles had stopped by the road. One cyclist, then another, doused their lights.

Head down, arms covering his eyes, he stumbled deeper into the pines. Then he stopped, listening for the heavy thud of motorcycle boots.

Nothing.

On his hands and knees, he skittered backward into the dense cover of miniature trees. Then he stopped, listening. The only sound was the swish of rain on the boughs of pines, their smell pungent in the dark.

Hurriedly, he jerked the cell phone from his pocket.

Hunching to protect it from the rain, he called 911, speaking in an urgent undertone. Then he heard the snarl of motorcycles from the road, loud at first, before they faded into the night.

★ ★ ★

Kneeling, Chase stayed in hiding, the rain through the branches soaking his back. Then he heard the siren of a squad car, its blue swirling light cutting through the boughs.

Two more cars arrived. Slowly, Chase stood and began edging through the pines.

Holding a flashlight, a large, distinctive form in a wide-brimmed hat was moving toward him. Then Sheriff Al Garrett appeared behind the light. For a moment, he inspected the man in front of him. "You look a mess, Congressman. Once we get out of this rain, maybe you can tell me what happened."

Sitting in the car beside Garrett, Chase felt relief wash over him. Then, as best he could, he reconstructed his panic and fear for the sheriff and deputy sitting in the back seat.

"So you couldn't make out anyone," Garrett said.

Chase shook his head. "I only saw one of them for second, and he was wearing a helmet. But you know my default position—White Lightning. Nothing else makes sense to me."

As often, Chase found the sheriff's expression impenetrable. "I'll go talk to Parnell. Maybe his motorcycle will still be wet, and we'll find a weapon that fired at you with its barrel still hot. But even if it's him, the man's not stupid, just crazy with hate. Too bad he's got so much company."

"Yeah," Chase responded. "And they've all got the right to bear arms."

Garrett fished out the fob for his car. "I'll drive you to the office, get your statement, then take you back to the hotel. We'll get the GBI to go over that car for bullets."

He started the engine, then turned back to look at Chase. "Next time you decide to go visit somewhere, let me know. Seems like there's at least one person in this county who'd be sad if anything happened."

48

Entering his hotel room, Chase bolted the door. Then he stripped off his damp, mud-streaked clothing, threw it in the corner, and went to the shower.

For a time he had no way of determining, he let the hot water run over him, easing the tension from his body, his thoughts muddled by a residue of fear and dissociation. He had managed to give a coherent statement to Sheriff Garrett, he judged, and to simulate calm for as long as required. But now, alone, he did not feel like a congressman, or a father, or any notion of himself in some formerly familiar reality. Being hunted by men with guns ran through his consciousness, separating a past that felt suddenly distant from a future too obscure and chaotic to grasp.

He stayed there amidst a cloud of steam, suspended in disbelief. Finally, he turned off the shower, wrapped a towel around his waist, and went back to the bedroom.

There was a knock on the door.

Instantly, Chase experienced how the last three hours had altered his responses. His first thought was that some white man with a gun had walked through the lobby, taken the elevator, and come to the door intending to kill him. Then he remembered that Garrett had stationed a deputy to assure that only employees and guests could come upstairs.

Unbolting the door, he left the chain in place, peering through the crack.

It was Allie.

Surprised, he let her in, locking the door behind them. When he turned back to her, he saw that her face was suffused with worry. "How did you get up here?" he asked.

"Al Garrett called me. He seems to think I care about what happens to you. So he had a deputy follow me here."

Chase managed to smile. "Guess we're running out of secrets."

Instead of responding, she came to him, hugging him so fiercely that it filled him with surprise. After a moment, his arms circled her, and she laid her face against his chest. "I'm OK," he told her. "Just scared."

"So am I."

They stayed there for long minutes, silently holding each other, as if creating warmth against the cold. Then she looked up into his face, gently running the tip of one finger down the length of his chest. "Just let me lie against you," she said.

Together, they walked to the bed.

He lay there, looking up at her. Then, to his surprise, she began to undress, eyes still meeting his.

In the light of his bedside lamp, she was slender and beautiful, the woman he had loved before. What felt different was the catch in his throat.

She slipped down beside him. Turning on his side, he drew her close, feeling the warmth of her skin, the softness of her breasts against his chest.

For a long time they did nothing, said nothing.

"We still fit," she murmured.

The words brought everything back to him, how much he had wanted her, how it had felt to love her. Dimly, he felt the reunion of past and present dissipate the terror living inside him, until that, too, felt less real.

"Do we?" he asked.

★ ★ ★

Holding him, Allie remembered yet again those terrible moments on the sailboat foundering in chill, roiling waters, desperate to transfer the warmth of her body to his to keep him from dying, knowing then that she loved him. It would be only two weeks until she disappeared from his life.

And now, because of the reason she had done so—their child—he was here.

Her lips met his, gently at first, then longer. "As far as I know," she answered.

As he looked into her face, she unwrapped the towel around his waist. Then, gently, Allie touched what she had uncovered, an offer of herself that required nothing more.

Feeling him respond, she recalled their first time, the beautiful, fateful night of wine and pizza and Black Juliet. He was no longer that boy; she was no longer that girl. But both still lived within them, she understood, and they were meeting again, deepened by all that had happened to them since, the realization of all they had missed.

When he slipped inside her, their eyes met again. Then her hips rose to meet him with the desire of years.

She wrapped her legs around him, as if to pull him deeper, her movements divorced from any thought but wanting him. Then the world went black.

They were moving together, slowly at first, then almost savagely, as to take from each other what they had lost. She felt the inside of her tightening, the muffled cry rising to her throat, before the shuddering spasms running through her made her cry out.

★ ★ ★

Quiet, they lay together.

After a time, Chase felt astonishment and disbelief become acceptance. At least for tonight, this was their reality. "You look the same to me," he told her.

She kissed him, a smile on her lips. "They say when you're older and you meet someone you loved years before, you look at them and see the person they were. Fine with me if you look past the crow's feet."

"They're fine with me, too," he answered. "Both of them."

Suddenly she grinned, summoning her dimples. He touched the side of her mouth. "Haven't seen *those* in years."

"Haven't fucked me in years, Congressman."

The irreverent remark was so at odds with their shared sense of the moment that he laughed aloud. "Just whose fault is that, Alexandria Hill?"

He said this without rancor, and he could see that she knew this. But it reminded them both, he felt certain, of the person they had made together. Though soft, her expression became serious again.

"Why did you come here?" he asked.

Her gaze turned inward. "When Al called me, the first thing I thought of was you nearly dying on that boat, how it felt to almost lose you. I felt that again. But when I put down the phone, I realized it was so much more than that." She touched his face. "Ever find yourself wishing you could live an alternate life?"

He considered his answer. "More often, lately. Even considering the life I've lived until now. There are people missing from it, I'm beginning to think."

"Like who?"

"Like a family, Allie. Like you."

★ ★ ★

Holding her, Chase began thinking again of how afraid he had been and would be tomorrow. But tomorrow would bring more than fear. "It's gotten lost in all the excitement," he told her, "but I had an interesting visit with your mother."

She turned over to look at him. "What was *that* like?"

"Eventful. Even before she asked if I was Malcolm's father. Turns out she's a student of smiles and orthodonture."

"Can't say I'm surprised. What did you say?"

"You know what she's like—back in college, you told me often enough. What do you suppose I told her?"

Allie absorbed this, quiet. For a few hours in this room, however shadowed by worry and foreboding, they had found a cocoon of renewal. But for Malcolm, alone in a cell, nothing had changed, and the devastating sadness of that overcame her again. "I know we need to tell him," she said. "I just have to think about how."

"We both do," Chase answered. "Soon, so we can tell him on our own terms." He thought again of why she had come to his room, the fear she had banished, but only for a time. "We also need personal security. These people know who I am, and you're out in public for Blue Georgia. Even if I were cavalier about getting shot, which I'm certainly not, this is the wrong time for Malcolm to be missing a parent."

Suddenly, Allie felt relief coursing through her. "It won't be easy to tell him," she finally answered. "But I'm glad there are two of us now."

49

So as not to be seen, Allie left before dawn, pausing to kiss Chase at the door. "If you're wondering," she told him, "I have a lot of regrets, for both of us. But last night isn't one."

"Nor for me."

Alone again, Chase struggled to absorb the events of the last 24 hours—Harris' demand for the death penalty, his own quietly wrenching visit with Malcolm, his appearance in court with Allie, the revelatory conversation with her mother, the two men on motorcycles trying to kill him, and the renewed enmeshment with Allie that augured pain, promise, and uncertainty with no end in view. At the heart of this was the son in need of a father and in fear for his life.

Making coffee, Chase decided to visit him again. He would do better this time, he resolved, though he was not quite sure how.

His cell phone rang.

"Hi, Chase," the cheery voice said. "It's Tom Temple."

Surprised, Chase felt instantly on edge. Though Tom had been one of his housemates during senior year, over time the relationship had become amiable but distant. He could not remember when they had last talked on the phone.

Swiftly, Chase resurrected a politician's bonhomie and, with it, the name of Tom's second wife. "Great to hear from you, Tom. How's Kathleen?"

"She'd say she's good. I'd say she's pregnant again. My wife seems to think that kids are a profit center."

"You'll just have to work harder, pal. That way you can send all ten of them to Harvard."

Tom chuckled. "You're scaring me. But that's what I deserve for marrying someone twelve years younger without getting a vasectomy." Abruptly, his tone became less jovial. "I wanted to alert you to something."

Though Chase knew at once what had happened, he said lightly, "They've asked you to chair a new capital campaign?"

"That you can afford. This is about a call I got just before leaving the office yesterday."

There was no point in dissembling, Chase realized. "Print or cable?"

"Fox. They wanted to know what I remembered about you and Allie Hill. Once Kathleen told me you'd appeared with her in court, it wasn't hard for me to draw a straight line from Harvard to Georgia."

"What did you tell them?"

"Nothing. I developed instant amnesia and a double-digit IQ, and said I was drawing a blank. It struck me as unseemly to mention Allie staying over that spring."

"Thanks, Tom. I appreciate this. Some of these people can go pretty low."

"No worries, Congressman Brevard. You always cleaned up your own dishes, and I thought she was nice. But it won't be too long until they find some Republican whose memory is sharper. You guys were never touchy-feely in public, but still."

"But still," Chase answered, "is all they'll need."

★ ★ ★

As he hung up, his first reflex was to call Allie. But, too quickly for his own liking, he subordinated this to the cold calculus of politics. That their most painful moments could be picked over in public by gleeful and malicious predators—the men and women who made their money catering to the basest instincts of millions coarsened by racism and rage—created its own harsh imperatives. The first was for Chase to stop deceiving the man he paid to help him deal with such things.

"Malcolm Hill is your son," Jack Raskin repeated in a voice so stunned that Chase had never heard it before. "All along, you've been playing with matches and lying to me."

"Not lying," Chase answered evenly. "Just omitting a material fact too personal to share. It seems pointless for you to personalize that."

He felt Raskin straining to call on his reserves of professionalism and patience. "There's little in politics that stays personal," he retorted, "and damn few secrets. Now that you and Ms. Hill are about to burn at the stake, you're asking me to put out the fire."

"No. Just to put aside your hurt feelings. I care deeply about this woman, and our son. This will be devastating for both of them, and there are vultures in the media who'll think that degrading all three of us is a spectator sport. I need your dispassionate advice about making that no worse than it will be."

There was a brief silence. "OK," Raskin said in a clipped tone. "Two basics. The first is obvious. This won't keep, and your congressional seat is on the line—not to mention your fleeting hopes of becoming a senator. Your only decision is how to tell the story before somebody else does, and to whom."

"And the second?"

"You can't do this alone."

"I know that, too," Chase responded. "But that's not up to me, is it?"

★ ★ ★

They met by the pond again, sitting beside each other in the sunlight of early afternoon. But this time they feared more than discovery, and two bodyguards from Blue Georgia watched them from just out of earshot.

As he told her about the call from Tom Temple, Allie listened without visible reaction, save for a small, mirthless smile.

"It was bound to happen," she said. "Remember when I wondered why you expected things to turn out better than they were bound to? Seems like it's contagious. I knew better than to want you to come with me to the courthouse, but I did."

Strange, Chase thought, how distant their night together suddenly felt. "I wanted him to see me," Chase answered.

"So did I." Pausing, she studied the grass at her feet. "Maybe I shouldn't have put off telling him, but I was afraid of how he'd take it. Now it's mixed up with telling the world."

"That's why we need to go see him. Today."

"I know. But first we need to talk about what's coming for all of us." Abruptly, Allie's tone became businesslike. "I'm sure you've already called to your political people. So I'm also sure they advised you to do the television stations of the cross in public, before your enemies can reach for the hammer and nails."

She was as seasoned as he, Chase reminded himself, and at least as tough-minded. "Jack did say something about 'controlling the narrative.'"

She gave him a swift, knowing look. "Did he also mention how much you needed me? If he didn't, you should fire him and find someone else to overpay."

Despite their circumstances, Chase emitted a brief laugh. "You might as well tell me the rest. It'll save me the trouble, and you're admirably concise."

She stood, pacing. "OK. Your guy Jack doesn't want the media having two shots at us, each of us telling our own story. He thinks if you do this right, you might have a chance of bailing out your career. That makes me indispensable."

Chase looked up at her. "Yeah, that's pretty much it. Except for the part about doing it only once, on local TV, and telling everyone else who wants us to go pound sand."

She stopped, standing in front of them. "What did you say?"

"That I couldn't ask you to do an ersatz version of Harry and Meghan."

The briefest of smiles came and went with the dimples at the corner of her mouth. "Princess Allie. Should've thought of that. Did you boys discuss how much I need you to play Prince Harry?"

Abruptly, Chase saw them as two people who were finding their way back to each other, reduced to negotiating their roles in strip-mining for public consumption the most painful corner of their life. "It came up," he acknowledged.

"Of course it did. My story works better if you're my partner, not some random guy I slept with in college." She sat beside him again. "I know we both hate this. I can't even describe how much I do. But we chose this life. I've got donors, too, foundations to worry about. Blue Georgia—everything I've worked so hard to build—depends on how well I handle this. But you know what else is important to me? You.

"You came here because of me and a son you never knew about, risking everything you've worked for—Congress, the Senate, maybe more. I won't let you go down while I stand by and watch, all because of something I decided without you ever knowing." She paused again, looking at him intently. "Which brings us back to Malcolm, doesn't it? I'm not sure your mastermind has thought about how whatever we do affects his chances at trial, but I'm sure you have."

"Yeah. Quite a lot in so short a time."

"So tell me."

"All right. Controlling the narrative means dealing with archetypes. I can either be an ambitious politician pandering to Blacks, or a father standing by his son. You can be a woman who didn't care about whether Malcolm had a dad, or a mother who sacrificed her own happiness because you thought that best for me. We can be two people who care only about ourselves, or parents united in caring about Malcolm."

"In other words," Allie said, "a family."

"Uh-huh. You and I both know that real families are complicated. But that's not the archetype. People want to believe that families are loving and nurturing, because that's what they want for themselves. So that's what we'll give Malcolm on television." He slowed his speech, feeling the burden of all that they faced. "Too many people imagine him as an executioner from some scary rap video. We need to start changing that dynamic. That begins with making the best of this mess in public, like it or not. I just hope we can make him understand."

Allie touched his face, enough like her son's that she saw them in each other. "I just hope he'll accept you," she answered. "At least in time. Both of you deserve that."

50

When the door of the visiting room opened, Allie perceived at once Malcolm's confusion and surprise.

Though he had seen them together before, in court, she knew that their presence here, as a couple, augured something more portentous. She and Chase had debated whether Allie, alone, should tell their son the truth of his origins. But there was no easy answer, and very little time. So they had decided to come together, in the hope of birthing a new understanding of Malcolm's life that, with whatever awkwardness and uncertainty, would now involve the three of them. At least if Malcolm chose.

She crossed the room, swiftly hugging him as Chase watched, hands in his pockets. Looking up at Malcolm, Allie saw the first glimmer of comprehension stealing into his eyes.

"Can all of us talk?" she asked.

Stiffly, he sat near the end of the table, his mother at the end, Chase across from him. Malcolm looked tired, she saw, the bruises of sleeplessness darker.

He looked from one adult to the other before focusing on his mother. "What is it?"

Briefly, she glanced at Chase before turning back to their son. "You've always wanted to know who your father was," she said. "I'm sorry I never told you."

For a moment, he looked away from both of them, his thoughts unfathomable. Then, slowly and, it seemed, reluctantly, he turned to Chase, as if the fluorescent lights glaring down at them had begun hurting his eyes.

Silent, Chase nodded. In that moment, Allie saw with fresh poignancy that the hope softening his expression had heightened his resemblance to their son.

Almost imperceptibly, Malcolm seemed to flinch.

Quickly, Allie touched his arm, the protective reflex of a mother. "Chase didn't know," she told him. "Please, let me explain."

★ ★ ★

For uncounted minutes, Malcolm listened to a story about two people he didn't know—a young Black woman from the rural South in the North's most elite and rarefied college, and a privileged white man whose father was French and whose mother came from a wealthy family in Boston—who, despite all the differences in where they had come from and what they wanted, had fallen in love so completely and yet so fatefully that the girl, discovering she was pregnant, had chosen to run away.

But the story had been no part of Malcolm's life. The life he knew began in Georgia, and the man who had loved him was his grandfather, now buried in a cemetery for Blacks.

Suddenly, this polished congressman sitting across from him claimed to be the embodiment of what Malcolm had always craved—a living presence with a face and a name and love to give him, the only person who could salve the inextinguishable pain of knowing that he lacked what so many other boys took for granted since he had first learned the word and all it meant: "father." A father who loved him, looked after him, was proud of him. A father whose own life would be inexpressibly sad without the joys of being with Malcolm at every step from boy to man. But all Malcolm had ever been was the careless mistake of a privileged white man who had impregnated a Black woman from Georgia, then proceeded to live his own life without a backward glance.

He looked from one to the other. "You lied to me," he said. "Both of you. I wondered about him, all right. But I didn't think you'd lie."

She touched his arm again. "Chase never lied…"

"Bullshit." Malcolm rose from his chair, looking down at them. "He was your friend, you told me. Not my father. Why are you telling me now?"

The man composed himself. "After yesterday, the news media started contacting friends from Harvard. We wanted to tell you before they did." He glanced at Malcolm's mother, as if asking permission to speak for them both. "I'm a politician," he continued. "I don't get to have a private life. To say I'm sorry you're all caught up in that doesn't begin to cover it."

Shaken, Malcolm tried to absorb his sudden sense of betrayal. "I think I get it," he said cuttingly. "I'm not just a birth control mistake; I'm a political problem—Congressman Chase Brevard's dirty secret, the Black son who killed a white cop. Bet you wish you'd used a rubber."

At the corner of his vision, Malcolm saw his mother wince. In a seeming act of will, Chase made his face go blank. "Your mother doesn't," he said evenly. "For whatever it's worth to you, neither do I. But now both of us have to go on television—tomorrow, in Atlanta. If we don't, the wrong people will make up any story they want."

He could feel his mother watching his face. Softly, she said, "You have every right to be angry. But we were going to tell you, just at a better time. We wanted for the three of us to work through this on our own."

"Too late for that," Malcolm cut in. "Instead, I get to watch the two of you on television."

"Please," she implored him, "don't blame Chase. This is happening because he put you above everything else in his life—Congress, his own ambitions, people telling him he could be president..."

She stopped abruptly, as if reading his expression. But Malcolm was already gripped by the sheer enormity of realizing he was at the mercy of forces beyond his understanding, the choices and priorities of a man and woman in which he had no voice. Savagely, he said, "Maybe he just missed fucking Black women."

His mother's face froze. "You can think of me what you like," Chase interposed, "but there's only one person in her life your mother has always put first."

"I don't need you to tell me about her," Malcolm snapped. "I don't need you to be here. So go run for president." He turned to his mother, the person he had most trusted before she had burdened him with this stranger's needs and ambitions. "Take him and go. Just go, before I ask my watchdogs to come and get the both of you out of my life."

She stood, her face twisted with pain. "I'm your mom, Malcolm. You can never get me out of your life."

For an instant, Malcolm experienced a furious pleasure in dividing her from him. Then he felt himself falling into a pit of exhaustion, a free fall with no bottom. "Just go," he repeated dully.

Silent, his mother stood, perhaps waiting for Chase Brevard to rise from his chair. Belatedly, he did, so mechanically that it suggested an act of muscle memory divorced from whatever he was feeling.

As they left, his mother turned in the doorway. The man did not. Then they were gone, the door closing behind them with a heavy metallic sound, and Malcolm was alone.

★ ★ ★

Parked outside the county jail that housed his and Allie's son, Chase stared at it through the wire fence. Beside him, Allie slumped in the passenger seat, the fingers of one hand touching her eyes. "It was just too much for him."

"My being there was the worst part," Chase said bluntly. "But for me, you'd have told him yourself. I should have known better."

Allie shook her head. "I can't count the times I should've known better. I should have reached out to you years ago. I could have told him about you when he was ten, or twelve—maybe during some summer when we had time to sit on the porch and talk for as long as we needed, just letting him take it in. His grandfather and grandmother could have helped. I could've told him what you were like. You could've come to see him…"

"Allie, stop."

She shook her head. "Instead, we spring this on him when he's in jail, emotionally and physically exhausted, then say we have to go on television because the alternative is worse—for us." Her voice filled with anger turned inward. "Over and over again, I decided for him, and for you. So I turned your life upside down, and trashed whatever remaining sense he had of his."

He covered her hand. "Don't take too much on yourself. You couldn't have seen this coming nineteen years ago, or three weeks ago—no one could've. All this happened because a racist cop stopped him on a country road at night.".

"And who put him there? Me."

"If you want to have an orgy of self-recrimination, Allie, I've got all sorts of time. Congress is in recess, and we don't have to be in Atlanta until tomorrow."

She exhaled. "He was just so angry. The things he said…"

"He's hurt. It gives an instinct for the jugular, and the desire to use it. When I first came down here, I was harsher to you than I needed to be. I couldn't see past my own grievances."

"You had good reason. So does he."

"Based on more recent events," Chase responded, "I seem to be getting over it. We've got the same weakness, and it's terminal. Loving Allie Hill."

She was quiet again—accepting the truth of this, Chase hoped. For him but, especially, for their son.

"Know where you really screwed up?" he asked. "The president thing."

She gave him a sideways look. "I knew that was stupid as soon as I said it."

"Yeah, only my mother believes that. Annually, after my father puts too much whiskey in their eggnog. The man hates Christmas."

She turned in the passenger seat to look at him. After a moment, she said, "I know how hard that was for you. I'm sorry."

Harder than you know, he thought, "I'm OK," he answered. "I didn't expect that much, and why would I? Anyhow, I brought it on myself. I should probably stay away for a while."

"Maybe. But it's so hard to know. He's always wanted a father."

Just not me, Chase almost said, and stopped himself. "When do you plan on seeing him next?"

"After we get back. I'm going to call Al Garrett later, ask him to keep a watch on Malcolm. I think it's time to see if I can arrange a therapist."

"Past time," Chase answered. "With all he's gone through, I think he's PTSD waiting to happen. He's begun having flashbacks about Bullock. Startle responses, too."

She looked at him in surprise. "He told you that?"

"Yes."

"Then maybe you were making more progress than you know. In the best of times, he would never have trusted Robert with anything like that." She paused. "When are you going back to Washington?"

"Monday. After tomorrow, that should be an interesting experience."

"Any idea how it will go?"

"None. Call me after my first day on the floor of the House."

"I will."

Chase looked at her, seeing the signs of exhaustion. "The two of you will be OK, Allie. You've been his mother for a long time."

They fell quiet again, with their own separate thoughts.

In the silence, Chase glanced at his watch, and saw that it was already past six o'clock. "I should drive you home. I know you have some work calls to make, and we've got a pretty long day tomorrow. We're working parents, after all."

★ ★ ★

Alone in his room, Chase thought of the son who did not want him.

Beneath the realities he had accepted, he asked himself, what had he hoped for in the depths of his subconscious? Some archetypal rapport with Malcolm that would have counterbalanced all he was risking? The first glimmer of gratitude that Chase had materialized from nowhere to fill the role of father? If so, it was hard to measure what in all this was worse—its narcissistic romanticism or its emotional obtuseness. He should have learned from his own youth that true fatherhood was not a matter of blood, but the accretion of acts that, over time, took root in the heart of a son.

By that measure he had much to do, and the chance to do it had, perhaps, already vanished in the slipstream of the past. In the future, his son might never be free, and there would be precious little room for Chase to make a difference in a life too crabbed for relationships, and that might end before his own.

Even so, he had learned, a man who resolves to be a father does not reckon the cost or prospects of success. The only choice was to move forward, doing the next thing he could, and then the next. Or not. There was much to weigh in the balance of his own life.

But there was someone else to think of—too carelessly neglected in his absorption with Malcolm, Allie, and himself.

Picking up his cell phone, he called the number he still stored in his contacts. When she answered, he said, "Hi, Kara."

"Chase?" she answered in a tone of surprise. "I'm really glad to hear from you."

"I know it's been a while. I'm sorry."

Briefly, she was quiet. "I just wish I knew what's going on with you. I got back to the hotel last night and saw the clip of you and Allie Hill. You never mentioned you even knew her."

"From a long time ago, at Harvard. That's why I'm calling."

"This must be pretty serious then."

"Serious enough. I wanted to tell you myself, before you hear about it on the news tomorrow evening." He paused. "Remember the last morning we were together, after your birthday? We were watching *Morning Joe*, and they put up the picture of Malcolm Hill."

"I remember. I was looking at his photograph, and suddenly you went quiet."

"More than quiet, Kara. I'd just realized something that explains everything I've done." Pausing again, he willed himself to finish. "Malcolm's my son."

51

Allie and Chase sat next to each other on the Swedish modern couch of an Atlanta television studio, with interviewers sitting a space apart—a plainspoken Black television anchor, Jennifer Kent, and Nancy Feldman, a white reporter from the PBS station in Boston.

The premise for the disclosure of Malcolm's paternity was Jack Raskin's. Only one interview, one hour long. No further comment from Chase or Allie. Local television only—to go on national TV would look cheap and exploitive. Candor without pathos; warmth without overwrought sentimentality. Concern for Malcolm over career or causes. Allie would take the lead—the decision from which everything followed had been hers, and only she could explain it. The common imperative for her and Chase was to garner public sympathy while enduring a ritual whose indignities they despised.

With a faintly accusatory air, Jennifer Kent asked Chase, "Congressman Brevard, why is this interview the first time you've acknowledged that Malcolm Hill is your son?"

As planned, Allie touched Chase's arm, as if to prevent him from answering. Then she turned back to Kent. "I never told him, Jennifer. Three weeks ago, he saw Malcolm's photograph on the news and saw himself. Chase came to Georgia as soon as he could."

Kent's eyebrows shot up. "For eighteen years, you concealed from the congressman that he had a son?"

"Yes," Allie answered, carefully softening her voice with regret. "He never knew Malcolm existed. That was my doing."

"Why?" Feldman interposed in an incredulous tone. "Didn't you think he had the right to know?"

Allie looked at her directly, as if they were two women talking only to each other. "I questioned my decision every day for every one of those years. I feel guilty about Chase, and even more guilty about depriving our son of a father." Through the briefest of pauses, she suggested the depth of her misgivings. "But we were only twenty-one. My decision was about who we were then—where we came from, and what we wanted to do with our lives."

Watching Allie, Chase was struck by her pitch-perfect presentation; only he could know how much this performance was costing her. "Was this a casual relationship?" Feldman asked.

Allie's lips compressed, a sign of annoyance she swiftly banished. "Never for Chase, I know." Looking at Chase, she added softly, "And never for me. Not then, and not now."

Meeting her eyes, Chase joined Allie in pretending they had no audience. But they did, and he could not know whether the affection in her eyes was truly intended for him, or to draw in those watching.

Allie turned back to their interviewers. "When we first met, I saw a good-looking guy with a great smile and so much money that I thought he just floated above other people's worries. What I discovered was that he was way more aware of himself and others. Me included." Glancing at Chase again, she summoned the wisp of a smile. "I'd tease him, or complain to him, or mock him for being a rich white elitist. It never seemed to bother him. Instead, he did the most surprising thing for a man that age, maybe any age—he listened, and worked at understanding who I was. He made me feel like the most special woman he'd ever met."

Briefly touching his hand, Allie kept watching the reporters. "So I started trying to understand *him*. Not just who he was with me, but who he was. I'm the least surprised person in the world that Chase cares more about our son than his own career."

Kent leaned forward. "According to you, he only discovered that he was a father because of charges against Malcolm for his alleged murder of a white sheriff's deputy."

Allie stared at her, erasing the softness from her expression. "Malcolm didn't *murder* anyone," she snapped. "He defended himself against a racist who was stalking him at night for the crime of helping people of color to vote. As a mother, it's tearing me up inside. As someone who's dedicated her life to making this country what it can and should be, it makes me unspeakably angry and sad. I don't think you, or anyone but Chase, can understand how that feels. So forgive me if I resent the premise for your question."

Watching Kent's reaction, a brief and clearly involuntary display of surprise and defensiveness, Chase realized that Allie intended to take over the interview. "But you were asking, Jennifer, why I deprived Chase of a son, and Malcolm of a father. So I'll go back to the beginning, the decision that changed everything for all of us, and the reasons I made it."

Glancing at Chase, she modulated her tone to one of somber remembrance. "Toward the end of our time together, we went sailing on Martha's Vineyard. Chase fell overboard in a sudden squall. The water was cold, and he nearly died from hypothermia. I desperately tried to make him warm, all the time thinking I couldn't let his life end this way. But God answered my prayers, and he lived.

"That's when I realized I loved him. Even then, I thought I might never love anyone else that much, except perhaps my own child." Pausing, she turned to Chase, looking into his eyes as if she needed him to know and remember what she was about to say. "I even considered staying up north to be near him, at least for a while. Maybe, I told myself, with a little more time we could see if there was a life for us somewhere."

In his surprise, Chase wondered if she was using this public ordeal to tell him what she had never been able to say. Then he remembered, yet again, that she had once been an actress, Black Juliet, long before she became a public persona so gifted that she could take an audience in her hands. Wondering what was truth and what was performance, he sensed that she was giving a performance illuminated by truth, made all the more affecting by the calculated device of facing him at the optimal moment. As she turned back to the reporters, their expressions attentive and respectful, Chase realized how completely Allie had taken control—in part by giving them the theater they wanted.

"Then I found out I was pregnant," she continued, "as much because of my own carelessness as his. As a matter of personal belief, I was going to keep our child. I knew that if I told Chase, he'd offer to marry me. I knew that he'd want to. But he had a future in Massachusetts, and I was committed to working for change in Georgia."

Her voice became quieter, as if she remembered how grounded her choice was in her feelings for Chase. "I wanted him to live the life he deserved. I told myself that he'd find someone whose own life wasn't so different, someone who loved him and belonged in his world. So I told him our relationship was just too hard, and ran out the door and back to Georgia for my parents to help me raise their grandchild, sick with thinking Chase would hate me for the rest of his life." For an instant, her voice caught. "When Malcolm was born, I wanted him there so much, I nearly gave in to it. But I didn't.

"How could I ask him to give up his dreams when I couldn't give up my own? How could I tether him to a woman and child in Georgia, the last place on earth that was right for him? How could I claim the right to change the course of his future?"

Pausing again, she shook her head in wonder and dismay. "Because of this tragedy involving our son, I ended up doing that very thing. Part of me feels terrible about that. But not all of me. Because Malcolm and I don't have to go through this alone. Most of all, because he now has a man who cares for him at a time he most needs that."

"What is the future of your relationship with Congressman Brevard?" Feldman asked.

Allie gave her a mildly incredulous look. "Our son is facing charges of capital murder. If that's not enough, both of us have responsibilities to others we asked for long ago: Chase, to his constituents in Massachusetts; me, to all the people in Georgia who racists and reactionaries don't want to vote. There's no time for us to consider the future of our relationship." Turning to Chase, she added, "I'm just grateful we have one again."

★ ★ ★

With this, Allie saw, Feldman decided to home in on Chase. "That raises the question of your political future, Congressman Brevard. There's been speculation that you plan on running for the United States Senate in 2024."

Chase gave her a thin smile of irony. "Sorry, Nancy, but I've been a bit distracted. That's what fatherhood will do for you, I've discovered. I'm a little more concerned with what happens to our son than I am with some theoretical race two-plus years from now. Ask me again once Malcolm goes free."

"As we speak," Feldman rejoined, "the voters of the Fourth District of Massachusetts are already asking. What do you say to them?"

Chase paused to compose his answer. "That I deeply appreciate their confidence and the opportunity they've given me to represent them in Congress. I take that very seriously. But I also believe that most people in my district will understand what I'm experiencing right now.

"Three weeks ago, a young man I didn't know became the most important person in my life. The second most important is his mother. We both know that Malcolm is innocent, just like we know that the deputy targeted him because of Allie's work." His voice became at once fatalistic and firm. "I don't know how I'll feel about politics if this case doesn't turn out like it should—all because the right-wing stalkers in politics and the media see our son as an opportunity to scavenge for money and votes, and to destroy all that his mother has worked so hard to accomplish for others…"

"But you're on the ballot this November," Feldman interrupted. "That's less than five months away."

"So I recall. I'll leave worrying about my future to the voters in my district. With the help of my terrific staff, I'll do my best under the circumstances to keep up with my responsibilities in Washington. But my most pressing concern is to do everything I can, whatever that may be, to help Malcolm get his life back. If some people don't like that, too bad."

Watching him, Allie experienced Chase on two levels—admiration for his gifts as a politician and, much more deeply, an overwhelming relief that he had become her partner in caring for Malcolm. But Feldman pressed on. "But realistically, Congressman, what can you do to affect your son's very adverse situation?"

"Legally, or personally? As to his case, probably not much—he's got a very good lawyer for that. But part of what you call my son's 'very adverse situation' is that his beloved grandfather died, and that he had no father. Now he does." He paused, looking at the camera, speaking past Feldman to an audience of one. "I want to claim Malcolm as my son in reality, not just by birth, and I want him to want that. But these things take time. I intend to give it."

★ ★ ★

On the drive back to Cade County, neither Allie nor Chase spoke for a while. In the passenger seat, Chase watched the exurbs of Atlanta become countryside.

"I keep thinking about Malcolm," Allie said at last. "Yesterday and now. What he's thinking and feeling, all alone in that cell. What he'll think when he sees us on television, if he hasn't already. Compared to that, our national mortification is nothing."

He watched her weave in and out of traffic more aggressively than normal, as though to dispel how soiled she felt. "We did the best we could. Both days."

"Did we? Anyhow, I liked what you said at the end. I hope Malcolm hears it."

"So do I." He turned to her. "But for the setting, I appreciated everything you said. Including the things I hadn't heard before."

She shot him a glance. "That I thought about giving in back then, staying up north? Yeah, I thought that part was especially poignant."

Chase hesitated. "But was it actually true?"

Considering her answer, Allie seemed to exhale. "Of course it was. Which made leaving you all the harder." She changed lanes again, passing a truck and another car. "Anyhow, now we're America's semisweethearts. At least on reality TV."

"And our reality now?"

For a moment, she was quiet. "I don't know whether this is reality," she answered, "or the foolish wish of a Black girl from Georgia, who discovered at Harvard that she's more of a romantic than makes any sense. But when I woke up to you yesterday morning, before I remembered why you were here, I wanted that wish to be our reality."

★ ★ ★

Two hours later, sequestered in Chase's hotel suite with a guard outside the door, he and Allie had dinner from room service and watched their televised images dominate cable news in a seemingly endless loop.

Chase took another sip of his martini, feeling the quick medicinal hit of gin course through his limbs. "Jesus, I'm tired."

Narrow-eyed, Allie sipped her glass of red wine, watching and listening intently as commentators interspersed clips of their interview with presumptively sagacious assessments of their performance and its impact on Allie's leadership of Blue Georgia, Chase's political future, and—least important, it seemed—the murder charges against their son.

By consensus, except on Fox, they had proven to be a compelling couple, and flash polls from Atlanta and Boston showed public opinion running in their favor.

"Allie Hill and Chase Brevard," opined a commentator, "provided a master class in the art of molding public opinion. She, in particular, showed a level of vulnerability that made her strikingly dimensional and appealing."

Abruptly, almost angrily, Allie turned off the television. "I never want to do anything like that again. Ever. The mercy is that it's actually working."

Chase drained his drink. "It'll keep on working. Especially once your communications director discloses that we were both shot at, and Al Garrett confirms it. Nothing like a near-death experience to arouse public sympathy."

She turned to him, her expression weary. "Here we are," she said with muted bitterness, "hiding in a hotel room with a guard at the door, watching ourselves sell our souls on television while we calculate the public relations benefits of being shot at. It's like a virtual reality experiment in dehumanization, with the three of us as subjects, and no exit as long as the legal system is holding Malcolm hostage. You must be sorry we ever met."

If nothing else, Chase thought, this was a day for telling truths. "I was, sometimes. But not now, looking at you, even after all this. It's the damnedest thing, Alexandria Hill."

Her eyes softened. "Would you like me to stay over?" she asked.

"Very much."

"Then so do I." Allie touched his hand, this time not for the cameras. "That way I can wake up to you again."

52

On the screen appended to the wall of his cell, Malcolm watched clips of his mother and Chase Brevard revealing to America how he had come to exist.

He felt humiliated, conflicted, and, despite himself, compelled to watch. They had loved each other, it seemed clear, and perhaps still did. But what struck him hardest was when this man said that he wanted to claim Malcolm as his son.

He had come to Georgia, risking his career. Perhaps, like Malcolm, this congressman had discovered how it felt when a piece of you was missing.

There was a knock on the door, and Sheriff Garrett came in. He had no gun on; it was as if he had come to visit. Looking up at the screen, he said, "Mind if I watch with you?"

Malcolm shook his head. Sitting beside him, Garrett contemplated the clips.

Finally, they ended. Malcolm turned off the television.

"Must be something," the sheriff said. "Watching that."

"Yeah. It's something."

Garrett was quiet for a while. "Me, I never had a father. Mine never showed."

Malcolm turned to him, surprised. "What's that like?"

"Strange. Not a day goes by I don't still wonder about him."

"Are you still angry?"

Garrett's heavy shoulders shrugged. "At your age, I was. But now I've got two boys of my own. So I've put those feelings into being for them what I never had. The man cheated himself is how I try looking at it."

Malcolm considered this. "What do you think about *him*?"

"The congressman? Got shot at, and he's still here. That tells me something." Garrett paused for a moment. "I've been on both sides of it, yours and his. You want what I wanted then; he seems to want what I've got now. The way I look at it, you two are the only chance each other has."

"You saying I should accept him?"

Slowly, Garrett shook his head. "No. All I'm saying is that he showed up here, with you in trouble, saying he wants the job. So you've got something else I didn't—a choice."

Feeling the sheriff's solid presence, Malcolm had the painful realization that what he wanted was a father like Al Garrett, a familiar Black man who reminded him of Wilson Hall. But what he had instead was a white man with whom he had nothing in common, yet who had left his inescapable imprint on Malcolm's face and, with the woman who seemed to love them both, the essence of who he had been since birth.

"It's a lot to think about," Malcolm said, and all that had happened overwhelmed him again. Still, he was glad the sheriff had come. The loneliness was feeling impossible to bear.

★ ★ ★

It was Friday; Chase intended to stay until Tuesday morning, when Congress would be back in session. He meant to spend time with Allie when she wasn't busy working and hoped, perhaps vainly, to see Malcolm.

In the meanwhile, his hotel room became his workspace. He talked to Jack Raskin, who allowed that Allie had done him some good, had Zoom calls with his staff and scheduler to keep up with his duties, and monitored the cacophony stemming from the interview. His office was inundated with calls and emails—most favorable, but commingled with some calling him a cop hater and others that were rankly racist. The unsourced assertion that he patronized Black prostitutes rocketed through right-wing websites; other fabrications, directed at Allie, marked the sordid intersection of bigotry and misogyny—including that Malcolm had resulted from her serial copulation with eight members of the Sophocles Club in less than an hour.

By now he was accustomed to falsehoods and ugliness directed at him. But, though other colleagues had experienced the slandering of parents, siblings, spouses, or children, Chase had not, and that these effusions were directed at Allie and Malcolm seared him far more. So he was grateful when the speaker of the House called to check in.

"I've been wondering how you were," she said. "Not just wondering—worrying. This must be pretty overwhelming for you, Allie, and your son."

This was like her, Chase thought—she was so tough and savvy that people forgot she was a mother and grandmother capable of thinking about her members as people, not just votes. "Sorry," he said. "Usually your wards have more parochial problems. Can't think of anyone who got shot at and announced that he was the father of a kid on trial for murder. At least not in the same week."

The speaker laughed briefly. "Or ever. Maybe we should talk about ways I can help."

★ ★ ★

Entering the visiting room, Allie stopped, looking at Malcolm with a tentative expression before sitting beside him.

He felt her studying his face with a mother's unabashed scrutiny. Only her uncertainty about touching him suggested all that had happened since the moment she and Chase Brevard had appeared here together.

"You look so tired, baby."

He shook his head, not in denial but at its futility. "I can get you someone to talk to," she said. "To help support you through all of this."

Malcolm inhaled. "Whatever."

"Not 'whatever.' I'm sorry we told you like that." She hesitated. "We both are."

"You're both right."

Her expression became one familiar to Malcolm since childhood, especially in moments of estrangement—a mother resolved to say what she must. "We're also sorry about the interview. But what we said was true."

She was careful, Malcolm recognized, not to single out what the man had said about Malcolm. But her meaning was clear. In a tone suspended between curiosity and accusation, he demanded, "Why is he so important to you?"

His mother regarded him with a look of caution. "Do you really want to talk about this?"

"What the fuck do you think, Mom? I'm the product of your great love affair, and now he pops up in our lives."

"He didn't just pop up. He came here for both of us…"

"He came here because he loves you," Malcolm snapped. "Do you still love him?"

She seemed to compose herself. "Yes. It's complicated, but yes."

He waited for his own emotions to settle. "All right. Mind telling me why?"

★ ★ ★

Looking into her son's face, Allie wondered where to begin.

Certainly not with "Because I've always loved him," or "Because he's a part of me," or "Because I still desire him," or "Because he's always loved me despite all my faults," or "Because no matter how much I love being your mother, I've been so damn lonely," or "Because beneath all our differences, he feels like my person." Though all those things and more, she had rediscovered, were true, they were not for a son to hear.

"There are so many reasons," she said. "But I'll start with the one that's most important to me now. Because he's part of us—you and me."

"He never was before."

"Not for you. But from the beginning I could look at you and see him." She looked down, trying to find the words to explain. "You knew half of who you are, the part that came from me. But I could see so clearly all that came from him. And it was my doing that you never could." Her voice became pinched. "I felt so guilty about that. So when he came here, angry as he was at me, he felt like the piece that had been missing for us both."

After a moment, she looked up at him. "But the biggest things were watching Chase discover that he wanted to be your father, no matter what it cost him, and me discovering that he was the man I'd imagined him becoming at Harvard. Not just a politician on the rise, who's way better than most, but a fundamentally good and caring person who for some reason—maybe me—never had a family, but then looked at us, amidst all this fear and misery, and saw one. Who looked at you and saw a son." She paused, feeling her own emotions. "For as long as I live, baby,

I will never be able to tell you how much that means to me. But that's the heart of it. Because he's part of us, Chase cares about the person I love most."

★ ★ ★

So much of this, Malcolm realized, was unfathomable to him. But he remembered well enough the pain of knowing, without anyone saying so, that he was the reason that she and Robert had not worked.

"Not like Robert, you mean."

He watched her consider dissembling and then realize that this was pointless. "No. Not like Robert."

"I never liked him."

"He never gave you much reason." His mother paused for another moment. "It's not just a matter of blood, but spirit. Your grandfather was tied to you by blood, but also because he had a loving and generous heart. As different as they are, so does Chase. One of the things that hurts me now—your grandmother, too—is thinking how much, in the end, they would've liked each other. I'm sorry that will never happen."

Malcolm tried to imagine his grandfather with Chase Brevard, and could not. "You want me to see him, don't you?"

"Only when you want to. You've got a lot to take in. Chase understands that."

Malcolm struggled to understand himself, and then gave up. "No point in putting it off," he said.

★ ★ ★

Captive to confusion, Malcolm stared across the table at the man he could not believe was his father. Yet he could see it—in the man's face, his build, the movements of someone at home in his own body. Except for an almost imperceptible wariness, the congressman seemed to have recovered his composure.

"I don't need to stay long," he told Malcolm. "I just wanted to let you know that I'm still here."

"You mean this is all fine with you," Malcolm retorted. "And I'm the only one who feels like it's pretty weird."

Briefly, the congressman betrayed the trace of a smile. "Absolutely. Every week or so another white congressman from Massachusetts wakes up and finds out he's got a Black son in Cade County, Georgia, who doesn't know anything about him. We've got a whole support group for that."

For a moment, Malcolm simply stared at him.

Abruptly, Chase Brevard's smile vanished. "The other day, I told you 'sorry' doesn't cover how I feel. Weird doesn't either. The one thing I'm sure about is that I want to work toward being your father. That makes you the only support group that matters." He paused. "I've got a day job. But I'll be back and forth from Washington to be with you and your mother."

Hearing this, Malcolm felt a strange kind of relief, and had no way of expressing it. "Fine," he answered dismissively. "Seems like she needs you."

53

On a bright Sunday morning, Janie and Allie Hill parked downtown to join Chase for the four-block walk from the Winthrop Hotel to the Friendship Baptist Church.

At the suggestion of Janie, who had spoken with their pastor, Allie had carefully choreographed their familial procession. Chase walked between the two women, security guards conspicuously stationed in front and behind, while television cameras recorded the scene through the open windows of the vans gliding beside them. Nearest the street, Janie Hill walked with her head held high and her eyes straight ahead. "It's time for us to appear as a family," Janie had decreed, and Chase understood that she, like her daughter, was a strategist with her own steely pride, and a public face she called on as circumstances demanded.

But this family's church was far removed from the Episcopal redoubt where the Brevards made obligatory appearances, despite the acidic grousing from his rigorously atheist father about the ceremonial pieties of inbred Anglicans.

The spacious, modern structure had high ceilings, but little architectural complexity and no decor save for stained glass sconces on each side of the church. Rows of recessed lighting from the white ceiling illuminated long rows of leather pews trimmed with burnished wood, bisected by a green-carpeted aisle that stretched to a raised platform, on which stood a black metal pew. Behind it were two large screens on the wall, and an elaborate sound system that pumped modern gospel music as the congregation filed in, noting one conspicuous novelty at the rear of the church—more camera crews from two cable networks that would broadcast the service nationwide.

The celebrants already seated watched Allie, Janie, and Chase as they passed between them toward the front of the church. Many gazed with

open curiosity; more than a few nodded and smiled at Chase, conspicuously the only white person there. Most were dressed in Sunday finery,
and the celebrants included more women than men—all ages; some
stout, some slender, some in between—with everyone responding to the
pulse of the music. Mixed in were small children, including pretty girls in
cornrows and bright dresses who made him imagine Allie as a child. One
boy of perhaps three was stretched out dead asleep in the pew amidst
the voices and noise all around him, testament to a tired child's gift for
oblivion.

Chase and the women took their place. As five singers in yellow
dresses came forward to render gospel songs with swaying bodies and
resonant voices, the congregation stood and began to clap. Standing
with the others, Chase clapped as seemed called for. Glancing over, Allie
gave him a smile of fondness and amusement. This might be yet another
performance, but she seemed glad to have him become part of her world.
If only for a time.

Despite everything, so was he.

★ ★ ★

After perhaps a half hour—a swelling chorus of gratitude for God, Jesus,
community, and a release from the cares of the week—Pastor William
Moore stepped to the pulpit.

A big man with a round face, steel-gray hair, and a sonorous voice,
he scanned the congregation with an air of implacable authority before
offering a few words of greeting and fellowship. Pausing, he gazed down
at Chase.

"We are honored," he continued, "to have Congressman Chase
Brevard here among us come with the rest of Malcolm Hill's family. I
see Malcolm's grandmother Janie Hill, who helped build the church in
which we celebrate today, and whose husband, Wilson, looks down from
above. I see Janie's daughter, Allie, who has helped change this county, this
state, and this country in ways that have made all of us so very proud."

Chase heard the random humming, murmuring, and clapping of
affirmation. "That's right," a man called out.

"But until now," the pastor intoned, "something was missing. Some*one*
was missing. But no more. The congressman has come forward to stand
beside Allie, to assume the role of father, and help his son Malcolm as a
father should."

Listening, Chase was at once moved and professionally admiring, as
the pastor began striking the notes of passion, challenge, and redemption with a voice that varied from a carefully modulated hush to a rich

baritone at once operatic and perfectly clear. "He has come through hatred and gunfire to join us who seek justice, at no little cost to himself. He has come here even though he and Malcolm's mother are pursued by evil men who hide in the darkness. He has come here because he discovered a son whose very life is in jeopardy. He has come here because that son is wrongly accused. He has come here to ensure that Malcolm regains the freedom he deserves."

"*Yes*," a woman cried out, more voices rising behind her.

The pastor's voice cut through them. "There have been bullets fired at Malcolm's mother and father. No one has stepped forward to claim these cowardly actions. But we know what this is—the work of white nationalists, the modern-day Ku Klux Klan, bearing in their stunted souls the same age-old evil..."

Amidst the outcry of disapproval, Moore continued. "But I promise you—I promise you—that evils done in darkness will come to light, and that their authors will stand before us stripped of their disguises. Just as I know that some blessed day, Malcolm will have justice and that America will be able look at this family—this mother, this father, their son—and think about love instead of about race."

Listening, Chase felt Allie's fingers interlace his. "I know you will support them," the pastor concluded, "as Christians and as a congregation. So welcome, Congressman, to your home in Cade County for however long you're among us." He looked out at his flock. "Please rise, everyone, and let this man and his family feel our care and our love."

Chase looked around, Allie's hand still in his. No one was sitting.

With this, he knew, the pastor had helped rally the Blacks of Cade County, alter the environment in which Malcolm's trial would occur, and make its outcome a matter of national concern. All that was calculated, part of a strategy to counterbalance the voices of fear and anger calling for Malcolm's life. But at bottom, Chase understood, this was an expression of what Allie had described to him at Harvard—the awareness of a community that indifference, as well as injustice, was their enemy. The consciousness that had brought her back to this place.

Tonight, when they were alone, he would tell her that.

★ ★ ★

After the service, Allie, Janie, and Chase stood on the lawn as the parishioners came up to greet them, men shaking his hand, women placing their hands on his arms in a swift embrace, quietly speaking their blessings or good wishes. Standing to the side, their bodyguards watched them as cameramen recorded the scene.

"You've got Malcolm's smile," a white-haired lady told Chase.

Smiling again, he responded, "I always thought it worked the other way around. But either way, I'm glad I found him."

Suddenly, he felt a hand clasping his shoulder and saw Jabari Ford's complex look of irony, compassion and, perhaps, respect. "Truth to tell, Congressman, I did kind of wonder. But really, who knew?"

He walked away to his own family, a pretty wife in a bright red dress with an equally pretty daughter and a younger boy chafing in what might be his first suit—looking, Chase supposed, much like Malcolm once had.

Who knew?

54

For Chase, his return to Washington marked a divide in his career, and in his life.

On the floor, many of his Democratic colleagues made a point of being warm and supportive, and the speaker of the House invited him for coffee. "I've been talking to our caucus," she said. "I think there are things we can do for you." But Lucy Battle and a few of her ideological allies were notably aloof, and the ostentatious scorn of many Republican House members confirmed something Chase had long believed—that for them, partisan hatred was not merely an act but a way of being. One tweeted a deepfake image of Chase holding a gun to George Bullock's head; tweeting a photograph of Chase and Allie leaving the courthouse, Dorothy Turner Dark wrote, "I never said that Chase Brevard was in bed with cop killers. Only their mothers." Death threats began inundating his office.

The greatest salve for Chase was doing what his constituents had sent him here for—working on a bill to fortify rural healthcare, another to aid his state's troubled fishing industry. But the politics of his job were increasingly rancid: The head of the police union in Boston called his statement that Malcolm was innocent "an abuse of his public platform not excused by his personal concerns," and a local talk show host said that "protecting cop killers is Chase Brevard's idea of family values." His Republican opponent in November put Malcolm's mug shot on his website with the heading "My dad is your congressman."

Beneath the initial tide of support from his district, Jack Raskin cautioned Chase, lurked trouble. The Republican Congressional Campaign Committee, which had heretofore considered Chase a lock for reelection, was spending money to cut down his margin of victory—the better to hamstring him should he run for the Senate in 2024 and, if he sustained more damage, to defeat him in November. His constituents had begun receiving a flyer with a photograph of Chase arriving to visit Malcolm in the Cade County jail, accompanied by the caption "This is your absentee congressman on paid family leave." His internal polling numbers dipped slightly, with independent voters expressing nascent doubts about his commitment to the job.

"I know this is hard," Raskin told him. "But you can either spend your weekends campaigning in your district and showing your face in the state, or visiting your quasi family in Georgia—including a son more voters than not still think is guilty of killing a cop. Every day in Cade County leaches support."

This was true, Chase understood. Any voter who saw him as standing up for Allie and Malcolm would have supported him before; in terms of cold political analysis, he had begun tiptoeing on quicksand—certainly with respect to the Senate. So instead of resisting Jack's advice, he thanked him for his candor.

But the strangest part was his late weeknights in Georgetown, which distilled how completely his life had changed. There was a security guard at his door, and he was otherwise alone. A month before, Kara might have been with him, or at least on the telephone from Iowa. But like any sensible woman who watched the interview, she had no doubt concluded that Chase belonged to Allie Hill and, perhaps, always had.

In any event, when not enmeshed in work, Chase thought continually of Allie and their son. After nineteen years of silence, it was Allie he called now, every night. Her days, she reported, were consumed by visits to Malcolm and the myriad demands of running Blue Georgia: hiring a new field director, targeting key areas for vote-by-mail drives, intensifying her phone calls to ensure that donor support did not flag and—an added expense—augmenting security for her offices. But, aside from seeing her mother, what free time she had at night was suffused with worry for their son.

"I think he's deteriorating," she told Chase on a Wednesday night. "Al Garrett has begun scheduling an hour for him in the exercise area, with no other prisoners around. But the other twenty-three hours he's living with his own despair. You know about Jabari's co-counsel, right?"

"The white guy from Atlanta? Only that Jabari thinks he's good."

"He's off the case," Allie said flatly. "Emergency heart surgery, no trial work anymore. I know Jabari's the one who matters most. But Malcolm is taking it as a sign from God."

It wasn't *that* bad, Chase knew, but it was an unexpected and unwelcome problem. Ford couldn't carry the load of defending a capital case alone and, as Allie and Malcolm well knew, one key part of his strategy was presenting a racially mixed jury with a white co-counsel. "He'll find someone else down there," Chase assured her. "How are *you* doing?"

Chase heard her calibrating her answer, in part to avoid creating more pressure on him. "Under the circumstances," she answered, "I'm managing. I'm where I'm supposed to be, doing what I'm supposed to do. It's you I worry about."

"How so?"

"A lot of reasons. I've always been Malcolm's mother, and I've loved him since before he was born. But you've had everything in your life turned inside out, eating away at your obligations and ambitions in the place you ever call home, all because of a woman and a son who live six hundred miles away." She paused. "When I'm not thinking about Malcolm, I'm thinking about you. I read things; I hear things. They're turning on us, just like we both knew they would. Maybe it's time to pay more attention to the people who can send you back to Washington."

Her voice was calm, that of a friend giving sensible advice to another friend. But he imagined her, as alone as he was, and all he wanted at that moment was to hold her.

"Would you like me to come back?" he asked.

She was quiet for a time. "I always want you to come back. But that's way easy for me to say, and not the issue."

"What makes you think it's so easy for me to stay away?" He paused, much as she had. "Maybe I can even help Malcolm. There are other weekends I can spend in Massachusetts."

★ ★ ★

When he arrived in Cade County around noon on Friday, Chase went directly to Ford's office.

Ford had sandwiches waiting on the conference table. Sitting across from Chase, he said, "Just wanted to say this in person, Congressman. If I ever begrudged your meddling, I don't anymore. Anyhow, you've turned out to be less of a pain in the ass than you could've been."

Chase laughed. "Believe it or not, that's one of the kindest things I've heard all week."

"Oh, I believe it. You should listen to my answering machine. Lynching's too good for me, 'cause it's too quick." Ford's expression and tone became sober. "I'm not so scared for me as I am for my wife and kids. Some of these people know where we live."

Chase thought of Ford's family at church. "I'm sorry."

For a moment, Ford simply looked at him. "I'm thinking you're more than sorry. You and Allie are the only people around who know exactly how I feel."

In the context of their sometimes edgy relationship, Chase realized, he had not given due thought to the mounting stresses on Ford. "They're lucky to have you," he answered. "Me, too, if I can throw myself in."

"Why not?" Ford responded. "You're his father."

"How's he holding up, do you think? Allie's pretty concerned."

Ford took a bite of his sandwich, contemplating the question. "Wish I could tell you he was better. But for an eighteen-year-old who's never left home and family, being locked up alone to obsess over how you got there is high-grade psychological torture. Imagine *that* as your first formative experience—constantly remembering George Bullock with his forehead blown off instead of scoping out girls at Morehouse." He gave Chase a curious look. "Making any headway with him?"

"Not much."

"Hope you can. Aside from Allie and Janie, I'm the biggest figure in Malcolm's life. Too big. In his mind, I'm all that's standing between him and a pack of white people trying to inject him with poison."

The bald truth of this remark made Chase put down his sandwich. "Allie said something about how much losing your co-counsel worries Malcolm. Given that he never met the man, I found that kind of unsettling."

Ford frowned. "I think it's more the concept. I'm only one man, and Malcolm knows that there are countless white people out there calling for his death. I think he wants someone to help me carry the load, and thinks maybe a white man can reach jurors I can't. Can't fault the logic, or the preoccupation with race. But the obsession's another bad sign of what's going on inside him."

"Any luck finding a replacement?"

"Not so far. Jack Harper was about perfect—a big white Southerner with terrific cross-examination skills and the ability to ingratiate himself with country folk. Too damn bad he had a congenital heart problem." Ford's voice became sardonic. "That's the other thing. Jack never expected to live all that long, so he was less afraid that some white nationalist would blow his brains out on the courthouse steps. None of the other folks I'm talking to have mentioned that, but you sure can hear them thinking."

Chase could imagine it all too easily. "Will you be able to find someone good?"

Ford sat back in his chair, warming to the sour task of summarizing his difficulties. "There's no lack of capable progressive white lawyers in Georgia with a functioning conscience. But then you start adding whether they're available; jury-likable; qualified by experience to handle a case of capital murder; OK with sitting second chair in the most nationally notorious, racially charged case in sight; and don't mind leaving home to spend a chunk of time in a county crawling with white nationalists carrying military-grade weapons, one or more of whom may be the people who already took shots at the defendant's Black mother and white father—with Dad gaining ground on Mom as a magnet for hate."

As if hearing his own summary, Ford spread his hands in a gesture of perplexity. "In this economy, I can underpay some smart and idealistic kids to do the donkey work back here at the office—looking up cases, organizing exhibits, keeping track of our witnesses. Joe Briggs can help research the backgrounds of prosecution witnesses. But replace Jack Harper at the defense table with someone near as right? Not so easy."

"Yeah," Chase said, "I can see the problem."

"Figured you would."

Finishing his sandwich, Chase stood. "Thanks for your time. And the lunch. The idea of sitting at some diner on Main Street is losing its appeal."

"And here I thought you were a man of the people," Ford rejoined. "Going to see Allie?"

"I was. But now I'm thinking I'll try to sit down with Malcolm."

★ ★ ★

It was strange, Chase thought. Even a few days away from a teenager he didn't know had underscored the changes in Malcolm.

This slump in his body was a portrait of depression, the eyes above dark circles looked like burn holes, and the high cheekbones he had inherited from Chase and Jean Marc Brevard seemed far too close to the skin. He was still doing push-ups, Allie said, trying to maintain the discipline of fitness. But his powers of concentration were diminishing; though he had started both of the novels Chase had left with him, he had not read much of either.

"Anyhow," Chase said, "here I am."

Listlessly, Malcolm nodded. But his gaze stayed focused on Chase. "Have you seen your friends?" Chase asked him.

"Some. But it's hard for me to find anything to talk about." His son's voice fell. "If I told them what was in my head, they'd think I was crazy. They're still trying to be nice and all, but..."

The sentence dwindled, all the more poignant for what was unsaid—he and his friends were becoming different species, and there was nothing Malcolm could do but feel and see the gulf opening between them.

Wondering what to say, Chase decided that it was better to meet Malcolm where he was than to worry about exacerbating his anxieties. "Your mom says you're afraid Jabari won't find another co-counsel."

At once Malcolm's eyes grew keener. "Why shouldn't I be afraid? What white guy wants to help a Black man defend a Black cop killer who posts a video saying Blacks should murder white police?"

The bald remark, Chase thought, was at once self-lacerating, racially stark, and destructive of hope—well beyond the reach of palliative words. All Malcolm had now was too much time to think, twisting his justified fear of the justice system into a psychological straitjacket from which he had no means of escape. Chase wondered if there was a therapist in the world who could help.

Finally, bereft of responses, he said that Jabari Ford had given him a little reason to believe. "We'll find you another good lawyer to help Jabari defend you."

Malcolm was staring at him now. "Will *you?*"

The instant premonition of mutual anguish sparked Chase's nerve ends. "Help find a lawyer?"

"No," Malcolm said harshly, "help defend me."

Chase felt the ground opening up beneath him. Desperately buying time, he asked, "As a lawyer?"

"My mother says you were good." Leaning forward, Malcolm bored in. "*You* said you were good. You put away a white cop for killing a Black man."

Suddenly, all Chase wanted was to escape this moment. *I worked hard to become a congressman*, he wanted to say, *and I don't want to throw that over because you're too desperate to comprehend anything but your own suffocating misery.* "That was in Boston," he temporized. "Ten years ago. I'm not even licensed to practice in Georgia."

Though all these things were true, Chase swiftly understood how hollow they would sound to Malcolm's ear. "I want to help you," he continued urgently, "any way that makes sense. But I'm a stranger here. I doubt that many jurors, whites in particular, would take to a lawyer from Massachusetts who happens to be your father. Even if they could, I've never defended so much as a case of jaywalking. I'm rusty. I wouldn't trust my own judgment in the pressures of a trial like this one even if I *weren't* your father. No lawyer on earth would defend his son on a charge of capital murder."

Across the table, Malcolm's jaw clenched, and his eyes looked wounded. "I've been thinking about this, over and over. Seems like I should matter to *you* more than any lawyer alive. Even Jabari."

Chase felt pinned by his own words, all his good intentions turning against him. "Jabari won't want me."

"Then talk to him." Abruptly, Malcolm stood. "On television you said you wanted to be my father, right? In reality, not just in blood. So be one."

There was nothing left to say, Chase realized, nothing to do but buy time, searching for ways that Allie or Ford could help extricate him from this mutation of instant fatherhood. "I'll talk to Jabari," he said, realizing as he left how synthetic this had sounded.

55

Sitting in the light of Allie's front porch, she and Chase felt the heat of the day diminish in a gathering dusk that turned the guard patrolling her grounds from man to shadow.

"I'm sorry," she said. "For both of you."

He shook his head in dismay. "I felt myself reacting like he was some selfish adolescent asking for something unreasonable, instead of a scared teenager in emotional free fall. But this is such a terrible idea."

Allie considered him. "For you, as a politician and maybe as a lawyer. But not for a son in jail who's always wanted a father." She took both of his hands in hers. "Every step you take toward Malcolm opens up another that is even harder for you. But this one is especially cruel—to him, and to you."

"And for you?"

"The cruelty for me is that I love you both."

Chase took her hands in his. "I care about him, too, Allie."

"I know you do. And the last thing I've wanted is for you to give up your political career. That's what you've worked for, the place you belong." Her voice grew softer. "So tell me this. If I told Malcolm what I just told you, would it really help you face him, or deal with what's in your own heart?"

Chase looked down. "No. I don't think it would."

For a moment, her eyes closed. "Good," she said gently. "Because I don't think I can. When I think about Malcolm, and about this, you and I are different."

He tilted his head. "How so?"

Allie seemed to gather herself. "Because of the decision I made, for all three of us, nineteen years ago. Because I'm his mother. Because for the last eighteen years of my life, Malcolm has always come first." She looked into his eyes again. "I'm sorry, Chase, but he still does. Whatever blame I bear, I can't be part of something else that hurts him."

"You're worrying about his emotional state," Chase rejoined. "So am I, a great deal. But you don't try to relieve that by diminishing his chances at trial."

Allie's shoulders slumped, and Chase could feel her misery for them both. "I'm not saying you *should* help take on Malcolm's defense. I know this is a very hard case. I know it will be hard on you, in so many ways. I know you're out of practice as a lawyer. Maybe I can't judge how that would affect you in the courtroom, from moment to moment, but I know you wouldn't be what you were a decade ago."

For an instant, Chase felt her words as a reprieve. "That's about *should* you," she continued. "But *could* you? I've always teased you about believing you can make anything turn out. But you almost always do, at least when you want to, because succeeding is embedded in your nature."

She met his eyes again. "So do I think you could step up with our son's life at stake, and be better than good enough whenever you're called on to be? Yes, I do."

Chase looked at her intently. "But does what *I* do really matter? Malcolm's fate rests on Jabari's shoulders, not whoever he signs on as his co-counsel. By comparison, the white lawyer sitting next to Malcolm will be window dressing for the jury—as long as he's got a Southern accent instead of sounding like a Bostonian from Harvard. It's better for everyone if I'm sitting in the first row next to you."

"You *are* out of practice," Allie interjected. "Don't you see that you've just turned your argument back on itself? You've just said your involvement as a lawyer won't determine Malcolm's fate. So isn't what really matters most to you, and to Malcolm, all that really matters?"

"Not if the jury hates me."

The faintest trace of a smile surfaced in her eyes. "Do you really think they would? You're not some Northerner anymore. You're Malcolm's father."

Yet again, Chase felt cornered by his lover, their son, and a reckoning he had never asked for. "That cuts both ways, Allie. What do *you* want me to do?"

For a moment, she looked away. "That can't matter to you. Once I answer, one way or the other, it could poison whatever's between us. So could the consequences of whatever you decide."

This was right, Chase knew. But all he could do was acknowledge this through silence.

"I love you," Allie said, "with all of me that's free to love you. But please, you shouldn't stay with me tonight. Nothing we do or say can help either one of us, and you need to be alone with this."

★ ★ ★

"I wish I could say you're spoiling my day," Jack Raskin said late that evening. "But it's too late for that, and this is too big. The only reason you're calling at this hour is that you're actually thinking about doing this."

Chase sat back on his bed, silently acknowledging the justice of this. "I'm sorry, Jack. I know I've been redefining the phrase 'thankless job.' But it's not like he's some spoiled kid asking Dad for a new Mercedes. That was *me* at eighteen."

"OK, Chase. I know he's in a uniquely terrible place, which means you both are. But what he's asking of *his* dad is to give up not just the Senate but your House seat. I don't see how you'd have any choice but to resign."

"Yeah, that's how it seems to me."

"How it seems to me," Raskin responded, "is that resigning would be spiritual suicide. You're not some grocery clerk. You're a gifted politician who ran for office, as they say, not just to be someone but to do things that matter to you and a whole lot of other people.

"Who are you, if not Congressman Chase Brevard? Do you go back to being a lawyer? You left the law as soon as you could. How about becoming a lobbyist? If you can't stand *them*, how could you stand yourself? Or you could run a nonprofit, like a lot of defeated incumbents who sit around wishing they still had real power and feeling like a Xerox copy of themselves. Or maybe you could take refuge in that favorite dodge of failed politicians, 'spending more time with the family.' Only you don't have one, except for an old girlfriend and a son facing murder charges in a place you don't belong…"

"Enough, Jack. I get the point."

"You called me," the consultant persisted. "So I might as well make a clean sweep of the obvious. Even if you didn't have to resign, you're not the best lawyer to defend this case, or even anywhere near the top quartile. At best, you'd look like your judgment completely abandoned you.

At worst, you'd be a narcissist with a white savior complex, risking your son's life out of unbridled vanity and self-regard."

Though Chase had considered all of this, hearing it from Raskin deepened his gloom. "That about covers it. But Malcolm *is* my son, and he's asked me to help him. I can't just blow that off in a couple of hours."

"Believe me," Raskin rejoined, "I get that. But he's eighteen years old, and the pressures he's facing have completely distorted his thinking." His tone became at once authoritative and sympathetic. "I *am* a father, Chase. I've been one for thirty-one years now. One of the hardest but most necessary parts of the job is telling a kid that what they most want in the moment isn't the right thing for them, or maybe for you. The fact that Malcolm has no idea of your life, and really can't care, makes this one all the harder—a parental do-it-yourself. But it doesn't change your obligations—to him, and to the imperatives of your own life."

As often, Chase thought, Jack's advice had a merciless clarity. But, yet again, only Chase would live with the consequences of following it—or not. "I understand," he said. "But just as an exercise, draft a resignation statement for my eyes alone. Maybe, like hanging, reading my own suicide note will concentrate the mind."

★ ★ ★

At nine o'clock the next morning, Chase met with Jabari Ford.

The lawyer appraised him over the rim of his coffee cup. "Doesn't look like you got much sleep."

"I didn't."

Ford shook his head. "Never thought I'd feel sorry for a rich congressman from Massachusetts, let alone one who's fortunate enough to be Allie Hill's boyfriend. But I truly do. Can't imagine being you right at this moment, and wouldn't want to be."

Beneath this, Chase felt Ford's compassion. "So what about a smart Black lawyer from Georgia, whose client wants to stick him with the exactly wrong co-counsel?"

For a moment, Ford studied him. "Do *you* want to be stuck?"

"Of course not." Chase paused "Truth to tell, I want you to put me out of my misery."

Standing, Ford walked to the window facing his desk, drawing the blinds down halfway to block the morning sun in his eyes. Turning, he said, "In other words, you want me to intervene with Malcolm. Tell him all the reasons I don't want you to do this."

Like Raskin and Allie, it seemed to Chase, Ford had a gift for confronting him with unvarnished truths—perhaps because his own choices were so limited, and his motivations so obvious. "It shouldn't be hard," Chase answered. "We both know that I'm the opposite of what you're looking for. But somehow Allie thinks that my being Malcolm's father might buy him some sympathy."

Sitting again, Ford pursed his lips. "Wouldn't be so sure about that. Back in the day, the white folks around here would call what you and Allie got up to at Harvard a premeditated act of miscegenation. Not a popular thing with some even now, especially given the uncomfortable fact that so many of their forefathers did the same thing, only without the consent of whatever Black women they preyed on. And others might look at you and see a Yankee telling them how to render justice on a Black son who murdered a heroic son of Georgia."

Leaning back, Ford put his hands behind his head, gazing up at the ceiling. "But I'll say this much for Allie. I mean to have some parents on the jury, Black and white. The idea that you're defending your own son could resonate with one or two."

"Maybe, maybe not," Chase answered. "But we're only talking about this because a young man who always wanted a father is in deep legal and emotional trouble, and in sheer desperation is making this a perverse parental loyalty test."

For a moment, Ford seemed to consider a photograph of his own son before turning back to Chase. "True enough, Congressman. But the two of you don't have any experience with each other to call on. No surprise he's trying to work out who you are, and whether you mean what you say." Pausing, Ford grimaced in commiseration. "What's such a bitch is that he's in jail facing murder charges. So you can't work it all out over time, going to baseball games together or visiting him at college or sharing a Thanksgiving or two so you fit in the family picture. You've got only one proving ground for that—the Cade County courthouse."

Chase studied the carpet. "I keep thinking of him throwing my words back at me: 'You want to be a father, so be one.' But that doesn't make me the right lawyer."

"Sure doesn't. But while we're on the subject, I finally got curious enough to go on YouTube and find the video of you cross-examining that cop up in Boston." Ford looked at Chase keenly. "You didn't just knock the man off his stride. You destroyed him."

In his surprise, Chase was quiet for a moment, recalling how those moments had felt. "What you saw," he told Ford, "was a case of assisted suicide. Kerrigan's lawyer should never have put him on the stand. That's why I keep worrying about Malcolm testifying in his own defense. If I could do that to a reasonably cunning Boston cop, imagine what Harris could do to a desperate teenager afraid for his life."

Ford's eyes glinted. "You're doing it again."

"What, exactly?"

"Strategizing over Malcolm's defense. As best you can, you try to be deferential. But you just can't help yourself."

Chase shrugged. "It's a reflex."

"It's more than that, Congressman. I can see you remembering the time when nobody you saw was better than you—or smarter than you. Based on that video, maybe all that was true. Anyhow, I know the feeling firsthand. Any day I walk into a courtroom."

"So what you need," Chase answered, "isn't me. It's a white guy from Georgia."

"I agree with that. But two more of those turned me down yesterday afternoon. And they weren't near as good as Jack would've been."

"Sorry. Believe me, I was hoping you'd find someone."

"So was I. Instead, Malcolm went and found someone for me. Even if he's not who I wanted." Ford leaned forward. "I can't tell you about your career. I sure as hell can't decide what you should do about Allie and Malcolm—except to say that it's what makes this particular situation different for me. So, for me, it doesn't come down to whether I want you, but whether I can live with you.

"I don't want to unduly sentimentalize our relationship, but these days more often than not I don't mind you that much. And off the evidence of that videotape, in terms of pure trial skills I could do worse. In short bursts—a cross-examination or two—with enough preparation you might come close to being that good again. That would take some of the weight off me." Pausing, Ford finished in a fatalistic tone. "Bottom line, if for whatever reason Malcolm wants me to petition the court for you to be co-counsel, I will. That puts the decision back onto you."

In the end, Chase knew, this was how it must be. "I've got a lot of thinking to do," he finally said.

"I know," Ford responded bluntly. "So while you're at it, I'll tell you what bothers me most about going through a trial with you. It's the fact that you *are* his father. You can tell me all you want that you'll defer to my judgments. But there's no way that won't get tied up with all your feelings about Malcolm, and no way we'll always agree. If we end up sitting together at the defense table, I hope we stay out of each other's way."

"I don't want to be *in* your way," Chase answered. "I'll let you know what I decide."

56

On returning to his hotel, Chase received a text from the scheduler for the speaker of the House, asking if the speaker could call him at one o'clock. Affirming the time, Chase reflected that he had far more to tell her than she could have expected.

He still could not reach a decision. But the speaker was the one remaining person to whom he owed an explanation of his dilemma. Until he spoke with Malcolm, he would not call Allie again.

Restless, he considered going for a run, then remembered Sheriff Garrett's admonition that this was no longer safe. Instead, he went to the hotel gym and ran hard on the treadmill for over an hour. When he came back, drenched in sweat, it was past eleven thirty.

Ordering a Caesar salad from room service, Chase imagined viewing himself from above—a displaced congressman distractedly eating another solitary meal, preoccupied with a life-changing decision that no one else would, or could, help him make. His only clear plan, a career in politics, had been threatened by choices made without him—first by Allie and then, fatefully, by their son. Chase had sought none of this.

Yet, Malcolm *was* their son, the only child of the woman he had loved most, part of the only relationships in his life that resembled a family of his own—or, at least, someday might. *His* son.

His son, Chase repeated to himself. No matter what happened with Allie. Or *to* Allie. If she fell victim to the worst, all Malcolm would have left was an aging grandmother—and Chase.

Jack Raskin had been right about the politics, and about who Chase had become. But Allie and Ford had been right in another crucial sense: If it came to a trial and Chase resolved to stand beside Malcolm, with enough preparation he could become more than capable of doing his part. He could never delude himself that refusing Malcolm's plea was the selfless act of a father concerned with the quality of his son's defense.

Putting aside his half-eaten salad, he began composing his thoughts for the speaker.

★ ★ ★

With her usual concision, the speaker explained the purpose of her call—her plan to help Chase and, by extension, protect Allie and Malcolm. Though she had always worked to advance his career, what she proposed far exceeded his expectations. The gratitude he felt merged with the pain of knowing that what she had proposed might be rendered irrelevant if Chase so decided.

"It's not nearly enough," he responded, "to say I'm grateful. But I'm afraid there's something more I have to tell you. I've been forced to consider resigning."

"How?" she asked swiftly. "By what?"

As best he could, Chase recapitulated Malcolm's request, Allie's ambivalence, and Ford's straightforward assessment. "I don't want to let you down," he concluded. "I know we've got a paper-thin majority, and that you need every vote. But I can't just peel off to moonlight in Georgia, and right now I can't tell you where I'll come out."

Briefly, the speaker was silent. "Just give me a minute to ponder."

Another moment passed. "OK," she said firmly. "I think I've got the answer. I'll need to talk with the leader and majority whip. But I'm very sure our caucus will go along."

★ ★ ★

It was past five o'clock when the speaker called back and, when their conversation was done, Chase did a brief Google search before calling Jack Raskin.

"You could just do that?" Raskin asked in an incredulous tone. "Just take a leave of absence instead of resigning?"

"Yup. It's been done before. All I need is the support of a majority of House members, meaning Democrats, and none of them wants my seat lying vacant from now until November. For that matter, the speaker wants me to stay on the ballot. So do I."

"How does that even work?"

"I wouldn't get paid for serving as co-counsel, so performing part-time legal services for my own son isn't an ethical problem. When it comes time for trial, I'll have to go on leave from the House. Until then, I can fly back and forth whenever the speaker needs my vote."

"What about campaigning for reelection?"

"No time. I'll just have to depend on the kindness of voters."

"That's not much of a survival plan."

"Maybe not. But it beats resigning my seat or rebuffing my son."

"It doesn't beat *losing* your seat," Raskin retorted. "Voters aren't the most forgiving people on earth. Especially when their congressman is transitioning from dedicated public servant to dilettante with an off-brand family in Georgia. You do realize you'd be kissing off the Senate."

Yet another unhappy truth, Chase thought. "Sure seems like that— Lucy will be all over this. But at least I wouldn't be giving up my career."

"Not voluntarily. So please tell me there's at least some hope you'll ditch your second career, and let Malcolm find a real lawyer with a license to practice in Georgia."

Chase considered his answer. "I haven't quite crossed the Rubicon yet, or whatever river there is down here. But write me up a statement explaining all this to my constituents. Placed side by side with a suicide note, unpaid family leave may look pretty good. At least to me."

★ ★ ★

It took another sleepless night before Chase could visit Malcolm. He had spoken to no one, except to briefly tell Allie that he would decide in the morning. But it was not until seeing Malcolm that he truly decided.

As Chase entered the visiting room, his son looked up at him with a hopeful expression he struggled vainly to conceal. The dark bruise of weariness beneath his eyes contrasted even more sharply with his light brown skin. But Malcolm said nothing, perhaps was afraid to.

For a moment, they sat there in silence, examining each other's faces, so different and yet so alike. "It's as you said, Malcolm," Chase told him finally. "I want to be your father. So if what you need from me is to be a lawyer again, I'll be that, too."

He wished this felt better, more real, wished for Malcolm to help. But all his son said, quite softly, was "OK." Perhaps Chase only imagined, or wished to imagine, the sheen in his eyes.

57

In the dark of her bedroom, Allie lay her head on Chase's shoulder as the afterglow of lovemaking eased through her body.

The faint smell of his hair, the feel of his skin, the way their bodies fit—all these were both familiar and startlingly new. Bereft of light, their sensory haven could as well have been his bedroom at Harvard. But it was not, and with a clarity of perception both wistful and sweet, Allie understood that she had experienced nothing like these feelings between the morning she had left him and the night at his hotel, nineteen years later, when she had given into them again.

At twenty-one, neither had written on the blank slate of their lives to come. Now they had, and so they had returned to each other as different people whose choices had pulled them in opposite directions, even as the son they had begun to share had brought them together to confront his wrenching passage toward an uncertain, possibly tragic, future. She could not predict how this would affect them, save that she knew that what would become of them was inseparable from what would become of Malcolm.

"What are you thinking?" she asked.

Gently, Chase kissed the top of her head. "Other than that I love you? That's always a good question these days. No end of things to think about, for both of us." For a moment, he was quiet in the darkness, and Allie could feel him parsing his thoughts. "Actually, I was thinking about Malcolm. Remembering the expression on his face when I entered that room this morning, neither of us sure of what I'd say. And wondering what I would have said if the speaker hadn't made this a little easier."

"I'm glad someone could. And I'm pretty sure I know what you would have done."

"Please, enlighten me."

"You'd have resigned. That's why you told the speaker you were considering it."

He laughed softly. "Selfless as usual? Good to know. So what were *you* thinking?"

"A lot about us. But I keep coming back to Malcolm, and that I'm glad for what you decided. In spite of all the difficulties for you."

"I know all about those. So tell me about the 'glad' part."

Allie considered how to express what she felt. "I'm glad," she finally answered, "because I'm *selfish* as usual, at least in my role as Malcolm's mother. I want him to have a father, and I want him to have *you* for a father. I know you, so I know you'll care more about defending him than anyone else could, which means you may turn out to be better at it than anyone except Jabari." Her voice softened. "If you had refused our son, I would have understood your reasons. But it would have ended us."

"Would that have mattered so much to you?"

"What do *you* think?" she asked with commingled exasperation and affection. "Who asked you to come out here? What were we doing fifteen minutes ago? Did you think that was just my tender way of saying 'thanks'?"

"No. That was my tender way of saying 'you're welcome.'"

He needed more from her, Allie thought, and this morning he had freed her to give it. What surprised her was the emotion in her own voice. "The truth, then," she said softly. "That was my tender way of saying 'I love you, and I'm so glad you're here that it hurts.'"

★ ★ ★

At ten o'clock that morning, Chase and Allie sat in her living room to watch CNN carry a live appearance by the speaker of the House.

She stood at a podium, flanked by the majority leader, a shrewd and seasoned veteran of countless legislative battles, and the majority whip, a tough-minded Black man from South Carolina whose influence and savvy had made him one of the most powerful legislators in Washington. Arrayed behind them was an ideologically and ethnically diverse sampling of the Democratic caucus drawn from across the country, symbolizing that the speaker was acting on behalf of a unified party. Lucy Battle was among them, Chase noted with interest and amusement, looking like a captive in a hostage video, leaving him to imagine the priceless moment when the speaker had ever so politely invited her to come.

"We are here this morning," the speaker read from a prepared statement, "to support our friend and colleague Congressman Chase Brevard.

"As has been widely reported, Congressman Brevard has answered the call of conscience to stand by his son, Malcolm Hill, as he faces a charge of capital murder stemming from the fatal shooting of a sheriff's deputy in Cade County, Georgia. We make no statement with regard to the merits of that charge. Nor do we minimize the loss suffered by Deputy Bullock's family. But we are aware of the inflammatory, politically motivated, and potentially prejudicial attacks on Mr. Hill by some politicians and members of the media. We are also aware that certain political figures in Georgia have called for the death penalty without the benefit of hearing the evidence at trial.

"We cannot help but note that Malcolm's mother, Alexandria Hill, has drawn partisan ire for her groundbreaking work in broadening participation in the democratic process by people of color, and that her son was participating in that work. We further note that the shooting followed a traffic stop on a dark road, late at night, without witnesses."

"Here it comes," Chase told Allie.

"Within the past week," the speaker continued, "a gunshot was fired into Ms. Hill's home, and Congressman Brevard was fired upon by armed motorcyclists as he drove alone at night on the same road where Mr. Hill was stopped—an apparent attempt to take our colleague's life. Given the confluence of these highly disturbing events, we request that the Department of Justice and FBI investigate both shooting incidents, and that the department's Civil Rights Division monitor the proceedings against Mr. Hill to ensure that the underlying investigation is thorough, and that any trial that occurs is conducted fairly and equitably."

To the speaker's left, Chase saw the majority whip nodding for emphasis, no doubt reflecting his own bitter memory of civil rights workers, many his friends, being jailed or beaten by police; his knowledge of the uphill battle Black defendants often faced in his home state; and how often the death penalty was imposed on Black defendants.

"Again," the speaker said firmly, "we do not prejudge the outcome of this case, or the conduct of the legal authorities in Georgia. But when a matter becomes so inflamed, when the voices of hatred drown out the voices of restraint, when threats of violence become violence in reality, then we must be concerned about the impact on the justice system itself. We all learned on January 6, 2021, how imperiled our legal, political, and electoral institutions have become, and how vigilant we must be in their defense.

"Given these circumstances, Congressman Brevard has resolved to participate in his son's defense, and was actively considering whether doing so required his resignation. But we do not believe that responding to a family emergency exacerbated by the irresponsible behavior of others means that his constituents, or this country, should be deprived of a talented and dedicated public servant…"

"Look at Lucy," Allie suggested, and Chase saw that Battle's eyes had half shut, as if she were praying for levitation.

"There is nothing," the speaker concluded, "in the rules governing this body that requires him to do so. Accordingly, I've suggested to the congressman that he request a leave of absence when, and if, the demands of a pending trial require him to do so. At that time, I'm confident our caucus will vote unanimously to grant that request. In the meanwhile, we extend him our full support as he balances his public and personal obligations."

As she left the podium, Chase felt even more grateful than he had imagined. In ten minutes, this formidable woman, supported by his colleagues, had acted to protect the rights of his son, to engage the Justice Department in assessing the case, and to balance the political pressures on the prosecutor and judge with the uncomfortable awareness that every step they took would attract national scrutiny. And, as a footnote, she had preserved the possibility, if not the certainty, that his national career was not yet over.

"Thank God," Allie murmured. "For all of us."

★ ★ ★

The following afternoon, Ford and Chase appeared before Judge Tilly to request that Chase be allowed to serve as co-counsel in Malcolm Hill's defense.

That the hearing occurred by Tilly's fiat suggested to Chase that, in the judge's mind, the matter was far from routine and that, perhaps, he wanted to make this point in public. Someone had alerted the media and, as before, reporters crowded the benches. In the first row, Allie and Janie Hill waited for the judge to appear, both giving Chase brief smiles of encouragement.

To Chase's surprise, two sheriff's deputies brought Malcolm into the courtroom.

Wearing an orange jumpsuit, Malcolm looked confused. As the deputies led him to the defense table, he cast a sideways look at Chase before staring at the floor.

"Did they tell you what this is about?" Ford asked him.

Eyes remaining downcast, Malcolm shook his head.

"All rise!" the courtroom deputy called out.

With an air of ceremony that appeared to be supplemented by arthritis, Tilly took the bench. Silent, he eyed the media with a squint that, in its traces of wariness and irony, suggested his awareness that the speaker of the United States House of Representatives had put a target on his back.

"As all of you know," the judge began in the refined locutions of a white Southern patrician, "Congressman Brevard has petitioned the court to appear as co-counsel for the defense in *State of Georgia versus Malcolm Hill*. Because of the unusual circumstances of this request, the court has arranged for Mr. Hill to be present. They also require us to make some preliminary remarks."

After scanning the assembled reporters, Tilly appeared to take stock of Malcolm, then rested his eyes on Chase. "There may be a sense among some here," he continued in his driest tone, "if only those unfamiliar with our legal system in Georgia, that this county is a legal backwater insensitive to its obligations of scrupulous fairness to defendants in capital cases. In reality, our state is on the cutting edge in ensuring that defendants in death penalty cases have fully and highly qualified counsel. That exacting standard requires the court to exercise great care in ruling on this petition."

Beside him, Chase felt Malcolm tensing, even as he himself began to feel a concern about where the judge was going. In that moment he realized that, for him, the matter was settled—he wanted to represent his son.

"Congressman Brevard," Judge Tilly continued, "after reviewing your credentials it's clear that, a decade ago, you were an experienced trial lawyer who successfully prosecuted several homicide cases. Even then, however, you had never represented a single defendant in any matter, let alone in a death penalty case. In fact, you couldn't have, because the Commonwealth of Massachusetts doesn't believe in such things." He paused, peering down at Chase. "Any objection so far, Congressman? I want to make sure that I'm not slighting your qualifications."

The judge meant to play with him, Chase understood at once, though he could not yet be certain of why. "No objection, Your Honor."

"Good," Tilly responded, "although I must say that your absence from the courtroom, and your lack of any relevant experience on this side of the table, in itself gives me serious pause. But that's not the heart of things. So let me start by confirming for the record that you're the defendant's father."

Once again, Chase felt Malcolm's surreptitious glance. "I am," he said firmly.

Tilly gave him a sharp look. "So, Congressman, am I also correct in concluding that this relationship is the one and only reason you've decided to renew your relationship to the law—despite the stakes?"

Instantly, Chase perceived that, whatever his racial and social predispositions, Tilly was a smart and sophisticated judge skilled in using his advantages as lord of the courtroom. Slightly muting his air of deference, Chase responded, "Not 'despite,' Your Honor. Because."

"But isn't that precisely the problem? You're not standing with the defendant because of your objective qualifications. You're here because of a familial and emotional attachment, however recent, that could impel you to make dubious judgments in the crucible of a capital murder trial. As suggested by your willingness to set aside your own inexperience..."

"Your Honor," Ford interjected, "if I may speak to that question?"

"Thank you, Mr. Ford," the judge interrupted tartly. "But no. For the moment, I prefer to stick with the real parties of interest. Father and son." He turned his attention to Chase again. "Comments, Congressman?"

Abruptly, Chase caught himself wanting to show Malcolm that he could not be bullied. Then he realized the judge was baiting him to make that very point and, perhaps, to expose him to his own weaknesses.

"The presence of Mr. Ford," Chase responded evenly, "goes to the heart of this petition. He may not have a speaking role today, but he certainly will at trial. As I understand the law of Georgia, the court is required to determine whether Mr. Ford is qualified by experience to serve as lead counsel for the defense. It has. Thereafter..."

"Thereafter," Tilly cut in, "the court has some latitude in determining the qualifications of co-counsel. Part of which involves the defendant's own preferences as to who serves in that role. Isn't that what you were about to argue?"

Immediately, Chase understood the judge's purpose. Tilly intended to rest the ultimate burden of this hearing not on Chase, but on Malcolm. "Partially," Chase parried. "That Mr. Ford is willing to accept me as co-counsel also carries weight..."

"Mr. Ford," Tilly snapped, "is not the defendant in this case. So I won't pause to examine whether he's more sanguine about your presence here than your qualifications would suggest."

Stung, Chase reminded himself of a lesson he no longer had the luxury of forgetting—in the courtroom, the lawyers are ever at the mercy of the judge. Turning to Malcolm, Tilly adopted a gracious, almost paternal, manner. "Mr. Hill, I imagine you may be wondering why the court wanted you here today? Is that correct?"

It took a moment, Chase saw, for Malcolm to realize that the judge had called on him to speak. "Yes, sir." Briefly, he angled his head toward Chase. "It seems like you're asking if I want him to represent me."

For a moment, quiet, the judge seemed to be listening for something he could not quite hear. "For the record, Mr. Hill, you mean by the word 'him' to indicate your father. Congressman Brevard."

Malcolm hesitated, as if the formulation sounded strange to him. "That's right. The congressman."

"Your father," Tilly persisted.

Malcolm looked down. "Yes, sir."

"That's why the court wanted to hear from you today." The judge sat back, clearing his throat. "I'm a father myself. In fact, I'm now the father of a father with an eight-year-old son of his own. So I know from experience that, even under the best of circumstances, the father-son relationship can be a complex thing.

"These are far from the best of circumstances, and I don't have to be a family therapist to know that the relationship between you and your father—the congressman—may be very complicated for you both. No matter how good a lawyer he is, or was, those complexities could certainly affect his abilities to represent you in a capital murder case with the effectiveness you deserve." The judge glanced at Chase, then turned to Malcolm again. "Do you understand that, Malcolm?"

After a moment, Malcolm looked up at the judge, his new and deeply unwanted authority figure. "Yes, sir."

The judge nodded. "In light of that," Tilly inquired gravely, "do you truly want your father to represent you in this matter?"

The courtroom was excruciatingly quiet, Chase thought. Taut, he watched Malcolm as his face seemed to freeze, saw his hands clench and unclench, felt Malcolm's mortification at being compelled to confess his own needs in public, to claim Chase as his father in a courtroom before he felt this in his heart.

Malcolm seemed to swallow, and his response was close to inaudible. "Yes, sir. I want him to be my lawyer."

The judge studied him, then nodded. "Very well," he told the courtroom. "In light of Mr. Hill's request that Congressman Brevard serve as co-counsel, and the congressman's prior experience as lead prosecutor in homicide cases, the court will grant the petition."

Briskly, he rapped the gavel.

"All rise!" the courtroom deputy called again. Watching Tilly vanish through the door to his chambers, Chase realized how surgically the judge had accomplished his multiple objectives: making a scrupulous record; exposing Chase's inexperience; imbuing him with a wary respect for Tilly himself; elucidating the problems with a father representing a son; delicately exposing the nascent and painfully complicated relationship between Chase and Malcolm; and, ultimately, grounding his ruling in the legal terra firma of a defendant's right to the counsel of his choice. But what concerned Chase most was the reaction of his son.

In the tumult of the courtroom, Malcolm slowly turned to Chase.

Nothing happened. Though his son looked at him intently, his emotions were indecipherable, and he did not speak. Instinctively, Chase restrained himself from touching him.

Quickly, the deputies came for Malcolm. Leaving with one to each side, Malcolm did not look back, as if consumed by his own thoughts. Allie followed, vainly trying to reach him in the crush of reporters. The person who reached out to Chase was Jabari Ford.

Resting his hand on Chase's shoulder, he said quietly, "Well, that's done. I wish you good luck with him, Congressman. With all of it, really."

PART SIX

The Offer

58

In late October, Ford and Chase met to strategize about the preliminary hearing before Judge Tilly that, for worse or better, would define the shape of the trial.

In the preceding four months, Chase had commuted from Washington to Georgia with occasional stops in Boston, keeping up with critical votes while helping Ford hire experts, interview prospective witnesses, work with investigators, and supervise three young lawyers they had hired to perform research and assist in trial preparation. He could feel a lawyer's habits of mind returning, and he and Ford collaborated respectfully and with minimal friction. But there were hard issues looming—potential conflicts over whether to seek a change of venue, prospectively avoiding Judge Tilly and, critically, whether Malcolm should testify in his own defense.

The shape of that defense seemed little changed. Despite the efforts of Joe Briggs and other investigators, they had uncovered nothing more about George Bullock's racial attitudes or potential associations with groups antagonistic to Blacks. Nor did the prosecution's case seem different from what it had been three weeks after the shooting: introducing physical evidence from the scene; establishing Malcolm's intoxication; and then using Billy Palmer and the Double-XX video to establish Malcolm's propensity for violence, hatred for law enforcement, and murderous intent in the darkness of Old County Road. In Chase's mind, as in Ford's, race was the thirteenth juror, potentially the deciding factor in a factually ambiguous prosecution.

Chase's personal life narrowed. In Washington, he worked late nights to keep up, occasionally going to social functions or to dinner with colleagues. There was no question of seeing Kara; even had they been able to navigate a path to mere friendship, an awkward task, she had relocated to Iowa for the duration of her client's Senate campaign. His emotions were consumed by two people in Georgia: Allie and their son.

To ease his life in Cade County, he had rented a furnished apartment on the second floor of a commercial building on Main Street, which allowed him to set up an office, cook for himself, and be with Allie on the nights when she was free. As much as possible given the ratcheting pressures of Allie's work, they settled into a domestic routine, at once oddly comfortable and familiar, yet shadowed and often defined by the trial looming ahead. Their future, like Malcolm's, was contingent.

Both worried about their safety. They, and Malcolm, remained the epicenter of hatred for right-wing politicians, conservative media, and the fever swamps of the internet. Unlike Allie, Chase did without security guards, except when he drove at night, reasoning that the specter of an FBI investigation would make white nationalists like Charles and Molly Parnell more cautious. But neither the sheriff's department nor federal investigators had been able to connect the shots fired at Chase or Allie to the Parnells, White Lightning, or anyone else. It was a strange existence, Chase thought, living in suspension in a strange place, with his present, and perhaps his future, tied to the son he had discovered by accident.

When in Georgia, he visited Malcolm often. While his son was often listless and clearly depressed, his weight had stabilized, he had begun working with a capable Black therapist, and he was able to sleep with the help of medication. Despite Chase's fears, he did not crack up: He seemed to have an inherent strength, likely derived from his mother and her family, and visits from Allie, Janie, and Chase served as a distraction that helped sustain him. But he was already changed—he continued to have nightmares and other symptoms of PTSD, and lived in unremitting fear of a lifetime in prison or a squalid death by lethal injection. His days were agonizingly slow—long hours spent in a solitary cell obsessing about, and awaiting, the trial that would define his life, even as he relived the terrible moments that had caused it.

His interactions with Chase were largely uneventful and unemotional. Occasionally, Chase could sense Malcolm feeling out who Chase was, and what they might become to each other. But for Malcolm, Chase discerned, it was hard to imagine a father-son relationship growing in a lifetime of freedom on the other side of a trial for capital murder.

Sometimes awkwardly, they killed time talking about books and baseball. Now and then, Chase would describe his political career—about which Malcolm displayed some genuine curiosity—or would share bits and pieces of his life, including a family tree that Malcolm clearly regarded as existing on some other planet populated by an alien race. Compared to Malcolm's grandfather, a French professor of literature did not seem to strike Chase's son as a heartwarming figure, or even anyone of interest; nor did a grandmother who, instead of serving warm, heaping meals in her kitchen, employed the graduate of a culinary academy to prepare haute cuisine for her dining room table. Nor did Chase's parents, with whom he barely spoke, and who did not evince any interest in meeting a grandson in jail whom they clearly regarded as an accidental human, unrelated to them, who had consumed their son's life and derailed his career.

But the one thing Chase clung to was that, over time, Malcolm seemed to take his presence for granted. Chase was a consistent figure; he kept coming back to Georgia, kept working on Malcolm's defense, kept visiting him in jail. Malcolm had a mother, a grandmother and, well, someone else.

"You've made a difference," Allie assured him on the morning of his meeting with Ford. "He was born into us, my parents and me. You're the one who chose him."

★ ★ ★

When Chase arrived at Ford's office, he found the lawyer watching television in his conference room. "There's been a late-breaking development," Ford said sardonically. "Albert Tilly is a racist. Sort of shatters my faith in mankind."

Chase sat down beside him. On the screen was a dim photograph of a young man on horseback in the uniform of a Confederate officer. "What's this?" Chase asked.

Ford sipped his coffee. "That photograph is from the early 1970s. Turns out that the judge's college fraternity had an annual event called Old South Weekend. They elected Tilly to dress up as Robert E. Lee and deliver a stirring speech about preserving the values of the Confederacy and the primacy of whites."

"Sweet Jesus Christ."

Ford shrugged. "Saved Albert the trouble of slathering on eight pounds of blackface. According to the *New York Times* and MSNBC, that assignment went to the freshmen who served the brothers and their dates at the Saturday-night banquet. At least until their faces fell in their plates."

On the surface, as often, Ford's reaction to racism was laconic and matter-of-fact, its subtext "What else is new? This is the reality we live with." But Chase wondered about how soul-wearing it must be to have yet another confirmation, however unsurprising, of the intractable bigotry against which he fought—in life and in court.

"This is no good," Chase said.

Watching the screen, Ford held up his hand for silence. "A half hour ago," the female anchor was reporting, "a repentant member of the fraternity spoke to MSNBC."

Standing on his front lawn, a white-haired man faced a reporter. "I remember Al Tilly very well," he said in the scratchy voice of age, "and this was in character. The young man I knew thought the way things were before the civil rights movement was the way things should be."

The anchorwoman reappeared. "This morning," she continued, "Judge Tilly released a brief statement acknowledging that he's the college student in the photograph and saying, quote, 'This deeply embarrassing incident from a half century ago does not represent what is in my heart, or how I feel about the African American citizens in my county or my country. Perhaps the chief virtue of aging is the opportunity to outgrow who you were as a young person, in the hope of becoming wiser and better. I understand that some will judge me by my past instead of my present. That is their right. All I can do is promise to render impartial judgment in all matters before me, regardless of politics and, especially, regardless of race."

"Good, Albert," Ford remarked. "I feel better now."

"We have to think about recusal," Chase told him. "It's not just his turning us down on a subpoena for Bullock's social media. It's what I've learned about him. He's a smart son of a bitch who could find sixteen ways to help the DA bury Malcolm."

Ford turned to face him. "Sure, if he wanted to. We need to investigate whether Tilly's done or said things closer in time that show him up as a bigot for life. But I can tell you right now, we won't find any. Upper-class whites like Tilly don't grow out of racism, but they sure do grow more polite. At least in public."

"Doesn't matter," Chase answered. "He's busted in public. If we ask him to step down, he'll have to."

"Go to the coffee station," Ford suggested. "Pour yourself a cup, and we can talk about all this."

Chase did, returning to sit across from Ford. "That photograph is like a gift from God," he said. "Why not use it?"

Ford adopted the patient attitude of a professor explaining higher math. "To begin with, there are too few white Southerners of his age and station who weren't like Tilly in college, and none of those fine people are judges in this county. The three other white men who sit on our bench are just as bigoted as Albert, if not more, and varying degrees of stupid. At least Tilly's smart and knows the law."

"That makes him smart enough to shaft us."

"Sure. But how bad will he want to?" Ford gave him a fractional smile. "Back whenever it was you practiced, how much time did you spend trying to psychoanalyze the judges in Boston? Like, to pick a random example, the one in the Kerrigan case."

"Hours. Days. Who doesn't?"

"So you see where I'm going with this. Tilly's not just smart, he's proud. You see how aware he is of the spotlight. Now this. He knows full well that the media will be all over him, and that every smartass legal analyst on television will be looking at everything he does." Ford sat back, taking a sip of coffee. "I'm no sentimentalist who believes in white redemption, but maybe this is his chance to show he's a better man. So what can he do that we care about most?"

Chase considered the possibilities. "Evidentiary rulings and jury selection. Based on the Bullock ruling, I've got a bad feeling about category one."

"I understand. But at least Tilly will stick to the law, and he actually knows what it is. So let's take jury selection." Ford cradled the coffee cup in his hand. "Under the Batson case, the Supreme Court says it's unconstitutional to try to pick a jury based on race. But jurors in this county are aligned by color. So every lawyer tries to find six different excuses to do just that while pretending not to, and some judges let them do it. The prosecution of those three white men in South Georgia for killing Ahmaud Arbery took place in a county with an abundance of Blacks, but only one Black on the jury.

"Forget what Dalton Harris says about this place being halfway to better in matters of race—if he could get by with it, he'd pick a jury so white it would blind you. I don't even pretend that I wouldn't like twelve Black folks. But the best I can hope for is enough of them to give me a shot at hanging the jury, assuming I can't get Malcolm acquitted."

"What are the chances of that?" Chase inquired.

"A lot depends on the judge and the jurisdiction. In Cade County, the jury pool is divided roughly fifty-fifty between Blacks and whites. After all this embarrassment, I think Tilly will bend over backwards to give Malcolm a representative jury, and I don't think there's another judge around here who will." Ford put down his coffee cup. "If we let this go, we're telling the man we take him at his word that he'll be fair. Short of people like Charles Parnell, I don't know too many racists who won't deny they are one—including to themselves. This is our judge's big chance."

"You know him," Chase answered. "I've only seen him. But sometimes 'proud' is a synonym for 'I won't bend to pressure from outsiders.' He has to live in this place, after all. Off the top, he strikes me as the type who'd rather hold his head up at the country club than look good on MSNBC."

"Assuming you're right," Ford answered, "that goes double for his colleagues. At least Tilly's under pressure to appear race-neutral."

Chase took a swallow of harsh black coffee. "For me, that raises the question of whether we should ask for a change of venue. I'm guessing he'd grant it, for the same reason you think he'd cut Malcolm a break on jury selection. Besides, I think he'd love for someone to give an excuse to get rid of this case. Who wouldn't want to give Rosemary's Baby up for adoption?"

Ford emitted a short bark of laughter. "Think you're right about that. But what are our grounds?"

"Prejudicial publicity. Anything that works."

Ford's look of amusement persisted. "No wonder you've succeeded in politics. Sure are shameless enough. Skip all the fascists out there polluting the legal environment to railroad Malcolm—between you, me, Allie, Reverend Moore, and your friend the speaker, any citizen of Georgia who hasn't heard about this case is in a coma." He spread his hands. "We have to do that, no question, or get buried. But based on your deep knowledge of our state, give me your idea of a dream venue for Malcolm."

It was a good question, Chase knew. "Ideally? Maybe Atlanta."

To Chase's surprise, Ford actually smiled. "Guess you saw a lot of Black folks at the airport. Anyhow, dream on. I'd kill to try this case in Atlanta. But there's no way that happens. If he grants our motion, Tilly decides where the case goes. Under the law, he'll look for a county that is demographically similar, which may mean one with fewer Blacks and more judges who are bad for us than not." Abruptly, his face grew somber. "It's a crapshoot, Congressman. We'd be rolling the dice for your son's life. At least staying here, we know what we've got."

"Which is what, exactly? Other than a bitterly divided community with a toxic racial and political environment and an oversupply of white nationalists carrying weapons who'll wind up at the courthouse." Chase paused, adopting a tone of pointed irony. "Not that it matters, but on a purely personal note, I'm the one who got shot at. And Allie, of course."

"Like I said," Ford responded coolly, "these people know where I live. Not a day passes I don't think about my wife and kids. So, on a purely personal note, I'd rather take this fucking show on the road than have it playing anywhere near them. But it's not my job as a lawyer to let that influence my defense of Malcolm Hill.

"Except for college, Allie has lived here all her life. So has Janie, so did Wilson. More Black people than not in Cade County love and respect the whole family. They watched Malcolm grow up. They know he was an honors student, saw him play football, never heard he was any trouble for this except for the fight with Billy Palmer." Ford looked at Chase intently. "That's the other thing. Most people in my community don't trust the local white cops. Some of them know that Billy's father, Woody, is a racist pinhead, and we can let the Blacks on the jury know about him leaning on Malcolm…"

"Not unless Malcolm testifies. You already know that I don't think he should."

Ford gave an elaborate shrug. "Maybe he will, maybe he won't. Some of it depends on how strong the prosecution case looks once Harris puts it on. Maybe we can lean on reasonable doubt without calling Malcolm. But this much I know: He'll want to tell the jury what happened that night, and he's scared he'll go down if he doesn't. So is his mother."

"Yeah," Chase said resignedly. "I'm aware of that. As a matter of domestic tranquility, I've been ducking the whole subject. But the day of reckoning approaches."

"Not yet," Ford rejoined. "But we do need to decide right quick whether we try to dump Tilly or seek a change of venue." He leaned forward, resting both arms on the table. "Right now I say no to both. I think Tilly will give me the jury I want and, worse comes to worst, that I can hang this case in Cade County. If I'm right, unappealing as it may seem, there's no place like home."

This was the break point for Chase—the place where, no matter how grave his misgivings, he was called upon to subordinate his judgment to Ford's decisions that would affect Malcolm's fate. "If we keep the judge," he retorted, "that means he rules on our pretrial motions: whether we can exclude the Double-XX videotape; whether we can keep Billy Palmer off the stand; and whether, if all else fails, we can introduce Bullock's postings about how Democrats and voting rights workers are stealing the presidency. With Tilly on the bench, I'll give you odds we go zero for three."

"Maybe," Ford swiftly responded. "Maybe even probably. But what makes you think we'd do better with some other judge? Tilly knows the law of Georgia, and so do I. We're swimming upstream on all three motions." He looked at Chase intently. "Here's my version of an odds-on bet: The jury won't hear a word regarding how Bullock felt about Blacks."

"Why not?"

"You already know why not. Beginning with the pretrial hearing, Harris is going to fight like hell to keep Bullock's postings out of evidence. At trial, he won't put on a single character witness, from the governor to the guy who cut Bullock's hair, to say what a fine upstanding churchgoer he was, let alone how much he loved Black people. Dalton's way too smart for that—he'd be opening the door to us introducing evidence on the man's racial attitudes, and he already knows there's a problem." Ford jabbed the table with his forefinger. "I'll do my damnedest to sell the argument about Bullock's postings. But we may be left hoping they seep into the jury pool through the media. Unless we decide to let Malcolm take the stand."

Ford had laid down his marker, Chase understood. Ford was lead counsel—he knew the law, knew the judges and prosecutor, knew how to read the jury pool, knew the ways of the place where he had lived since birth. He would listen to Chase as he cared to. But he, not Chase, would determine the strategy for saving the life, and the freedom, of Chase's son.

When Chase picked up his cup of coffee, he found it was cold. "Let's talk about the motions," he suggested.

59

On a cloudy but unseasonably warm morning in late October, Ford and Chase appeared for the pretrial hearing before Judge Tilly.

Once again, Sheriff Garrett had assigned deputies to clear the path to the courthouse, separating the media and antagonistic crowds of demonstrators: whites carrying signs saying "Death To Cop Killers" and "Blue Lives Matter" or, among Charles and Molly Parnell and White Lightning, AR–15s; a racially mixed crowd, led by a tall Black man with a bullhorn leading cries of "Free Malcolm Hill." Inside the courtroom, reporters dominated the crowd that packed the benches. Allie and Janie Hill sat behind the defense table; for the first time, Dorothy Bullock and her son and daughter were sitting near the prosecutor's table. Stationed beside one of his assistants, a tall and composed Black woman who appeared to be in her early thirties, Harris looked like the Southern aristocrat he was, transformed by obligation into an aristocrat of the courtroom.

"All rise," the courtroom deputy called, and but for the sound of everyone standing, silence descended.

Assuming the bench with a preternaturally grave demeanor, Tilly nodded toward the lawyers. "Good morning, Counsel. Before we get to the various motions, the court wishes to address a few preliminary matters. The first of which we deeply regret."

Immediately, Chase appreciated anew how smart Tilly was—he could see too well what the judge intended. "This court," he continued, "is well aware of the publicity regarding certain matters in my past. We understand, as well, that they may be matters of concern in the present.

Therefore, we are obliged to ask whether the prosecution or defense wishes to request our recusal."

By his manner, Chase thought, Tilly was suggesting that he would recuse himself if asked—thereby placing the burden on Ford. Promptly, Harris responded, "The prosecution does not."

The judge peered down at Ford. "Mr. Ford?"

Trapped in his own misgivings, Chase watched as Ford said calmly, "Nor does the defense."

Tilly nodded, his face becoming an emotionless mask. "I'm also aware, Counsel, of the passions within our community aroused by this case. So I must ask whether either party wishes to seek a change of venue, and to advise that the court would give such a motion serious consideration."

By raising these matters so directly, Chase understood, Tilly was compelling the defense to expressly acquiesce in his dominion over the case. The moment struck him as potentially fateful and, for Malcolm, ominous.

"We do not," the district attorney answered.

With this, the question of whether the case would be tried in Cade County, and whatever would flow from its resolution, rested with Jabari Ford. For an instant, Chase sensed Ford feeling the weight of his own uncertainties. "Your Honor," he said, "the defense does not request a change of venue."

It was done, Chase thought.

It had taken all of his self-discipline not to tell Allie how he felt. But to do so would have alienated Ford and unsettled her still more. Stifling his own emotions, he instead had repeated Ford's reasoning without revealing his own belief—that this judge's legal rulings would stack the odds against their son.

Tilly sat straighter, as if reassuming his command of the courtroom. "Finally," he said, "several television networks have requested that they be allowed to televise the trial itself. The court is concerned that this might further inflame the environment surrounding these proceedings. However, it reserves the option of sequestering the jury to protect jurors from exposure to prejudicial publicity. With that in mind, we wish to hear the sentiments of the prosecution and defense."

Beneath his impassivity, Chase surmised, Tilly himself was conflicted: Gavel-to-gavel television coverage would expose not only his rulings but his demeanor to immediate and unrelenting scrutiny; to shrink from it might suggest that he feared revealing his own bias or inadequacy. Here, at least, Ford and Chase had made the same calculation—both about the judge and, for similar reasons, the district attorney.

"Mr. Harris?" Tilly asked.

For an instant, the prosecutor glanced toward Ford and Chase. "In light of the court's ability to sequester the jury, we defer to the defense."

"Your Honor," Ford said promptly, "this is a case of national importance. We believe that televising the trial will maximize public understanding of its events, including the nature of the prosecution, the defense, and the rulings of this court. For those reasons, we support the request."

From the slight narrowing of Tilly's eyes, the brief compression of his lips, Chase saw that the judge understood Ford's purpose—to balance the pressures from the whites of Cade County with the merciless spotlight of national judgment, exponentially increased by the instantaneous omnipresence of television. "Very well," he said after a moment. "The trial will be televised."

At the slight stirring among the spectators at these first pivotal events, Tilly cracked his gavel, the sound of his authority resonating through the courtroom. "The next order of business is the defendant's motion to preclude from the trial a video by a performer known as Double-XX. Do you wish to speak to this, Mr. Ford?"

Standing, Ford advanced to a podium facing the bench. "We do, Your Honor. There is no evidence whatsoever that Malcolm Hill was looking to confront a law enforcement officer on the night in question. To the contrary, Deputy Bullock initiated these events by stopping the defendant on his way home. But for that, we would not be here today."

Ford paused, and then continued slowly and emphatically. "What a seventeen-year-old minor posted on Facebook over a year ago sheds no light on the shooting itself. To introduce a single inflammatory video, recorded by a third person speaking in generalities, is far more prejudicial to a fair trial than probative of anything—let alone that Malcolm Hill intended to kill Deputy Bullock. In fact, there is no evidence that this video moved anyone to commit any act of violence, anywhere..."

"The court understands your argument," Tilly said in an unimpressed tone. "We read your papers." Facing the district attorney, he said, "Mr. Harris?"

As Harris stepped forward, Ford returned to the defense table, seemingly impervious to the judge's peremptory manner. "*Our* papers," the prosecutor began forcefully, "contain a verbatim text of the videotape. It calls on Blacks to randomly murder white police in so-called revenge for the death of a Black person who dies anywhere, for any reason, in any confrontation with a white law enforcement officer. In short, the race-based execution of a white police..."

"I've also read your papers," the judge interrupted. "That's our practice. Please tell me what the law is."

Harris stiffened. "Intent is an element of a capital murder charge. Deputy Bullock was killed by a bullet from the defendant's Glock 19. This videotape goes to the defendant's state of mind—his intentions—at the moment of the shooting." His tone, slightly lower, suggested confidence returning. "In the Ahmaud Arbery case, the judge allowed prosecutors the option of introducing social media evidence that the white defendants charged with Mr. Arbery's murder were motivated by racial prejudice. By comparison, the videotape posted by the defendant is far stronger evidence of his intention to kill a law enforcement officer. Indeed, it's the nearest thing to a signed confession…"

"By Mr. Double-XX, perhaps," Tilly interjected. "You needn't stretch the point, Mr. Harris. But before I rule, perhaps you should comment on the defendant's motion to preclude the testimony of Billy Palmer."

★ ★ ★

Gripping her mother's hand, Allie watched the judge with mounting trepidation.

"Logically," Harris responded smoothly, "the two evidentiary questions are of a piece.

"According to Billy Palmer, his violent confrontation with the defendant occurred directly after an angry civics class discussion concerning the death of George Floyd, in which Malcolm Hill was a prominent participant. Mr. Palmer asserts that he was wearing a 'Back the Blue' T-shirt to support his father, a member of the Freedom Police Department. He further states the defendant accosted him with angry words about the police, before striking him with an unprovoked punch so forceful that it broke Billy's nose—leading to Mr. Hill's suspension from Cade County High School.

"In tandem with the Double-XX video, this incident demonstrates the defendant's hatred of police and propensity for violence. Both are probative of the defendant's state of mind at the moment his gun fired the fatal bullet."

Stomach knotted, Allie felt the anguish of knowing that what Malcolm would have said about the shooting—that he was being stalked by a racist cop filled with hatred for Allie herself—had no role here. At the corner of her vision, she saw Dorothy Bullock's grim look of satisfaction.

"Mr. Ford?" the judge prompted Jabari.

Again, Ford stepped to the podium, a trim and resolute figure. "Your Honor, a fight between two high school students sheds no light whatsoever on the death of Deputy Bullock. To allow Mr. Palmer's testimony would open up a swearing contest between him and the defendant over entirely ancillary matters—what motivated their confrontation, and who said what to whom."

For the first time, Ford's timbre suggested controlled anger. "I can tell you right now that Mr. Hill's account would be quite different, including that Billy Palmer called him by a racial slur so familiar and yet so inflammatory that—under the law—it's rightly considered a provocation. That the defendant responded to a hateful word popular with white racists cannot—I repeat cannot—be used to convict him on a capital murder charge based on unrelated circumstances thirteen months later."

Suddenly, Allie had a jarring perception: The two incidents *were* related. But the link was not Malcolm's propensity toward violence, but the bigotry shared by two racist whites. Unless Malcolm testified in his own defense—exposing himself to cross-examination by Dalton Harris—he could neither refute Billy Palmer's testimony nor tell the truth of George Bullock's actions. Already, the rulings at this hearing were threatening to enmesh him.

★ ★ ★

"So your papers contend," the judge was saying to Ford. "But, at the least, wouldn't you agree that the videotape and Mr. Palmer's testimony are logically related—as are the court's rulings on them both?"

Ford hesitated—surely perceiving, as Chase did, that the judge's probe was both an opportunity and a trap rooted in Georgia's rules of evidence. "The more telling relationship," Ford responded, "is between the prosecutor's advocacy for these two pieces of supposed evidence, and his opposition to our motion to admit social media evidence of George Bullock's racial and political attitudes."

Gripping the podium, Ford looked intently at the judge. "Deputy Bullock's Facebook postings," he urged, "go to the heart of our defense. They aren't some videos by someone else—or a fight between two high school students with conflicting accounts. They're about the *only* videotape that *would* be relevant to the shooting—if it weren't missing. They're about the phantom videotape from the body and dashboard cameras George Bullock chose not to turn on—in violation of department policy. They're about Deputy Bullock's belief that minorities and voting rights activists stole the presidential election of 2020—and why he chose that night to operate in the dark.

"It's no coincidence that Malcolm Hill and his mother are *both* those things—African Americans engaged in voting rights work. It's no coincidence that Alexandria Hill runs the largest voting rights group in this state—the obvious target of George Bullock's antagonism. It's no coincidence that the prosecution wants to exclude the postings that confirm this antagonism—neatly reversing the arguments he made five minutes ago. Because they're not only relevant to what happened on Old County Road that night—they're the *only* evidence that is. Effectively, Mr. Harris is asking this court to rig the trial before it begins."

The judge's eyes seemed to narrow. "Logically, Mr. Ford, it's an interesting and even appealing argument. But I assume that the district attorney will affirm his view of what the law requires."

Harris stood without leaving the prosecution table, as if the outcome were already assured. "I do, Your Honor. Deputy Bullock made a lawful traffic stop of the defendant, pursuant to the true and reasonable belief that he was intoxicated. As a matter of Georgia law, the only relevant question is Mr. Hill's state of mind at the moment George Bullock died at his hands.

"Set aside that Deputy Bullock's garden-variety political predispositions are shared by millions of Georgians." Taking one step forward into the well of the courtroom, Harris spoke with quiet force. "The legal crux is this: Unless the defense can show that Malcolm Hill was aware of these attitudes, they are completely irrelevant to what he intended when a bullet from his gun shattered his victim's forehead and ripped through his brain. Indeed, these postings are a textbook definition of 'more prejudicial than probative'—given that they are probative of absolutely nothing."

To Chase, Harris looked confident, almost serene—another sign that he would be a smart and formidable opponent. Should he win on all three points, the choice he would place before Ford was clear: discredit the physical evidence offered by the prosecution about the shooting itself before dismantling Billy Palmer on the witness stand, or call Malcolm as a witness in his own defense.

He was counting on Judge Tilly to help him, Chase thought sourly. After all, Tilly knew the law.

★ ★ ★

Awaiting the judge's rulings, Allie saw her mother close her eyes, bending her head in the attitude of prayer.

Folding his hands, Tilly surveyed the courtroom, speaking slowly so the court reporter could transcribe his words. "The three motions before us today," he began, "present difficult questions.

"First, there's whether to allow the Double-XX video posted by Malcolm Hill to be introduced as evidence against him. On one side, it has nothing directly to do with the events of the shooting. On the other, it may show the propensity of the defendant for violence toward police, or to resist lawful arrest.

"The fact that Mr. Hill had his own gun in the car, and that it fired the bullet that killed Deputy Bullock, is of critical importance. I'm going to allow the videotape into evidence and let the jury sort out whether it speaks to the defendant's intent."

Numb, Allie imagined what would soon become reality: jurors judging Malcolm by the words and demeanor of an angry Black rap singer. Instinctively, she looked toward Chase but could not see his expression.

"Next," the judge continued, "the prosecution wants to call Billy Palmer regarding his fight with Mr. Hill. Again, this does not directly bear on the events of June 22, 2022. But it may relate to the defendant's attitude toward law enforcement officers, and therefore to the prosecution's argument that the shooting was not a matter of accident or self-defense.

"The fact that Mr. Palmer was purportedly wearing a 'Back the Blue' T-shirt, and that his father is a local police officer, suggests that this confrontation could have been about more than racial antagonism. Therefore, the court will leave it to defense counsel to cross-examine Mr. Palmer, and to the jury to make a judgment about his credibility and demeanor."

In her despair, Allie saw the judge train his gaze on Jabari Ford as a new harshness entered his tone.

"Finally, Mr. Ford, we take up your argument for admitting Deputy Bullock's Facebook postings into evidence. As Mr. Harris suggests, they don't differentiate him from millions of his fellow Georgians. They certainly don't, in themselves, indicate a predisposition to abuse his authority. But that's not the central problem with your motion."

Fixing Ford with a gelid stare, he continued, "As you're well aware, in 2013 the state of Georgia adopted the Federal Rules of Evidence to govern our criminal proceedings. Those rules call for disparate treatment between evidence regarding the intentions and motivation of the defendant in a homicide case, and the intentions and motivation of the victim."

The judge's voice became quietly caustic. "A decade ago, you could have cited the prevailing law of Georgia to support your position—specifically, that Deputy Bullock's purported attitudes were relevant to his motives for stopping Mr. Hill. No longer. You no doubt believe that creates an imbalance between the prosecution and defense, and the court might even agree. But we both know the law very well, and this court is obligated to follow it.

"Implicitly, the prosecution argues that the late Deputy Bullock is not on trial here. That is the law, unless and until the defendant offers evidence that the defendant was aware of, and felt endangered by, the deputy's supposed attitudes at the time of the shooting. Motion denied."

Helpless, Allie and her mother held each other's hands more tightly. Perhaps Janie was thinking, as was Allie, of the long, harsh, and sometimes lethal history of Black men before white judges, now reaching out for the Black man they loved most.

★ ★ ★

In other words, Chase thought of Tilly, *you're trying to force us to do exactly what Harris wants—put Malcolm on the witness stand.*

But the judge was not through with Jabari Ford. "That's what bothers this court about your motion," he told Ford. "You *do* know the law, and therefore you know that no sentient judge should grant it. You didn't expect *this* court to grant it. But you *do* expect that the men and women sitting behind you with notepads and tape recorders will run to their newspapers, websites, and cameras to let prospective jurors know that the victim harbored racial prejudice, and suggest to their readers and viewers that the court is repressing evidence of bigotry."

Tilly stopped abruptly, staring at Ford as silence suffused the courtroom.

Perhaps, Chase thought, the judge was extending this moment as a warning; perhaps he was waiting to extract Ford's apology. But Ford merely looked back at him with an expression so blank that it suggested an unspoken insolence or, at least, indifference. Allie had been right about him—Ford willed himself to be as impervious to fear or pressure as human nature allowed.

To Chase's surprise, after a time the judge's eyebrows lifted slightly, and the merest hint of a smile played at one corner of his mouth. "So what's your preference, Mr. Ford? In your papers, you suggested that the defendant wants the earliest possible trial date. But this is a capital murder case, and the court has just made three key evidentiary rulings adverse to the defense. Perhaps you want more time to prepare."

The thought had occurred to Chase. But, again, it was Ford who spoke—truthfully—for Malcolm. "I'll confer with Mr. Hill," he responded in a voice so calm that only the slightest edge suggested that anything had passed between himself and Tilly. "But an early trial is exactly what he wants. Until it's over, he'll be locked up in the Cade County jail for something he didn't do. He's innocent, and he wants to be free."

The judge seemed to shrug, a fractional twitch of shoulders in black robes. "I can't prejudge the outcome, Counselor, but I can accommodate your client's timetable." He turned to Harris. "Pending defense counsel's further consultation with the defendant, Mr. Harris, are you content with a trial date of three months from today?"

"Quite content, Your Honor."

Content with everything, Chase read from the prosecutor's serene expression. And so, it appeared, was the judge—as well he might be after the day's proceedings.

"All right, gentlemen," Tilly said. "I believe that concludes our business."

"All rise," the courtroom deputy called out again, and behind him Chase heard the babble of voices, the jostling of bodies as reporters rose to report Malcolm Hill's adverse, perhaps terminal, day in court. As Dorothy Bullock embraced her daughter, he saw Allie clasp her mother's shoulders, bracing her against what both had just witnessed.

Filled with an anger and a frustration he could not express, Chase turned to Ford. But the lawyer was occupied arranging the papers on the table, carefully placing them in his leather briefcase. Chase said nothing.

60

The next morning, Dalton Harris invited Ford and Chase to his office. The district attorney was courteous and calm. Only when he had waved his visitors to the chairs across from his desk, and they had declined his offer of coffee or soft drinks, did he get to the point of the meeting.

"I won't dwell on the hearing," he said politely. "Given the law, I'm sure you expected what happened." Facing Chase, he added, "I know this is difficult, Congressman. Whatever my obligations, I appreciate that this tragedy impacts two families."

Glancing at Ford, Chase felt the buried tension in the room. "It would compound the tragedy," he told Harris, "if my son goes to prison, or worse, for something he didn't do."

Harris' expression remained equable. "I argued the law. The judge followed the law. We can't establish an alternative legal system to accommodate Malcolm's defense."

"The law isn't a straitjacket," Chase retorted. "You've got plenty of discretion about what cases to bring, and on what basis. You opposed our efforts to explore Bullock's electronic devices for evidence of bias, or to introduce the evidence we found on our own. But for that, the jury could consider whether Bullock was a racist who went off the grid."

"You're perfectly free," Harris responded coolly, "to call Malcolm as a witness. He can give the jury his own version of George Bullock..."

"It's one thing," Ford interjected, "for us to put Malcolm on the stand. It's another for you to prevent us from corroborating what you call *his* version of George Bullock. The only Bullock you want the jury to see is a dead man with half his forehead blown off. Seems like you'll do damn near anything to make sure they don't know who he actually was."

Harris sat back in his chair. "I didn't make your client post that video or break Billy Palmer's nose. Seems like you'd do damn near anything to keep all that from the jury..."

"All right," Ford cut in. "Let's hear it."

Harris folded his hands. "Very well. In exchange for a plea of guilty, I'm prepared to drop our demand for the death penalty."

"That's nice. Just what sentence is Malcolm supposed to agree to?"

"Life without parole."

At once, Chase felt Ford's hand on his arm. "So," Ford said to Harris, "a slow death instead of a quicker one."

"We all die in our own good time," the district attorney replied calmly. "I've yet to meet a defendant who doesn't prefer that to lethal injection."

"Then I hope they were guilty." Ford's tone became silken. "I've been wondering how the powers that be in this county were going to jump. Now I know.

"With all the national publicity, they don't want to give Malcolm the death penalty—bad for business. But all of you know that letting Malcolm go free would threaten your primacy in the white people's hierarchy. You figure a life sentence would pacify most whites except for the Parnells and their like, and maybe provide some modest relief to people who support Malcolm but worry about the outcome. All Malcolm need do to help you keep the lid on is agreeing to die of old age in some Georgia state penitentiary..."

"He'd be agreeing to live," Harris shot back.

"Call it living if you like." Standing, Ford stared down at Harris with none of his usual equilibrium. "I'm obligated to convey your offer. I've always been lawyer-like in our dealings, a fine upstanding member of the Cade County Bar and a proverbial credit to—let us say for the sake of polite ambiguity—my profession. But I just want to tell you how contemptible this is. Or would, if I'd ever learned the vocabulary at Cade County High School."

Harris stood to face him. "That's totally uncalled for."

"I wish." To Chase's surprise, suddenly Ford's voice became rough with emotion. "You already know that Bullock was a racist, and probably dirty. I imagine you suspect that Malcolm Hill is telling the truth. For sure you know that the physical evidence doesn't contradict him. But you've got just enough extraneous shit to try and sell the jury on Malcolm as a Black cop killer.

"So don't ever tell me you run a nice, clean office because you don't embezzle money. What you're doing by the book is one step up from a lynching. As far as I'm concerned, you should come to court in a white robe instead of a pinstripe suit..."

"Enough," Harris interrupted. "I won't be insulted. We're through here, Jabari."

Chase rose from his chair, standing next to Ford. "Not quite," he told Harris. "As one elected official to another, I've got something to add. You're looking to pacify all the racists in town by making my son choose between death and a living hell, all for a crime you must doubt he committed. You may hang on to your office, but there's no way you're fit to hold it." He stopped, summoning his next words slowly and succinctly. "I'd quit public life before selling my soul as a condition of survival. But it seems like yours should be discounted for excessive handling."

Ford put a hand on Chase's shoulder. "Guess we're through *now*," he told Harris. "My co-counsel and I need to tell Malcolm all about your generous offer."

★ ★ ★

Outside the courthouse, Ford and Chase stood on the grass. "Never done that before," Ford said quietly. "Just lose it."

"Why not? I did."

"You're his father. I thought I was going to keep you from going off on Harris." Staring at the ground, Ford shook his head. "I always knew that bottling things up came at a cost. But Black folks have plenty of practice, and Black lawyers in this place get even more. Guess this was the moment I got too sick of it to care."

"No matter, Jabari."

Ford looked up at him. "How are *you* doing?"

Chase tried to find the words. "Sick. Angry. Scared for Malcolm. Devastated for Allie. And completely unsurprised by what just happened."

"Yeah, I sensed it coming the moment Tilly started ruling on our motions." Ford paused. "I could feel how pissed off you were at me. There was just nothing I could say."

"You'd already said it—you predicted how the judge was going to rule. I just couldn't help reacting to the reality of it." Chase looked him in the face. "We may have more disagreements. I *am* his father, and I've got my own instincts. But you made a reasonable judgment about Tilly giving you a jury to work with. As of now, that's in the rearview mirror."

Ford nodded. "How do you think Malcolm will take this?"

"Not well. I didn't, and I'm not the one who's been locked up with PTSD running laps in his head. Imagine him deciding on this. Before we see him, I'd like to tell Allie."

"Want me to be there?"

"No need."

"Didn't think so." Ford shoved his hands in his pockets. "I've known Allie Hill pretty much the whole nineteen years you two weren't speaking. So I know how much better off she is with you here."

★ ★ ★

Sitting beside Chase on the porch, Allie gazed at the fields where she, then Malcolm, had played as children.

"There are so many things I'm remembering," she told him. "Bringing Malcolm home from the hospital. Watching him grow. Seeing him love and be loved by the same two people who'd always loved me. Thinking about why I came back here." Her tone became weary. "It wasn't just about all the racists who don't hide what they are. People like Harris are why I exist. They always have been racists, and now they hold my son in their hands."

"What will you tell him?"

"I only know what I want him to say. All my life I've raised him to claim the life he deserved. All that time, I was so afraid I'd lose him." Her shoulders squared. "They can kill his body, or kill his soul. I'm frightened of the first and can't abide the second. But he's not just my child anymore."

Pondering her implicit question, Chase took Allie's hands in his. "I want him to fight this," he told her. "But once I say so, I own a piece of risking his life. So would you. Every day of a trial will be even harder on us both."

"I know. But that doesn't really matter, does it?"

That was the heart of it, Chase knew. "Compared to Malcolm," Chase answered, "nothing can."

★ ★ ★

In the visiting room, Malcolm sat at the end of the table, with Chase Brevard and his mother sitting on each side, and Jabari beside her.

Leaning back, Malcolm hugged himself. "I'm afraid, all right?"

His mother touched his arm. "All of us understand, the best way we can."

Malcolm shook his head, a captive to misery and fear. "I don't want to spend my life in prison. I don't want to never go to college, or fall in love, or have a family of my own. I don't want to never sleep in my own bed again, or sit on our porch, or taste Grandma Janie's cooking…"

"I understand," his mother repeated softly. "I was there…"

"I don't want them to fill me with poison," Malcolm went on. "I don't want to feel my life slip away while the three of you watch me dying through a glass window. I don't want either one of those things happening because of some racist."

Allie fell quiet. "None of us does, baby," she finally said. "But only you can say what happened that night."

★ ★ ★

Watching Malcolm and Allie, Chase, like Ford, remained silent. He felt every moment of their son's anguish, and hers, as his own.

Finally, Malcolm turned to him. "What would *you* do?"

Across the table, Allie glanced at Chase and nodded.

Chase steeled himself. "I can't decide for you, Malcolm. But there's only one way for you to get back in the world. That means trusting Jabari and me to do all we can. Speaking as a father, I'd go to trial in a heartbeat before I let these people make their lives a little easier by stealing yours."

For a long time, Malcolm simply looked at him. In a tight voice, he said, "You mean that, don't you?"

Chase met his eyes. "That's why I came here. True, I love your mother. But you're the only son I've got."

Malcolm said nothing, did nothing but continue to study his face. At length he angled his head toward Ford. "I guess it all comes down to me testifying."

Ford glanced at Chase. "Maybe," he answered. "But that's another decision only you can make."

Quiet, Malcolm looked from Ford to Chase and, finally, to Allie. "OK, Mom," he said at last. "It's like you always told me. No matter how hard it is, sometimes there's only one way to stand up for yourself. The only way I've got is going to trial."

PART SEVEN

The Trial

61

In late January, Jabari Ford and Chase Brevard arrived at the Cade County courthouse to commence their defense of Malcolm Hill for his alleged murder of Sheriff's Deputy George Bullock.

Sheets of rain soaked the ground, and the thunder that followed jagged yellow lighting came so close that the earth seemed to tremor. Deputies in rain gear lined the front of the courthouse and the steps climbing to its entrance, and Al Garrett had cordoned off a section of lawn on each side with a chain-link fence. To further prevent violence, the governor had sent state troopers in combat gear to man the barricades, interspersed with members of the prison riot squad bearing clear shields.

Despite the deluge, reporters and demonstrators filled the lawn beyond the fencing. Near the street jammed with sound trucks, angry whites wearing "MAGA" caps and carrying flags and placards massed with armed members of White Lightning led by Charles and Molly Parnell, some carrying hand-lettered signs saying "Death To Cop Killers." For a last moment before exiting the car, Ford and Chase watched them through the shimmering, rain-spattered windshield. "Some of these people," Ford observed somberly, "aren't from anywhere near here. It's like all the demagogues and haters made Cade County their spiritual home. God save Malcolm Hill from America."

The lawyer looked exhausted, Chase thought. "How's *your* family doing?"

In profile, Ford's eyes narrowed in something resembling a wince. "OK, for now. We've got neighbors with shotguns sleeping on the floor of our living room. I try telling myself that no lynch mob full of racists will come to the house, looking to harm my wife and children. But then I see these people, and I ask myself whether I could save my family if the old days came back. It's the primal fear of Black husbands and fathers." He glanced at Chase. "And Allie?"

"She didn't sleep all night. It's hard for me to watch. But neither of us wants to be alone."

For a moment, Chase thought again of all that had happened to them both, the centrifugal forces of present and past. He was still a congressman, albeit on leave: Though the Fourth District of Massachusetts had narrowly reelected him, the House Democrats had lost the majority— making Chase, in Jack Raskin's estimate, all the more important to the future of his party and, perhaps, the country. But consumed by his son's defense, Chase had effectively abandoned his nascent campaign for the Senate, and he could not see past the trial that awaited Malcolm. As for Allie, the new voting law that retarded voter access had led to wrenchingly close races across the state, including a loss for Governor, accelerating the tension between her needs as a mother afraid for her son and the inescapable pressures of leading Blue Georgia.

"Showtime," Ford told him, and they got out of the car beneath their umbrellas and headed toward the courthouse.

★ ★ ★

Together, they climbed the steps to the entrance between a phalanx of deputies.

As reporters thrust sound mikes from beyond the barricades, a man shouted, "Kill them!" At the corner of Chase's vision, Molly Parnell appeared dressed in a White Lightning jacket and brandishing an AR-15, her mouth distorted with hate as it spewed venomous words he read as, "Go fuck your nigger."

"Sort of redefines the phrase 'femme fatale,'" Chase murmured to Ford. "You wonder what breeds human garbage like that." It was a relief, he discovered, when they passed through security and their footsteps began echoing in the hallway.

★ ★ ★

Entering the courtroom, Chase paused to reorient himself.

It was modern, spacious, and devoid of architectural imagination. Four chandeliers hung from brass chains, and Judge Tilly's raised wooden bench loomed above the left corner, stationed in front of the door to his chambers. To the right of the bench was the witness stand and, directly in front, a desk for the court reporter. Behind it was an American flag, and facing it was a table for the prosecutor, to his right, and one for the defense.

Separated by a wooden railing and bifurcated by a carpeted aisle were six rows of wooden benches, once again packed with reporters and spectators, who now included, as the prosecutor and judge well knew, a veteran lawyer from the Department of Justice. Beneath the paintings of judges in black robes, armed sheriff's deputies again lined the walls. To each side of the courtroom were television cameras positioned to capture the judge, lawyers, and witnesses, for an increasingly violent and embittered nation; but not the members of the jury who, for the duration of the trial, were sequestered at the Winthrop Hotel while not in court.

They waited in the jury box, their composition a tribute to Ford and, Chase was compelled to acknowledge, to Albert Tilly. On the cusp of jury selection, Tilly had sternly informed the lawyers of his resolve to assure that the list of potential jurors from across Cade County accurately represented the race and gender of its residents. The judge had proven a rigorous supervisor: Working from a diverse jury pool of roughly two hundred people, he brought in the prospective jurors one at a time and, after extensive questioning by Harris and Ford, asked questions of his own.

The painstaking process had taken two weeks. The result was a twelve-person jury of eight men and four women—seven whites and five Blacks. There were, by Ford's reckoning, three likely foremen: Stephen Hewitt, a white computer science professor from the local community college; Robert Franklin, the first African American loan officer at the Cade County Bank; and Nettie Gray, a brunette whose precise and punctilious manner reflected her position as chief financial officer of Freedom's only department store. All had sworn that they could serve impartially; all, as required by law, disclaimed any moral objection to the death penalty. Collectively, Ford had opined to Chase, they were better than he might have expected, and the best he could do.

"Never would've happened," Chase had deadpanned, "if I hadn't insisted on keeping Judge Tilly. I could sense his finer qualities from the moment I saw him."

★ ★ ★

Ford and Chase took their seats in the courtroom, leaving a chair between them for Malcolm. From the prosecution table, Harris nodded with perfunctory courtesy. Beside him was Amanda Jackson, a Black assistant district attorney in her midthirties. In Ford's estimate, she was not only able but a shrewd choice: At least for the Blacks on the jury, she would serve as a counterweight to Ford himself and, symbolically, to Allie.

Turning, Chase located Allie and her mother in the first row behind them. A few hours before, he had held her, restless in the dark. Now, however sleep-deprived and worried, she smiled at him. Janie, too, briefly smiled. With Malcolm, Chase thought, these two women, Black mother and daughter, had become his family in Georgia.

Across the aisle were Dorothy Bullock and her children. Ignoring Allie and Janie, George Bullock's widow stared fixedly ahead. But Fay Spann, sitting beside Bullock's daughter, pinned Malcolm Hill's mother with a poisonous stare.

At the preordained time, 9:55, two sheriff's deputies escorted Malcolm to the well of the courtroom. He was dressed, Chase saw, in the subdued charcoal-gray suit Allie had bought to accommodate the weight loss sustained during his imprisonment in a room with one overhead light, books, a television, and a bed. In descending quiet, he walked between the rows of spectators fixated on every step, taking his place between Ford and the man everyone knew was his father.

To Chase, Malcolm looked older than his years. But his face was set with the resolve reminiscent of Allie's at her worst moments of adversity. Touching his shoulder, Chase said under his breath, "We'll be OK."

Turning, his son started to answer. Before he could, the courtroom deputy called out, "All rise," and the capital murder trial of Malcolm Hill began.

62

Ascending the bench, Judge Albert Tilly was a portrait of genteel gravity. "The prosecution," he told Harris, "may deliver its opening statement."

Allie watched the district attorney approach the jury, wondering what impression he would make. In his gray suit, gray tie, and white shirt, he seemed to affect the clothing and demeanor of a serious man attending a memorial service, and the tone of his opening remarks suggested reverence and regret.

"We are here," he began, "because a leading member of our community is dead.

"Deputy Sheriff George Bullock spent three decades in law enforcement. He gave his days, his nights and, finally, his life, to make Cade County safer. On the night he died, he was simply doing his job, as he had every day of his career. He stopped an unknown driver on a routine DUI, never knowing that this was the last traffic stop he would ever make. Because the man behind the wheel was Malcolm Hill."

Helpless, Allie fortified herself to hear a sanctimonious reimagining of the sneering deputy who had trapped her son on a dark country road—a compendium of pious lies calculated to persuade twelve men and women who did not know either person that Malcolm deserved to spend his life in prison, or to die. Her mother, Allie saw, had clasped her hands tightly together, as if listening might become unbearable.

"Only one gun was fired that fatal night on Old County Road," Harris continued, "the Glock 19 that Malcolm Hill had purchased a week before. George Bullock died with his gun still in his holster, from a single bullet fired at such close range, there were burn marks on his face." Harris paused, scanning the jury, and suddenly his voice rose in anger. "That's what happens, ladies and gentlemen, when you're murdered up close and personal—*very* personal—by an angry young man filled with hatred for any law enforcement officer who happens to be white.

"You don't have to take my word for that. Take Malcolm Hill's."

Turning abruptly, Harris walked to the prosecution table, picked up a remote, and aimed it like a gun at a television screen beside the witness stand. "*This,*" he told the jury, "is a video posted by Malcolm Hill one year before he murdered George Bullock."

Harris clicked the remote, and the opaque glass filled with the image of Double-XX.

Allie was shaken again, this time by watching the jurors fixate on a rapper personifying menace in quasi-military gear, a black handgun dangling from his finger, words echoing in the courtroom as he called for the random murder of police. With a twitch of Harris' finger, the rapper's lethal smile froze on the screen. As Allie watched, the Black juror in whom Jabari reposed considerable hope, Robert Franklin, looked from the frozen face of the rapper to the frozen expression of her son.

"*That,*" Harris told the jury, "is Malcolm Hill's message of violence and hate, an X-ray of his bitter soul."

★ ★ ★

"But there's more," the prosecutor said, and Malcolm knew what would follow.

"Barely more than one year before the murder," Harris told the jury, "Malcolm Hill broke the nose of a classmate with a punch so vicious that it left Billy Palmer lying in a pool of his own blood."

Moving swiftly to the easel, the Black woman with Harris placed a blow-up of a white kid with straw-blonde hair, a broken nose, and empurpled eyes swollen half shut. "*Fucking nigger.*" *That's what Billy called me,* Malcolm wanted to say.

"What did Billy do to deserve this?" he heard Harris ask. "He wore a 'Back The Blue' T-shirt to class. You see, Billy's dad is a member of the Freedom Police Department, and the offending T-shirt was Billy's way of supporting him. But it made Malcolm Hill so angry that he sucker-punched Billy before he could defend himself." The prosecutor's voice lowered. "Just like George Bullock. Except this time, Malcolm Hill bought himself a gun. And so this community lost a good man, and his grieving family lost a loving father and husband.

"Now, the defense will tell you that the physical evidence is ambiguous. That you can't tell for sure who fired the Glock 19 Malcolm Hill kept in his car." Harris' tone became scornful. "They may even ask you to believe that somehow this seasoned officer shot himself in a scuffle, shattering his own forehead and imploding his own brain. But you can be very sure of *this*—that George Bullock died trying to defend himself against Malcolm Hill and that, tragically, he failed…"

Malcolm clenched his hands. "*Afraid it's just you and me, Malcolm,*" the cop had said. "*A respected law enforcement officer, and the bastard son of a socialist whore…*"

"And here's something else you can be sure of," Harris told the jurors. "There is no right—none—to kill a law enforcement officer in the lawful discharge of his duties…"

His nightmare was returning, and Malcolm could say nothing.

★ ★ ★

Sitting beside his son, Chase saw Malcolm's jaw tighten.

"The defendant," Harris was saying, "has an absolute right not to testify in his own defense, including with respect to the circumstances of George Bullock's death. But you have no obligation to make up a story for him…"

At once, Ford was on his feet. "The defense requests a bench conference, Your Honor."

Swiftly, Tilly looked from Ford to Harris. "Please come forward, Counsel."

Harris, Jackson, Ford, and Chase clustered at the port of the bench. In a furious undertone, Ford said, "The prosecutor's last statement violates the constitutional prohibition against suggesting that a defendant's failure to testify implies guilt…"

"I did nothing of the kind," Harris cut in. "I'd be happy to have the court reporter read back my exact words."

The judge's eyes narrowed slightly. "What curative do you suggest, Mr. Ford? That the court declare a mistrial? Is that what your client would want?"

Absolutely not, Chase knew, and so did Ford. "As an alternative, Your Honor, we request that the court admonish the jury to ignore Mr. Harris' remarks."

"But in what words exactly?" Tilly pursed his lips, considering the problem. "As a matter of semantics, Mr. Harris is correct. At this moment, I'm struggling to come up with a verbal formulation that doesn't underscore the impression you're trying to avoid."

The judge was right, Chase thought. Cleverly, Harris had implied that Malcolm's silence would indicate guilt without quite saying so. Frustrated, Ford answered, "Then we request that the court direct Mr. Harris to avoid the subject altogether."

Turning to Harris, the judge eyed him with an air of disapproval. "The defense is correct that you're skirting the line. I advise you to back away from it. Please proceed."

Returning to the defense table, Chase caught Malcolm's look of bewilderment. But he, like Ford, understood that Harris had won their first skirmish. His purpose was to intensify the pressure on Malcolm to testify, and his words had come very close to Chase's own in the opening statement of the Kerrigan case. He sometimes still wondered what role his verbal subterfuge had played in Kerrigan's disastrous decision to expose himself to cross-examination.

Moving closer to the jury box, Harris concluded with a respectfully artful plea. "Members of the jury," he acknowledged, "this case won't be perfect. No trial involving human beings can ever be perfect. But the evidence before you will establish a perfect truth: that Malcolm Hill murdered Deputy George Bullock for lawfully performing his duties. We ask that you return the only truthful verdict—guilty on all counts."

With this, Chase thought, Harris had done his job. Too well.

63

Rising to give his opening statement, Jabari Ford walked over to the prosecution table, picked up the television clicker, and aimed it at the screen. "Mind?" he asked Harris, and banished the frozen image of Double-XX before the prosecutor could respond.

"Your Honor," he said to Tilly, "we don't require young Mr. Palmer, either. We'll have a few words about how he came to look like that a little later."

To Chase's eye, the judge's scrutiny of Ford combined annoyance at his presumption with a certain veiled amusement that he was inflicting some modest reprisal on Harris. "Yes, Mr. Harris," he told the prosecutor, "defense counsel is entitled to address the jury free of distractions."

Stepping forward, Amanda Jackson removed the photograph and leaned it against the prosecution table. Watching Ford approach the jurors, Chase wondered how he would begin. They had discussed the opening extensively—including Chase's concern that, by repeating in detail Malcolm's account of the shooting, Ford would implicitly promise that Malcolm would testify in his own defense. But Chase was far from sure of where Ford would choose to go.

"Mr. Harris," Ford began, "has told you a story about Malcolm Hill. It might sound pretty compelling—until you start thinking about all the prosecutor decided not to tell you.

"Listening, you might've thought that Malcolm was out looking for trouble on Old County Road, just hoping some random law enforcement officer would stop him. Truth to tell, Malcolm had been out drinking beer with friends, the end of a long day spent passing out absentee ballot applications to folks who want to vote in our elections. The only so-called crime he committed, and one he regrets, was a mistake known to many of us: drinking the proverbial one too many.

"Far from being some criminal, Malcolm was an honors graduate of Cade County High School who'd never had a lick of trouble with the law. The future that Malcolm Hill was looking towards was not some revenge fantasy from a video, but a freshman year at Morehouse College spent playing football, cracking the books, and maybe meeting a nice girl or three." Ford paused for emphasis. "And the thing he worried about—the reason he bought a gun—was not because he was looking for trouble, but because he was afraid that trouble would come looking for him."

★ ★ ★

Good, Allie thought.

Drawing himself up, Ford focused his attention on Robert Franklin. "Now, most of us might think that helping people vote is the most American thing there is. And that's true. But that's the life's work of Malcolm's mother, Allie Hill. And Malcolm knows that his mother has received so many death threats that she lost count long ago."

Abruptly, Ford's tone became at once melancholy and stern. "It's a terrible thing, and no surprise. Because, like Malcolm, all of us know that the history of Black folks seeking the rights granted other Americans is drenched in their own blood.

"Like Malcolm, all of us know that those crimes were committed by men who chose to operate in the dark. So let's talk about another thing Mr. Harris didn't tell you—all about how George Bullock chose to operate on Old County Road the night he flagged down Malcolm Hill.

"He never called in a traffic stop to the sheriff's department—in violation of departmental policy.

"He never turned on his body camera—in violation of departmental policy.

"He never turned on his dashboard camera—in violation of departmental policy.

"Because Deputy Bullock flagrantly and repeatedly violated departmental policy, there is absolutely no videotape of what he said or did to Malcolm Hill—in violation of department policy."

Ford crossed his arms, looking from Nettie Gray to Stephen Hewitt, both parents of teenage boys. "In short, this experienced law enforcement officer deliberately and repeatedly ensured that he could operate in the dark—that neither anyone in the sheriff's department or anyone on this jury would ever witness his interactions with Malcolm Hill."

Ford's slight smile of scorn was no smile at all. "So here's the story the prosecutor wants you all to make up about George Bullock—that this thirty-year veteran just happened to inadvertently make one rookie mistake after another. That, having stopped an eighteen-year-old Black teenager on a deserted stretch of road, he suddenly developed amnesia about everything a deputy in this county is supposed to do. Because, really, what else has the prosecutor got?"

Watching her son, Allie saw Malcolm listening intently, and thanked God for Jabari Ford.

★ ★ ★

Listening to Jabari, Malcolm felt his shoulders relax.

"Mr. Harris," Ford went on, "didn't even try to tell you that the physical evidence says anything about whether Malcolm Hill intended to shoot Deputy Bullock—or even why or how the gun went off. Because it doesn't.

"So what does my friend the district attorney have left? Trying to prejudice you against Malcolm Hill by introducing extraneous stuff that has absolutely nothing to do with this case—a high school altercation and a video made by somebody he doesn't even know.

"Let's start with Billy Palmer." Walking to the prosecution table, to Harris' clear astonishment Ford picked up the blow-up of Billy's injured face and turned it toward the jury. "He looks pretty bad, I think we'd all agree. But it's the kind of thing that happens after a white boy calls a Black boy a 'fucking nigger.'"

Several of the jurors, Malcolm saw, looked startled at hearing the words uttered in open court. "Yeah," Ford said conversationally, "it's ugly to hear those words out loud. Didn't enjoy saying them. Maybe that's why Mr. Harris chose not to mention them when he brought out Billy's picture. But there are times when a picture is definitely *not* worth a thousand words. Or even two.

"So I'll say them again: 'fucking nigger.'"

Pausing, Ford looked from one juror to the next. "Some of you are white. Some of you are Black. But we all live here.

"I doubt the white folks on this jury think it's OK for Billy Palmer to call Malcolm Hill a name that sears the souls of Black folks, reminding them of all the days and ways that some people have treated them as less than human—and still do." He softened his voice. "And I doubt that the Black folks on this jury believe, as Mr. Harris has asked you to believe, that punching Billy Palmer for calling him a 'fucking nigger' means that Malcolm Hill is guilty of murdering George Bullock.

"It means no such thing. What it *does* mean is that the prosecutor is asking you to end Malcolm Hill's freedom, and perhaps his life, for defending his dignity. God help us."

Ford spread his hands. "What has Mr. Harris given you so far? A rogue deputy. Physical evidence that tells you nothing. And an altercation between a Black teenager and a white teenager who called him a racially charged name every Black on this jury despises, and every white on this jury knows better than to use.

"That leaves you with—what? A videotape."

If only, Malcolm thought, *I had pulled my finger back instead of pressing a key*. He hoped he would not spend the rest of his life, however long, reliving that moment in prison.

★ ★ ★

This, Allie thought, was the minefield. There was never a day when she didn't fervently wish that he had listened to her warnings about social media more closely, or that she had monitored him more carefully.

"The prosecution," Ford told the jury, "has complete access to all of Malcolm Hill's social media devices. But they can't show you a single word by Malcolm himself advocating violence against anyone, let alone calling for reprisal against police.

"Like many other young men of his age and race, Malcolm is rightly concerned about the unjustified shootings of Blacks by police. But Malcolm's own way of seeking change was not through violence, but through encouraging more people of color to participate in our democracy. Through ballots, not bullets."

Ford glanced toward Allie, calling attention to her presence. "That's his mother's way," he continued. "And that was *his way* the night that George Bullock accosted him in the dark. He is not the stereotype of an angry Black man conjured by Mr. Harris from a single video, but an actual eighteen-year-old who spent long and hot summer days acting on the ideals he was raised with.

"All this leads you back to the gaping holes in the prosecutor's account of the only thing that matters here—what actually happened that night on Old County Road." Pausing, Ford fixed Harris with a long, silent look, and then his voice hard with anger. "He can't tell you why Deputy George Bullock went off the grid. He can't tell you what happened in that car. And apparently he can't bring himself to tell you, although he should, that he should *never* have brought this case. For this prosecution is worse than a mistake—it's an injustice unsupported by the evidence, and unworthy of the justice system he has pledged to uphold…

"Your Honor," Harris called out. "I object. These personal attacks are an unwarranted and prejudicial aspersion on my character…"

"Approach the bench," Tilly interjected. "All of you, right now."

★ ★ ★

Silent, the four lawyers stood before the judge. Chase could see the red mottles of anger on his concave cheeks.

Glaring down at them, he said sotto voce, "There'll be no more of this. The next lawyer who commences a character attack is the first one I'll hold in contempt. As for you, Mr. Ford, I'd be particularly careful. You've certainly gotten your own back."

"With respect, Your Honor," Ford responded, "I doubt I'll live long enough to ever get my own back. But I apologize for publicly voicing my private evaluation of what the lack of evidence against Malcolm Hill may suggest…"

"Then stick to 'not guilty,'" the court snapped. "What the prosecutor did in his opening was too cute by half. But you were going for slander." Silent, he looked into the eyes of each of the lawyers. "Enough. Get back to being professionals, or risk being humiliated in front of the jury. That, I can assure you, you do not want. Proceed, Mr. Ford."

With his usual composure, Ford walked back toward the jury box as the others returned to their seats. Calmly, he said, "Ladies and gentlemen, we were talking about the evidence. Or lack of it.

"At the end of the trial, Judge Tilly will instruct you that to convict Malcolm Hill you must find him guilty of murdering George Bullock beyond a reasonable doubt. I respectfully submit that you cannot. That is why the evidence—or lack of it—requires that you set this young man free to continue his life."

He paused for a moment, soliciting through his gaze a bond with the jury. "Ladies and gentlemen," he concluded simply, "Malcolm and I thank you for listening."

Filled with admiration and relief, Chase thought Ford's argument close to perfect—he had implicitly raised the specter of racial bias, and nailed the case for reasonable doubt without committing to Malcolm as a witness. That decision, mercifully, would come later.

Leaning close to his son, Chase murmured, "No reasonable doubt about who's the best lawyer in the courtroom. Yours."

Chase hoped that would be enough. But watching Malcolm's face, he saw that hearing this was enough for now.

64

As Sheriff's Deputy Nick Spinetta took the stand, Chase observed Malcolm watching him closely, and realized that it was his son's first real opportunity to see the man who had arrested him in the darkness of Old County Road.

It was fortuitous for Harris, Chase thought, that the sequence of events that night made Spinetta the prosecution's opening witness. The deputy was in his early thirties, clean-cut and handsome, with chiseled Italianate features, wavy brown hair, dark and candid eyes, and the respectful demeanor of a cop who did his duty and followed the rules. Swiftly, Harris established that Spinetta had moved to Cade County after marrying his wife, Susan, a local girl; that they had two young children, an eight-year-old boy and a six-year-old girl, who were enrolled in the charter school; and that he had garnered several commendations in his eight years with the sheriff's department. He would be easy for jurors to like and believe.

But there was another reason Spinetta's testimony on direct examination would be difficult for the defense, and Chase could feel Malcolm preparing himself. His recurring nightmares and memories of the dead man's face, hard enough in themselves, were about to be refreshed.

Moving to the night of the arrest, Harris struck a tone of professionalism edged with sympathy. "How would you describe your relationship with Deputy George Bullock?"

Folding his hands, Spinetta glanced toward Dorothy Bullock and her children. "George—Deputy Bullock—was my mentor after I joined the department. Pretty soon we became close friends—Dorothy and Susan, too. As far as our families go, we still are."

Harris nodded gravely. "And you were out on patrol the night Deputy Bullock died."

A brief narrowing of the eyes lent the deputy a slightly pained expression. "Yes, sir, I was. Our shifts overlapped."

"And were you in contact with him during that time?"

"On and off. It was a slow night, so sometimes we'd be talking on our cell phones. Just seeing what the other was doing."

For the jury, Chase thought, the answer would sound casual enough. But he wondered what more Spinetta knew about Bullock's movements and intentions that night, and what the deputy might be leaving unsaid. Sitting on the other side of Malcolm, Jabari Ford had begun taking notes, interrupting himself to look keenly at the witness.

"After the shooting," Harris asked, "were you the first person to arrive at the scene?"

Spinetta's brief grimace, Chase thought, would register with the jury—he was a professional but also human, and George Bullock had been his friend. "I was there first," the deputy affirmed softly.

"Was there a particular reason for that?"

"Yes, sir, there was. We'd been talking on the phone, and suddenly George says he's going after somebody." Spinetta paused. "That was the last time we spoke."

"Did you try to call him again?"

"I did."

"How long was that after your last conversation?"

"According to my cell phone, about eleven minutes. George's phone rang and then went to voicemail."

Surreptitiously, Chase watched the jury register that, in those eleven minutes, George Bullock had died. "What did you do next?" Harris asked.

"I called into the department to find out where he was. All I knew was that George said he was on Old County, but once you turn on your roof light or siren, the department can place you."

"For what reason, Deputy Spinetta, did you decide to find Deputy Bullock?"

"George was an experienced officer. He'd made hundreds of traffic stops, busted I don't know how many drug dealers. But stops are inherently dangerous." Pausing, Spinetta stole a look at Malcolm. "You may not know who you're stopping, or whether they've got a gun."

Harris nodded again, as if to underscore the sense of a tragedy looming. "When you arrived at the scene, what did you see?"

"There were two cars parked by Old County Road. George's squad car was parked maybe ten yards behind a white Honda Civic." Pausing, Spinetta seemed to prepare himself to give an emotionless account of what, for him, had been a terrible moment. "I got out of the car with my gun and flashlight out. There was no one in Deputy Bullock's car. Then I saw a young Black man sitting in the gravel beside the white Honda."

"What did you do next?"

"I approached him."

"Would you say his demeanor was calm?"

Ford's head snapped up from his notes. "Objection, Your Honor. Leading the witness."

"Sustained," Tilly told Harris.

For an instant, Harris' expression betrayed annoyance that Ford had interrupted his rhythm. Turning back to Spinetta, he inquired in a grudging tone, "How would you describe his demeanor?"

Spinetta paused to consider his word choice. "I'd say he was subdued. His hands were covering his face, and he didn't look up."

"What else did you observe?"

"When I bent down beside him, I saw a pool of vomit on the gravel, and he smelled like beer. It was clear to me he'd been drinking."

"At that point, did you restrain him?"

"Yes, sir. I handcuffed his arms behind his back."

"Did you also get a good look at his face?"

"Yes, sir. With my flashlight."

There was no mystery, Chase thought, about the Black man's identity. But the moment had inherent drama, and Harris intended to milk it. Angling his head toward Malcolm, he asked, "Is the man you saw present in the courtroom?"

"He is."

"Can you identify him for the jury?"

For Chase, the next moment was like a series of freeze frames: Spinetta turning to Malcolm, his son; Malcolm compelling himself to meet the deputy's gaze; the jury following it from the witness to Malcolm, the twelve faces forming a frieze of their own as Spinetta said tonelessly, "The defendant. Malcolm Hill."

But this was nothing, Chase knew, compared to what Harris had prepared for them next. Glancing toward the prosecutor's table, he saw a rectangular cardboard box beside Amanda Jackson's chair.

"Once you secured the defendant," Harris asked, "what did you do next?"

Reflexively, Spinetta looked toward Dorothy Bullock. "I got up to inspect the defendant's car."

"How did you do that?"

Spinetta grimaced. "The first thing I did was point my flashlight inside."

Prompting him, Harris gave a brief nod. "What did you see?"

"I saw George—Deputy Bullock—slumped in the passenger seat."

"And what was his condition?"

"He wasn't moving." Spinetta's voice lowered. "There was blood on his face. Half of his forehead seemed to be missing."

Ford stood. "May we approach the bench, Your Honor?"

To Chase, Judge Tilly's expression suggested, at most, a weary tolerance of wasted time. "Please come forward, Counsel."

The four lawyers did so. With raised eyebrows, Tilly inquired, "Yes, Mr. Ford?"

"Obviously, Mr. Harris is about to produce gruesome photographs of Deputy Bullock. But why? As we've said before, we're perfectly willing to stipulate to the fact that the deputy died from a gunshot wound to the head. Moreover, the very next witness—the medical examiner—will testify to that. These photographs are nothing more than an attempt to inflame and prejudice the jury..."

"I understand your argument, Counsel," the judge interrupted. "Mr. Harris?"

Harris shot Ford a look. "I'm sure Mr. Ford regrets that his client dispatched Deputy Bullock in so unsightly a way. But these two blow-ups are the best evidence of what Deputy Spinetta saw, and the jury is entitled to see it as well. We don't choose evidence based on whether or not it's unpleasant. Murder is unpleasant."

"So it is," the judge told Ford tartly. "The prosecution is entitled to reasonable latitude. Let's get this over with."

As the lawyers returned to their places, Amanda Jackson picked up the cardboard box. In sequence Chase saw the look of muted horror on Malcolm's face, the stiff attention of Allie and her mother, Nick Spinetta crossing his arms, Dorothy Bullock grasping the hands of both children, the jurors seeming to brace themselves against some dreaded unknown. Briefly, Chase placed his hand on his son's shoulder.

Removing the first blow-up from its cardboard container, Jackson placed it on the easel. Except for a brief gasp, perhaps from Dorothy Bullock, the courtroom was utterly still.

The blow-up was of George Bullock's head. The left side of his forehead was gone, exposing blood and brain matter. His eyes were badly swollen, and there was a red welt on his cheek that appeared to be a burn mark. Viscous-looking streams of more blood commingled with brain matter bisected a patch of soot on his face that Chase knew to be gunpowder. George Bullock had entered the courtroom, horribly disfigured by death at close quarters.

Amidst his distress for Malcolm, Chase understood very well what Harris was doing—as a prosecutor, he had done it himself, using photographs like this to rouse the emotions of jurors. Horrors so graphic call out for revenge.

Sitting beside him, Malcolm covered his face, and a tremor ran through his body.

Facing Spinetta, Harris asked, "Does this photograph accurately depict the condition of Deputy George Bullock at the time you found him in the passenger seat of Malcolm Hill's car?"

The deputy puffed his cheeks, expelling a breath, and then rearranged his features in a stoic expression. "Yes, sir. That's how George looked."

That's how he looked, Chase thought, in Malcolm's nightmares.

In the jury box, Nettie Gray had gone pale. Behind her, Robert Franklin turned to see Dorothy Bullock, his mien sympathetic and appalled. He would never ask himself, Chase thought, whether she was deliberately offering herself as a symbol of suffering and loss to help convict Malcolm Hill.

After a long moment, Amanda Jackson placed a second photograph on the easel.

Mercifully, perhaps, this depicted the dead man's torso, not his head. There was blood spatter on his shirt. But Chase's attention went to the gun in his holster.

"And does this photograph," Harris asked Spinetta "accurately show the position of Deputy Bullock's gun?"

Spinetta nodded heavily. "It does."

The implication, Chase knew, was plain enough. George Bullock had never taken out his gun. He had been not simply murdered, but executed.

"No further questions," Harris said.

65

Apprehensive, Chase watched Jabari Ford rise to cross-examine Nick Spinetta.

Turning to Harris, Ford said, "I won't be needing your photographs."

Harris glanced up at the judge, who nodded. As Amanda Jackson stepped forward to remove the photographs, Chase could feel Malcolm's relief, and his own.

Approaching Spinetta, Ford began his questioning in the conversational manner of someone who expected an honest law enforcement officer to give honest answers—no matter the circumstances.

"When you arrived at the scene, Deputy Spinetta, did Malcolm Hill resist arrest?"

The deputy glanced of Malcolm. "He did not."

"Did he try to run away?"

"No. He hardly moved."

Ford angled his head. "Sounds like he was in shock."

"I'm not a doctor, Mr. Ford. So I can't really say."

"Would you say that Malcolm seemed stunned?"

Spinetta placed a finger to his lips. "I guess that's fair. Of course, he'd been drinking and thrown up. I don't exactly know what you call that, except inebriated."

"Did Malcolm say anything?"

"Yes," the deputy responded dismissively. "He said to me, 'It was an accident.'"

Ford stood straighter. "Did you report that to anyone?"

"Yes. That night. I told the investigators from the GBI."

"Ever tell anyone else?"

"Sheriff Garrett." Spinetta glanced toward the district attorney. "And Mr. Harris."

Chase watched Ford consider another question, and then decide to change tack. "By the way, Deputy Spinetta, were the headlights on Malcolm Hill's car on or off?"

"They were off."

"Do you know who'd turned them off?"

Spinetta gave him a puzzled look. "I assumed that the defendant had."

"You assumed," Ford repeated. "So it's also possible that Deputy Bullock turned off Malcolm's headlights."

"It's possible. But I don't know why he would."

"What about Deputy Bullock's headlights?"

Spinetta frowned in thought. "They were off."

"And his roof lights?"

"Off."

Leaning close to Malcolm, Chase murmured, "This is good."

"What about your headlights?" Ford asked Spinetta. "Were they on or off?"

"I kept them on."

"For what reason?"

"I didn't know what was happening out there. I needed to see whatever I could."

Ford crossed his arms. "Let me see if I get the picture here. It was a dark night with a quarter moon. On that stretch of Old County, there aren't any streetlights or houses around. The headlights on Malcolm Hill's car were turned off, and every light of Deputy Bullock's squad car. So until you showed up, it must've been pretty dark out there."

"It was."

"In fact, isn't it fair to say that the area around the two cars was pitch black?"

For the first time, Spinetta looked unsettled. "I guess that's fair."

On the bench, Chase noticed, Judge Tilly followed the questioning with a look of keen interest. "To summarize," Ford continued, "the only illumination in sight came from your squad car. Is that correct?"

"Objection," Harris called out. "Asked and answered."

"Overruled," the judge said promptly. "You may answer, Deputy Spinetta."

Spinetta turned back to Ford. "That's right."

"Who do you suppose turned off George Bullock's headlights?"

The deputy hesitated. "I don't know."

Ford smiled a little. "Seems like you've only got two choices. Think Malcolm Hill did that?"

"Not really, no."

"Doesn't seem very logical, does it, to think that Malcolm got out of the car, threw up, got to his feet, went to Deputy Bullock's squad car, turned off the headlights, went back to his car, sat down beside it, and commenced looking—as you put it—stunned."

"Objection!" Harris snapped. "Calls for speculation."

Instantly, Chase thought this a mistake—when the opposition is doing damage to your witness, the better course, more often than not, is to look like nothing is happening. "Overruled," the judge said again.

"No," Spinetta answered slowly. "That doesn't seem logical."

"So the logical conclusion is that Deputy Bullock turned off his own headlights. Seem right to you?"

"Yes."

In the jury box, Chase saw, Stephen Hewitt was taking notes again.

"When you make a nighttime traffic stop," Ford asked, "do you keep your headlights on or off?"

"On."

"Ever turn them off?"

"No."

"Because you want to see what's around you?"

"Yes."

"What about your roof lights, the blue flashers?"

"I keep them on."

"For the same reason—seeing better?"

Again, Spinetta nodded, and Chase saw him become caught in the rhythm of Ford's questioning. "Yes. Same reason."

Ford cocked his head. "Is another reason that, in case of trouble, you want other law enforcement officers to see you?"

Spinetta hesitated. "That's true."

"And you also want those officers to see what's around them when they arrive at the scene."

"Yes."

"To your knowledge, did Deputy Bullock make a practice of turning off his headlights during nighttime traffic stops?"

Spinetta paused again. "I don't have any reason to think he was any different than the rest of us."

"When you assess the situation as potentially dangerous, do you sometimes call for backup?"

"Sure."

"Did Deputy Bullock call for backup that night?"

"No."

"Did you ever have any occasion to provide backup for Deputy Bullock during a nighttime stop?"

"Several."

"Were his headlights always on?"

"As far as I remember, yes."

Ford placed his hands on his hips. "Can you think of any reason why Deputy Bullock wanted to turn off his headlights after stopping Malcolm Hill?"

Spinetta spread his hands. "I can't."

"No? Could it be that Deputy Bullock didn't want anyone to see what he was about to do?"

"Your Honor," Harris interjected. "I really must object. This question only calls for speculation, but it insinuates something for which there is no foundation in the record."

Tilly thought for a moment. "Sustained."

Unruffled, Ford contemplated the witness. "After Al Garrett became sheriff, did he establish departmental policies with respect to the use of body and dashboard cameras?"

"Yes. We were supposed to turn both cameras on before any interaction with the public."

"Does that include traffic stops—day or night?"

"Especially. Those come with the increased possibility of incidents or conflict. The sheriff also uses the videos from dashboard or body cameras to ensure that we're conducting ourselves appropriately."

"Do those policies also relate to the fact that, to provide more coverage of the county, deputies go out on patrol by themselves?"

"Yes."

Ford nodded briskly. "So those videos are the only way the sheriff can know whether his deputies are behaving in an appropriate and lawful manner."

"That's correct."

"Are there any exceptions to those policies?"

"None. Sheriff Garrett has been very clear about that."

"And is one of his concerns to ensure that there are no abuses of authority related to race?"

For an instant, Spinetta looked toward Malcolm. "Yes."

"Since those policies were instituted, have you always turned on your body and dashboard cameras before stopping a motorist?"

"I have."

Steepling his fingers, Ford gave Spinetta a sharp look. "On the night in question, did Deputy Bullock turn on his dashboard camera?"

Spinetta slowly shook his head. "When I got there, it was off."

"And when you found Deputy Bullock in the passenger seat of Malcolm's car, was his body camera on or off?"

"Off."

"Is it also departmental policy for a deputy to call in a traffic stop to headquarters?"

As if abashed, Spinetta looked down. "Yes."

Ford stepped closer. "But he didn't do that either, did he?"

"No."

Spinetta, Chase noticed, had begun answering in monosyllables—less out of hostility, it seemed, than reluctance. "Do *you* always call in traffic stops?" Ford asked.

"Yes."

"Do you have any information as to whether, before the stop, Deputy Bullock knew that the driver was Malcolm Hill?"

"I don't."

"Do you know whether Deputy Bullock had been following Malcolm?"

"Again, I don't."

"You don't know one way or the other."

Spinetta seemed to hesitate. "No."

"*He was,*" Malcolm whispered urgently.

"At any time in your relationship," Ford asked Spinetta, "did Deputy Bullock ever mention the name Malcolm Hill?"

The witness seemed to squint. After a moment, he said, "I don't recall him doing so."

Ford's tone sharpened. "What about Malcolm's mother, Allie Hill?"

Swiftly, Harris stood. "Objection, Your Honor. I request permission to approach the bench."

As Chase rose to join the bench conference, Malcolm tugged his sleeve. "You know what he said about her."

"I do," Chase whispered. "But there's a problem."

When Chase reached the bench, Harris was addressing the judge. "You've already ruled on this, Your Honor. This goes to George Bullock's political beliefs. Unless the defense can establish that Malcolm Hill was aware of them at the time of the shooting, they're irrelevant."

"Your Honor," Ford shot back, "we've just established that Bullock violated departmental policy six different ways, all to get Malcolm alone in the dark. What else do we have to do to make *his* intentions relevant?"

The judge pursed his lips. "Unfortunately for you, Mr. Ford, establish a predicate in the mind of Malcolm Hill. Maybe you will, perhaps through his testimony. Until you do, this line of questioning is out of bounds under our rules of evidence." He leaned forward. "You've done a very nice job of hijacking Mr. Harris' witness to drive home your point. But for now you're just going to have to make your argument by inference. Objection sustained."

It was the first day of trial, Chase thought, and already the pressure on Malcolm to testify was building. Including within Malcolm himself.

Once more, Ford approached the witness. "Are you aware of any other instances in which, by violating departmental policy, Deputy Bullock went off the grid—in other words, eluded supervision?"

Spinetta's gaze seem to turn inward, as if he were troubled. "Seems like there's already an answer in your question, Mr. Ford. If any deputy wants to avoid supervision, it would be pretty hard to know."

"Including during drug busts?"

"Objection," Harris said loudly. "No foundation. Completely irrelevant. And, I might add, needlessly insinuating."

Tilly leaned forward. "Sustained. Mr. Ford, move on."

Ford put his hands in his pockets. "During your eight-year friendship with Deputy Bullock," he asked Spinetta, "did you form any impression of his attitude toward Blacks?"

"*Objection.*"

"Sustained," the judge said harshly. "You're right on the edge, Counselor. Do not take another step."

For what seemed to Chase a dangerously long time, Ford gazed back at the judge without responding. Then he turned back to the witness.

"Let's return to the night in question, Deputy Spinetta. You found Deputy Bullock in the passenger seat. Was there anything else in that seat?"

"Yes. Absentee ballot applications."

Ford gave him a curious look. "Was it departmental policy for deputies to approach motorists from the driver's side?"

"Yes."

"Did it strike you as unusual to find Deputy Bullock on the passenger side?"

"I don't know. I don't know how he got there, or why."

"Do you have information about why or how the defendant's gun went off?"

Spinetta shook his head. "If you mean do I know what happened in the car, I don't."

Ford moved closer yet. "In other words, you don't have any factual basis for contradicting Malcolm Hill's statement that the shooting was an accident."

"I know that George never took out his gun," Spinetta rejoined.

"That wasn't my question," Ford responded. "So let me repeat it. Do you have any factual information that would contradict Malcolm Hill spontaneous statement to you that the shooting was an accident?"

Spinetta gazed up at him. "No," he said finally. "I don't."

Pausing, Ford let the answer linger in the courtroom. "Thank you, Deputy Spinetta. No further questions."

With that, Chase judged, Ford had done all the damage anyone could.

★ ★ ★

As Harris stood, Chase watched him make a critical calculation of whether attempting to extract extenuating circumstances from the witness was riskier than asking a few brief questions.

"In your experience, Deputy Spinetta, despite departmental policy, do deputies sometimes forget to turn on their body or dashboard cameras, or call in the stop?"

Spinetta seemed to relax. "It still happens."

"In your observation, do those three things tend to happen together?"

"They can. Typically, it's because of excitement—a deputy too caught up in the moment. Sometimes things happen fast, and when it's night you're a little more on edge. We have a lot of drug dealers coming through the county, and they can be pretty dangerous."

Harris nodded. "In those moments, can that kind of adrenaline rush happen even to experienced deputies?"

"It can," Spinetta affirmed. "No matter how long you do this work, I've never seen anyone stop having nerves."

Harris stopped to consider his next question. "With respect to Malcolm Hill, you said that he seemed to be intoxicated."

"Clearly."

"Would stopping an intoxicated driver seem urgent to a reasonable deputy?"

"Yeah, it would. You don't want impaired motorists endangering other people's lives. Or their own."

"Would you say that stopping intoxicated motorists is an important part of your job?"

"I would."

"One last question, then," Harris said sternly. "Does an intoxicated motorist have any right whatsoever to refuse to comply with a lawful order, or to resist a lawful arrest?"

"No one does." Looking toward Malcolm, Spinetta responded in a tone that struck Chase as almost elegiac. "That's the kind of behavior that makes our job so dangerous. It's how law enforcement officers wind up dead."

66

The second prosecution witness was a lean man in his midfifties, with graying ginger hair and beard, clear blue eyes, a professorial manner, and a pleasingly soft Irish accent that lent a further air of erudition. Watching him take the stand, Chase felt Malcolm tense at the prospect of more photographs.

Once again, cameras from the three major cable news channels broadcast the trial. Again, Dorothy Bullock and her children were in the first row of spectators—determined, it seemed to Chase, to personify their pain for the jury. But Allie and her mother were focused intently on Malcolm, as if wishing they could protect him.

"Can you identify yourself for the record?" Harris asked the witness.

"I'm Dr. Steven Connell, a medical examiner for the Georgia Bureau of Investigation."

"Thank you, Dr. Connell. Could you summarize your professional background?"

Not if the defense could help it, Chase thought—it was self-defeating to challenge the superior credentials of the prosecution experts, particularly Connell, or to let Harris dwell on them.

Casually, Ford interjected: "Your Honor, we are familiar with Dr. Connell and will stipulate to his qualifications as a pathologist."

"I think that should save time," Judge Tilly told Harris. "Why don't you proceed?"

Harris gave Ford a quick, knowing glance before turning back to the witness. "Dr. Connell, did you perform the autopsy on Sheriff's Deputy George Bullock?"

"I did."

"Could you describe for the jury the steps you took prior to conducting the autopsy?"

"Certainly." Turning to the jurors, Connell spoke in the pleasantly dispassionate manner of a professional accustomed to clarifying his scientific process for laypeople. "Before the autopsy itself, I examined the body with respect to the gunshot wound; burns or gunpowder on his face, hands, or clothing; and any other injuries that might indicate a struggle—bruised knuckles, broken nails, or scratches on his face or hands. In the course of doing so, I also photographed Deputy Bullock's head, face, and uniform."

Already, Chase noticed, the respectful demeanor of the jurors was mixed with a wary anticipation of graphic and unpleasant testimony. Reflexively, Nettie Gray glanced toward the empty easel beside the witness stand.

"With respect to the autopsy itself," Harris asked Connell, "what was your process for determining the cause of death?"

"I extracted a bullet from Deputy Bullock's skull. Further, I determined the trajectory and pathway of the bullet, as well as the approximate range of fire. As an ancillary matter, I also determined that there were no drugs or alcohol in his system that might have reflected impaired judgment or increased belligerence."

"In your professional opinion, what caused Deputy Bullock's death?"

Again, Connell faced the jury. "A single gunshot wound to the head from close range, resulting in severe damage to the brain."

"In the course of that determination, did you take digital photographs of the injuries to Deputy Bullock?"

"I did."

"What was your purpose in doing so?"

"To depict the wound, as well as the process through which I determined the cause of death. In my experience, a merely verbal description does not suffice."

Certainly not for the prosecution, Chase thought. There was no dispute as to the cause of death. But for Harris, there was also no substitute for graphic photographs of the damage to Bullock's head.

Briefly, Harris nodded to Amanda Jackson before facing the witness. "In preparing for your testimony, Dr. Connell, did you compare your photographs to the enlargements prepared by this office as trial exhibits?"

"I did, Mr. Harris. The enlargements accurately depict my original photographs."

★ ★ ★

Malcolm braced himself against nausea.

As the courtroom waited in collective silence, Jackson mounted a blow-up of George Bullock's face and head. Malcolm flinched. The enlargement was in close-up—shattered forehead; exposed brain tissue; lifeless, swollen eyes; burn marks; gunpowder; spatters of bone and brain matter on his face. Once more, someone gasped. A woman, Malcolm thought—maybe a juror, maybe Bullock's wife.

Standing to the side of the easel, Harris positioned himself to question the witness while focusing attention on the photograph. "What, if anything, Dr. Connell, did you conclude from the nature of the wound?"

The witness turned to the easel. "I noted the jagged edges of the skin around the wound. That indicates an angled shot. So does the damage to the skull, which is far more substantial than one caused from a straight shot to the forehead."

Malcolm looked away, remembering the terrible moment of struggle, the percussive pop, the man's ruined head. Even now, he did not know how the gun had gone off. But these people were making him sound like he was a killer determined to do the damage the jury saw now—never knowing that he was more sickened than they ever could be.

"Did you reach any other conclusions, Dr. Connell?"

"Yes," the pathologist responded in the same quiet tone. "The burn marks indicate a gun fired at close range, approximately four to six inches away. What appears to be soot is actually gunshot residue expelled from the gun itself. This also tells us that, upon firing, the gun was very close to Deputy Bullock's head." Turning to the jury, he added, "The swollen eyes reflect massive damage to the brain—as does the blood, brain matter, and bone fragments spattered on his face. All of that goes to the cause of death."

Malcolm could feel the awful silence in the courtroom, focused on a dead man with a shattered forehead and ruined brain, even as a television camera turned to capture his expression. He caught Chase glancing at him. "I'll be OK," he whispered. But he felt his stomach twitching, like when he'd thrown up beside the car.

Amanda Jackson came forward and replaced the enlargement with another.

This showed what appeared to be a metal rod stuck into the wound itself, a final indignity of death. Pointing toward the rod, Harris asked, "Can you explain to the jury what this photograph demonstrates?"

"Yes." The witness adjusted his tie, contemplating the disturbing image. "I inserted a metal probe through the bullet hole. As you see, the part that is still exposed points downwards from the wound. That indicates that the bullet traveled in an upward trajectory, from the right side of the deputy's head through the brain to the left side of his skull—the location from which I extracted it."

"Earlier in your testimony, Dr. Connell, you said that you closely examined the body for signs of a struggle. What did you find?"

Connell seemed to pause for a moment, as if to underscore the import of his answer. "Nothing," he responded incisively. "No broken fingernails. No bruises or scratches on the victim's face or hands. While there was gunshot residue on the victim's hands, that could simply reflect a gun fired at short range—or that the deputy was reaching out in an unsuccessful effort to defend himself."

Harris nodded his satisfaction. "In sum, Doctor, you found no evidence that affirmatively supports an accidental death—specifically, the assertion that the gun went off in a struggle between Deputy Bullock and the defendant."

"None."

Listening, Malcolm felt paralyzed. He did not have to be a doctor to understand what Harris was insinuating: that there had been no struggle—simply an act of murder, carried out at close range by a Black man with hatred in his heart.

"No further questions," Harris said.

★ ★ ★

Sitting with Janie, Allie watched Jabari Ford approach the witness. This time he did not ask that the photographs be removed.

"Let's get to it, Dr. Connell. You have no idea how that gun came to be fired, do you?"

Connell hesitated. "Not literally, no. An autopsy can't tell you that. But I did testify to the absence of definitive evidence that there was a struggle for the gun."

Ford frowned. "I'd like to deconstruct that answer. First, when you say 'not literally,' you're really saying that you don't know how that gun came to be fired."

"That's right. I can't know."

"OK. When you talk about 'the absence of definitive evidence,' do you mean that you found no evidence that *could* support a struggle for the weapon?"

The witness paused to consider the question. "Are you asking about the gunshot residue on Deputy Bullock's hands?"

"Seems like a good start. Isn't it true that the deputy could have gotten GSR on his hands because he was grappling for the weapon?"

Tense, Allie awaited Connell's answer. "Yes," he conceded, "that's one possibility."

Ford walked over to the easel. "So these photographs, however horrific, tell the jury nothing about whether the shooting was accidental or deliberate."

"Not in themselves, no."

Now Ford moved from the easel to an angle that compelled Connell to face the jury. "Nor can you, Dr. Connell, tell the twelve men and women charged with judging Malcolm Hill whether this was a murder or an accident."

After a moment, Connell faced the jury. "No," he answered. "I cannot."

★ ★ ★

After the trial adjourned for the day, Ford and Chase returned to the office to plan for the next prosecution witnesses.

Before doing so, they took a half hour to scan the three cable news channels. The trial led every newscast. The legal analysts on CNN and MSNBC complimented Ford's performance; the lead commentator on Fox accused Ford of "not just using the race card, but dealing the whole deck."

"You did a nice job on Connell," Chase said. "No matter what Fox says about you."

Settling into a chair, Ford shrugged. "Just got the man to admit the obvious—like with Spinetta, he wasn't there. Truth is, the only person alive who knows what happened is Malcolm. This is really getting to him, isn't it?"

"Yeah," Chase acknowledged. "While you're up there, I'm sitting with him. He's being forced to relive what happened, and watch Harris twist it, without being able to say a word. But that doesn't mean we should put him on the stand."

Ford gave him a skeptical look. "If we don't, who are our witnesses?"

Chase prepared himself for an argument. "The ones Harris is putting on. We've got more of them to go, but so far you're two for two. Based on Spinetta and Connell, I don't think a sane juror could get past reasonable doubt."

"I agree with that. But Harris is going to conclude with Billy Palmer and the videotape. Things could look a good bit different then."

"Maybe," Chase allowed. "There's nothing much we can do about Mr. Double-XX. But I think we can put a dent in Billy. Malcolm says the kid's no genius."

"Not sure he needs to be. Who's prosecution's most important expert?"

Chase considered this. "The ballistics guy, probably. Depending on what he says, he could make an accidental shooting harder to sell."

Ford smiled a little. "You want to take him? Trying homicides, you must've seen a lot of these people."

At once, Chase was jolted. A deep part of him shrank from standing up in court after ten years, in front of Allie, Malcolm, and the world, to shoulder some part of the responsibility for saving Malcolm. But he could not ask Ford to cross-examine every prosecution witness—he had far too much to do.

"If that's the best way I can help you," Chase answered.

Ford gave him a long look of comprehension. "I know this isn't easy," he said at last. "He's your son, and you haven't done this for a while. But they won't call Mr. Ballistics until Thursday, so you've got the next two nights to prepare."

67

The next day, Assistant District Attorney Amanda Jackson presented her first witness for the prosecution, her matter-of-fact demeanor suggesting that prosecuting Malcolm Hill was simply part of the job, not the subject of misgivings.

The witness, Joel Stein, was a chubby, balding man in his forties whose calm and straightforward manner reflected who he was—a veteran of numerous trials as a crime scene investigator for the GBI, with additional expertise in DNA evidence. Quickly, Jackson moved to the heart of his testimony.

"On the night of Deputy Bullock's death, Mr. Stein, did you respond to the scene?"

"I did, with two other members of my team. There were a number of deputies already there, standing near a white Honda Civic. Inside was Deputy Bullock."

"How did he appear?"

Stein grimaced, a frown tugging at the ends of his mouth. "He was deceased, obviously. He had a substantial gunshot wound to the head, and his face was in the condition described by the medical examiner. After obtaining a search warrant for the car, we proceeded to take photographs of his head and torso, enlargements of which were shown in connection with the testimony by Deputy Spinetta."

"After taking the photographs, did you obtain physical evidence from the body?"

"Yes, ma'am," Stein answered. "We bagged the deputy's hands so they could be swabbed for gunshot residue. We also requested that the sheriff's department bag Mr. Hill's hands, so that our people could swab them as well."

"What else did you do?"

"We observed that Deputy Bullock's service weapon was still in his holster. Thereafter, we located a gun on the floor of the passenger side—a black Glock 19. We photographed it, bagged it, and removed it from the scene. That way we could inspect it for fingerprints and DNA before our ballistics expert performed his own inspection."

"Were you able to find out who owned the gun?"

Stein looked toward the jury. "Yes. Roughly two weeks before, Malcolm Hill had purchased that Glock at Freedom Guns, just a couple blocks down Main Street."

"Did you subsequently determine whether there were fingerprints on the Glock 19?"

"There weren't any," Stein replied promptly. "That's pretty common."

Jackson moved closer to the witness, standing so that Stein was facing the jury. "Did you find any DNA evidence on the gun?"

"We found trace DNA from the defendant and the victim."

This, Chase knew, was a critical point. For the prosecution, Stein was a mixed blessing—they needed him to establish certain forensic evidence essential to proving elements of the crime, including such basics as identifying the gun and its owner. But in the process, they were compelled to elicit facts potentially helpful to Malcolm's defense. No doubt Harris had been happy enough to give this witness to Amanda Jackson.

"Did you later determine," she asked Stein, "whether there was gunshot residue on the defendant's hands?"

He nodded briskly. "There was. In fact, there was a goodly amount, suggesting that the defendant had one or both of his hands on the gun at the time that it fired."

As Robert Franklin took notes in the jury box, Jackson let the answer linger for a moment. "No further questions," she said.

★ ★ ★

As Ford walked toward Joel Stein, Malcolm fidgeted in his chair. He had begun holding a pen in his hand, Chase noticed, twisting it between his thumb and forefingers.

Ford stopped a few feet from the witness, hands on his hips. Without preface, he said, "So there was gunshot residue on the hands of both Malcolm Hill and Deputy Bullock."

Briefly, Stein hesitated. "That's correct. In fact, on both of the deputy's hands."

"We already know that the deputy's DNA was on the gun itself."

"Yes. On the handle."

"And where was Mr. Hill's DNA?"

"Also the handle. As well as the barrel."

Ford gave him a curious look. "Obviously, Deputy Bullock left *his* DNA on the Glock 19 the night of the shooting."

"It seems obvious to me that he did."

Ford showed the same brief smile that, Chase realized, a smart witness should take as a warning. "So when did Mr. Hill's DNA get on the barrel?"

"How do you mean?"

"I mean which day or days of the 'roughly two weeks' that Mr. Hill had owned the gun?"

Comprehension seemed to slightly widen Stein's eyes. "I can't know," he conceded.

"Uh-huh. So for all you know, Deputy Bullock was aiming the gun at Malcolm, and Malcolm Hill managed to deflect it."

Stein considered the question with a look of intense concentration. "It's possible. But with the angle of the bullet, how does that make sense?"

"Isn't the real problem, Mr. Stein, that you're assuming Malcolm pointed the gun at Deputy Bullock, and that's how *his* DNA got on the handle?"

"I might have. But all I'm testifying to is the DNA evidence, which is that both men left DNA on the handle of the gun."

Ford stepped closer to the witness stand. "But when? Let me try a not-so-hypothetical hypothetical. As a predicate, you agree that there were absentee ballot applications on the passenger seat—some of which ended up with Deputy Bullock's blood on them."

"That's true."

"Suppose I told you that the gun was under the absentee ballot applications, and that Deputy Bullock reached for the applications, uncovered the gun, grabbed it, and tried to aim at the defendant. Is there any evidence of which you're aware that contradicts that hypothetical?" Ford smiled again. "Oh, and please don't hurry to answer. You may need some time to sort out your previous suppositions."

Stein put curled fingers to his chin. "I don't know the basis for your hypothetical," he said at last. "But at this point, I can't think of evidence that directly contradicts it."

"What about evidence that supports it? For example, did you find fingerprints on the applications themselves?"

"The defendant's." Stein paused for a moment. "And Deputy Bullock's."

By now, Chase had perceived the brilliance of Ford's cross-examination, because he had grasped where it was going. But it was not yet apparent that Stein had.

"So you're willing to concede," Ford continued, "that Deputy Bullock reached for the ballot applications?"

"Perhaps, but not necessarily. Another possibility is that he touched them while falling after receiving his wound."

"In either case," Ford said easily, "that raises another interesting question. Exactly what was Deputy Bullock doing inside Malcolm Hill's car?"

"I don't know," Stein responded impatiently. "I wasn't there."

"Then let me be more precise. Before you searched the defendant's car, you got a search warrant, yes?"

"Of course," Stein said. "The law requires it—" He stopped abruptly.

"Did Officer Bullock?" Ford asked.

Briefly, Stein shook his head. "I don't know."

"Actually, Mr. Stein, he did not. Nor, I think you'll agree, did he turn on his body or dashboard cameras."

Stein hesitated again. "That's true. He didn't."

"So we don't have video or audio telling us whether Deputy Bullock just fell into those papers, or tried to grab them without the benefit of a search warrant."

"That's also true."

"In fact, Deputy Bullock's various omissions have deprived us of visual evidence regarding how the shooting happened?"

Swiftly, the witness glanced at Jackson. "Objection," the district attorney called out. "Asked and answered."

"Overruled," Tilly said at once. "You may answer, Mr. Stein."

"We have no video," Stein acknowledged. "That would be the best evidence of how the shooting occurred."

"Then let's get back to what evidence we *do* have. Would you say that there were roughly equal amounts of GSR on the hands of both Malcolm Hill and Deputy Bullock?"

"That's true."

"Does that suggest," Ford prodded, "that they struggled for control of the weapon?"

Stein nodded. "It's among the possibilities."

"You also testified that neither Malcolm or Bullock left fingerprints on the gun, and that the only trace DNA was on the handle of the gun."

"That's true."

"Indeed, Mr. Stein, you don't even know who pulled the trigger."

"No," Stein said with open annoyance. "But why would Deputy Bullock shoot himself?"

Ford stared at him. "He wouldn't, deliberately. But isn't it also possible that Bullock had his finger on the trigger, and the gun went off in the struggle?"

Stein rubbed the fingertips of one hand against the other, for the first time glancing at the television cameras that stared back at him. "That's conceivable," he said finally.

"It's more than conceivable," Ford rejoined. "Can you offer me any evidence that expressly suggests that Mr. Hill, instead of Deputy Bullock, pulled the trigger?"

"I can't."

"I didn't think so," Ford snapped. "So let me ask you one final question. Based on your work, can you offer the jury your opinion as an expert as to whether the shooting was deliberate or accidental?"

This time, Stein's tone mimed resignation. "As you well know, Mr. Ford, I can't."

"I do know, Mr. Stein. That's why I've got no more questions. At least for you."

As Ford sat down, Chase saw the jurors following him, for this moment the courtroom's center of gravity. Placing his hand on Malcolm's shoulder, Chase whispered to Ford, "You're now three for three."

★ ★ ★

Late that evening, Chase worked at the desk in his apartment, outlining his first cross-examination in a decade. Finally, after midnight, he crawled into bed next to Allie.

She, too, had not slept. The tension of the trial had drained the passion from them both. What was left was worry for Malcolm, their need for each other's presence. Quiet, Chase held her in the dark.

"I was thinking about Jabari," he said at last. "I don't know if I was ever that good."

She, too, was quiet for a time. Then she turned and, quite gently, kissed him. "I know you'll be fine, baby. And so does our son."

68

The following day, Dalton Harris called the chief firearms inspector for the Georgia Bureau of Investigation to the witness stand. Larry Elder was a native Georgian in his midforties with a lean frame, a calm demeanor, and the sharp-eyed look of a hunter. On the easel was a blow-up of the Glock 19.

Sitting between Ford and Chase, Malcolm could see how sinister the gun would look to the jury—black and blunt, made for killing. While it was not in dispute that Malcolm's gun had fired the fatal shot, Ford had explained, the prosecutor had to go through the formality of proving this to the jury. But, in the prosecutor's telling, Malcolm had chosen it to deliberately murder George Bullock.

"The Glock 19," Elder explained, "is a very popular weapon. Although powerful, it's relatively small and therefore easy to conceal. Because it has an internal firing pin, you can fire it quickly. You don't need to cock the hammer—you simply put your finger on the trigger and give it a light squeeze."

"Is it a reliable handgun?" Harris asked.

Elder nodded. "Extremely reliable. It simply doesn't misfire. This gun will always do what you want it to do."

But it hadn't, Malcolm thought. *It just went off.*

"How would you describe its capacity to inflict death or serious bodily injury?"

"High. That's the point of the gun."

The jury, Malcolm saw, was serious and attentive. "Is this enlargement," Harris asked the witness, "an accurate depiction of the gun you were asked to inspect?"

"It is."

"Could you describe the steps you took to evaluate the Glock 19 shown here?"

"Yes." Again, Elder faced the jury. "First, I inspected the gun to make sure it was firing properly. It was. I checked the trigger pull—the amount of pressure necessary to fire the weapon. Then I fired the weapon, and matched the bullet to the bullet extracted from the victim's skull."

"And what did you conclude?"

"Beyond doubt, this is the weapon that killed Deputy Bullock."

"Thank you," Harris said. "No further questions." But in that moment, Malcolm felt the larger implications—inspired by the Double-XX video, Malcolm had purchased a particularly deadly weapon with malicious intent, and then turned it on a deputy who had never drawn his gun. Now the task of undermining this had fallen to the man Malcolm had asked to represent him.

★ ★ ★

After a brief pause to steady his nerves, Chase touched Malcolm's shoulder and rose from the defense table to cross-examine Larry Elder.

Briefly, he registered Harris' look of mild surprise, the curiosity on the faces of the jurors, his son's worried gaze. He tried to focus on nothing but the witness.

With a calm he did not feel, Chase asked, "Did you determine the make of the bullet extracted from Deputy Bullock?"

Elder nodded. "It's a Remington 115, full metal jacket."

"Does it have a hollow point?"

"No."

"In other words," Chase continued, "it's a conventional bullet, not one designed to inflict maximum damage on a human being."

"That's right. It will kill you at that range, sure enough. But it's not made to create the lethal damage a hollow point would."

"And only that one bullet was fired, correct?"

"Correct."

With this, Chase felt himself following a once-familiar path. It was a cardinal rule of cross-examination to know the answers before he asked the questions, the better to draw the witness into a rhythm of acquiescence. "As compared to a revolver," Chase asked, "how much pressure does it take to pull the trigger on a Glock 19?"

From Elder's expression, Chase divined, he understood where this was going. But he was an expert, not an advocate, and by reputation was committed to accuracy over partisanship. "Relatively less," he answered.

"Therefore it also requires a lighter touch."

"That's right."

Chase paused for a moment. "As a result, the gun in question could have fired accidentally, in the course of a struggle between Deputy Bullock and Malcolm Hill."

The witness glanced at Harris. "Yes," he acknowledged. "That's possible."

This was a point for the defense, Chase felt certain, that the prosecution had anticipated—and that, quite likely, they hoped might end the cross-examination. But, if the next questions went as he hoped, he had hardly begun. Casually, he inquired, "What's the normal trigger pull on a Glock 19?"

"Four to six pounds of pressure."

"And what was the trigger pull on Malcolm Hill's Glock?"

"Two to three pounds."

"In other words," Chase prodded, "roughly half the pressure required to fire the normal Glock 19—if not less. Did you determine why the defendant's gun was so much easier to fire?"

Elder shifted in the witness chair. "The Glock the defendant purchased from Freedom Guns was a used gun. The prior owner had modified the gun to make the trigger pull lighter."

Chase nodded toward the enlargement. "So this particular Glock had what you would call a hair trigger."

"Pretty close to that, yes."

"Does that further increase the chances of an accidental shooting?"

"It could, yes."

Chase felt himself gaining confidence. Part of this was preparation—he had committed to memory every feature of the Glock 19, before consulting with the defense ballistics expert on the particular properties of Malcolm's gun. "So let me ask you this, Mr. Elder. If two people struggling for this gun touched the trigger simultaneously, would that lighten the trigger pull still more?"

"Yes. Theoretically, it would cut the trigger pull in half."

"Which, in turn, would further enhance the possibility of accidental shooting."

"Yes."

Chase moved closer to the witness. "Does the inherent design of a Glock 19 also increase the risk of an accidental shooting?"

"It does."

"For what reason?"

Elder turned to look at the enlargement. "The Glock 19 is the best in the world, made right here in Georgia. But it has no external safety—everything works off the trigger."

"Would you say that accidental firings of a Glock 19 are quite common?"

"They are. Everything works off the premise that you won't touch the trigger."

"Is fear of accidents why the American military doesn't use Glock 19's?"

"That's correct."

"Thank you, Mr. Elder," Chase said easily. "Did your work on this case also include studying the autopsy report and related materials?"

Immediately, Chase sensed the close attention of Judge Tilly and, with that, the prosecutor's heightened alertness. "It did," Elder responded. "I went over the autopsy report, the autopsy photos, and the victim's uniform on the night of the shooting."

"Did you focus on particular aspects of the autopsy relevant to your opinion?"

"Several."

"Including stippling—the question of whether unburnt powder from the Glock adhered to Deputy Bullock's skin and clothing?"

"That's right."

"Had it?"

"Yes."

"Specifically, on his hands?"

"Again, yes."

Chase felt himself reflexively becoming the trial lawyer he once had been. Moving, he positioned himself so that Elder was looking in the direction of the jury. "What does that tell you?" he asked.

"Stippling only travels about two feet. Its presence on the face, hands, and clothing suggests that the gun was fired at very short range."

"Does that also suggest that Bullock could have had his hands on the gun?"

"Could have? Yes."

"Were there other indications that the gun was very close to Deputy Bullock when it went off?"

Again, the witness glanced at Harris. "The soot from the gun. Soot only travels about twelve inches, and it was present on the victim's face, hands, and shirt."

This, Chase intuited, had been the focus of considerable discussion between Harris and his witness. "Did you also fire Malcolm Hill's Glock 19 to determine how it distributes stippling and soot, and therefore determine the approximate distance between the muzzle of the gun and the deputy's wound?"

"Yes. I fired it into a cotton cloth. Based on the pattern, I concluded that the gun was fired approximately four inches from the entry wound."

"Does a shot at such close range also enhance the possibility that the defendant and Deputy Bullock were wrestling for the gun?"

Elder hesitated. "Obviously, they were close enough that either or both could have touched the gun."

"Did you also determine the distribution of gunshot residue, otherwise known as GSR?"

"I did."

"GSR comes out of the top of the gun, true?"

"True."

"So that you'd expect to find GSR on the hands of whoever fired the gun."

"That's right."

At the corner of his vision, Chase saw Stephen Hewitt scribbling notes. "There was GSR on Deputy Bullock's hands, correct?"

"There was."

Chase's questions came more swiftly now. "In fact, there was a roughly equal amount on his hands as on Malcolm's, correct?"

"Yes."

"You're further aware, I assume, that the deputy's contact DNA was found on the handle of the gun."

"I am."

"Independent of the other evidence we've already discussed, does that suggest that they were both grappling for control of the weapon?"

"It could, yes."

Chase skipped a beat. "Or Deputy Bullock had aimed the gun at Malcolm Hill?"

Elder hesitated again, as if considering the possibilities. "Again, it could."

Chase angled his head, miming curiosity. "Under ordinary circumstances, does the cartridge containing a bullet eject from a Glock 19 once it's fired?"

"It does."

"And when you test-fired the defendant's gun, did the cartridge eject normally?"

"It did."

Chase placed his hands on his hips. "But on the night of the shooting, the cartridge did not eject from Malcolm's Glock 19."

"No," Elder responded slowly. "It was still stuck in the weapon. The slider on top of the gun that opens automatically to permit ejection didn't open far enough."

"What does that suggest to you?"

Elder seemed to frown. "That someone had their hand on top of the slider, preventing it from opening."

Chase paused, drawing out the moment. "Doesn't that suggest Malcolm and Deputy Bullock were struggling for control at the *exact* moment the Glock discharged?"

Again, the witness looked pensive. "That's a logical explanation."

"Given that the cartridge ejected normally when you fired the gun yourself, isn't that the *only* logical explanation?"

Elder spread his hands in a shrugging gesture. "I can't think of another."

Thus far, Chase thought, Harris and Elder should have anticipated the thrust of his cross-examination. But this was less true, he hoped, for where he was going next. "There's another point of interest," he told the witness. "So bear with me for a moment."

Returning to the defense table, Chase took a second Glock 19 out of his briefcase, conscious as he did so of Malcolm's deep attention. Then he walked back to Elder, placing the gun in his hands. "Can you identify the make of this weapon for the jury?"

"Certainly. It's a Glock 19."

"Just hang on to that," Chase responded. "In the meanwhile, I have a hypothetical question. Suppose that the autopsy report showed that the bullet entered Deputy Bullock's forehead from straight in front of him, with the gun held at the same level as the entry wound. What might you conclude about the nature of the shooting?"

Elder considered the question. "It might, and I emphasize 'might,' suggest a deliberate shooting by someone capable of aiming the gun."

"All right. Suppose the gun entered the deputy's forehead from a downward trajectory, indicating that the gun was fired from above him. Would that suggest that Deputy Bullock was in a vulnerable position, enhancing the possibility of a deliberate shooting?"

"It could, yes."

"But according to the autopsy report, that's not what happened."

"No. It's not."

"In fact, the bullet entered Deputy Bullock's forehead on an upward trajectory, indicating that the gun was fired from below him."

"That's what the medical examiner found."

"And according to Dr. Connell, the bullet also entered the right side of the deputy's forehead."

"That's correct."

"So, just to be clear, the bullet traveled on an upward trajectory."

"Yes."

Chase cocked his head again. "Suppose I tell you that Malcolm Hill is right-handed. If he pulled the trigger to deliberately shoot Deputy Bullock in the forehead, what is the likely direction of the bullet?"

The witness hesitated, and Chase saw comprehension stealing into his eyes. "Either straight, or entering from the left side of his forehead."

"Thank you," Chase responded. "Before we go any further, could you make sure the Glock 19 you're holding is empty?"

Silent, Elder checked for cartridges. "It is."

"Mind handing me the gun?"

Elder passed the gun. Taking it, Chase held the Glock in his right hand and, extending his arm across the witness' chest, twisted his hand backward and upward at a crooked angle roughly four inches from the right side of Elder's forehead. "Is this the angle at which a right-handed person would have to fire the gun to deliberately shoot Deputy Bullock as shown in the autopsy report—an upward trajectory through the fore-head?" Abruptly, Chase twitched the trigger, causing a metallic click. "In other words, like that."

Elder blinked. "I suppose so."

"Isn't that an extraordinarily awkward way for a right-hander to deliberately shoot someone?"

Elder seemed to collect his thoughts. "It would be. But not necessarily if you were wrestling for the gun."

"Exactly," Chase said. "So we're back to that—wrestling for the gun. Assuming that Malcolm Hill is right-handed, would you agree that the trajectory of the bullet increases the likelihood of an accidental shooting in the course of a struggle?"

"It seems like I just said that."

"Actually, you did. So let me summarize your testimony. The Glock 19 is prone to accidental shootings. Moreover, the likelihood that George Bullock's death resulted from an accident is enhanced by the following factors: the modification of the gun to have a virtual hair trigger. The presence of GSR, stippling, and soot on Deputy Bullock's hands. The fact that the cartridge didn't eject. The upward trajectory of the bullet through the right side of the forehead. And the fact—which I can assure you, *is* a fact—that Malcolm Hill is right-handed." Chase paused for effect. "Would any one of those factors support the possibility of accident?"

"They could, yes."

"Taken together, do all these factors substantially increase the possibility that Deputy Bullock died as the result of an accidental shooting?"

"Objection," Harris called out. "Counsel's summary misstates the prior testimony."

"Overruled," the judge said promptly.

Chase turned back to the witness. "Yes," Elder responded at last. "They do."

"Thank you, Mr. Elder. No further questions."

Returning to the defense table, Chase saw the hint of a smile in Jabari Ford's eyes. As he sat beside Malcolm, his son whispered, "That was good."

At once, Chase felt relief washing over him. "Good enough," he whispered back.

★ ★ ★

Immediately, Harris was on his feet. "Mr. Brevard listed a number of factors to suggest that this was an accidental shooting. Isn't every one of them equally compatible with the conclusion that Deputy Bullock tried to protect himself by seizing the gun, and that the defendant fired before he was able to do so?"

"Yes," Elder answered emphatically. "Depending on the circumstances, all of them could line up that way."

"Mr. Brevard also made quite a point of the trajectory of the bullet, and that the defendant is right-handed. But isn't it also true that in his scenario the two men were, of necessity, moving?"

"Of course."

"Therefore," Harris continued, "Deputy Bullock could have turned the right side of his forehead toward the gun, rather than the defendant twisting his arm at a supposedly awkward angle."

It was a critical point for the prosecution, Chase understood. "That's certainly true," Elder answered promptly. "A lot depends on the movements of both the defendant and the victim. They surely weren't frozen in place."

"So that, depending on the position of Deputy Bullock's head, the defendant could have fired the shot from directly in front of him."

"That's also true. With respect to the trajectory of the bullet, a lot depends on the position of the victim's head relative to the gun."

"Thank you," Harris said promptly, and sat down.

Briefly, Chase considered asking another question. "Anything more?" the judge asked.

Swiftly, Chase reached his decision. "No, Your Honor. Thank you."

"Very well. We will adjourn for lunch until one o'clock."

"All rise," the courtroom deputy commanded, and a cacophony of noises broke out.

Leaning across the defense table, Ford murmured to Chase, "Good call just then. Looks like you haven't entirely lost it."

"Not entirely," Chase answered.

Turning to Allie, Chase saw that she was still sitting with her mother, head downcast, a portrait of tension relieved. "Let's get some lunch," he told Malcolm. "I'm starving."

69

Over the noon break, Chase, Ford, and Malcolm ate sandwiches in a waiting room for witnesses. After lunch, Ford slipped out to make phone calls or, Chase sensed, to give him time with Malcolm.

Across the table, Malcolm regarded him curiously. "Didn't seem like you were nervous at all."

Thinking of how apprehensive he had been, Chase smiled at this. "That reminds me of something your mom told me at Harvard—'That's why they call it acting.' In politics we do it all the time."

Malcolm appraised him. "Maybe so. But I've never really seen you lose your cool."

For the first time, Chase felt Malcolm feeling out his characteristics, perhaps to try them on for size. "Life never gave me much reason to," he answered. "So equanimity came easy to me. Later on I figured out that staying calm is useful. But sometimes I have to force myself."

"Like when?"

"Like today. People tell me you're competitive. When it matters to me, so am I. If I have to live with losing, I will. But there are times when I absolutely hate it."

"What did you ever lose that mattered to you all that much?"

Looking at his son, Chase reflected on the answer. "Your mother," he finally said. "And you, it turns out." He paused before adding, "I don't want to lose you again, Malcolm. That's what you saw today."

To Chase, his son's contemplative quiet felt less like doubt than consideration. In time, Chase hoped, it might ripen to acceptance. But only if Malcolm went free.

★ ★ ★

The afternoon session, Allie had warned her mother, was unlikely to go as well. As the prosecution toxicologist began to testify, she took a moment to study their new environment.

The jury seemed even more attentive, she thought. But the three jurors Jabari and Chase had focused on—Stephen Hewitt, Robert Franklin, and Nettie Gray—remained opaque. Filing into the courtroom, Dorothy Bullock looked wounded, as though fearful that the justice system would betray her and her children. Outside the courthouse, Allie had spotted Fay Spann talking vehemently into the microphone of a Fox News reporter, and Charles and Molly Parnell had marshalled a brigade of armed militia holding a flag emblazoned with a bolt of white lightning. The first days of the trial seemed only to have heightened its tensions.

On the witness stand, Dr. Sharon Williams began ensnaring Malcolm in his own misjudgments.

From the outset, Williams seemed persuasive, a pleasant but precise gray-haired woman in her late fifties, with thirty years of experience as a toxicologist for the Georgia Bureau of Investigation. "Dr. Williams," Harris asked, "please describe how you evaluated whether the defendant was intoxicated at the time of the shooting."

"Certainly," Williams responded. "Shortly after Mr. Hill's arrest, we obtained a warrant and took a sample of Mr. Hill's blood. Since that time, the blood sample has been in the continuing custody of the GBI. Pursuant to our standard procedures, we gave it a barcode, tracked it, and followed everyone who looked at it. We also locked it away, to ensure the integrity of the sample."

"Was the test you used to determine the defendant's level of intoxication consistent with generally accepted scientific methods?"

"It was. Our department has very strict protocols."

"What was the result of the test?"

Almost imperceptibly, Williams frowned. "The sample showed a blood alcohol content of point zero seven percent."

"What does that suggest," Harris asked, "about the defendant's level of intoxication at the time of the arrest?"

The judge, Allie noticed, was following the testimony with a keen interest befitting a critical piece of proof. "The blood draw," Williams answered briskly, "occurred roughly an hour and a half after Malcolm Hill's arrest. The average elimination rate—that is, the speed at which the blood alcohol content dissipates—is zero point one five per hour. On that basis, we can estimate that the defendant's blood alcohol content at the time of his arrest was between point zero eight and point zero nine."

"What is the legal drinking age in Georgia?"

"Twenty-one."

"How old is the defendant?"

"Eighteen." Williams glanced at the jury. "Mr. Hill was below the legal drinking age—for these purposes, a minor under the law."

"And under the law, Dr. Williams, what is the blood alcohol content in which a minor is deemed to be intoxicated?"

"It's point zero two. At the time of the arrest, the defendant exceeded the standard by roughly four times."

Glancing at the defense table, Allie saw that Jabari and Chase had both assumed the bland expression of defense lawyers when testimony is going badly for their client. But Malcolm had no such training—he stared down at the table, seemingly fixated by the cost of his own carelessness. Vainly, Allie thought of all the times she had warned him against drinking too much, the danger to a young Black man of mistakes caused by disinhibition. But perhaps the worst of this, now, was the impression Harris was creating for the jury: that Malcolm was a lawbreaker, spurred by illegal alcohol consumption to act out his hatred of police on George Bullock.

"For what reason," the prosecutor asked Williams, "is the standard different for an eighteen-year-old like Malcolm Hill"?

"They are presumed to be more vulnerable to alcohol."

Harris nodded. "But in this case, Doctor, you believe that Malcolm Hill met the adult standard for intoxication at the time of his arrest."

"I do. Again, that standard is point zero seven, which matches the blood alcohol content of his sample at the time his blood was drawn. As I previously noted, based on the average elimination rate, I believe that the blood alcohol content at the time of his arrest was at least point zero one percent above the legal limit for adults."

"At either rate—point zero seven or point zero eight—how would that level of intoxication affect the average adult?"

Williams folded her hands, seeming to marshal the symptoms of inebriation. "In the average person, you'd expect slurred speech, loss of judgment, and an impact on driving that includes divided attention, a slowing of reflexes, an increase in reaction time, and impairment of depth perception. Overall, the probable effects on behavior include a loss of memory and, in particular, a decrease in impulse control."

"Malcolm Hill," Harris continued, "is approximately six feet one inch tall and one hundred eighty-five pounds. How might his size affect the potential impact of alcohol?"

"Not much, if at all. That's a pretty average size for an adult male."

"And, if anything, the impact of alcohol on the defendant would have been greater at the time of the shooting—correct?"

Allie saw Jabari stir, as to object, and then think better of it. "It surely could have been," Williams answered. "But even were he an adult, he was still legally intoxicated at the time of the blood draw."

"Would that level of intoxication," Harris asked quickly, "increase the defendant's impulse toward violence?"

At once, Jabari stood. "Objection, Your Honor. The question calls for speculation, and goes well beyond the proper scope of expert testimony."

"Sustained," the judge said. "Please reframe your question, Mr. Harris."

Harris drew himself up, as if to emphasize for the jury the importance of this testimony. "Could that level of intoxication, Dr. Williams, increase the inclination toward violence of an average adult?"

"Certainly," Williams answered. "An increased tendency toward violence is consistent with the diminution of impulse control. Regrettably, it takes no time at all between impulse and action to pull the trigger of a handgun."

Beside her, Allie felt her mother's sharp intake of breath. With a satisfied expression, Harris said, "Thank you, Dr. Williams."

★ ★ ★

Watching Ford's neutral demeanor as he approached the witness, Allie divined that he viewed her with caution, and simply hoped to get what he could. "Dr. Williams," he began. "Just to be clear, you have no idea whatsoever about how the shooting actually happened."

Again, Williams folded her hands. "That's correct."

"So you also don't know what impact, if any, the defendant's consumption of beer had on how that gun came to be fired."

"I don't."

Ford stuck his own hands in his pockets, adopting a casual posture. "I note that you testified about the impact of intoxication on the average person. Is that because you can't testify as to whether—if at all—Malcolm Hill's judgment and impulse control were impacted at the time of the shooting?"

"That's right. I can't."

"Or whether Malcolm was driving in a way that might have suggested that he was impaired?"

"Again," Williams conceded, "I can't."

"So you can't shed any light on whether Malcolm's driving was a factor in Deputy Bullock's decision to stop him."

"Objection," Harris called out. "There's no foundation for the question, and it calls for speculation. Obviously, Dr. Williams can't put herself in Deputy Bullock's mind. All she can do, as she has done, is testify very clearly about the impact of that level of intoxication on an average adult. Let alone on an eighteen-year-old."

Tilly turned to Ford. "Sustained. Anything else, Mr. Ford?"

As Ford hesitated, Allie sensed him searching for a way to end his examination on a more positive note. "To summarize, Dr. Williams, you can't offer an opinion on whether the blood alcohol level you found impacted the defendant's driving at the time he was stopped, or his behavior at the time of the shooting."

"Objection," Harris said again. "Asked and answered."

"I was asking for a summary, Your Honor," Ford responded. "I think the jury should be very clear on the limitations of Dr. Williams' opinion."

Briefly, the judge pondered his ruling. "Overruled," he directed. "You may answer, Dr. Williams."

Ford stepped forward. "Before she does so, Your Honor, can I ask that my last question be read back so that the jury has it clearly in mind?"

Allie saw Tilly's eyes narrow, as if in appreciation of what Ford was trying to do. Finally, he said to the court reporter, "Please read back the question."

Summoned briefly to center stage, the plump blonde woman glanced at the cameras newly focused on her. In a hesitant voice, the reporter read: "To summarize, Dr. Williams, you can't offer an opinion on whether the blood alcohol level you found impacted the defendant's driving at the time he was stopped, or his behavior at the time of the shooting."

Williams paused for a moment, seemingly replaying the question as the jurors watched intently. "That's right," she answered. "I can't express a specific opinion on either issue."

"No further questions," Ford said at once.

★ ★ ★

Afterward, Chase and Ford sat in Ford's conference room, taking stock of the day and the trial.

"About the toxicologist," Chase said, "there's nothing more you could have done with her."

"I know," Ford answered glumly. "I'm just sorry Malcolm's paying for being a dumb kid. The price is way too high."

The harsh truth of this struck Chase again. But for George Bullock's decision to stop him, and the reasons for that, it would not have mattered that Malcolm had drunk too much beer, or had been carrying a gun in his car—actions that, Chase suspected, had at one time or another characterized a good half of the males in Georgia. But proving Bullock's motives remained beyond reach.

"Williams wasn't great for us," Chase said at length. "But taken together, the prosecution experts have gone a long way toward making our case for reasonable doubt. If Harris could have gone straight to Billy Palmer and Double-XX without having to prove that George Bullock is actually dead, he would have."

"True enough," Ford responded. "But according to the witness list, our fun is over. Come Monday, Billy is up next, followed by the GBI social media person to show that video again. After that, things will look different. Then *we* have to decide what witnesses to put on, and in what order."

If any, Chase thought but chose not to say. There was an earlier matter to decide, and he had been thinking about it more seriously since cross-examining Larry Elder. Finally, he said, "I want Billy Palmer."

Ford stared at him in surprise. "Why?"

"It's like I've been saying about Malcolm facing Dalton Harris. Billy is an eighteen-year-old kid; I'm a former prosecutor. I may be out of practice compared to Harris, but I'd bet that Malcolm is way smarter than Billy on the best day Woody Palmer's boy ever lived." He looked back at Ford intently. "I don't just want to discredit him, Jabari. I want to dismantle him."

Ford shook his head in demurral. "That seems like a real problem to me. What you did to Elder was surgical, not personal. Malcolm's your boy, and this cracker son of a pinhead cop is out to get him. That's way too emotional for any father to handle. Leave Billy to me."

Chase leaned forward, resting his elbows on the table. "I promised from the outset that you'd call the shots and I'd stay out of your way. I meant that. But tell me this—how long have you known me by now?"

Ford calculated. "Eight months, give or take."

"OK. So in that time, Malcolm's been charged with capital murder, I've been shot at, Allie's been shot at, I've been under all sorts of political pressure, I decided to claim Malcolm as my son, Allie and I have had to parade our personal life on television, and I took a leave of absence from Congress to participate in the trial. During all that, how many times have you seen me lose it?"

Briefly, Ford considered this. "Once. When Harris offered Malcolm LWOP."

"I was just following your example," Chase rejoined. "You'd already lost it, and I didn't want you to feel alone." He paused, then continued in a different tenor. "Look, you're right that I'm angry at the whole idea of Billy Palmer. But I can make it work for me."

Ford gave him a look of deep concern. After a time, he said, "That's a lot on your shoulders, Chase."

It was the first time, Chase realized, that Ford had ever used his given name. "I know," Chase responded. "But you're a dad, Jabari. If Malcolm were your son and you thought you were capable of cross-examining Billy, could you leave it to anyone else?"

Silent, Ford seemed to gaze off into the distance. "No," he finally answered. "I couldn't."

"I thought so," Chase said. "Because that's the other thing that's happened in the last eight months. Malcolm's my son now, no matter what he makes of that."

Ford studied the table for an indeterminate time, saying nothing. At length, he nodded, seemingly as much to himself as to Chase. "OK, then. At least let's think about how you might cross-examine this kid. I've got some ideas that could work."

70

Watching Billy Palmer take the witness stand, Malcolm remembered the moment that now threatened to end the life he had known.

It was the spring of their junior year, a few months after Malcolm turned seventeen. Classes were over for the day: Malcolm had track practice; Billy, a baseball game. In the brief moments before they were due to go their separate ways, Malcolm went to his locker to retrieve his track shoes, and saw Billy sauntering toward him down the hallway.

Billy was still wearing his "Back the Blue" T-shirt. The day before, during the murder trial of that Minneapolis cop, the cable news channels had shown the video of him asphyxiating George Floyd; an hour before, in civics class, he and Malcolm had been on opposite sides of a frequently bitter discussion about the trial.

Though Malcolm despised Billy as a racist and a moron, he decided to ignore him. But from Billy's expression, a slight twist of the lips, he had a point to make.

He stopped only two feet from Malcolm. "Like my T-shirt, Malcolm?"

Malcolm turned to look at him. In that moment, Billy Palmer personified the inbred bigotry of the stupid whites who had tormented Blacks for generations, the son of a beady-eyed cracker dressed up in the petty authority of a Freedom town cop, the man who had stopped Malcolm for the crime of driving through a white neighborhood on his way to visit his grandfather's grave.

Filled with anger and contempt, he answered, "Not as much as you liked watching that cop murder a Black man. Bet your idiot father thought it was a training video."

Billy stepped closer, his face inches from Malcolm's. "At least I got a father, you stupid fucking nigger."

Before he could stop the molten rage shooting from his brain through his body, Malcolm wheeled, and with all the strength he possessed, slammed his closed fist into Billy's face.

The punch landed flush. As the shock numbed his arm, Malcolm heard and felt the crunch of bone and cartilage. Billy was sprawled on the linoleum floor, blood spurting from his ruined nose as he moaned in shock, "You fucking nigger..."

Speechless, Malcolm perceived with astonishment what he had done. Suddenly Billy Palmer no longer seemed worth hating. But it was too late.

★ ★ ★

Now, almost two years later, Billy Palmer was worth hating again. In that split second between thought and action, Malcolm had armed him with the power of legalized revenge.

Sitting on the witness stand, Billy was a tall, slender teenager with blue eyes, lank blonde hair, a fresh haircut, and regular features save for a slightly crooked nose, dressed in a nondescript gray suit that, like Malcolm, he had surely purchased for graduation. Though perhaps only Malcolm could feel the intensity with which his antagonist wished to ruin his life, he sensed Chase Brevard, seated next to him, watching Billy with a fixity so complete that Malcolm felt less alone.

The Black prosecutor, Amanda Jackson, began questioning Billy in a calm and respectful voice, as if unwilling to unduly distress the victim of an unwarranted trauma. "Before this incident," she asked, "did you ever have any altercation with Black people, in or out of school?"

Billy shook his head. "No, ma'am."

"Did you ever have disciplinary problems at high school?"

Perhaps for the jury, Billy's Southern inflections carried a tone of regret Malcolm had never heard from him. "No, ma'am," he repeated. "Because my dad is a policeman, he always told me I needed to set a good example."

Jackson sharpened her tone, spelling out each word. "At *any* time before the assault, did you *ever* address any Black person in racially disparaging terms?"

"Never," Billy said emphatically.

That, Malcolm felt quite certain, was a lie—that day the words had come to Billy's lips far too easily. But he had no way of proving that.

Again, Jackson spoke with an air of gravity. "On the day of the assault, did you call Malcolm a racially degrading name?"

Billy looked toward the jury. "No, ma'am. I never did."

"He's lying," Malcolm whispered to Chase. Placing his hand on Malcolm's arm, Chase kept watching Billy.

"Did you exchange words before Malcolm hit you?"

Billy turned back to her. "Only he did. Malcolm Hill."

To Malcolm, the courtroom felt too quiet. "What did the defendant say?" Jackson asked.

For the first time, a trace of anger entered Billy's voice. "I was wearing a 'Back the Blue' T-shirt. I was just passing him in the hallway and he reached out to stop me. He said if I wore that T-shirt again, he'd rip it off my back. Then he called my dad the kind of cop who wanted to kill Black people."

Helpless, Malcolm looked toward the jury. *He's making this up*, he wanted to tell them. But since the night of the shooting, he had lost his power to speak. He could only watch the jurors being drawn into Billy's lies.

"Did you respond to him in any way?" Jackson asked Billy.

"No, ma'am, I didn't want any trouble. I was going to pitch for the baseball team that day, and this scout from Mercer was coming to watch me." Billy touched his nose. "All I did was try to take his hand off my arm. He hit me before I could see it coming."

"Were you injured?"

Billy's jaw set. "I had to go to the emergency room. But he'd broke my nose so bad, it was hard to breathe. A surgeon had to fix it."

This time it was Harris who put a giant photograph on the easel— Billy with his ruined nose, his eyes slits in swollen purple skin. "Looking at this enlargement," Jackson asked, "does it accurately reflect the picture taken when you went to the ER?"

Studying his image, Billy seemed to wince. "That's only what I looked like. I could hardly see, and my head hurt so bad, I was three days getting back to school. They couldn't operate until summer."

"For the record," Jackson said sympathetically, "you couldn't pitch that day."

"No, ma'am. Not for the rest of the season."

"Did the school take any disciplinary action?"

"They talked to both of us, and then they suspended Malcolm for hitting me."

Jackson nodded. "But not you."

Billy sat straighter. "No, ma'am. I didn't do anything. I wasn't looking for a fight. He just blindsided me because of a T-shirt."

Jackson waited a moment, letting his answer linger for the jury. "Thank you, Billy," she said almost gently. "No further questions."

71

Hands in his pockets, Chase approached Billy Palmer with a noncha-lance designed to conceal the depth of his loathing. Briefly, he registered Dalton Harris' astonishment that it was Chase, not Jabari

Ford, who had risen from the defense table, its reflection on the face of Judge Tilly himself.

Everyone in the courtroom, including the jury, surely knew that he was Malcolm's father, about to commence the cross-examination of a key witness against his son. But no one could know that over the long weekend during which he had designed his cross-examination, Chase had seen only Ford and Joe Briggs. He had watched none of the nonstop coverage of the trial on cable and, consumed by his task, had barely slept. To leave him alone, Allie had gone home for the weekend.

"Compared to this," he had told her, "Joe Kerrigan was nothing."

"I know," she had answered. "I'm Malcolm's mother."

Now, on the cusp of this crucial moment, Chase felt grandmother, mother, and son watching him with anxiety, Ford's self-reproof for allowing him to take it, the undertow of his own misgivings for having sought this responsibility in a nationally televised drama where the stakes were Malcolm's freedom and, perhaps, his life. In a final act of will, he dismissed all of this and focused his attentions on Billy. Through his veneer of politeness, the boy regarded Chase with apprehension.

In an even tone, Chase asked him, "Are you familiar with the George Floyd case, Billy?"

"Objection," Jackson called out.

Apprehensive, Chase kept his eyes on Judge Tilly. So much depended on how much latitude Tilly gave him, and whether Chase could use it to unnerve Billy Palmer. "With three or four questions, Your Honor, I'm confident that I can show relevance."

"You may answer," Tilly told the witness.

For a moment, Billy simply stared at Malcolm's father. "I've heard about it," he responded. "Everyone has."

But he had more than heard of it, Chase knew, and not just in civics class. Joe Briggs had done his work well, including among Woody Palmer's drinking companions.

"Did you see any part of the trial on television?" he asked.

Again, Billy seemed to hesitate. "Some of it."

Chase took a step closer. "Including the video of the defendant, Derek Chauvin, with his knee on George Floyd's neck?"

"Yeah," Billy answered. "I saw that."

"In fact you discussed that video the very next day, in civics class."

"Yeah." Billy stopped, as if to amend his manners. "Yes, sir. We did."

"When you first saw the video, where were you?"

"At home."

"Were you watching alone?"

"Objection," Jackson interposed again.

This time Chase gave her a short, sideways look before turning to the judge. "I find these objections puzzling, Your Honor. For the record, I'm attempting to probe the sentiments Mr. Palmer brought to his encounter with Malcolm Hill."

"Overruled," Tilly said, addressing Jackson. "Defense counsel should be allowed to pursue this subject without undue interruption."

What a look of chastisement, Jackson sat down. Chase sensed that she, too, was feeling the pressures of unremitting scrutiny fed by the cameras. But Harris' calculations in asking her to present this particular witness were clear enough.

Turning back to Billy, Chase asked, "Again, when you first saw the video of George Floyd dying, were you watching alone?"

Billy glanced at Jackson. "No." He paused, then added, "My dad was there."

Chase regarded him closely. "Anyone else?"

Billy hesitated yet again. Immediately, Chase sensed that he might not have revealed to the prosecutors what the defense already knew, leaving him to make his own calculations under the pressure of cross-examination. Finally, Billy said, "I think a couple of my dad's friends were there."

"So they'd remember what all of you said about the video."

"Objection," Jackson interpolated, reasserting herself with a trace of anxiety. "The question lacks foundation and calls for speculation."

"Sustained," Tilly said. But from Billy's wary expression, Chase saw that he had accomplished his purpose—to make this callow witness cautious about lying.

"During the course of that conversation," he asked, "did your father express an opinion about the prosecution of Derek Chauvin?"

Once more, Chase observed Billy Palmer in the process of thought. "He said it was wrong," Billy allowed.

"Is that all?" Chase inquired more sharply. "Or did he give a reason for saying so?"

At this, Billy's instincts seemed to take over. "He said that George Floyd was a drug addict and a criminal. He thought it was all political."

"Just that? Didn't your father say, in words or substance, that the prosecutors were pandering to Blacks?"

"I don't know what you mean by that."

"Then let's try this. Did your dad say that they were prosecuting Derek Chauvin to suck up to Black people?"

Chase watched Billy wonder what he knew, and from whom. Vaguely, Billy responded, "He may have said something like that."

"Did he also say that they were using the George Floyd case to smear all police?"

Again, Billy cast a surreptitious look at Jackson. "I guess so."

Moving still closer, Chase mimed curiosity for the jury. "Who is 'they,' Billy?"

"I don't know what you mean."

"According to your father, do the people who don't like police include Blacks?"

Another pause. "Some of them."

"During that discussion, did your dad and his friends mention Black Lives Matter?"

To Chase's satisfaction, Billy had begun looking unnerved. "I think so."

"In fact, didn't your dad say that Black Lives Matter was trying to tear down police?"

"I think maybe he said that."

For a moment, Chase scrutinized him in silence. "Let's move to the next morning," he said. "Did you wear your 'Back the Blue' T-shirt to school?"

Briefly, Billy flicked his hair, as if it were obscuring his vision. "That's right."

"And that was the day of your encounter with Malcolm Hill, yes?"

"Yeah," Billy said more loudly. "But I was just supporting my dad."

"Really? Has your dad ever been accused of roughing up a Black person?"

"Not that I know about."

Chase shot him a look. "Or stopping a Black person for driving through your neighborhood?"

"I don't know."

"I think you do, Billy. But let's put that aside for a moment. Were you really wearing that T-shirt to support your father, or the policeman accused of murdering George Floyd?"

"My father," Billy insisted.

Pausing again, Chase recalibrated his tone to one of mild curiosity. "By the way, are the majority of your classmates Black or white?"

"Black."

"Were you aware that some had strong feelings about the murder of George Floyd?"

"I guess so."

"In fact, the whole of your civics class that day was spent discussing George Floyd."

A flicker of disapproval crossed Billy's face. "Pretty much."

"Do you remember what your Black classmates said about the case?"

Briefly, Billy folded his arms. "It sounded like they were against the police."

For an instant, Chase wanted to say *They're against murder, you bigoted little shit.* But he was living in two dimensions now, anger feeding his purpose. "What about you, Billy? Did *you* express an opinion?"

"I might have."

"Might have? Didn't you in fact say that the prosecution was all politics?"

"Yeah, I think I said that."

"During this discussion, were you concerned that wearing a 'Back the Blue' T-shirt the day after the video of George Floyd's murder might offend your Black classmates?"

"I didn't care," Billy said with his first intimations of anger. "They've got their opinions, and I've got mine."

"Did Malcolm Hill have the right to object to your wearing that T-shirt?"

"He didn't have the right to punch me."

"That wasn't my question, Billy. Didn't you approach him by his locker?"

"That's not how it happened."

"No? Didn't you go up to him and demand to know how he liked your T-shirt?"

"Objection," Jackson said swiftly. "Asked and answered."

"Overruled," the judge responded with some asperity. "The witness may answer."

Billy looked from the judge to Chase. "I can't remember what I said."

"Really? Less than an hour ago, you told the jury you never spoke to Malcolm. In fact, weren't his first words a response to your question about whether he liked your T-shirt?"

"I don't remember," Billy repeated.

Chase stared at him. "Specifically, didn't he respond by asking whether your father thought the film of Derek Chauvin killing George Floyd was a training video?"

Billy stiffened. "All I remember is him insulting my father."

"Do you remember how you responded?"

"No."

"Were there any other kids close enough to hear?"

"I don't think so. The ones who saw him hit me were further down the hallway."

"But you do remember saying something to Malcolm, don't you?"

Billy hesitated, as though wondering if—somehow—someone he didn't know about had overheard him. That Chase knew about his conversation at home was clearly unnerving. "All I remember is him punching me."

Chase studied him with an air of disdain. "So let's refresh your recollection, Billy. Just before he hit you, didn't you call Malcolm Hill a "stupid fucking nigger?""

"No," Billy insisted.

"Why? Because you've never used that word in your life?"

Billy shrank back, shoulders hunched. "I don't remember ever saying that."

"Wait a minute. I distinctly recall you telling Ms. Jackson that you'd never called any Black person a racially disparaging term. You did say that, didn't you?"

"I guess so."

"Because you don't consider calling a Black person a 'fucking nigger' disparaging?"

Stubbornly, Billy shook his head. "I never said that."

"In fact, doesn't your father routinely refer to Black people as 'niggers'?"

Billy scowled. "Maybe once or twice."

"Think he was using the word 'nigger' as a term of endearment?"

"I don't know what he was thinking."

Chase tilted his head, as though viewing Billy from another angle. "But just to be clear, you're not denying that you sometimes refer to Black people as 'niggers.'"

"Like I said, I don't remember saying that."

"Is that because, unlike your dad, you don't refer to Blacks as 'niggers'? Or only because you usually don't call them 'nigger' to their face?"

"I told you. I don't remember saying that."

Chase conjured a look of incredulity. "Who would you say is your closest friend?"

Abruptly, Billy looked trapped. "Objection," Jackson said again. "Irrelevant."

Turning to the judge, Chase spread his hands. "The prosecution chose to call Mr. Palmer as a witness in a capital murder trial. Does the court require argument on this?"

"We do not," Tilly replied incisively. "Please answer the question, Mr. Palmer."

Billy's face set. "It's hard to say."

"I'm sure you're very popular, Billy, but who hangs out at your house the most?"

"Maybe Bo Morris. Or Grady Jarvis."

"Are they white or Black?"

"White."

"OK. If I had them brought here under oath and asked if you ever use the word 'nigger,' what would they say?"

"I don't know…"

"Really?" Chase cut in. "I thought you never use that word."

"Asked and answered," Jackson said in rising voice.

"Overruled," Tilly snapped. "The witness may answer."

Billy shifted. "I already said I don't remember."

"Is that because you say 'nigger' so commonly, you don't remember a specific time?"

Billy's voice tightened. "That's not true."

"So do you now remember calling Malcolm Hill a 'stupid fucking nigger'?"

"No," Billy insisted. "I don't."

"Did you ever discuss Malcolm with your friends?"

"I don't remember."

"Do you remember whether you disliked Malcolm Hill?"

"He *punched* me out…"

"I meant before that day."

Billy frowned. "I guess I didn't like him much."

"For what reason?"

"He was always mouthing off in class. I thought he was too full of himself."

By now, Chase hoped, more jurors than not had begun seeing Billy as evasive and resentful of Blacks. But that was not yet enough. More quietly, he asked, "You just don't like Black people very much, do you?"

Billy's mouth became a stubborn line. "That depends on who they are."

"In other words, you like some but not others?"

"Sure."

"Again, isn't it also true that at Cade County High School, there are far more Black students than white?"

"That's right. Way more."

"So who were your Black friends in high school?"

"Objection," Jackson said. "This is no more relevant than questions about Deputy Bullock's racial attitudes."

Chase faced the judge. "Respectfully, Your Honor, the prosecution should be careful before their argument turns on them. For now, I'll point out that Mr. Palmer testified that the punch was unprovoked, and that his racial attitudes had no bearing on his confrontation with Malcolm. Among other things, this goes to credibility."

"Overruled," Tilly said yet again.

"OK, Billy," Chase said promptly. "Have you had time to remember the names of your closest Black friends? One or two will be good enough."

Billy shifted in his seat. "It's hard to say."

"We can narrow it down. Which of your Black friends have you had over to your house?"

"I don't remember any."

"That wouldn't go over with your dad very well, would it?"

Again, Billy hesitated. "I don't know."

"You really don't? Which neighborhood does your family live in?"

"Eastwood."

"Would you say there are quite a few law enforcement officers in your neighborhood?"

"I think so."

"In fact, that's where Deputy Bullock lived."

Billy's eyes narrowed. "Yeah. About two blocks away." He glanced toward where, Chase assumed, Dorothy Bullock sat watching. "His family still does."

Chase decided to take a chance. "Did the Bullock family ever come to your house?"

Billy paused yet again. "Maybe once or twice. Like, for a barbecue out in the backyard."

"Are you aware of any Blacks living in Eastwood?"

"Objection," Jackson said. "The defense has had a great deal of latitude in cross-examining this witness. But his knowledge of Eastwood is totally irrelevant."

"I'll withdraw the question," Chase responded easily, "and substitute another." Turning back to Billy, he asked, "Prior to your confrontation, did your father stop Malcolm when he was driving through the neighborhood?"

"Yeah, he told me that."

"Do you know whether your father cited him for anything?"

"I don't know."

"What did he tell you?"

"I don't remember."

"Wasn't it because he didn't like Black people driving through Eastwood?"

"I told you. I don't remember."

Placing his hands on his hips, Chase appraised the witness. "I have to say, Billy, that for a young man you have a really terrible memory—or a really convenient one. So let me ask you this: Just before you called Malcolm Hill a 'stupid fucking nigger,' didn't you ridicule him for not having a father?"

Billy hesitated yet again. During the entire trial, Chase thought, he had never heard a deeper quiet. Silent, he watched Billy consider anew whether someone might have overheard him. "I might have said something," Billy mumbled.

"Seems like you were misinformed," Chase observed mildly. "By the way, are you going to college this year?"

For the first time, Billy glanced at Malcolm, a look of spite changing his face. "Not this year. I was hoping for a baseball scholarship."

"I guess you didn't get one."

"No."

"And you blame Malcolm for that, don't you?"

"Sure. That scout from Mercer never saw me pitch."

Once again, Chase assumed an expression of curiosity. "Was Mercer the only college that expressed interest?"

"Yeah."

"You pitched your whole senior year after that, didn't you?"

Billy crossed his arms. "After what Malcolm did to me, nobody came around."

Chase permitted himself a faint, fleeting smile. "Well, you've certainly gotten back at him, haven't you? But has it ever occurred to you, Billy, that you're just not good enough to compete at the college level?"

"Objection," Jackson said. "This kind of badgering is grossly unfair to the witness."

Chase turned to her. "I certainly don't want to be 'unfair' to *this* witness," he responded with the barest trace of contempt, "let alone debate whether calling him to testify was unfair and, if so, to whom. Anyhow, I'm done with him."

Quickly scanning the jurors, Chase saw the look of satisfaction on Robert Franklin's face. When he sat down, he felt Malcolm grasp his wrist beneath the table.

★ ★ ★

Immediately, Amanda Jackson was on her feet. "Your father wears his uniform every day, doesn't he?"

Billy sat straighter. "Yes, ma'am. Every day he puts himself on the line. We still talk about those two officers who got killed, and their families."

"And that wasn't the first day you wore that T-shirt to school, was it?"

"No, ma'am. It sure wasn't."

Jackson nodded with satisfaction. "And the reason you wear it is not to antagonize anyone, but to express pride in your dad."

"That's right." Billy shot Malcolm a brief glance of spite. "Look at what it cost me."

But for the demands of decorum, Chase would have laughed at the expression on Dalton Harris' face. He resolved to forgo further cross-examination.

72

Over the noon break, Ford and Chase ate sandwiches in a conference room, taking stock of how the trial stood.

"Saw that hug Allie gave you just now," Ford observed. "Don't think I could have questioned Billy Palmer any better."

The deep relief Chase felt made Ford's compliment almost as welcome as the look on Allie's face. Only now did Chase allow himself to fully contemplate the risk he had taken. "Sure you could have," he answered. "Once Tilly let me go after him, Billy was semicooked. He's stupid to begin with, he'd clearly lied to Harris about how racist he was, and he didn't know we had a line on what he and Woody had said about the George Floyd video. You could see him wondering what else we knew."

Ford smiled a little. "Yeah, it was fun to watch him squirm. But here's why it wound up being smart to let you have him, all against my better judgment—you're Malcolm's dad. Maybe Albert Tilly cut you some slack because you're a classy white guy, maybe it's that Woody and Billy Palmer aren't *his* kind of white guy. But I don't think Tilly wanted to be the judge who cut off Malcolm's father on CNN."

He paused before continuing, serious now. "Yeah, give me the same leeway and as a lawyer I could have discomfited Billy just fine. But only you could do that as his father, and I could see it mattered to him. I think that puts the two of you in a different place."

Remembering Malcolm gripping his wrist, Chase hoped that much was true. But he did not know whether his cross-examination of Billy

Palmer would make a real difference in the trial itself. There was too much left to go, too many decisions yet to make—including whether Malcolm would testify in his own defense. While Chase hoped that his deconstruction of Billy would serve as a counterexample, he decided not to press the point. The conflict he sensed coming would arrive soon enough.

But, perhaps, Ford had read his thoughts. "Problem is," he told Chase, "in terms of the prosecution case, we just had our high point. In an hour or so, the GBI social media expert will take Mr. Double-XX out there for an encore, doing his best to make Malcolm look bad, and maybe even rehabilitate Billy. Without that video, we could all go home, and come September Allie could pack Malcolm off to Morehouse. At least if he's ready after ten months in lockup having nightmares about Bullock."

Ford's unspoken admonition, Chase sensed, was that Malcolm would need to testify—both to explain the video and the shooting, and as an emotional imperative. But Chase contented himself with saying, "I don't envy you this particular cross-examination."

Ford shrugged. "True that," he said. "You get all the easy ones."

★ ★ ★

By midafternoon, Malcolm felt his optimism receding into worry and despair.

The prosecution's social media expert, Dr. Mary Blaine, who had a PhD in computer science, was a plump and placid-seeming Black professional of indeterminate age who, if anything, seemed to regret the need to verify the video he had so carelessly posted. Beside her was the television screen on which, once again, Double-XX would appear before the jury to urge that Blacks kill white police.

Sitting on each side of Malcolm, Chase and Ford had assumed the bored expressions that he had learned signaled trouble. Malcolm could not bring himself to look toward his mother—or the jurors.

"After securing the defendant's laptop and cell phone," Harris asked Blaine, "what steps did you take?"

Briefly, the witness seemed to frown at her own work. "Among other things," she answered, "I reviewed the defendant's texts, emails, and social media sites since 2018, as well as his visits to websites and other sources of information."

"What did you find?"

Blaine clasped her hands. "Most commonly, the websites Mr. Hill frequented concerned allegedly abusive police practices involving Blacks. He regularly followed the Black Lives Matter movement and its leaders, and sometimes posted their materials on Facebook. He also tracked a wide variety of sources involving the specific deaths or shootings of Black men and women in encounters with police, including Breonna Taylor, George Floyd, Tamir Rice, Eric Garner, Philando Castile, and Michael Brown."

Watching Blaine, Malcolm sensed that she was independently familiar with these incidents and found them troubling. Moving past them, Harris asked, "Did you also find a video by a rap artist known as Double-XX?"

The witness' expression became as neutral as her tone. "I did. In June 2021, Mr. Hill posted it on his Facebook page."

"In other words, only a year before the fatal shooting of George Bullock."

"That's correct."

At a nod from Harris, Amanda Jackson stood, clicker in hand. "Thank you, Dr. Blaine," Harris said. "I'd like to play a video and ask if you could identify it for the jury."

Once again, Double-XX filled the screen.

Repetition, Malcolm discovered, only enhanced his sense of how incendiary the video would seem to others. The rapper's gangsta posturing. The propulsive rhythm of the words. The black handgun dangling from his finger—apparently a Glock 19. The demand for the random shootings of white police in reprisal for the death of Blacks—now linked to Malcolm's assiduous attention, to the cases of Blacks killed by cops. In the imaginings of jurors, this could have become Malcolm's ongoing obsession, until he acted out a rapper's instructions by murdering George Bullock.

Concluding the video, Double-XX told the jury: "If a white cop dies after any time another white cop kills a Black, that's deterrence."

Jackson hit a button, freezing his image. In the silence, Harris asked Blaine, "Is that the video the defendant posted on his Facebook page?"

"Yes."

"Did the defendant ever take it down?"

"He did not."

Once again, Malcolm cursed himself for having half forgotten the video's fateful existence. "To be clear, then," Harris prodded, "this video advocating the murder of police remained on the defendant's Facebook page on the night a bullet from his Glock 19 took the life of Deputy Bullock."

This time, Malcolm thought, the witness' manner betrayed weary resignation at her role in Harris' drama. "That's correct," she answered without inflection. "It was."

★ ★ ★

Apprehensive, Allie watched Jabari Ford rise to question the witness. Leaning close, her mother whispered in protest, "That video isn't like our baby." As if hearing her, without seeking permission Ford took the clicker and banished Double-XX from the courtroom. Only then did he turn to Blaine.

"Dr. Blaine," he asked politely, "did Malcolm Hill himself ever post a comment on this video—let alone endorse the sentiments expressed?"

"He did not," she answered firmly. "All he did was post it."

"You testified to performing an exhaustive search of his emails, texts, and postings for approximately four years—in other words, since he was roughly fourteen years old. Did you ever find anything else that suggested the commitment of violent acts against police?"

"Nothing."

"You also mentioned that the defendant followed cases where police had harmed or killed Black men and women. In many of those cases, were the victims unarmed?"

For an instant, Allie imagined the hint of satisfaction in Blaine's eyes. "Many," she answered. "One of the themes running through those cases is that the victims were defenseless."

Glancing at Harris, Allie saw the briefest look of irritation. "Is it correct," Ford asked the witness, "that not all of the cases that Malcolm followed involved misconduct by police?"

"That's true."

"Indeed, Dr. Blaine, the cases of Trayvon Martin and Ahmaud Arbery involved the fatal shooting of unarmed Black men by self-appointed white vigilantes."

Harris stood. "Objection, Your Honor, to the characterization of the whites involved in those incidents."

Tilly raised his eyebrows. "What term would you prefer, Mr. Harris—'guardians,' 'watchdogs,' 'protectors of the peace,' or something else? The three men who killed Mr. Arbery were convicted of murder. The witness may answer."

"That's correct," Blaine promptly told Ford. "Both cases involved the death of unarmed Blacks at the hands of white civilians."

Ford nodded. "In the course of your review of materials accessed by Malcolm Hill, did you also find a case where a white sheriff's deputy in Georgia was arrested for communicating with the leader of a white nationalist group?"

"Objection," Harris said again. "The question is beyond the scope of direct examination, as well as the opinion expressed by this witness."

"Not so," Ford answered promptly. "The proper scope of cross-examination covers the entirety of Dr. Blaine's examination of information consumed by the defendant. It's not confined to the single piece of evidence Mr. Harris chose to offer."

The judge nodded briskly. "Objection overruled."

Briefly, Blaine glanced at Harris. "I did," she told Ford. "Two newspaper articles accessed by Mr. Hill involved alleged misconduct by a deputy in Wilkinson County."

"What did that case involve?"

"Several things," Blaine answered. "The deputy in question was accused of beating Blacks in custody." For an instant, the witness' gaze flickered toward Malcolm. "According to the articles, he told the leader of a white extremist group that he meant to charge Black people with felonies to keep them from voting, and to intimidate voting rights workers—or maybe worse."

"Specifically, Dr. Blaine, did one of the articles report that the deputy had threatened to 'kill or castrate' canvassers who registered Blacks?"

Again, the witness glanced at Malcolm. "That's correct."

"Thank you," Ford said. "No further questions."

It was the most Jabari could do, Allie thought. He could not change the video, or erase its adverse implications for her son. Instead, Ford had laid the groundwork for explaining why Malcolm had purchased a lethal handgun—not to murder a law enforcement officer but to protect himself from one.

But only if Malcolm chose to testify.

From the bench, Judge Tilly was addressing Harris. "Is this your final witness, Mr. Harris?"

"It is," the district attorney responded calmly. "The prosecution rests."

73

At ten o'clock the next morning, Jabari Ford asked the court to dismiss the prosecution of Malcolm Hill for the murder of George Bullock.

With the jury absent, he stood at a podium in the well of the courtroom. The rapt spectators who crowded the seating area included Allie and Janie Hill, Dorothy Bullock and her children, Fay Spann, locals of varied races, and a throng of print and television reporters ready to supplement the cameras instantaneously broadcasting the proceedings to millions of Americans.

Outside, Chase felt certain, the throng that had greeted them as they arrived—demonstrators supporting Malcolm; white militia led by the Parnells—remained to await Tilly's ruling. Sitting beside Malcolm, he could feel his son's tension.

"Your Honor," Ford concluded, "the prosecution case has failed on its own terms. Even if you interpret the evidence most favorably to the tendentious theories it espouses, it has not—and cannot—prove beyond a reasonable doubt that Malcolm Hill committed an act of murder. Under the law, we respectfully submit, this court is required to dismiss these charges with prejudice."

"Mr. Harris?" the court said. "Do you feel the need to respond?"

In itself, the wording of the inquiry put Chase on edge. "Briefly, Your Honor," Harris responded in a confident manner. "The court saw that video, and so did the jury. The operative question is simply this: whether there is evidence sufficient for rational jurors to find the defendant guilty. The fact that there may be opposing interpretations regarding some of the physical evidence does not support an acquittal. That's all the more true when there's substantial evidence of the defendant's intention to commit murder, including his penchant for violence and loathing of law enforcement officers. Under the law of Georgia, this motion must be denied."

This line of argument reflected what Chase had expected. Despite the problems with this case, Harris hoped to get past this motion, force Malcolm to testify and, having wounded him, persuade the jury that an angry and inebriated Malcolm Hill had murdered George Bullock. The one thing that would surely end his public career would be to lose here and now.

With an air of command, Judge Tilly surveyed the courtroom, its inhabitants, and the cameras that had followed him to this critical passage. In somber tones, he said, "We must agree with the district attorney, Mr. Ford. In trials like this, the evidence is frequently ambiguous. That's what trials are for, and juries—to sift the evidence, including that regarding the defendant's intent at the time of the victim's death, and then measure it against the appropriate legal standard for conviction. Motion denied."

Sitting close to Malcolm, Chase felt his son slump in his chair. There was a brief murmur from those watching before Tilly cracked his gavel. "With that," he said to Ford, "is the defense ready to proceed?"

Briefly, Ford glanced at Chase. "May it please the court, we request until tomorrow morning to consider whether to call witnesses. And, if so, whom."

The time for decision was here, Chase knew. Within minutes, every legal analyst on cable would be talking about whether the defense would call Malcolm Hill.

"Very well," Tilly responded. "The court will reconvene at ten o'clock tomorrow morning. At that time, we will either hear from the first defense witness or commence closing argument."

★ ★ ★

Moments later, Chase and Ford sat across from each other in his conference room.

Chase felt torpid and dispirited. "It's not that either of us expected to win," he told Ford. "What made it so hard was knowing that Malcolm has gotten his hopes up, and then watching him return to jail without knowing if he'll ever see freedom again. I could feel the life going out of him, and know Allie was seeing it, too." His voice softened. "I keep thinking about the two of us at Harvard, with me not knowing she was pregnant, and wishing that somehow I could go back and redirect all our lives."

"But you can't," Ford answered. "So time's up, Chase. You don't want to call witnesses, do you?"

Chase forced himself to refocus. "No. I don't."

"Didn't think so," Ford said crisply. "But you'd better spell that out for me."

"It's pretty simple. Any DA who's not an idiot could get this case past a motion to dismiss. But Harris has had his shot, and I don't think he's close to proving his case beyond a reasonable doubt. If we rest our case without calling witnesses, that's the message we'd be sending to the jury."

Ford looked askance at him. "So, you'd hang Malcolm's future on reasonable doubt. We just go to the jury, without him ever saying a word in his own defense. Without anyone saying anything in his defense." He leaned forward. "Are you really willing to take that kind of risk?"

"Not happily. But anything we do is a risk—especially calling Malcolm, which is exactly what the prosecution wants us to do. I can't dismiss the not-insignificant chance that Harris could tear him apart. You saw what I did to Billy."

"If I hadn't," Ford rejoined, "I was pretty sure you'd remind me. Look, I know it's a risk. But like you say, Billy Palmer is a moron. Your and Allie's son isn't, I think you'd be the first to acknowledge. No matter how you feel, he's the one whose life is on the line."

"I know that all too well, Jabari. But once we put him on, we can forget about everything else. It will all come down to how the jury sees him." Chase paused, then began speaking with all the urgency he felt. "What has Harris got? His experts can't tell them anything about Malcolm's intent. I'm pretty sure the Black jurors saw Billy Palmer for who he is. That leaves the videotape, and you did an optimal job of using Blaine to provide an alternative explanation for why Malcolm bought that gun. Why effectively erase all that on the chance that calling Malcolm makes things better?"

Ford's eyes narrowed in thought. "I tend to agree with you about the experts. I think we dented Harris' enough that we don't need to call our own. But no witnesses at all? Setting aside Malcolm, I can think of two: Al Garrett, and a formidable woman you pretty much know better than anyone. Alexandria Hill."

Surprised, Chase studied him. "In terms of sheer presence, I'd take both Allie and Garrett. But what would you call them for?"

"Several things. First, presence matters. You're right that the Blacks on the jury have seen one version or another of Billy Palmer all their lives. But what about somebody they can actually identify with in a positive way?

"Al Garrett is an authoritative Black man, and he can spell out a lot better than Nick Spinetta how many departmental policies Bullock violated, and why they exist. And if we don't call Malcolm—or even if we do—Allie's the best character witness we've got. She may be his mother, but most of the Blacks on the jury respect her like pretty much no one else. I think that they not only hope to see Allie; they want to." Ford looked at Chase intently. "Put her on, and she can tell the jury all that Malcolm knew about death threats, white nationalists posting his picture and directions to their house. If you don't think that resonates, you need to spend more time here."

Silent, Chase parsed his thoughts. "I get all that," he answered. "But they could rough her up about the things she didn't know about her son—like his posting that video and buying a Glock."

Ford gave him a thin smile. "She'll get by. I can see you betting against half of your newfound family, however imprudent that might be. But Allie? Do you really want to do that?"

Chase emitted a brief, halfhearted laugh. "Not particularly."

"Smart man. So here's the rest of my thinking about Malcolm. For this whole fucking case, George Bullock has been a cardboard corpse. We know he was a bigot, but they won't let us prove it." Ford jabbed the table with his finger. "Call Malcolm, and suddenly the jury hears about all the things he said and did—knowing who Malcolm was, hating

Allie, turning off those headlights. You don't think that our man Robert Franklin isn't going to snap to attention?

"But here's the other thing—once we roll out the real Bullock, which we can only do through Malcolm, we can ask Tilly for more slack in asking someone like Spinetta who Bullock really was. Harris sure can't keep on saying that's irrelevant to what happened on Old County Road."

Chase hesitated, weighing the known risks against what, to him, were speculative benefits. "I understand," he finally responded. "But suppose Spinetta comes back and says that the real George Bullock loved Black people, and never said a racist thing. You just don't know, but the man was Bullock's friend."

Slowly, Ford nodded. "True. Still, I think there are multiple reasons we end up calling Malcolm. But I'm willing to wait on deciding until after the jury sees Garrett and Allie. Suit you?"

It was more of a concession, Chase understood, than Ford needed to make—perhaps only a courtesy. But, for now, he would take it.

"Suits me," he answered.

74

As Chase lay on the bed, contemplating the multiple implications of calling Malcolm as a witness in his own defense, Allie stepped from the shower.

Entering the bedroom, she wore nothing. For an instant, the image froze in Chase's mind. She was achingly lovely, and the superficial domesticity of the moment seemed especially poignant. In another life, this could be their reality. But reality awaited them in the courtroom where, tomorrow, Allie would testify on their son's behalf.

The twisting path to this moment had begun nineteen years ago, at Harvard, on the night of Black Juliet. Now both Chase and Allie carried the years within them. They were the same, yet very different, their essences rooted in lives that were the accretion of events and choices made with no thought that the two of them would, or could, ever be together. Yet they were, and the comfort they felt in each other's presence was at once real and ephemeral, subject to events over which they had no control, as well as to the pull of the commitments each had made over time, transforming who they once had been into the separate people they were now, and would be in the future.

However fraught the space that had allowed them to first fall in love, this temporal cocoon was even more fragile. There was another person now, Malcolm, whose fate was inextricably tied to theirs and that reality, depending on the outcome, would affect their relationship with each other, and with him, in differing and perhaps conflicting ways. Every day was precious, yet there was no time to consider that, let alone to savor it. The reckoning all of them faced was too overwhelming, for Malcolm most of all.

Naked, Allie paused to look at him. "What are you thinking?"

So many things, he could have said. *I was hoping our son doesn't testify, knowing you feel otherwise. So, inevitably, I turned to regretting, yet again, the crosscurrents in our lives, and what they might do to all three of us.*

"I was thinking you were beautiful," he answered.

She smiled a little. "So why don't you hold me for a while? I wouldn't mind that."

Sitting up, he held out his arms. Then she curled up against him, skin to skin. "This is nice," she murmured.

He kissed her hair. "Always was."

In a moment or two, Chase knew, their talk would turn back to the trial, what she needed to accomplish for them all. But, for an instant, they had this.

★ ★ ★

Sitting with her mother in the front row of the courtroom, Allie watched Sheriff Al Garrett settle into the witness stand. Even here, the sight of him was somehow reassuring.

His sheer bulk, all mass and muscle, seemed to render his surroundings a little smaller, and an erect military posture combined with an unwavering gaze seemed to make him even more imposing. But however tough and unflinching Al Garrett could be, beneath his laconic manner lived a compassionate and even gentle soul.

As a child, he'd had very little—a missing father, a fitfully loving but feckless and distracted mother, no money to speak of. In many ways, his father figure had been the army, and he had returned to Cade County with an iron self-discipline and a resolve to follow the rules while making them a little kinder, a little better. The authority figure he had become still preserved within the wistful, lonely boy whom the adult Sheriff Garrett remembered with a compassion he extended to others. He was that all-too-rare person, Allie knew—a good man who had willed himself to be so.

On the stand, as elsewhere, he evinced the fatalism of someone who did not expect life's surprises to be pleasant. The widespread respect he enjoyed in the county for fairness, including from many whites, was mirrored in the attentiveness of the jury. Within the constraints of his office, Allie felt certain, he would do what he could to help Malcolm. But she knew him well enough to sense when he did not like his circumstances. She felt that now, and wondered what the reasons might be.

Questioning him, Jabari Ford began with his tenure as sheriff. "When you took office, Sheriff Garrett, what steps did you take to improve the relations between Blacks and whites in your department?"

Garrett settled in, back still straight, giant hands folded in his lap. "I did several things," he answered in his baritone voice. "I made sure that my deputies dealt with all races, both inside and outside their duties as law enforcement officers. My white deputies went to civic functions held by Blacks, and vice versa. There's not much of that around here, and I thought it would be good for the community, and good for my officers."

He looked toward the jury, as though he saw them as another opportunity for public education. "I acclimated young Black deputies to being trained and supervised by whites, and did the same for new white deputies who were mentored by Blacks. I hired more officers of color, both men and women. The whole idea, as best as I could do it, was to create a department where law enforcement wasn't defined by race."

"Did you also take steps to reduce the incidence of racially motivated abuses?"

"I did. More generally, I also wanted to ensure that my deputies interacted with members of the community, Black or white, in a lawful and appropriate manner."

Ford moved to the side, as though to assure that the jurors remained focused on Garrett. "What specific steps did you take to help accomplish that?"

"There were several," Garrett answered firmly. "Because of manpower and budgetary constraints, each deputy patrols the county alone. To make sure that they conducted themselves appropriately, I gave them dashboard and body cameras that also have an audio function. Then I made it a rule—no exceptions—that every deputy had to turn on both cameras before making a traffic stop, and turn on their body camera during any encounter with a member of the public."

"Were you able to monitor whether your deputies followed the policy?"

"Definitely. We have specialists who monitor our technology twenty-four hours a day—dashboard and body cameras, when lights and sirens are employed. Whenever a deputy turns on a siren, a specialist contacts me. After that, I can download video and audio from the cameras to look at traffic stops and other interactions. That way I can review the conduct of our deputies, and make sure they're accountable."

"Was one of your concerns to determine whether deputies exhibited racial bias toward members of the public?"

"Absolutely."

It was only a matter of time, Allie knew, before Ford reintroduced Deputy George Bullock to the jury. "What procedures do you follow if a deputy may have violated your procedures, or otherwise operated outside the law?"

Again, Garrett faced the jurors. "First, I've got a zero-tolerance policy. Most folks in this county can remember a time when deputies would just pull over some motorist outside the city limits, maybe in the dark, so they could act out their own bigotry or abuse their authority. Those days are done with. If the deputy doesn't turn on his cameras or otherwise follow regulations, he answers to me—I automatically assume that the deputy acted inappropriately, and investigate the circumstances. If it happens once too often, like more than once, their job is on the line."

Malcolm, Allie saw, was riveted to the sheriff—as was Dalton Harris. In the same even tone, Ford asked, "During your tenure as sheriff, did you meet with Deputy George Bullock to discuss what you considered to be his questionable conduct?"

Harris stood at once. "Objection, Your Honor. What the victim did or didn't do in unrelated circumstances is completely irrelevant to the issues in this case. Not to mention potentially prejudicial."

On the witness stand, Garrett turned toward the judge. "Sustained," Tilly said promptly. "Move on, Mr. Ford."

Looking back at Garrett, beneath his impassivity Allie read a hint of frustration. "Sheriff Garrett," Ford asked crisply, "did Deputy Bullock comply with departmental policy when he stopped Malcolm Hill?"

Quickly and incisively, Garrett answered, "He did not."

Glancing at Dorothy Bullock, Allie caught her stare of anger at Jabari Ford. "In what respect?" Ford asked.

"Several," Garrett answered. "He never called in the stop. He never turned on his dashboard camera. He never turned on his body camera. He never interacted with the department in any way."

Ford nodded. "Would you expect that kind of noncompliance from a thirty-year veteran of the sheriff's department?"

"I wouldn't expect it from anyone in my department. Even rookies know the rules. But it was especially notable in a deputy as experienced as George Bullock."

"In terms of evaluating his conduct on June 22, 2022, what were the results?"

"We have no video or audio evidence of Deputy Bullock's interactions with Malcolm Hill. Effectively, he was operating in the dark."

"Were you able to investigate the reasons for his behavior?"

"I was not," Garrett said flatly. "Deputy Bullock was dead at the scene, and the GBI took over the investigation."

"Did the GBI ask you for information about Deputy Bullock?"

"Yes. They asked what our system showed about the movements of his patrol car in the moments before he stopped Malcolm Hill."

"And what did they reveal?"

"According to the GPS, he'd been waiting by the side of Old County Road, a couple miles outside of town. Before he turned on the siren, it looked like he'd been following Malcolm for several minutes."

"In terms of visibility, Sheriff Garrett, how would you characterize the stretch of road where Deputy Bullock stopped the defendant?"

Eyes narrowing slightly, Garrett seemed to consider how to phrase his answer. "About as dark as it gets. No lights, no buildings close to the road. It's all woods and fields."

For a moment, Ford paused, letting the jury imagine the scene. In a tone of curiosity, he asked, "In the course of its investigation, did anyone from the GBI ask for your evaluation of George Bullock's performance as a law enforcement officer?"

"Objection," Harris said promptly. "Irrelevant. Again, the question has nothing to do with the night in question, or with Malcolm Hill's motives or intent at the time of the shooting."

"Sustained," the judge snapped, and trained an admonishing stare on Ford. "You're well aware of our prior rulings on this point, Counselor. Ignore them at your peril."

"Thank you, Your Honor," Ford said in tenor that, to Allie, suggested no more gratitude than she felt herself. Turning to Garrett, Ford asked, "Did you make the GBI aware of the departmental policies regarding the use of body and dashboard cameras?"

"I did."

"Did you also suggest to the GBI, in words or substance, that you were concerned about Deputy Bullock's reasons for not activating those cameras?"

"Objection," Harris interjected. "Irrelevant. Further, the question calls for speculation on a matter concerning which Sheriff Garrett has already testified that he lacks knowledge."

Ford shook his head. "Not so, Your Honor. By virtue of his position, Sheriff Garrett has all sorts of knowledge regarding Deputy Bullock. Moreover, he specifically testified as to his presumptions when a deputy violates department policy."

Expectantly, Garrett turned to the judge, as if awaiting permission to answer. "Sustained," Tilly ruled.

Watching Garrett, Allie again detected the fleeting hint of frustration crossing his face. Furious, she felt law concealing the truth of George Bullock.

"No further questions," Ford said.

Returning to the defense table, he gave Chase a glance that, to Allie, seemed intended to convey a message that only the two lawyers understood.

★ ★ ★

Standing, Harris approached the witness. "In your experience, Sheriff Garrett, do deputies sometimes forget to turn on their body cameras?"

Garrett's heavy shoulders moved in a minimal shrug. "They have."

"And in individual cases, have you determined that it was a case of forgetfulness or excitement, rather than malicious intent?"

"I have," Garrett answered, his expression stony. "In those cases, I took into account the experience of the particular deputy."

To Allie, the implications of the answer were as clear as, it seemed, they were to Harris.

"No further questions," he said.

75

That afternoon, Allie took the stand.

Uneasy, Chase watched her. Among the trial's many ironies was that between Malcolm's parents, he, not Allie, had heretofore occupied center stage. Now, at last, the jury would hear from the mother who had loved him from the first, fearful moments of his birth.

They had discussed her approach. She would speak to the jury and, as best she could, directly to Robert Franklin, the Black bank officer with a teenage son. *Surely*, she would try to convey, *you understand the dangers our boys face in common.*

Efficiently but sympathetically, Ford elicited from her the facts of Malcolm's life prior to the shooting. The closeness of his family. His love for his grandfather. The community service he performed through his church. His accomplishments—honors student, debater, all-conference athlete, class president, recipient of an academic scholarship to Morehouse. To Chase, her testimony was an affecting combination of quiet pride and love with an undertone of regret, as though her memories were now shadowed by the knowledge of what was to come.

Almost gently, Ford asked, "Before June 22, 2021, had Malcolm encountered any difficulties with the law?"

"None. His only encounter with the law was when an off-duty police officer stopped him from driving through Eastwood, on the way to visit his grandfather's grave."

This clear allusion to Woody Palmer, Chase knew, was arguably hearsay. But Harris did not object—clearly he had resolved to treat Allie Hill with due caution. "Did you discuss this incident with Malcolm?" Ford inquired.

Briefly, Allie regarded her son with an expression of tenderness and regret that, in turn, seemed to soften Malcolm's face. "I did. One of the hardest things for any mother of a Black son is to teach them a fear and caution they don't deserve to feel. How many white mothers, I wonder, have to teach their boys to say 'sir,' to keep their hands visible, to swallow insults—all so they don't wind up in jail, or dead? It's no wonder Malcolm followed the shooting of other Black men, or boys. Put him in the wrong place, at the wrong time, facing the wrong person, and he could be the next one. He grew up knowing that."

Listening, Chase thought of how lonely raising Malcolm must have been for her, how different his own life might have felt had he spent years fearing for his son for reasons that transcended teenage carelessness. Fruitlessly, he wished that they had always been a family, that he could have shared the difficulties faced by Allie and their son.

"Aside from the dangers peculiar to Black men," Ford asked her, "does your particular family face unique dangers?"

"Yes," Allie responded simply. "Because of my work."

"Could you describe that work, Ms. Hill?"

Again, she oriented herself toward the jury "I'm the CEO of the Blue Georgia Movement. It's dedicated to ensuring that all citizens of Georgia, particularly the poor and people of color, have the right to vote.

One of the sad paradoxes of our mission is that defending something so American generates so much hatred."

Ford nodded. "In the course of that work, do you receive death threats?"

Allie's expression became somber. "Yes. Especially since the election of 2020."

"How frequently?"

"It depends on how close we are to an election. In the months prior to November 2022, I was averaging four to five a week, mostly through anonymous emails or calls to my office."

The resignation in her tone, Chase thought, made the testimony more chilling. Looking toward the jury, he saw that Robert Franklin's expression was clouded. "Do workers for Blue Georgia also receive threats?" Ford asked Allie.

"Unfortunately, they do. Our offices also receive bomb threats and other forms of intimidation. Right after the 2020 election, armed members of a militia group known as White Lightning gathered in front of our office here in Freedom. As a result of all this, our budget for security alone runs well into seven figures."

Harris, Chase noted, seemed unusually still, as if bracing for a line of testimony about which he could do little. "Let's turn to Malcolm," Ford told Allie. "Was he aware of the threats against your life?"

"He had to be," she responded. "After 2016, I got advice from our security firm about how to protect my family—Malcolm, my mother, and my late father. We never went anywhere without texting each other to say where we were. We tried not to be alone in places we didn't know, or with people we didn't know—especially at night. We asked the neighbors to call us if they saw anything suspicious." Allie paused, then finished quietly, "Malcolm was thirteen years old, and part of a family security team to help protect each other. No one should have to grow up like that."

"Over time," Ford inquired, "did the threats against you intensify?"

"Yes. After the election of 2020, white nationalist groups posted my picture and directions to our home, saying that I was the woman who'd stolen the presidency. I had to show Malcolm, so that he'd know what was going on."

"How did he react?"

Silent, she looked back at her son. "Mostly, he was scared for me. I remember him asking if I was going to buy a gun for self-protection."

"What did you say to him?"

"That I hated guns. But he already knew that. They've taken too many lives, including Black lives."

Listening, Chase had a renewed sense of fate encircling Malcolm and his mother. "In earlier testimony," Ford said, "Dr. Blaine mentioned that Malcolm had accessed articles about a sheriff's deputy in mid-Georgia who texted a white nationalist about 'killing or castrating' voting rights workers. Did you discuss those with him?"

Allie bit her lip. "He discussed it with me. It was like the fifties and sixties, he said, when police and deputies stalked civil rights workers in the South. After that he got more worried about groups like White Lightning infiltrating law enforcement."

"Did the two of you also talk about the threats to canvassers for Blue Georgia?"

"We did."

"Do you recall the most recent conversation?"

For a moment, Allie gazed at her lap. "Yes," she answered softly. "It was in the spring of 2022, when he told me he wanted to spend the summer canvassing for us."

"How did you respond?" Ford asked.

"I didn't want him to do it. So I told him what I knew to be true—as my son, he was at greater risk of being targeted by anyone who hated me."

"What did he say to that?"

"He asked me where Blacks would be if they went and hid from everyone who hated them. *I* hadn't, he said, so why should my son?" She shook her head. "I was proud of him, and scared for him. But I let pride win out over fear, and helped put Malcolm in harm's way. No matter what happens, I'll live with that for the rest of my life."

Glancing at the jury, Chase saw Nettie Grey watching and listening with total absorption. The silence in the courtroom felt complete, almost suffocating. Sitting beside him, Malcolm clasped his hands together, gazing fixedly at the table.

"Did there come a time," Ford asked, "when Malcolm was specifically targeted by enemies of Blue Georgia?"

"There was," Allie responded in the same raw voice. "A right-wing website posted Malcolm's yearbook picture."

For the first time, Harris stood. "Excuse me, Your Honor. I've remained quiet out of courtesy to the witness, and sympathy for her personal situation as the defendant's mother as well as an activist in a time when disagreement has become far uglier than it should be. But I fail to see why these accounts, however affecting they may be, are germane to the events of June 22."

Instead of facing the judge, Ford spun on Harris. "Really?" he asked in a tone dripping with anger and incredulity. "You've spent the better part of this trial objecting to this or that testimony, claiming it isn't relevant to the defendant's state of mind on the night George Bullock stopped him on the darkest part of Old County Road. Now you're objecting to testimony so relevant that a six-year-old would understand it…"

"Enough, Mr. Ford," the judge cut in. "In responding to an objection, I'll thank you to address this court, not the prosecutor. But as a sixty-nine-year-old, I'm able to grasp your point. Mr. Harris' objection, if that's what it was, is overruled. Please continue."

"Thank you, Your Honor," Ford replied. "Please indulge me while I put up an enlargement of our own."

Returning to the defense table, he reached into a cardboard box similar to that used by the prosecution, extracted a Styrofoam rectangle, and placed it on the easel. Staring back at the jury was a blow-up of Malcolm's yearbook picture, bearing the caption "Allie Hill's illegitimate son."

"Does this enlargement," he asked Allie, "accurately depict a posting from the website of a group that calls itself Americans Against Replacement?"

Allie's lips compressed in anger. "It does."

"Did you show that to Malcolm?"

"Yes. I was even more afraid for him. So I asked if he'd consider working in our local office, at least for a while."

"What did he say?"

"That he refused to be intimidated."

"Do you recall the date of that conversation?"

"Distinctly." Allie seemed to draw a breath. "It was June 21. The day before the shooting."

Chase saw that the professor on the jury, Stephen Hewitt, had stopped taking notes and was staring openly at the enlargement and then at Allie. He, too, had a teenage son.

Ford was silent for a moment. Then he asked, "Did Malcolm tell you that he'd bought a gun for self-protection?"

Allie shook her head. "No. As I said, he knew how I felt about guns." Her voice fell off. "I hadn't told him that I'd started thinking about buying one. The threats just kept getting worse."

Again, Ford paused. "I'd like to turn to another subject. The prosecution has shown the jury a video Malcolm posted by a rap artist named Double-XX. Were you aware that he had done so?"

"No," Allie answered. "I wasn't. But now that I know *when* he did that, I understand why." She faced the jury, sadness suffusing her face and voice. "It was shortly after he first saw the video of George Floyd dying. He asked me when Black men were going to start defending themselves."

Ford moved to stand beside her. "Did he, at any time, say Blacks should indulge in random shootings of police to act as a deterrent to police violence?"

"He did not. He was very upset, like every other Black person who saw that sickening video. But he grew up knowing that *our* way, the way of our family, was to embrace nonviolence." Allie's voice grew firm again. "I don't know how many dinner table conversations we had, the four of us, talking about how violence only bred more violence, with Black people ending up on the losing end. That violence was not only wrong for its own sake, but because it would end up doing us great harm. That the only way to work for change was going from person to person, enlisting them in the process of building the better democracy they deserve."

She stopped abruptly, an anguished look surfacing in her eyes. "When he told me he wanted to help Blue Georgia, I knew he was continuing that work. That was another reason I said yes. Another reason I felt so very proud. In spite of everything that's happened to him, I still am."

"No further questions," Ford said softly. "Your witness, Mr. Harris."

★ ★ ★

Standing, Harris approached her, stopping at a respectful distance. "Just to be clear, Ms. Hill, your son didn't tell you about that video."

Allie composed herself. "No, he didn't."

"Nor did he tell you he had purchased a gun."

"No."

"On the night of June 22, did he tell you where he was?"

Allie hesitated. "He said that he was hanging out with friends."

"But did he tell you he'd been drinking?"

"No."

"Is he aware that the legal drinking age is twenty-one?"

"Yes. He knew that. He made a mistake."

Slowly, Harris nodded. "So you can't know what else he may not have told you, or anyone, about the events of June 22."

Allie regarded him coolly. "No, Mr. Harris, I can't. Just like you can't know what really happened after Deputy Bullock decided not to activate his body camera."

The lethal retort, Chase thought at once, left Harris off-balance. But it was too late to object, and to ask that Allie's response be stricken from the record would only make things worse. Nothing could strike it from the minds of the jurors.

Instead, seeking a graceful end to this, Harris turned to Tilly. "Given everything, Your Honor, it seems best to excuse Ms. Hill. I have no further questions."

76

In late afternoon, Ford, Chase, Allie, and Malcolm gathered around a conference table in the courthouse. The two deputies stationed outside, Chase thought, served as a reminder to Malcolm of the life that might await him. When the meeting was over, he would go back to the cell where he'd spent the last eight months, wondering if this imprisonment would end in another that lasted until death.

His son looked at once tired and fretful, glancing from one adult to the other. Tomorrow morning he would commence testifying in his own defense—or not. "Before we leave this room," Ford told him, "we have to know what you'll do. Your mother, father, and I all have opinions, and you should listen to them carefully. But in the end only you can decide."

"What do *you* think?" Malcolm asked him.

Ford considered him gravely. "That it's the biggest decision you'll ever make. All I can do as a lawyer is tell you the difference between testifying and going straight to the jury.

"Right now, our defense is based on reasonable doubt—the idea that Harris hasn't proven his case. I think we've done a pretty good job with that. But here's what we haven't done. We haven't said what actually happened that night. We haven't told the jury what Bullock said and did or who he really was. We haven't explained how that gun went off. Only you can do that."

Allie, Chase saw, watched their son intently. It seemed difficult for her not to speak. Turning to Chase, Malcolm said, "You're my lawyer, too."

Chase gathered himself, looking into his son's face. He had never seen Malcolm so vulnerable, and he found himself wishing that he did not need to speak. But he did.

"I'm also several other things," he answered. "I'm a dad who's just discovered his son. I'm a white guy who doesn't understand his place or its people. I'm somebody who spends a lot of time trying to imagine what it was like to be you before all this, and what it's like to be you now. I'm a man who loves your mother, and knows that she's listening to this with her heart in her throat. All that makes saying what I think impossibly hard."

Pausing, Chase willed himself not to look at Allie. "But you *are* my son, so I will. If it were up to me, you wouldn't testify tomorrow."

Malcolm's face tightened. "Why not?"

Chase glanced at the others. "For me, it's a matter of balancing risk and reward. I think Jabari has done a terrific job. As matters stand, I think we can win outright, or at least hang the jury. But once you testify, everything changes. For better or worse, you'd be taking the case off our shoulders and putting it on yours. Because nothing we've done until now will matter half as much as how you do tomorrow."

"So you don't believe in me," Malcolm said tightly. "Or maybe you just don't *believe* me."

Chase winced inside, fearing that every word he said would erode his son's fragile trust and, perhaps, his confidence. "I've always believed you, Malcolm. And I believe in you as a person. But what happens in a courtroom, as unfair as this is, has nothing to do with either of those things." He glanced at Ford. "You need to hear from Jabari. But I know he's familiar with something called sponsorship theory. Essentially, it's the idea that jurors tend to believe the testimony from a witness that is most damaging to the party who offers him up.

"Right now, that's working in our favor. We got Nick Spinetta to acknowledge you told him that the shooting was an accident. We got expert after expert to admit they can't say that you deliberately shot Bullock. We made that moron Billy Palmer look like the racist and liar he is. Add to that our own witnesses—Al Garrett all but said that Bullock was a rogue cop who made sure to stop you in the dark, and your mom explained all the threats that made you buy that gun. What does Harris have left? A fucking video. It's not enough. At worst, I think Jabari could hang this jury in his sleep.

"So ask yourself what Harris needs, and what he's clearly always wanted—a shot at you. You're ten times smarter than Billy Palmer. But you're eighteen years old. Dalton Harris is an experienced prosecutor with his career on the line, who's been thinking about little else except how to make you look bad in front of the jury. Don't give him the chance."

For a moment, Malcolm looked unsettled. "What do you think?" he asked Ford, and Chase felt the terrible burden of his decision.

Ford was quiet for a moment. "I think your dad wants what's best for you. I understand what he's saying, and there's sense in it. You never know about juries, but I think I can probably hang this one…"

"But what happens then?"

Ford gave a shrug of resignation. "More likely than not, Harris goes back to the drawing board and retries the case. Unless he decides to generously offer you a long stretch in prison with an eventual shot at parole. In either case, you stay where you are, waiting him out."

"I don't want that," Malcolm said.

"I know you don't," Ford answered. "But that's just the thing, isn't it? You want an acquittal, and you want to walk out of the jail and go eat a big plate of your grandma's cooking. All you want is your life back. So that's why you have to think about taking your chances, and taking the stand."

Abruptly, Malcolm's look of anger was replaced by deep consideration. "If I testify, do you think I've got a better chance of being acquitted?"

Ford gave something close to a sigh. "Yeah, I do. At least if you do as well as I think you can."

"Why's that?"

"I think the jury wants to see you. Once they do, they'll realize you're not the angry predator Harris wants them to imagine. Then they can start thinking about George Bullock. You tell them everything—that he turned off all the car lights. That he knew who you were. That he said disgusting things about your mother. That your work made him angry. That he threatened you might not live out the night. That he reached for the gun, and it went off in the struggle." Ford's voice gathered force. "Suddenly everything makes perfect sense—including why he never called in the stop or turned on his cameras.

"But here's another thing. I think once you testify about Bullock, all the crap about his political and racial views being irrelevant goes out the window. I believe the judge will let us put on the stuff from Bullock's Facebook page, and maybe take another shot at asking Spinetta and Garrett about who the man really was. I don't know about Spinetta, but I'm pretty sure Al's got more to say if Tilly lets him. If we're lucky, and we'd have to be, I think that would pretty much blow Dalton Harris out of the water."

Abruptly, Malcolm turned back to Chase with an accusatory stare. "You don't know what it's like to sit in jail for something you didn't do, day after day with no end in sight, never knowing if you'll end up in another cage. You don't know what it's like to wonder if they're going to kill you. You don't know what it's like listening to people call you a murderer, while you sit there like you've got tape over your mouth.

"You don't know what it's like listening to all the rules that say no one else but you can tell what that man really was." His voice rose. "I'm sick of being this person everyone talks about. I want to speak for myself."

Chase fortified himself. "So let me ask you this. Why did you take that gun out of the glove compartment?"

"You already know why. I was afraid he'd ask for my registration."

"And that's what you'd tell Harris tomorrow."

At the corner of his vision, Chase saw Ford's look of comprehension. "Yes," Malcolm said angrily. "It's the truth."

"I believe you," Chase responded. "But what happens when Harris asks why you didn't just take out the registration?"

For a moment, Malcolm seemed stunned. "I didn't think of it."

"So instead you took a deadly handgun out of the glove compartment, and hid the Glock where you could pull the trigger before Bullock knew what hit him. That's why he died with his gun in its holster." Chase softened his voice. "I'm sorry, Malcolm. I know it was an accident. But I used to be a prosecutor, so I also know there's always something you haven't thought of. So does Harris. He'll try to rattle you, make you lose your temper. He's the one in control."

Malcolm touched his eyes and then sat straighter, looking directly at Chase. "If I don't testify, they'll think I'm guilty."

For the first time, Allie spoke. "Chase," she said, "I'd like to talk with you for a moment. Just the two of us."

★ ★ ★

They stood in the hallway, face-to-face. "I'm sorry," Allie said. "But I couldn't watch that anymore. You're hurting him in there."

No one else, Chase thought, had her capacity to sting him. "I'm trying to help him, for God's sake. What I did just now was the last thing I wanted to do. But I'm reliably informed that parents do hard things. I don't want to sit there tomorrow watching Harris take him apart because I was too afraid of losing him to speak."

She looked into his eyes so intently that he felt the depth of her emotion. "I know you want to help. But our son is a young Black man who grew up in Cade County, and there are things about that you can't understand. There are things about *us* you still can't understand." Her voice quickened. "My parents taught me to stand up for myself. I always did. I taught Malcolm to stand up for himself. Now you're saying that he shouldn't when his life is on the line, that you've figured out for him that it's better not to.

"What if you're wrong? Could he live with himself in prison, or on death row, never having said what really happened? Could you live with yourself on Capitol Hill? Or as his father? I can tell you as his mother that I would taste the ashes in my mouth until the day he dies, and maybe for many years after that. Because I'm young enough to outlive him unless he dies as an old man in prison." Allie paused. "If we take away his right to speak, we'd be stealing his soul. And our own."

Shaken, Chase looked down at her. "What would you have me do?"

"Support him. Work with them tonight, helping him think about what Harris might do like you just did. But please, send him into that courtroom tomorrow as the best Malcolm Hill he can be. That's the best way to be your Black son's father."

Chase wasn't sure of that, or anything. All he knew was that he had said enough, and all that was left to him was to make the best of what would happen in the courtroom and among the three of them. "All right," he said at last. "Let's go back inside."

When they entered, both Ford and Malcolm looked up at them expectantly. But what struck Chase was the expression on Malcolm's face, hopeful and fearful at once.

Chase sat down beside him. "Your mom and I talked it over," he told his son. "The three of you are pretty persuasive, you most of all. What I want to do is help you prepare. Is that OK?"

Malcolm became quite still, as if to control his own emotions. "Yeah," he finally answered. "That's OK."

77

The following morning, at ten o'clock, Allie watched her son take the witness stand in his own defense.

The packed courtroom simmered with tension and antagonism. Among the spectators, Dorothy Bullock once again sat with Fay Spann. The omnipresent television cameras reflected what commentators identified as the trial's "defining moment."

Malcolm wore a suit, as he had to his senior prom and graduation. But this was one size smaller, to accommodate his loss of weight, and the other differences in Malcolm were wrenching to her. His face was too thin, accentuating the cheekbones he had inherited from Chase; the smile that had reminded her of Malcolm's father seemed a stranger to his lips; the playfulness lurking at the corners of his eyes had vanished; and his light brown skin appeared to have the pallor of someone who had barely seen the sun for almost nine months. In so many ways, he was a replica of the boy she had raised.

Still, his voice was steady, his demeanor resolute. However daunting the moment was, it seemed that Jabari and Chase had sent him to court with the most equilibrium he could manage. Though the atmosphere between Allie and Chase the night before had been strained, upon coming home from preparing Malcolm, Chase had tried to assure her that their son would be ready. "He's very smart," he told her. "He presents well, and you can feel his toughness as well as his heart. You're not his mother for nothing."

Wherever Malcolm's qualities came from, she thought, he needed them now.

The first part was easy enough. Smoothly, Ford led him through a life that, while shadowed by self-doubt and the absence of a father, featured a string of successes: student leadership, a school scoring record in football, class offices in all four years, a nearly flawless academic performance, Athlete of the Year in 2022, the scholarship to Morehouse, an unblemished record except for the fight with Billy Palmer.

"Before we get to the events on June 22," Ford said easily, "there are a couple of subjects emphasized by the prosecutor we need to address. The first is the video you posted by Double-XX. Maybe you can start by explaining why you did that."

"Yes, sir," Malcolm said in a calm, clear voice. "First of all, I wish I never had. I don't believe in what Double-XX said about shooting white police. But when I posted that I was angry about what police were doing to Blacks. I meant it as a kind of protest."

"Was there a particular event that motivated you?"

"There'd been a whole bunch of shootings where police officers killed unarmed Black men. Like Dr. Blaine said, I followed those cases. But when I posted that, I'd just seen the video of that policeman in Minneapolis killing George Floyd." Malcolm's tone grew quiet. "I just watched it, minute after minute, this white policeman with his knee on this helpless Black man's neck. He was so—I don't know—*relaxed*, like he had the right to do this with everyone watching because George Floyd wasn't human.

"I asked myself, 'Suppose that cop was just smart enough to do that in the dark, or that girl hadn't taken out her cell phone to record him? George Floyd wouldn't be this martyr. He'd just be another dead Black man no one remembers, and that white policeman would be free to go do it again.'That's when I got mad enough, just long enough, to post that video." Malcolm shook his head. "Problem is, once you post something, you give it a life longer than whatever feelings made you do it. It just never goes away, and so people can say it shows who you are."

That was good, Allie thought. "So why didn't you take it down?" Ford asked him.

Malcolm compressed his lips. "This is embarrassing to say. But I pretty much forgot all about it. Before June 22, I don't think I could've remembered much about what Double-XX really said."

"Now that you've seen it again, how do you feel about his actual words?"

"I don't agree with them. Black people should know better than anyone how wrong it is to kill someone for the color of their skin." Malcolm paused for emphasis. "If a white policeman kills a Black person for no good reason, we have to hold that officer accountable. There are way too many times our justice system doesn't do that. But killing innocent police is the worst kind of response."

Turning to the jury, Allie saw them listening carefully. "Just to be clear," Ford asked Malcolm, "have you ever posted anything else expressing similar sentiments?"

"No, sir. I haven't."

"Have you ever said anything like that to anyone at all?"

"Never."

The act of speaking after months of enforced silence, Allie thought, was making Malcolm become more like himself. She prayed it would continue.

"The district attorney," Ford went, "also spent a great deal of time on your fight with Billy Palmer. I want to get to that. But, before your altercation with Billy, did you have a separate encounter with his father, Woody?"

"Yes, sir."

"Could you describe how that happened?"

Malcolm's face clouded. "I was driving to visit my granddad's grave. I used to do that every week. Sometimes I'd just sit there and talk to him, kind of imagining he was still with me." Briefly, he stopped. "Anyhow, I was just going along through Eastwood when I saw this police car by me with a flashing light, and had to pull over. When the guy who stopped me came up to my window, I saw it was Woody Palmer."

"Did you know him on sight?"

"I did. I'd seen him a couple times at high school, dressed in his policeman's uniform."

"When he pulled you over, was he wearing his uniform?"

"No. Seemed like he was off duty."

Ford nodded. "After he stopped you, what did he say?"

"The first thing he said was, 'Afternoon, Malcolm. What are you doing out here?'"

"Were you surprised he knew you by name?"

Malcolm shook his head. "Not really. A lot of folks around here know my family, my mom especially, or know me from football. Anyhow, he might have heard about me from Billy. There'd been talk about race and police in civics class, and Billy and I were pretty much on opposite sides."

"When he asked what you were doing, how did you answer?"

"I said I was going to visit Granddad's grave out in Planting Field."

"How did he respond?"

Malcolm's voice hardened. "That I needed to find another route."

"Did he tell you why?"

"Didn't have to. We both knew why."

"How did you respond?"

Briefly, Allie caught the glint in Malcolm's eye. "I kept my hands on the wheel and minded my manners. I asked if he wanted to arrest me for driving while Black. But if he didn't, I was going to hang out with my granddad. All the man did was turn red. So I rolled up the window and went on my way."

Her son's quiet defiance made Allie proud, even as she worried about how it would sound to the jury. Glancing at Dalton Harris, she saw him studying Malcolm intently.

"That brings us to Billy," Ford said to Malcolm. "According to him, you two had a disagreement in civics class about the George Floyd case. After that, he says you stopped him in the hall and insulted his father. In his telling, he never said a word to you. Instead, he just tried to get away from you, and you sucker-punched him, ruining his baseball career." Ford permitted himself a smile. "At least that's the story he started with. Except for the part about baseball, it seemed to keep shifting…"

"Objection, Your Honor," Harris called out. "In all that verbiage, I've yet to hear a question. Instead, defense counsel is mischaracterizing Mr. Palmer's testimony."

"Which version, Your Honor?" Ford inquired innocently. "Anyhow, I was just working up to a question when Mr. Harris interrupted me."

For an instant, Allie thought, Tilly looked amused. "That's because he had a point, Counsel. Skip the preamble and get to your question."

Turning to Malcolm, Ford said, "Maybe we should start with the discussion in civics class that day. What did you and Billy say about George Floyd?"

"We were talking about the video," Malcolm responded. "Billy had decided to wear his 'Back the Blue' T-shirt that day, and came on with an attitude. He said that Black radicals were using George Floyd to make police look bad, when Blacks were the ones looting and causing all the problems with crime. So I said that the cop had murdered a Black man in cold blood, and that a lot of other police had killed unarmed Blacks because they could. The only difference was this one had killed a Black man on video."

"When was the next time you saw Billy?"

"I was getting track shoes out of my locker. I saw Billy kind of sauntering toward me, and decided to ignore him. But he comes up to me, standing right in my face, and asks, "How do you like my T-shirt, Malcolm?"

"He says you told him you'd rip it off if he wore it again. Is that true?"

"That's a lie."

"What did you say?"

"I remembered his dad trying to run me out of their neighborhood for being Black. So I asked him if his father used that film of George Floyd as a training video."

"What did he say next, Malcolm?"

Glancing at the jury, Malcolm hesitated before answering in a muted voice. "He said, 'At least I've got a father, you stupid fucking nigger.'"

In this moment, Allie could not know what the jury felt about hearing the words spoken aloud. But she saw the brief, wounded look in her son's eyes and knew what he was feeling—shame, remembered. Perhaps what had sparked his fury was not only being called a "fucking nigger"—though, for Allie, that was enough—but the searing reminder from a racist white kid that Malcolm had no father who loved him. She could only see the back of Chase's head, but he seemed to be quite still. In the jury box, Robert Franklin had turned toward him.

You have a father now, she wanted to tell her son. *I am so sorry I kept you apart.* That was among the many reasons she had interceded with Chase the night before. It was not simply that Malcolm needed to stand up for himself at the most crucial moment of his life, but that he needed Chase Brevard to support him. Should he ever be free, this would matter more than Chase could understand.

"What did you do then?" Ford asked Malcolm.

There was no perfect answer, Allie knew. The truth as she understood it—that Malcolm had swung his fist in instinctive outrage—might suggest to the jury a temper so reflexive that, inebriated, Malcolm had shot George Bullock for the lawful act of stopping him. His best hope was that the jury would feel Billy's words as an insult rendered too grievous by America's history of race to expect Malcolm, or any Black man, to swallow his pride.

"I swung my fist," Malcolm answered softly. "It was instinct. He was on the floor like a second later."

"When you saw him with a broken nose, how did you feel?"

Malcolm looked down. "I didn't know. He'd come up to me after civics class looking for trouble, and no white man should say those words to a Black man. But I wished I'd punched him in the stomach. Seeing him like that made me kind of sick."

"To be clear, you punched him because he insulted you."

"That's right. If he hadn't done that, nothing would've happened."

"In his testimony, Billy claimed that you punched him for no reason. Was that a lie?"

"A total lie."

"Specifically, he testified under oath that he never called you 'a fucking nigger.'"

"That's a lie," Malcolm said firmly. "That's exactly what he called me. He blames me for him not pitching that afternoon. He might as well blame himself, instead of coming here to lie about me."

It was the right answer, Allie thought—Billy had lied to the jury as an act of reprisal. "During cross-examination," Ford asked Malcolm, "Billy tried to say that he never called Black people 'nigger.' Do you believe that?"

"Not for a minute. That's a big word, and everybody knows what it says to Blacks. Saying it to me came way too easy."

Ford nodded in affirmation. "Let's move on to purchasing the Glock 19. When did you do that?"

Briefly, Malcolm seemed to wince. "About two weeks before what happened. June 8."

"Why did you buy it?"

Malcolm spread his hands—a gesture that, to Allie, said, *Where do you want me to start?* "All sorts of reasons," he answered. "The way our family always had to be so careful. The police who killed unarmed Blacks. All the threats to my mother and the people at Blue Georgia. That sheriff's deputy who was texting white nationalists about killing or castrating voting rights workers. The armed militia who threatened my mom's office after the election. The website that accused her of stealing the election, posting her picture and giving directions to our house. Any one of those things."

"But why on June 8?" Ford asked. "Was there a particular event?"

"I'd persuaded my mom to let me canvass for Blue Georgia. Like I said, people knew who I was, and that I was Allie Hill's son. I was putting myself out there."

"Why did you decide to work with your mom?"

For the first time, Malcolm looked toward his mother. "I was proud of her. I felt proud of what our family had always tried to do, help people get their rights. I'd come to believe, like she did, that helping people vote was the best way we could make change." For a moment, he hesitated. "I just knew how lonely she felt sometimes, how scared she was without ever saying it. I wanted her to know that I was with her."

For Allie, the words were a stab to the heart. *I never wanted you to take care of me,* she wanted to tell him. *I'll always be OK. A mother's job is to watch out for her son, and I didn't. That's the only reason you're here.* But all she could do was look at him with all the love she felt for this young man who, however conflicted, had a loyal and loving soul.

"At the time you purchased the Glock 19," Ford asked, "had you ever owned a gun?"

"No, sir. The only gun I'd ever touched was Granddad's old hunting rifle. He kept it around for self-protection after he stopped hunting deer."

"Do you happen to know why he stopped?"

Malcolm looked off into some middle distance, as if aware of the irony of his answer. "I stopped wanting to go out with him. We did everything together, him and me. But I didn't like killing things."

It was true, Allie knew. It was the one time Wilson Hill had been frustrated with his grandson—as far as he was concerned, the damned deer were overrunning Cade County, Janie could do wonders with venison, there were plenty of outlets for making deer into Bambi burgers, and here was Malcolm turning softhearted and softheaded. She had thought it pretty funny, then.

"Where did you buy the Glock?" Ford asked.

"Freedom Guns here in town."

"Why a Glock?"

"The owner recommended it. I didn't know anything about handguns, so I said sure."

"Had you done any research?"

"No. I figured the man would know what was best."

Ford cocked his head. "Why did you purchase a used gun, instead of a new one?"

"I just wanted to save money. Working for Blue Georgia, I wasn't making a lot."

"Did you know that this particular Glock had been modified to lighten the trigger pull?"

Malcolm looked down. "I didn't."

"Did you ever practice firing?"

"No. The owner showed me how to use it; that was all. I kept meaning to go to a shooting range, but I never had time. So I just put it in the glove compartment of my car."

"Between June 8 and June 22, did you ever touch the gun?"

"No, sir. Not once."

To Allie, and she hoped the jury, this was a critical point. Ford was doing a nice job of countering Harris' critical insinuation—that Malcolm was a predator who had purchased a Glock 19 to turn it on police.

"Just to be clear," Ford asked, "did you buy that gun with the idea of using it against a law enforcement officer, as Double-XX seemed to suggest in that video?"

Malcolm looked at the jury. "No," he said emphatically. "When I bought the gun, what Double-XX said a year ago was the last thing on my mind. What I was thinking about was all the threats to my mom."

Ford nodded. "On June 21, did you also learn that a right-wing website had posted your picture and identified you as Allie Hill's son?"

"Yeah." Abruptly Malcolm's tone was etched with foreboding. "She asked if maybe I wanted to work in an office, at least for a while. I said I wouldn't let them scare me off."

"Nonetheless, did that increase your concerns about your own safety?"

"It did. Definitely."

Ford paused for a moment. "OK, let's turn to the events of the next day, June 22. Was that a workday for you?"

Glancing toward the other side of the courtroom, Allie saw Dorothy Bullock tensing, her face set. Again, Janie Hill grasped her daughter's hand. "It was a Wednesday," Malcolm answered. "Our workweek runs Wednesday through Sunday. We can find more people at home on the weekend."

"How long did you work that day?"

"I started out at eight in the morning, and worked pretty much straight through as long as there was enough daylight. So twelve hours or so."

"What were you doing?"

"I was passing out applications for people to fill out, so they'd receive mail-in ballots. I went to one meeting at a church, but mostly I was going door to door."

However else people felt about mail-in voting, Allie thought, a long day toiling in the vineyards of democracy hardly sounded like a prelude to premeditated murder. Her son was doing well, she thought, speaking clearly, soberly, and respectfully. He sounded like who she knew him to be—a good kid, under pressure in a hard place. It was sickening to think that the jury might convict a counterfeit Malcolm, conjured by the prosecutor from a video and his righteous punch of a racist teenager.

"After you finished passing out ballots," Ford asked, "did you have other work to do?"

Malcolm nodded. "Every time we pass out a ballot application, we make an entry on our iPad with the person's name, address, and contact information. At the end of every workday, the canvassers have to send all that to the field director. So five of us got together at a house a couple of kids were renting on Peach Street, over in a Black section of town where we did a lot of canvassing. We just sat on the porch, finishing our reports, and someone said they'd get a couple pizzas and some beer."

"How did you respond?"

Again, Malcolm glanced at Allie, this time with a look of surreptitious guilt. "I knew my mom would want me home. But we'd had a long day, and it seemed like fun. So I called and asked her if I could hang out with some friends from work for a couple hours."

"What did she say?"

Malcolm hesitated. "I knew she wasn't all that happy, especially with the idea of me driving home late at night. But she finally told me to drive carefully, stay out of trouble, and get back by midnight."

Touching her eyes, Allie wished, as she had wished every day for the last nine months, that she had told Malcolm to come home right away. Silent, Janie squeezed her hand more tightly. "Did she say anything about not drinking alcohol?" Ford asked Malcolm.

He looked away. "She didn't have to. She'd mentioned it often enough before. But I just wanted to join in with the others, so I told myself I'd stop after a couple beers."

"Did you?"

Malcolm shook his head. "The evening stretched out, and we were talking about all sorts of things—politics, mostly, but also what we wanted to do with our lives. So I maybe had three or four."

"During that time on the porch, Malcolm, did anything else get your attention?"

Malcolm nodded, his expression darkening. "One thing. There wasn't much traffic on that street at night. But toward the time when I left, I saw this car or truck—I think it was a pickup truck—pass by the porch, driving so slow it seemed like the driver was checking us out. I mean that truck was just crawling." Malcolm's eyes narrowed in thought. "What seemed so strange to me was why someone would do that. We weren't playing music, and people in the neighborhood were out on their porches all the time. A few kids hanging out was nothing unusual. I couldn't imagine Black people paying us any mind, and you didn't see a lot of white people on that street, even in daylight."

"Could you see who the driver was?"

"No way. There aren't any streetlights, so I could barely make out that I thought it was a truck."

Ford's expression conveyed curiosity and concern. "Do you think whoever was inside could see your faces?"

"Sure. We were close enough to the street. The porch lights were pretty bright, and we were sitting right under them."

"Specifically, do you think that someone driving by that slowly could recognize you as Malcolm Hill?"

"Objection," Harris interjected. "Lack of foundation, calls for speculation. I don't even know if it's relevant to anything."

"Let's find out," the judge said promptly. "Objection overruled."

"I'm sure they could," Malcolm answered soberly. "I'd gotten used to all sorts of people I didn't know recognizing my face. But what I remember thinking about just then was that those white nationalists had put my yearbook picture up on their website."

"Did that cause you to react in a particular way?"

"Yeah, it spooked me enough that I decided to leave. I couldn't relax anymore."

"What route did you take home?"

Briefly Malcolm looked away. "From where we were, there's only one. Old County Road."

Ford had begun taking his time, Allie noticed, building a sense of events enveloping her son. Thinking about it made her skin crawl.

"Was there anything about Old County that concerned you?"

The timbre of Malcolm's voice diminished. "There are whole stretches that are real dark, with nothing close to the road."

"You remember the moon that night?"

"Yeah, we'd been looking up at it from the porch. It was only a sliver. So when I got out on the road, it was even darker."

"Once you were on Old County," Ford asked, "about how long would it have taken you to get home?"

"About a half hour."

"Did you see any traffic?"

"I remember one car coming the other way." Malcolm paused. "The only other thing I saw were these headlights behind me, maybe ten minutes after I hit Old County. A hundred yards back or so."

"Did you notice anything particular about them?"

"Not at first. But it seemed like they never got any closer or further away. It was like they were driving the same speed I was."

"For about how long?"

"Maybe another ten minutes." Malcolm's voice became quieter. "That's when I began to think they were following me. Every now and then, around a curve, they'd disappear. But then there they were again, no bigger or smaller, always the same distance behind me."

Ford nodded his encouragement. "What happened next?"

"Suddenly a blue flashing light appeared on top of the headlights. I knew they were coming for me, and realized I was on the darkest part of the road." Malcolm folded his hands. "When the siren started screeching, I pulled over to the side."

"What was going through your mind?"

Malcolm glanced toward the jury. "I was scared. I knew I'd been drinking, but I thought I'd been driving OK. What made it so bad out there was thinking this person was following me, and all I could do was wait for whatever happened."

"While you were waiting, did you do anything else?"

"I should have called my mother, told her what was happening. But then that car pulled up behind me. I didn't have much time." Malcolm began to speak more quickly, as if recalling the swiftness of events. "If this was a traffic stop, I figured he'd want to see my registration. But it was in the glove compartment with the gun. There were absentee ballot applications on the passenger seat. So I took out the gun and hid it beneath the papers. That way I could reach for my registration without anyone seeing I had it."

Listening, Allie could feel Malcolm's dread and panic as her own, a chill of premonition entering the courtroom. On the bench, Tilly's features were emotionless. "Why didn't you take out the registration?" Ford asked Malcolm.

"I should have. But things seemed to be happening so fast." Malcolm's voice lowered. "Suddenly whoever it was turned off his siren, his flasher, and his headlights. That's when I realized how bad this could get. Because the only light in all of that darkness came from my car."

78

Taut, Chase envisioned the darkness enveloping his son, imagined the sound of Bullock's heavy boots on gravel. "When you took out the gun," Ford asked him, "did you intend to use it?"

"No," Malcolm insisted. "I swear it."

"After the driver of the squad car turned off all of his lights, what did you do?"

"I just kept waiting with my hands on the steering wheel, like I had with Woody Palmer." Malcolm's voice resonated with remembered fear. "Then his shadow filled my driver's side window, and already it felt way different."

"Could you see his face?"

"No. He rapped on the window with his flashlight, then shined it in my eyes. 'Open the window,' he ordered. So I did."

"Did he ask for your driver's license or registration?"

"No. He just reached through the window and turned off my headlights." Malcolm looked haunted now. "Suddenly it was pitch dark all around us."

Ford waited a moment. "What happened next?"

"He told me to get out of the car and take a breath test."

"Did you comply?"

"No," Malcolm answered. "I didn't want to be out there with him. I knew it wasn't safe."

"Was that because he'd turned out the lights?"

"Yes." Malcolm's voice became tighter. "But I noticed something else. I knew from our training that deputies should turn on their body cameras. But I couldn't see the speck of light on his chest.

Ford nodded. "What did you say to him?"

"I asked him to follow me home. We could talk there, I said."

"How did he respond?"

"He laughed. 'No, Malcolm,' he said. 'We're staying out here where Mama can't see you.'" Distractedly, Malcolm touched the side of his face.

"That's when I knew for sure this wasn't just a traffic stop. The man had come after me."

"What did you decide to do?"

"I said I had the right to call my mother." Malcolm seemed to swallow. "I'll never forget what he said next. 'Afraid it's just you and me, Malcolm. A respected law enforcement officer, and the bastard son of a socialist whore who likes to take on men three at a time.'"

The first time Chase had heard this, he forced himself to stifle his own fury. But now he glanced at the jury, and saw Robert Franklin grimace. For a Black person in this county, Ford had told him, this portrait of George Bullock would be no great surprise. Chase wondered how much of a surprise Malcolm's account was to Dalton Harris.

"Did he say anything else?" Ford asked.

"He said I was just a mama's boy, busy rounding up Black people too stupid to vote." Malcolm paused again. "He didn't just know who I was; he knew what I did."

"By then did you have any idea who *he* was?"

"Only that he was a deputy. I still hadn't even seen his face. All I knew was that he hated us. Not just me and my family. Black people."

To Chase, the jury looked rapt now. Stephen Hewitt kept glancing up from his notes, as though compelled to watch Malcolm closely. "I kept looking in the rearview mirror," he continued, "hoping some driver would come along and see us, any kind of witness to what was happening to me out there. But there wasn't any.

"Suddenly, my cell phone rang. I knew it was my mom." Malcolm's voice slowed. "For a minute, I was relieved. Then I realized I shouldn't move my hands. So I asked if I could answer."

"How did he respond to that?"

"He said that out where we were, I didn't have phone privileges. I just sat there, frozen, until the ringing stopped. My hands were still on the steering wheel."

Chase gazed at his son and, for a moment, their eyes met. *Just stay with it*, Chase tried to tell him. *You're doing fine.* But the image of his son gripping the steering wheel as Allie tried to find him hit Chase hard, deepening his loathing for a dead man who might yet bring Malcolm down.

Ford moved closer to Malcolm. "After your phone stopped ringing, what happened next?"

Malcolm's shoulders sagged. "He stuck his arm through the window and turned his flashlight on the passenger seat. 'What you got there?' he asked me. I said the papers were absentee ballot applications. Then he accused me of violating Georgia voting laws, and told me to hand them over."

"Did you?"

Briefly, Malcolm's eyes closed. "I couldn't. The gun was underneath them."

"What did you do instead?"

"I told him I didn't want any trouble, and asked if I could see Sheriff Garrett."

"Did he say anything to that?"

"He said he knew I'd like to go see my mother's friend, but that wasn't how my life was going tonight. Unless I wanted to die I should stay right where I was. Then I hear his footsteps on the gravel again, and suddenly I can see his shadow through the passenger window.

"He jerks open the passenger door, and the inside light comes on. Then he leans into the car." Malcolm seemed to swallow. "Suddenly he's grabbing the papers, and I know he'll uncover the gun…"

He stopped abruptly. In the same even tone, Ford asked, "What did you do?"

"I couldn't do anything. It felt like I was paralyzed. Then he moves the papers and sees the gun in the light from the ceiling." Malcolm's voice quickened. "He starts reaching for it, and I know for sure he's going to kill me. So I take my hands off the steering wheel and try to grab it. We've both got our hands on the gun, and he's trying to turn it toward me.

"Our faces are so close, I can smell his breath. My head hits the steering wheel. He's over me now. I'm using all my strength to twist the gun in his hands. Then there's this pop…"

Once more, Malcolm stopped.

"Go on," Ford prompted.

Slowly, Malcolm nodded, responding in a hollow voice. "I feel his grip loosen, and there's something wet on my T-shirt. Then I see his face in the light. He's slumped in the passenger seat, just staring. A piece of his forehead is missing, and there's blood on his face. I knew right then he was dead."

"What did you do?"

"I turned away and stumbled out of the car. Next thing I was sitting in the gravel, throwing up." Malcolm shook his head in despair. "My phone rang again. I knew my mom was calling. But it was too late."

Quietly, Ford asked, "Did you mean for the gun to go off?"

"No. I don't even know how it did." Sitting straighter, Malcolm composed himself. "Like I told Deputy Spinetta, it was an accident. I didn't want to fight with him. I didn't want any part of it. All I wanted was to get home safe."

With the last poignant sentence, Chase felt yet again the terrible unfairness of Malcolm's tragedy. The accident that had ensnared him in a trial for capital murder had resulted from a malignant stranger's design, and only the stranger deserved to die.

"Thank you, Malcolm," Ford told Chase's son. "No further questions."

79

Sitting on the witness stand, Malcolm watched Dalton Harris rise from the prosecution table and walk slowly toward him.

He was at once focused on Harris and conscious of their place in a pit of legal combat intently watched by the judge; jurors; the other lawyers; spectators including his mother, grandmother, and George Bullock's wife and children; the sheriff's deputies assigned to guard his safety; the television cameras broadcasting his face and voice to millions of strangers who would know him by this alone. *Just keep watching Harris*, Chase had advised. *Preserve a calm demeanor. Don't play to the jury. Don't answer too quickly. If you don't understand the question, ask Harris to clarify it. If you find yourself anxious or losing your temper, take a breath before answering.* He did not need to say that Malcolm's freedom, and perhaps his life, might depend on how well he withstood the district attorney's assault.

For an instant, Malcolm thought of the tension he had always felt before playing football, and wished with a rush of nostalgia for the nights of innocence when the stakes of failure or success were simply a win or loss in a season of games played for pride, one moment in time on the way to a continuing life where its elation or disappointment would dissipate in the absorption of new events. But one practice he had followed before every game was to sit by himself, eyes closed, and say a brief, silent prayer from his childhood. Malcolm did that now.

Harris stopped in front of him, a portrait of poise and command and, to Malcolm, entitled indifference to everything but his own pride of place in the hierarchy of color. "Before you broke Billy's Palmer's nose," the prosecutor asked calmly, "did he threaten you?"

Malcolm took his first breath. "He called me a name."

"That wasn't my question. Before you hit him, did Billy threaten you with violence?"

Malcolm paused to think. But there was only one answer. "No."

"Did he try to hit you?"

"No."

"You didn't punch Billy in self-defense?"

Once more, Malcolm considered his answer. Though he kept his eyes on Harris, he felt the intense attention all around him, jurors reacting to his every word. "Not physically."

Already, Harris seemed like a chess player, making one move after another. "Why didn't you walk away?"

Malcolm stared back at him. "Because he called me a 'stupid fucking nigger.'"

"In other words, you hit Billy because you were angry."

"I hit him because he insulted me like no one should ever insult a Black person."

"In fact, you were so angry that you broke his nose."

"I didn't plan on breaking anything."

Harris adopted the patient manner of a lawyer extracting obvious truths from a reluctant witness. "But you hit him very hard, didn't you?"

"I just hit him, that's all. I was reacting to what he said. I didn't think about how hard I was hitting him."

"Did anyone else hear him call you that name?"

"Not that I know about," Malcolm responded. "But I did."

"But you were already angry at Woody Palmer, weren't you?"

"Yes sir, I was. I thought I should be able to visit my grandfather's grave without getting stopped for being Black."

"Weren't you also angry because Billy wore a 'Back the Blue' T-shirt?"

How should he frame his response? Malcolm wondered. "I thought it was disrespectful to do that the day after they showed that video of George Floyd."

"And roughly an hour before, in civics class, Billy said he thought the Black Lives Matter movement was using the video to disparage police."

"He said that, yes."

Harris' tone became sharper. "You were angry at his father, angry about his T-shirt, and angry at him for speaking out in civics class. Isn't *that* why you broke his nose?"

"No," Malcolm retorted. "If he hadn't called me that name, I wouldn't have hit him."

"So, it was just a reflex."

"That's right."

Harris studied him. "Would you have shot him by reflex if you'd had a Glock 19?"

"Objection!" Jabari Ford called out.

Turning, Malcolm saw Jabari on his feet, his expression angry. "Over-ruled," he heard the judge say.

Malcolm paused before facing Harris. "No, I wouldn't have wanted to shoot him."

"If it was a reflex, how do you know? I thought you hit him before you had time to think."

Malcolm felt off-balance. No one had expected the question, and now no one could help him. "I didn't bring a gun to school," he answered. "I didn't ask Billy to insult me. No matter how mad I was, I know the difference between a punch and a gunshot."

This time it was Harris who paused—quite deliberately, it seemed. "Then why did you post that video by Double-XX?"

Because I was angry, Malcolm wanted to say, and then felt the words die on his lips. "When I did it, it felt like a protest."

Swiftly, Dalton Harris took a television clicker from his suit pocket. "Please watch this."

Once again, Malcolm saw Double-XX fill the television screen. Once again, he heard the words he had so carelessly launched in his own name. Once again, Harris froze the rapper's image for the jury to see. "Is that your idea of a protest?"

Malcolm felt his face tighten, his tongue clumsy in his mouth. "I shouldn't have posted that."

"So let's take that video line by line. Do you believe that the 'white so-called justice system ain't nothin' but a killing field?'"

Why else am I here? Malcolm wanted to say. "No," he answered care-fully. "I don't believe the 'nothing but' part. What I was trying to say is that the justice system has failed Black people who've been killed by police. But I chose the wrong way to say it."

"Why didn't you take that video down?"

"Like I said, I forgot I posted it."

Harris summoned an expression of astonishment. "Is that the kind of video you just forget?"

Malcolm tried to frame the true answer. "Not right away. But June 22 was so much later."

"How many days after breaking Billy Palmer's nose did you post that video?"

"Maybe three or four."

"So you didn't feel so bad that it kept you from posting a video about shooting white police at random."

Malcolm hesitated. "I didn't think about it that way."

"Then let's return to the video. Do you agree with the statement that 'those motherfuckers'—meaning police—'won't stop until we start killing cops every time some cop kills a Black man'?"

"No."

"No? Did you ever post anything repudiating that statement?"

"I never said anything about that video."

"Even though Double-XX said it was OK to kill innocent police."

Malcolm felt trapped. "That wasn't what I meant."

But Harris kept pursuing him with the same relentless calm. "Double-XX also says, 'Don't matter which cop, long as they're white.' Did you understand that he was calling for the murder of innocent white police?"

"That's what he was saying, but those aren't my words."

"Did you further understand the words 'So start deterring, brothers' as a call for killing white police in revenge for allegedly unjustified shootings of Blacks?"

"I understood the words."

"So it was OK to kill some white policeman, even if he was, say, coaching inner-city kids in his spare time."

"No. I never believed that."

"No again? When you broke Billy Palmer's nose, weren't you acting out the instructions of that video? Billy Palmer was the nearest thing at hand—the son of a cop you hated, parading around in a 'Back the Blue' T-shirt. So you hit him with all the force you had."

"Objection," Malcolm heard Ford interject.

"Overruled," the judge responded. "You may answer, Mr. Hill."

Malcolm sat straighter. "The only reason I hit Billy was what he called me."

"Then help me understand the sequence. First, you saw the video of George Floyd. Next, you broke Billy Palmer's nose. Third, you posted the Double-XX video calling for the murder of white police. Is that correct?"

"I guess so. But that makes things sound different than they were. I don't think I'd even seen the Double-XX video when Billy called me a 'fucking nigger.'"

Harris appraised him. "So how long were you suspended from school for hitting Billy?"

"Three days."

"And during that time, you posted the Double-XX video."

"I guess so, yes."

"Because you considered that an appropriate thing to do after being suspended for breaking the nose of a policeman's son."

"I wasn't thinking about Billy. I was thinking about George Floyd."

"Why?" Harris snapped. "Because you'd already forgotten about hitting Billy? Just like you forgot about that video before you shot George Bullock?"

For a moment, Malcolm waited for an objection. But Ford had explained his strategy—unless there was a very good reason, he did not want the jury to feel that he was anxious about Malcolm's responses under cross-examination.

Disciplining himself to pause, Malcolm framed an answer. "When I posted that video, Mr. Harris, I hadn't forgotten about hitting Billy. But I'd forgotten about the video by the time Deputy Bullock stopped me. That was over a year later. All I knew is that the man had me out there all alone, and I was scared."

★ ★ ★

Good, Chase thought. But he could feel Ford's tension as clearly as he felt his own. Harris was as good as Chase had feared, and the heart of his cross-examination was coming.

"When you bought the Glock 19," Harris asked, "had you forgotten about that video?"

"Yes."

"Even though it called for shooting white police."

"I wasn't thinking about that video," Malcolm responded. "I was thinking about all the threats against my mom and our family."

He was poised, Chase saw with satisfaction, and equipped for any line of questioning they could anticipate. But Harris could attack from too many angles for them to predict every one.

"Who did you tell about buying a gun?" Harris asked.

"No one. I knew how my mom felt about guns."

"But if you needed a gun, why didn't you tell any of your friends?"

"I just didn't think about it."

"In fact, you hid it, didn't you?"

Malcolm shook his head. "I just put it in my glove compartment, that's all."

"All right. This morning you testified about sitting on the porch with your coworkers, drinking beer. You also claimed to see some sort of vehicle slowing down as it passed. Did you ever see that vehicle again?"

"I don't know. I couldn't see it very well to begin with."

"Did you know who was in the car?"

"No."

"So it could have been anyone, like a neighbor. Did you detect someone following you as you left the neighborhood?"

It was a key point, Chase knew. Though he and Ford suspected there might be some connection between the shadowy truck and what happened on Old County Road, there was no way to prove it.

Again, Malcolm hesitated. "Sitting here now I can't be sure."

"In other words, you can't connect this mystery vehicle to George Bullock's decision to stop you."

"I can't. It was more how I felt."

Harris placed his hands on his hips. "Isn't the word for how you felt 'intoxicated'?"

"I felt fine."

"You did know that you were well below the legal drinking age in Georgia."

Malcolm met his eyes. "I knew that."

"And you're further aware that Dr. Williams testified that you were legally intoxicated by the standards that apply to adults, and approximately four times over the level of intoxication that applies to people over twenty-one."

"Yes, sir, I know she said that."

"Do you have any reason to disagree?"

Just own it, Chase mentally ordered. Instead Malcolm insisted, "Like I said, I felt fine."

"But that's not what I asked. Do you have any reason to challenge the finding by an expert toxicologist that you were legally intoxicated at the time Deputy Bullock stopped you, under both the standard for a minor and the standard for an adult?"

Malcolm hesitated, then seemed to remember his instructions. "I don't."

"You further testified that you believe that George Bullock was following you, correct?"

"I'm sure he was."

Chase felt himself tensing further. The defense knew what was coming, but there was no way to avoid it. "Isn't the reason you're sure Deputy Bullock was following you," Harris prodded, "because you were driving while intoxicated?"

"He knew who I was…"

"Isn't it perfectly reasonable for a deputy to follow someone to determine whether they might be driving under the influence of alcohol?"

"If that's why they're doing it."

"Don't law enforcement officers have a right and duty to pull over motorists who they believe are endangering others because they're intoxicated?"

"Yes. But that's not why he did it."

"You do acknowledge that Deputy Bullock asked you to take a breathalyzer test."

"Yes."

"And that you refused."

"I was afraid." Malcolm's voice rose. "He'd already turned off his lights and my headlights, and I didn't think he was wearing a body camera."

It was the truth, Chase knew. But already Harris was putting on a clinic on why it had been so dangerous to put Malcolm on the stand.

"So tell me this," Harris said. "When did you first take your gun out of the glove compartment?"

★ ★ ★

Please, Allie implored her son, *be ready. I know Jabari and Chase prepared you for this.* She felt Janie clasping her hand.

In a lower voice, Malcolm answered, "When I pulled over to the side of the road."

"At that point, you hid it beneath the papers in your passenger seat."

"That's right."

"In other words, before Deputy Bullock even got out of his car."

"Yes."

"Just to be clear," Harris continued, "that was before Deputy Bullock supposedly turned off your headlights."

Malcolm hesitated. "Yes."

"Or asked you to take a breathalyzer test. Or even said a word to you."

Briefly, Malcolm seemed to glance at Chase. To Allie, he looked vulnerable. "Like I said, I thought he might ask for my registration. I wasn't thinking straight."

"That's too bad," Harris said. "Because if you'd taken out the registration instead of hiding the gun, George Bullock would still be alive."

Quickly, Ford stood on his feet. "Objection."

"Overruled," the judge said promptly.

Malcolm shook his head. "I don't know what would've happened. The man was looking for me."

Harris moved closer. "Didn't you take out that gun because this was your chance to shoot a law enforcement officer?"

"No," Malcolm insisted. "All I wanted was to get home. The shooting didn't happen until he reached for the ballot applications."

"Isn't all you needed to do was comply with Deputy Bullock's request to take a breathalyzer test?"

"He was looking for me. He knew who I was."

"You testified that lots of people in Cade County know who you are. Why would that bother you?"

Malcolm stiffened. "He threatened me. He insulted my mother."

"He threatened you," Harris said softly. "He insulted your mother. So did this intimidating figure ever take out his weapon?"

"He didn't have to. The man had me alone."

"Of course he did," Harris shot back. "He was patrolling alone, which is standard procedure, and you were driving alone while intoxicated. So we have to take your word that he said any of those threatening, insulting, and racist things."

"He did say them…"

Watching, Allie could feel the next question coming. Moving closer yet, Harris asked, "Just like Billy Palmer said those insulting and racist things."

"He did."

"Isn't it true, Malcolm, that every time you get in trouble for assaulting a white person, you make up a story about them saying racist things to you?"

For an instant, Allie saw fury and defensiveness flash through Malcolm's eyes. "It happened. Both times. It happens a lot if you're a Black person in Cade County. You make it sound like it never happens, or maybe you don't know that it does."

It was a strong response, Allie thought. But Harris seemed unfazed. "So George Bullock didn't stop you because you were intoxicated. He stopped you because you're Black."

"He was following me," Malcolm repeated.

"So let's take your stories at face value. If someone insults you, they pay the price, don't they?"

"No."

"Billy paid the price for insulting you, didn't he? Isn't that your story?"

"I told you what he called me."

"You have trouble controlling your temper, don't you? Especially when some white person gets crosswise with you."

Malcolm seemed to steady himself. "It depends on what they call me. Seems like that's something you don't know a whole lot about."

Careful, Allie thought. In that moment, she felt with piercing clarity what Chase had anticipated—in the crucible of the courtroom, Malcolm must walk the tightrope between competing emotions, subordinating his own humanity to the cause of survival.

"I await your instruction," Harris responded with lethal civility. "So maybe you can enlighten me as to how a thirty-year veteran of law enforcement was accidentally killed with your Glock 19, and with his own weapon still in its holster."

★ ★ ★

Watching his son, Chase could see and feel the ravages from nine months of imprisonment—the fatigue, the abraded nerves, the unbearable tension of fighting for his life against charges of which he was innocent, of breaking his silence where every word could be turned on him in deadly and unanticipated ways.

"Just to be clear," Harris asked, "you took out the Glock and hid it within arm's reach."

"I wasn't thinking about that. I was worried about what would happen if he asked for the registration papers."

"So you took out the gun instead of the papers."

Briefly, Malcolm fidgeted. "I didn't have to time to think."

For a moment, Harris simply stared at him. "Couldn't you have told Deputy Bullock you had a gun in the glove compartment? No law against keeping it there, right?"

"I guess not, no."

"But you didn't do that, did you? Because you wanted to turn it on Deputy Bullock."

"That wasn't my reason," Malcolm protested.

"You also say you didn't hand him the papers because you were afraid of uncovering the gun. Is that right?"

"Yes."

"Why didn't you just tell him that there was a gun under the papers, and keep your hands on the wheel?"

"I was afraid of him, all right?" Pausing, Malcolm looked bewildered. "He said it was just him and me. He wouldn't let me talk to my mother or see Sheriff Garrett, and then he was saying I might not live out the night."

"Deputy Bullock was the one who didn't live out the night," Harris retorted. "Isn't what happened that you waited for him to lean inside the car, and then grabbed the weapon to shoot him?"

"No, it wasn't like that."

"In fact," Harris pressed, "what really happened is that Deputy Bullock saw the gun in your hands, and reached for it just as you shot him. That's the truth, isn't it?"

"*No.*"

"*Yes,*" Harris said succinctly. "Now you're stuck with telling the jury that this thirty-year veteran of law enforcement shot himself with your gun."

"It was an accident."

"An accident," Harris repeated with lethal quiet. "It was all an accident. You were drunk by accident. You accidentally drove where George Bullock was waiting to follow you. You took out the gun by accident. You hid it near your right hand by accident. You refused his lawful orders by accident. And then you shot him by accident. Because you're not responsible for anything, are you? From beginning to end, you were the innocent victim of a racist deputy who was stalking you for reasons of his own."

"Objection," Ford swiftly interrupted "The question is not simply compound; it's multiple choice. The witness can't know which particular distortion of his prior testimony he's supposed to answer—if any."

"Sustained," Judge Tilly said promptly.

Harris barely paused. "After the shooting," he inquired, "did you call anyone to report what had happened?"

Malcolm shook his head. "I couldn't believe it."

"Because it was an accident? Or did you sit by the car, trying to put together a story that would make murder sound like an accident?"

"I was sick."

"Because you were drunk," Harris said flatly. "You didn't have much time, did you? But George Bullock was dead, so you figured you could get by with whatever story you told. Including turning a dedicated law enforcement officer who'd stopped you for drunk driving into a racist instead of someone you decided to murder."

Chase watched Malcolm pull himself together. "I'm not going to blubber on the witness stand," he had told Chase and Ford the night before, "like that white kid in Wisconsin." Now he seemed almost to pray before looking up at Harris. In a steady voice, he answered, "That's not how it was, Mr. Harris. What my mother said is the truth. The only reason you can get by with calling me a murderer is because George Bullock decided not to turn on his body camera. If he had, he couldn't have done all the other things he did. So maybe he wouldn't be dead."

It was the best possible answer, Chase knew. After a moment, Harris said, "He wouldn't be dead, Malcolm, because you couldn't have shot him. No further questions."

Immediately, Ford stood. "Your Honor, I ask the court to instruct the jury to ignore the prosecutor's last inappropriate and prejudicial remark."

"It was all of that," Tilly agreed, and faced the jury. "You're instructed to ignore Mr. Harris' last comment. It wasn't a question, nor is it evidence."

Briefly, Harris looked nettled. But, as he intended, he had crafted a passable exit line.

Sitting down, Ford leaned over to Chase. "I'm thinking to leave this alone."

"Agreed," Chase whispered back. "Malcolm's done all he could, and he's been up there long enough."

Promptly, Ford stood again. Summoning an air of confidence, he said, "No redirect, Your Honor."

"Very well," the judge said. "The witness is excused."

As if disbelieving that his ordeal was over, Malcolm stayed seated. Then he rose, looking toward his mother before returning to the defense table.

Placing a hand on Malcolm's shoulder, Chase said quietly, "You did well."

Malcolm was too weary to respond. But Ford had already commenced with the final step of his plan. "May it please the court," he said to the judge, "we request a bench conference."

80

The four lawyers—Dalton Harris and Amanda Jackson for the prosecution, Jabari Ford and Chase Brevard for the defense—formed a tight circle before Judge Tilly. "Your Honor," Ford said, "the defense wants to recall Deputy Nick Spinetta and Sheriff Al Garrett."

Tilly peered down at him. "On what grounds?"

"It's pretty straightforward," Ford answered. "Prior to the defendant's testimony, the court ruled that evidence of George Bullock's racial and political views was irrelevant to the defendant's intent at the moment of the shooting. But Malcolm Hill has now testified to statements by Deputy Bullock that were antagonistic to Blacks in general and voting rights in particular. That goes directly to whether the shooting was deliberate, or some combination of accident and self-defense."

Glancing at Harris, Ford concluded, "We believe that it's possible, even probable, that the witnesses we seek to recall could provide testimony that tends to collaborate Malcolm's account. As well as shed light on why Bullock repeatedly violated department policy in connection with the stop."

"I'm inclined to agree,"Tilly responded."Do you have a position, Mr. Harris?"

"Can I have until morning to reflect on that, Your Honor? And perhaps do some research."

Tilly paused briefly. "No harm in overnight reflection. But I suggest you think hard. Whether or not Mr. Ford is on a fishing expedition that comes back to bite him, today's testimony positions him to take his chances. I'll hear argument at nine o'clock tomorrow, outside the presence of the jury."

★ ★ ★

Shortly after nine that evening, Allie returned home from visiting Malcolm.

Reheating the pizza he had ordered, Chase poured each of them a glass of red wine and sat with her at the kitchen table. She looked exhausted, he thought, burdened by fears for their son compounded by his day on the witness stand.

"How is he?" Chase asked.

"Relieved, on one level. But he's also rethinking every answer over and over again. So am I." Pausing, she seemed search his expression. "Do you still think we committed the sin of pride?"

Chase shook his head in demurral. "I understood your reasons, and Jabari's. After today, I think you were right."

In truth, Chase was not at all sure. But it was done."Think back to his testimony on direct," he continued. "Malcolm made his fears not just real, but sympathetic. I think that will resonate with the jurors, particularly the parents of teenagers."

Allie touched his wrist."But you believe Harris hurt him, don't you?"

Chase considered how to avoid being so disingenuous that Allie would see through him. During cross-examination, he had sneaked glances at their three bellwether jurors—Hewitt, Franklin, and Gray—as Harris sliced away at Malcolm's account. They appeared to be listening and weighing, their expressions at once hyperfocused and enigmatic. That there were holes in the logic of Malcolm's story did not mean that the jurors would disbelieve him. But there *were* holes, and Harris had found them.

At length, Chase said, "Harris did what Harris was always going to do. Malcolm was never getting off the stand for free. But overall I think it's better that the jury has seen him, no matter how the judge rules on Garrett and Spinetta."

Allie was barely touching her pizza, Chase saw. "What are the chances they could actually help us?"

Unerringly, she had asked the question Chase kept asking himself. "About Garrett," he answered, "my sense has always been that he had problems with Bullock. But Spinetta's a family friend. Private conversations among friends tend to stay private."

"What if neither of them knows anything?"

Silent, Chase looked into her face, a study in the anxiety he was striving to conceal. Neither of them, he knew, would sleep tonight, consumed by doubts too painful to express.

Then they'll have hurt us, Chase could have answered. But no relationship can survive total honesty, he knew—including theirs, and especially now. The grace of avoidance is sometimes a mercy.

"Then it's a wash," he told her. "But I'm still glad Malcolm testified."

★ ★ ★

Looking at Harris the next morning, Chase knew that something was wrong.

It was nine o'clock, the preordained hour, and Judge Tilly was prepared to hear arguments on Ford's motion. From the barrage of questions he and Ford had endured upon entering the courthouse, Chase perceived that the burden of television commentary had focused on two questions on which opinion was decidedly mixed: the impact of Malcolm's testimony, and whether the verdict now turned on what Al Garrett and Nick Spinetta—if allowed—might say about Bullock. As on every day of the trial, Dorothy Bullock and her children watched from the first row.

But before the proceedings could start, Harris was on his feet. Through the prosecutor's usual self-containment, Chase perceived a level of urgency that suggested trouble.

"Your Honor," he said, "before we proceed, the prosecution requests that counsel meet with the court in chambers."

This was serious, Chase knew, as quite clearly did the judge. "Very well, Mr. Harris. We can gather in ten minutes."

In the tumult that followed, Chase glanced swiftly at Allie and Janie before murmuring to Ford, "What do you think *this* is about?"

"No idea," Ford answered, his eyes alight with anticipation. "But I'm thinking our motion kicked something loose. Whatever that might be, I'm pretty sure it's better for us than for them."

★ ★ ★

Judge Tilly's chambers were much as Chase had expected: a large mahogany desk; shelves with old lawbooks; traditional furnishings augmented by two tall Chinese vases; photographs of a dignified wife, well-dressed adult children, and more rambunctious-looking grandchildren; and a last semihumanizing touch, a twenty-year-old trophy from his all-white country club for winning its annual golf tournament. Gathering in front of his desk, Harris and Amanda Jackson sat to one side, Ford and Chase to their right.

Abruptly, Tilly turned to Harris. "Time to share the bad news, Dalton. I have the feeling you're about to throw the proverbial monkey wrench into these proceedings."

Without an audience, Harris looked somber. "Last night, at the instance of Sheriff Garrett, I met with him and Deputy Spinetta. Long story short, we came into possession of evidence potentially pertinent to the defense."

The judge's expression became glacial. "Don't keep us in suspense. Especially when it sounds like we may be looking at a mistrial."

The district attorney's voice was tight. "It turns out that Deputy Spinetta has been in possession of a personal cell phone belonging to George Bullock. Until last night, we were unaware of its existence."

"And just how," Tilly inquired coldly, "did Deputy Spinetta acquire it?"

The prosecutor grimaced. "Apparently, he removed it from Deputy Bullock's body shortly after arriving at the scene."

Startled, Chase heard Ford swiftly interpose, "Your Honor, we respectfully ask for an evidentiary hearing to determine how this happened."

"That's not necessary," Harris interjected. "Our office will be happy to share the circumstances with defense counsel, and give them access to the phone itself."

Ford shook his head. "With respect," he told Tilly, "the implications of this last-minute revelation are much larger than the contents of the cell phone. We need to hear from Deputy Spinetta about what he did, and why we're only hearing about this now. Mr. Harris' denials notwithstanding, the defense is entitled to explore what the prosecution could, or should, have known about this situation before bringing this case."

Once again, Chase realized, Ford was one step ahead of him. But not ahead of the judge. Clearly angry, Tilly faced Harris again. "And so is this court," he snapped. "We're near the end of the trial. Suddenly it seems that we may have an incomplete record of information relevant to the defense—especially in light of the defendant's testimony." His tone became withering. "I want to know why. By one o'clock this afternoon, I expect to have that cell phone in our possession, and Spinetta on the witness stand to respond to Mr. Ford's questions. Any problem with that?"

The question, Chase knew, was an invitation to self-destruction. Unhappily, Harris responded, "No, Your Honor."

"Good," the judge said caustically "I very much look forward to clearing this up on national television. See you at one."

Silent, the lawyers exited Tilly's chambers and reentered the courtroom. Quietly, Chase said to Ford, "I guess I've seen judges more furious, but I can't remember when. Of course it's been a while."

A smile played on Ford's lips. "I'd say Albert's face was a study. But then it's not every day a judge finds out he may have been presiding over a travesty with high Nielsen ratings. Depending on Spinetta, we may be fixing to blow Dalton out of the water."

"A mistrial?" Chase asked.

"No," Ford answered, and now he was not smiling at all. "Malcolm deserves so much better. And Dalton Harris deserves so much worse."

81

Taking the witness stand, Deputy Nick Spinetta looked drawn, subdued, painfully conscious of becoming the focus of a packed courtroom studded with television cameras. Noting his surreptitious glances toward Dorothy Bullock and her children, Chase sensed that whatever Ford might compel him to say under oath would be painful for them, and for Spinetta himself. He could only hope it might be helpful to Malcolm. As Ford approached the witness, Chase briefly placed a hand on Malcolm's shoulder, silently hoping that, with luck, this moment could mark the end of his imprisonment.

"Good afternoon, Deputy Spinetta," Ford began. "As the court explained, your testimony today is part of an evidentiary hearing separate from the trial, the purpose of which is to determine whether the trial should continue and, if so, on what basis. That's why the jury is not present. Do you understand that?"

With an unhappy expression, Spinetta nodded. "I do."

"So you also understand the gravity of your obligation to respond fully and completely, regardless of who or what may be impacted."

Including your own career, Chase thought. Briefly, Spinetta's chest seemed to move in a sigh of resignation. "I do," he repeated.

Ford nodded gravely. "During your prior testimony, you said that you went to the scene of Deputy Bullock's death because you hadn't heard from him for several minutes. Is that correct?"

"It is."

"And you further testified that you were able to locate his car through the department's monitoring system."

"That's right."

"And that, on arriving, you found Deputy Bullock dead in the passenger seat of the defendant's car."

Spinetta hesitated, seemingly all too aware of where Ford was going. "I did, yes."

The next question, Chase anticipated, would be about the cell phone. Instead, Ford said, "You also found Malcolm Hill sitting by the car, and arrested him on suspicion of murder."

"That's also correct."

Ford paused. "In the course of your friendship with Deputy Bullock, did he ever mention the defendant's mother, Alexandria Hill?"

★ ★ ★

Tensely watching, Allie saw Spinetta glance at Harris before turning to the judge. "Please answer," Tilly directed sternly.

Now Spinetta did not look at anyone. "George talked about her, yes."

To Allie, it felt like a wall of silence breaking. "What did he say?" Ford prodded.

Spinetta paused, and then seemed to reach a point of resolution. "He said she'd stolen the last election from America's rightful president."

Around her, Allie heard involuntary murmurs of surprise. "Didn't you think that information might be relevant to Malcolm Hill's defense?" Ford asked.

Again, the witness glanced at Judge Tilly. "When you asked me that before, Mr. Ford, I was instructed not to answer."

"All right," Ford said. But instead of pursuing Bullock's political and racial beliefs, as Allie had anticipated, he asked, "When you found Deputy Bullock's body, did you also see his departmental cell phone?"

"It was on his belt."

"That was the phone you called when you were talking with him that night."

"That's correct."

"But Deputy Bullock had another cell phone, didn't he?"

Spinetta nodded, and then remembered to answer aloud. "Yes."

"Where did you find it?"

"I heard a cell phone ping, like it was receiving a text. Then I saw it glowing in his shirt pocket."

"Were you surprised?" Ford asked.

"No," Spinetta responded in a lower voice. "I knew he had a second phone."

For a moment, Ford turned to look at Harris. "But according to the district attorney," he said to Spinetta, "Deputy Bullock gave up his cell phone several years ago."

"He did. But he had another phone no one knew about. Including Mr. Harris and Sheriff Garrett."

★ ★ ★

There it was, Chase thought.

"But *you* knew," Ford said to the witness.

"Yes." Spinetta hesitated, then added softly, "Because we were friends."

"Was this what drug dealers sometimes call a ghost phone?" Ford asked.

Spinetta looked down, his appealing face etched with reluctance. "That's right."

"For the record, Deputy Spinetta, how does a ghost phone work?"

"You buy the phone under a cell number not traceable to you, prepay the minutes in cash, and keep switching out phones. That way no one knows you have it."

"For what reason did a law enforcement officer need a ghost phone?"

This time, Chase thought, the longer look Spinetta cast toward Dorothy Bullock held a silent apology. In the same soft tone, he said, "George was having an affair. He used it to stay in touch with her. I said he could ruin his marriage and his family. But he wouldn't listen."

Watching Ford, Chase saw him reach the same realization that he had. "Was he using it that night?" Ford asked.

Pausing, Spinetta chose to look fixedly back at Ford. "*She* was. The pinging I heard was a text."

"When you heard that, did you remove the phone from Deputy Bullock's shirt pocket?"

"I did."

"Did you also read the text?"

Glancing at Harris, Chase saw from his expression that he already knew the answer. "Yes," Spinetta responded quietly. "It was still visible. She wanted to know if George was coming over."

For a time, Ford simply looked at him. "After you read the text," he asked with equal quiet, "what did you decide to do?"

Spinetta seemed to brace himself. "I made a snap decision. George was dead, and I didn't want his family to lose him twice over. I knew people would be swarming all over the place in minutes. So I turned off the phone and put it in my pocket until I decided what to do."

"In other words," Ford said, "you deliberately removed evidence from a crime scene."

Spinetta was quiet for a moment. "All I can tell you, Mr. Ford, is I didn't think it had anything to do with the case. I thought I was protecting Dorothy and the kids, allowing them to keep their memories of George. I was sure nobody else knew that phone existed." His voice fell off abruptly. "Instead of giving it to the GBI, I took it home and locked it in a drawer. I never even told Susan."

"Do you know the identity of Deputy Bullock's girlfriend?"

"Yes. I do."

Everything about Spinetta, Chase thought—his voice, expression, and posture—implored Ford not to ask the next question. But he had no better chance of that than of stopping the next sunrise.

"Who was she?" Ford asked.

"Molly Parnell."

The murmurs of surprise from those watching were followed by a stifling silence. Grasping Malcolm's arm, Chase whispered, "This may be it."

From the bench, Tilly looked from Harris to the witness. Calmly, Ford asked Spinetta, "What do you know about Molly Parnell?"

"She's a white nationalist, like her brother Charles. They lead the local version of a group called White Lightning."

Behind them Chase heard another stir. Turning, he saw Dorothy Bullock leaving the courtroom, holding the hands of her son and daughter, her face set and staring straight ahead. Impervious, Ford asked Spinetta, "For the record, is White Lightning the group of armed militia that threatened the offices of Blue Georgia after the 2020 election?"

"That's right."

"Did the reasons George Bullock needed to keep this relationship secret include Ms. Parnell's political beliefs? And, for that matter, his own?"

"Yes." Increasingly, Chase thought, Spinetta spoke with a certain stoic fatalism—the damage to himself, and to the Bullock family, was already done. "George was worried it could cost him his job."

"Seems like a reasonable fear. Did Deputy Bullock ever tell you how he'd become involved with Molly Parnell?"

Spinetta folded his hands. "According to George, they met at a rally over in Peach County. He was working security for the lady who was a United States senator then, just to pick up some extra money. White Lightning was doing her security, too, and it sounded to me like Molly had come on to George. Anyhow, they started seeing each other when they could—outside the county, or maybe late at night."

Ford paused to think. "In your understanding, did Molly Parnell have any influence on Deputy Bullock's racial and political attitudes?"

"I know she did," Spinetta said in a tone of regret. "Molly had ideas, he told me. George was never a big liberal, and he'd always had his views about Black people and crime. But it wasn't until he met Molly that he started carrying on to me about something he called the Great Replacement, where Blacks were supposedly working to replace white Christians and turn America into this crime-ridden country run by minorities who hated police. I thought that was crazy, too, even before he started saying violence might be the only way to save us. It was like Molly Parnell had set something loose in George he hadn't known was there."

"Is that when he began talking about Allie Hill?"

"It seemed like that. Especially after the presidential election."

"2020," Ford said, "was also the year Al Garrett became Cade County's first Black sheriff. Do you know how Deputy Bullock fell about that?"

Spinetta frowned. "From George's standpoint, it was a pretty tense relationship. He thought Sheriff Garrett was out to get him."

"Did he say why?"

"He believed the sheriff was watching him. According to George, Sheriff Garrett came pretty close to asking point-blank whether he'd ever stopped drug dealers, taken their money, and let them go instead of calling in the stop."

"Could Bullock have done that?"

Spinetta's eyes narrowed in thought. "I've got no reason to think he had, so you'd have to ask the sheriff what he was wondering about. But sure, he could have. He'd just have to know who he was looking for, and then figure out a way to go off the grid."

"Like with Malcolm."

Spinetta gave Ford a quick look of surprise. "To be honest, I never put the two together."

"Maybe not. But did Bullock ever mention Allie Hill in connection with Sheriff Garrett?"

"He did," Spinetta acknowledged. "He said that without her, the sheriff never would've been elected."

Leaning closer to Malcolm, Chase whispered, "That ties in with your testimony about what Bullock said when he stopped you." To his surprise, he saw tears surface in Malcolm's eyes, and imagined his son thinking that, at last, people might actually believe him.

"In light of all that," Ford asked sharply, "it didn't occur to you at the time Bullock died that he might have been following Malcolm?"

Spinetta sat back. "I considered that. But Malcolm was clearly intoxicated, so George had every reason to stop him if he was driving erratically. We'd been talking for hours that night, and he gave me no reason to think he was looking for anyone. Malcolm's name never came up. George was just sitting out on Old County Road, and I couldn't see how he'd even know that Malcolm was coming."

There was a logic to this, Chase knew, and feared that Ford would hit a dead end. "Could you tell the court," Ford asked Spinetta, "when and how you came to inform Mr. Harris about the existence of the phone?"

Spinetta seemed to gather himself. "Early on in the investigation, Sheriff Garrett held a meeting with me and the district attorney. He wanted to make sure I told Mr. Harris whatever I knew about George's political beliefs. So I explained how he felt about Allie Hill and the election."

"But not about Molly Parnell and the ghost phone."

"No. Not then." For the first time, the deputy's tone was tinged with a self-blaming irony. "I still didn't want to hurt Dorothy and the kids. Or maybe Susan and *our* kids. I just kept telling myself that George's affair had nothing to do with him getting killed."

★ ★ ★

Taut, Allie awaited the next question.

"What happened to change your mind?" Ford asked.

Spinetta squared his shoulders. "Sheriff Garrett happened," he answered. "Last night he called me to another meeting with the district attorney. He said it was likely I'd be recalled to testify, and that now was the time to come forward with anything else I knew about George Bullock. That he'd hate to see a verdict rendered without the jury knowing everything it should."

"How did you respond?"

"I said that I'd think about it very hard." Spinetta paused, as if contemplating the fateful moment anew. "I went home and told Susan. Then I opened up the drawer, took out the phone, and turned it back on. Once I saw it still worked, I opened it using George's usual password—his initials and birthday. Then I started scrolling through his texts. I thought they'd all be from Molly, but they weren't."

Ford waited a moment. "Who *were* they from?"

"Her brother. Charles Parnell. He was the one who'd been following Malcolm. The last text before Molly's said that Malcolm was heading home down Old County Road."

Allie felt herself shudder. "Right away," Spinetta continued. "I understood what had happened. Molly had recruited George for her brother, and now George had become one of them." His voice lowered. "I don't know what he meant to do with Malcolm. But if George had never met the Parnells, he'd still be alive, and Malcolm Hill wouldn't be on trial for murder. There was nothing left but for me to come forward."

Ford turned to Judge Tilly. "No further questions, Your Honor."

To Allie, the courtroom felt as quiet as a caught breath. For a moment, Tilly looked stunned, and then recovered his judicial authority. "In light of this testimony," he ordered," I want to see counsel back in chambers. Right now."

82

Gathering in chambers, the four lawyers were sober and subdued. A transparent evidence bag containing a black cell phone sat on Tilly's desk.

"If there's any doubt," Harris told him, "Deputy Spinetta accurately described the texts from the evening of June 22. Again, I want it clear that my office had no idea that this evidence existed."

Somber, Tilly looked from Harris to Ford. "So, Counsel, what to do. I imagine Mr. Ford is not without thoughts."

That was surely true, Chase knew. But he had no idea what Ford intended to say, and by itself a mistrial might leave Malcolm in jail awaiting Harris' decision on whether to retry the case.

"As I believe the court is suggesting," Ford answered promptly, "the proper remedy is to declare a mistrial. A member of law enforcement who served as the prosecution's first witness was in possession of exculpatory evidence not disclosed to the defense. It will take weeks, if not months,

406 | RICHARD NORTH PATTERSON

to investigate the full implications of this—including the connections between Deputy Bullock, the Parnells, and White Lightning. The trial is hopelessly tainted, and even if it weren't, the court can't hold the jury captive until the investigation is complete."

"Mr. Harris?" the judge inquired. "As unfortunate as this may be, do you see any other recourse? I'm hard-pressed to find one."

Reluctantly, Harris nodded. "So am I, Your Honor. The prosecution will agree to a mistrial."

"Then that's what we'll do," Tilly responded.

It was moving too quickly, Chase thought, and too neatly. Then he saw the hint of a smile in Ford's eyes. "Of course," Ford said easily, "declaring a mistrial is just the beginning. As a matter of law, my client has been in legal jeopardy since the jury was impaneled. To retry him would violate the constitutional provision against double jeopardy."

Tilly regarded him with an inscrutable expression. "What do you suggest, Counsel?"

Ford sat back in his chair, spreading his hands in a gesture that suggested that he was about to say the obvious. "Seems like the only solution is to dismiss the case with prejudice, and free Malcolm Hill for good."

Studying Tilly, Chase thought he detected the faintest trace of amusement. "It's certainly *one* solution," the judge responded, and turned back to Harris. "Clearly, Mr. Ford came here intending to offer you a choice. You can oppose his motion to dismiss, and hope I deny it, or you can say you're not opposed and let the defendant walk away."

Silent, Chase watched Harris perceive that he was standing on Ford's trapdoor. The thoughts behind his patent unhappiness were easy to read. For his constituents who had avidly supported Malcolm's prosecution, consenting to a dismissal would look incompetent and irresolute; for others, opposing it would mean that he was attempting to revive a tainted prosecution, redolent of bigotry, for a trial that he would have little chance of winning.

"I don't envy you, Dalton," Tilly observed. "From your perspective, this is not a pleasant choice. Before you make it, if you like I can perhaps offer a little guidance."

Glancing at Ford, Chase saw that they shared the same thought—that, quite deliberately, Tilly had reprised that classic moment from *The Godfather*: making an offer Harris could not refuse. With the air of a man entrapped, Harris responded, "Of course, Your Honor."

Tilly, Chase realized, had assumed an avuncular persona unseen in court but, perhaps, familiar to Harris. Watching, Chase began to imagine the two men having lunch at their country club, discussing in practical terms the realities and responsibilities they understood in common.

"To start," the judge told Harris, "you're in an increasingly difficult position. Next year you're up for reelection, and some folks will be unhappy no matter what you do. But what happens if you decide to retry this case—not just to you, but to this community?

"I don't think you can win it, and neither do you. But you'd look bad trying, and so would this county. This case just became a national embarrassment, and that's not good for a place that wants more businesses to relocate here. That may not be relevant legally, but you're not just the district attorney. You're a leading citizen of this community."

It was fascinating, Chase thought, to watch Tilly openly state the premises on which the local establishment operated, validating the assessment Ford had offered Chase on the first day they had met. But, through this prism, the judge seemed to be edging Harris toward a decision that benefited Malcolm Hill, and Ford's impassivity suggested a determination to conceal the fervent hopes they shared in common, still hanging in suspension while Tilly spoke to Harris as if no one else were there.

"People like the Parnells," Tilly continued, "aren't good for this community. It turns out that the late George Bullock wasn't very good for this community. Seems to me a little fumigation is in order, and it falls to you to start the job.

"So let's get back to the law. It's not just that you can't win this case—it's that you shouldn't. I've been on the bench for almost thirty years, and I'm not running for reelection. I want to retire with a clear conscience. So all I have to worry about is whether some outraged citizen tries to blow my head off when I'm standing over a putt on the eighteenth green."

Leaning forward, Tilly regarded Harris intently. "That leaves you. You can oppose the defendant's motion, and have a pretty good chance of prevailing, only to be stuck retrying this case. Or you can acquiesce, knowing there's no one to appeal my ruling. If you do, I'll grant it, and we can all go home—including Malcolm Hill. If you're lucky, some people will blame Deputy Spinetta for sandbagging you, and the diehards who still want this prosecution will blame him for defiling George Bullock's good name. If I were young Mr. Spinetta, I'd start looking for another profession in some other jurisdiction. But that's not your problem, nor is it mine. Living with ourselves is problem enough.

"So what's your pleasure, Dalton? Because in exactly one hour, I'm going to entertain the defendant's motion to dismiss. I can't tell you what to do, but I can tell you what I think. Under the circumstances, the estimable Mr. Ford has just done you a favor."

★ ★ ★

At a little past four o'clock, Ford, Chase, and Malcolm gathered at the defense table, awaiting Judge Tilly and, critically, Harris' decision. Standing with Amanda Jackson, the district attorney prosecutor had an opaque expression, and he did not look in their direction. The courtroom was jammed; among the spectators, only Allie and Janie Hill knew what had happened in Tilly's chambers, and what might happen to Malcolm.

All five of them, Chase knew, were filled with hope and afraid to hope. Both Ford and Chase rested a hand on Malcolm's shoulder.

When they had first gathered with his mother and grandmother in a conference room, the better for Ford and Chase to explain in private what Judge Tilly had said to Harris, Malcolm had struggled to absorb it. For too long now, imprisonment had been his reality, and the prosecution had blighted his future. Freedom had become too hard to imagine.

Finally, Malcolm shook his head, an expression of disbelief so profound that Chase found it painful to watch. "What you're telling me is that by tonight I could be having dinner at home."

"Maybe," Ford admonished. "We can't be sure yet. But if it happens, I imagine your mom can come up with something."

"Best to let me do it," Janie told Malcolm. "I cook better."

But beneath their efforts to buttress each other, the atmosphere was tentative and tense. However much he loved Allie, however dearly he wished for Malcolm to regain his life, Chase did not quite know what to say. He was acutely aware of being the only white person in the room and, relative to the others, still a stranger to their lives, unable to fully access the emotions of four Black people hoping for justice in a place they knew too well. All he could do was what he had done for the last nine months—be there.

When Janie suggested that everyone hold each other's hands in prayer, Chase joined them.

Now, as the minutes crept by in the courtroom, Malcolm watched the empty bench. Chase could feel the tension in his shoulders; the almost superstitious fear that freedom was a mirage that would vanish in an instant, just as it had vanished on a dark country road with the accidental twitch of a trigger.

"All rise," the courtroom deputy called out, and as those assembled stirred to their feet, Judge Tilly took his place.

To Chase, he looked remarkably composed, as though this hearing had not been proceeded by testimony so remarkable that it had changed the course of the trial.

"Please be seated," he said. "The first order of business is the defendant's motion for a mistrial. Mr. Ford?"

With a nonchalance Chase knew he did not feel, Ford walked to the podium.

"May it please the court," he said firmly, "the testimony of Deputy Spinetta necessitates a mistrial. On the virtual threshold of closing arguments, we've learned that the trial has proceeded without evidence critical to the defense—specifically, a cell phone that corroborates the defendant's account of his encounter with Deputy George Bullock. This, in turn, suggests that there may be further exculpatory evidence as yet unknown. There is simply no way to remove the prejudice to Mr. Hill, or to hold the trial in suspension pending further inquiry."

"Thank you, Mr. Ford," the judge responded. "Mr. Harris?"

Harris stood without leaving the prosecution table. "Now that we're in open court, I want to emphasize that we had no knowledge of this new evidence until yesterday evening. Nor did we have any reason to suspect the existence of an untraceable cell phone belonging to Deputy Bullock. If Deputy Spinetta had chosen to come forward, as was his duty, the decisions made by our office could have been very different."

Harris, Chase perceived, was taking the escape route suggested by the judge—blame Nick Spinetta. Nodding, Tilly responded, "As I understand it, Mr. Harris, the defendant's motion for mistrial carries no imputation of prosecutorial misconduct. Is that correct, Mr. Ford?"

Hardly, Chase thought. But for Malcolm's sake, Ford was prepared to play his role in Judge Tilly's kabuki theater. Rising, he said smoothly, "It is, Your Honor."

"Very well," the judge said. "That leaves the question of whether the prosecution opposes a mistrial."

For an instant, Harris hesitated. "We do not," Harris answered.

"With that," Tilly said formally, "the court declares a mistrial in the case of *State of Georgia versus Malcolm Hill*. Before we excuse the jury, are there any other matters on which counsel desires to be heard?"

Once again, Ford returned to the podium. "There is, Your Honor. Based on the finding of a mistrial, we believe that a second trial would violate the defendant's constitutional right to avoid double jeopardy. On that basis, we ask that this court dismiss this case with prejudice."

"Here goes," Chase said quietly to Malcolm.

Regarding Harris with judicial solemnity, Tilly inquired, "What is your position, Mr. Harris, on whether the prohibition against double jeopardy warrants dismissal of these charges?"

In the silence that followed, Chase heard Malcolm inhale, and saw his son's eyes close. "Having researched the law," Harris said wanly, "the prosecution cannot argue with certainty that this court can't grant a motion to dismiss."

A glint of humor surfaced in Tilly's eyes. "Decoding your double negative, is the court correct in understanding that you do not oppose defendant's motion?"

For a last moment, Harris paused. "We do not, Your Honor."

Sitting straighter, the judge surveyed the courtroom before addressing Malcolm. "Would the defendant please step forward?"

Malcolm looked startled. Then he collected himself, and walked to the foot of the bench.

"Mr. Hill," the judge said simply, "the court is dismissing all charges against you with prejudice. On behalf of the justice system of Cade County, we want to express regret about the circumstances under which you were brought before us. You are free to go."

The courtroom erupted in gasps and cheers. Turning, Chase saw Allie embrace her mother, Janie's tears of joy and disbelief. Then he felt the dampness in his eyes.

"Sweet Jesus," Chase murmured to Ford. "You did it."

"So I did," Ford answered, and then looked at Chase more closely. "I know," he said almost gently. "I know."

Turning, Chase saw Malcolm. Wordless, they looked into each other's faces. Then Malcolm stepped forward and rested his head against Chase's shoulder.

It was done.

★ ★ ★

Leaving the courthouse, Malcolm paused at the head of the steps, drawing a deep breath of chill winter air.

It was almost dusk. He had first arrived here for his arraignment on a rainy summer morning, by his count two hundred and sixty-nine days ago. Every day since had scarred him, for how long and how deeply he could not know. But somewhere in that time, a father had come to claim him.

He stood between Chase Brevard and his mother, with Ford walking beside her, his grandmother beside Chase. As in the courtroom, the cheers of his supporters were mingled with catcalls, though the Parnells and White Lightning were nowhere in sight. "You'll pay yet," a hateful voice shouted.

He tried to block it out. Soon, he would see the rolling fields of the only home he'd ever known, the one he shared with his mother; taste his grandmother's cooking; collapse into his own bed in the room that had been his since birth. Perhaps then it would seem real. Perhaps, in time, he would stop having nightmares, or flinching at sudden sounds. Perhaps, tonight, he would sleep a little.

Between the line of deputies flanking the steps, reporters shouted questions. To one of them, his mother said, "We'll have something to say tomorrow. For now, Malcolm's father and I are just grateful that he's free."

Surrounded by deputies, the five of them stopped at the foot of the stairs. Facing Chase, Allie told him quietly, "We need to take Malcolm home. I'll call you tonight."

Quickly, Chase braced Malcolm's shoulders. "You should get out of here," he said. "I'll see you soon."

★ ★ ★

Watching them drive away, Chase stood beside Ford amidst the deputies who Al Garrett had assigned to protect them. Tonight, Chase realized, he would be sleeping alone in a rented apartment where Allie's clothes hung in the bedroom closet, a remnant of their transient domesticity.

It was done. But Chase had no idea of what would follow. For now, it was enough to see Malcolm walk free.

"Let's go," Ford told him. "I've had enough of this place."

PART EIGHT

Beginnings

83

Two nights later, Chase took Jabari Ford to dinner.

His leave of absence was over. There were pressing votes pending in the House, and he had busied himself conferring with his staff and preparing to leave his apartment in Cade County. Tomorrow evening, he would drive to Atlanta, then fly to D.C. the next morning. But he felt suspended between the man he had been and whoever, because of Allie and Malcolm, he might have become. The case had been so consuming, its stakes so visceral, that at times he could hardly believe it was done.

He and Allie had long telephone conversations, much less about their future than Malcolm's. As best she could, Allie had plunged back into her work while trying to ease their son's passage to freedom and, in the fall, to Morehouse. He was sometimes restless and distracted, she told Chase. But the familiarity of home seemed restorative. On the first night, Janie had cooked his favorite dinner; afterward, he and Allie had sat on the porch in warm jackets, quiet, simply feeling the land around them. Neither spoke of the sheriff's deputies at the foot of the road.

Tomorrow morning, Chase and Allie planned to meet, and then he would spend time with Malcolm for the first time since the trial. But there was another person he wanted to see. And so, as on the first day they had met, Ford and Chase commandeered a table at the Winfield Hotel.

Both ordered the same cocktails—a martini for Chase, Maker's Mark and ginger ale for Ford. As they touched glasses, Ford remarked, "Guess this is better than where we started."

Chase smiled. "Was there a problem? All I remember is wondering how you could spoil perfectly good bourbon with sugar water."

Ford's mouth twitched. "Man, you really are exactly what you appeared to be—an elitist from up north. But at least you turned out to be a halfway decent lawyer."

"I was OK," Chase responded, "as long as you made the decisions. On all the big ones, you turned out to be right—keeping the judge, calling Malcolm as a witness, asking for another shot at Spinetta and Garrett. And the way you played Harris in chambers was pretty sublime. I think even Tilly kind of enjoyed it."

"God knows I enjoyed it. But the truth of things is that all of us owe Al Garrett big-time. After all our great lawyering, that's kind of humbling to consider." Ford's expression grew serious. "I keep thinking about how

close we came to having a trial that scrupulously followed the rules of
evidence and never got near the truth of what actually happened. Can't
help but wonder where Malcolm would be."

The thought haunted Chase. "I have no idea. But at least now the
Justice Department will zero in on the Parnells, and Bullock's a philan-
dering bigot instead of a white Christian martyr. I'm hoping that makes
Allie and Malcolm a little safer. You and your family, too."

"Amen to all that," Ford said fervently. "At least our town fathers
won't be funding a marble obelisk for St. George. I hear the widow
Bullock stormed out of court when I dragged the truth about him and
Molly out of Spinetta."

"Fuck her," Chase replied sharply. "If she could have, she'd have stuck
the needle in Malcolm's arm herself. As far as I'm concerned, she can
suffer for the rest of her life, and her evil husband deserves to be dead. I'm
just sorry my son has to live with all that for the rest of *his* life."

Ford frowned in thought. "Yeah, there's no erasing what happened to
him. The most we could do was get him his life back, and hope he makes
good use of it."

Chase pondered this. "All I know," he said finally, "is that I'll do my
damnedest to help him."

Ford was quiet for time, watching the couples and families drifting
into the ornate dining room. "So I guess you're going back D.C. the day
after tomorrow."

"No choice, Jabari. The world keeps spinning and time marches on.
That's what the Fourth District of Massachusetts reelected me to do,
and you'll notice I didn't say no." Chase took another sip of his drink.
"Speaking of which, there's something I wanted to mention."

"Which is?"

"Remember our first dinner, when you were talking about the barriers
to your own political ambitions? I distinctly recall you suggesting that I
floated into Congress based on one big case and a lot of family money."

Ford looked up at the ceiling, as if struggling for recall. "I may have
said something like that," he allowed.

Chase smiled. "Something exactly like that, actually. It was one of
your least obnoxious moments, because it's essentially true—leaving out
some bursts of hard work on my part. Anyhow, I've been watching some
cable news the last couple nights, and it's clear to me you're halfway
there." He paused for emphasis. "You're famous, pal. The case you just
won makes my prosecution of Joe Kerrigan look like moot court. Find
the right district, one the Republicans haven't gerrymandered to death,

and all you need to run for Congress is the money. I'd be happy to save you a seat."

Ford regarded him curiously. "All I need happens to be the one thing I don't have."

"But you could. I'd be more than pleased to talk to our congressional campaign committee, in the unlikely event you even needed my help. You're such an obvious natural that raising the money should be easy enough."

Eyes hooded, Ford studied the table. "I'm truly grateful you say that," he responded at length. "It's a compliment I don't take lightly. But I'd have to think about it. Watching what you and Allie went through got me thinking about what's best for my family. It's been nice getting reacquainted the last couple days." His tone became pensive. "Maybe we'd all be better off if I build on the career I already have. That would be trouble enough without putting them all through the meat grinder of politics. Being flayed alive isn't for everyone."

Or for most people, Chase thought—another reason, perhaps, that he had never found the right partner. "I understand," he answered. "Knowing what you have is a sign of sanity. Just let me know whatever you decide."

"You're sane enough," Ford countered. "Thing is, you never had a family."

"True. Sometimes I wonder about my own choices. But I keep on making them, don't I? The only one I'm sure I don't regret is coming here."

Ford nodded. "So what about the three of you, now?"

It was the question of the hour, Chase thought, perhaps of a lifetime. "I've got no idea. I know I want to be Malcolm's father, if he'll have me. About the rest, the things that separated Allie and me all those years ago still exist, and time has made them bigger. But after the last nine months, I know for sure that what we had was real, and still is."

"She does, too, it's pretty clear." Ford raised his glass again. "You deserve the best, Chase, whatever that turns out to be. You showed me a lot about yourself by sticking this out. Sure hope you get the good of that."

84

The next morning, Allie met Chase by the pond. "We always have our places, don't we?" she said. "Then it was an oak tree in Harvard Yard;

now it's a park bench in Cade County. Every now and then I look at you, and it's like the time in between just vanished."

But those years had defined them, she knew, and from his expression so did Chase. "How's Malcolm?" he asked.

Allie settled down close beside him. "You'll see. He's already gained some weight back, and the circles beneath his eyes are fading some. Yesterday his old girlfriend came out for a visit, and they spent a lot of time just talking. But there's so much still dammed up inside him." She shook her head. "His personal encounter with justice in America did him harm enough. But for Al Garrett, God knows what could've happened."

As so often, she saw him following her thoughts. After a moment, he said simply, "Electing people like Garrett is what you came back for."

Once again, Allie found herself wrestling with the complexity of her feelings. "So maybe my work helped save Malcolm. But the fact that he was doing it nearly cost him his life. All I know is, that will haunt me for the rest of mine, and that I'll be afraid for him, never wanting to say that."

Chase studied her. "He can make his own choices, Allie, just like you made yours. There's a whole world out there way beyond Georgia. I happen to live in it."

She smiled a little. "Oh, I remember. That seems to keep coming up." She paused "You'd like him to live there, wouldn't you?"

"I'd like him to try it, if he wants. He might be safer. But whatever happens with the three of us, I want to spend time with him. I can't help but think it could be good for us both."

This was hard, Allie thought—for so long she had been her son's only parent. But Malcolm had always wanted more, and now so did Chase. "I think it would be," she answered. "When his head clears, I believe that's what he'll end up wanting. Anyhow, I mean to encourage him."

A trace of melancholy entered his eyes. "I'm grateful for that. But why is this beginning to feel like a custody negotiation between parents who are separating?"

"Aren't we?" she asked, and felt the weight of her own sadness. "Isn't that what this is about?"

"I don't know," he answered. "I wish it hadn't been then. Does it have to be now?"

Allie looked down. "Back then, would you have come to Georgia with me?"

"Yes. If that was what you needed."

For a moment, Allie struggled to respond, and then the need to share her own complex truths overwhelmed her. "I don't know if I can ever tell you how hard this is for me. When you came back, I understood all over again why I'd fallen so much in love with you that spring. I felt lucky to have you back, and to feel who you've become. You weren't here just for me, but for a son you didn't know." Her voice thickened. "However terrible our whole situation, I even liked playing house. I'd walk through the door, and there you were. Like those fantasies I used to have."

"And so?"

"And so, twelve hours from now you'll be home in Washington, and as banal as it sounds, starting at eight tomorrow morning I've got four conference calls in a row." Fighting back her emotions, Allie took Chase's hands in hers. "Maybe we were made to love each other, and to have a son. But I'm not sure we were made to be together. You're a congressman from Massachusetts now, and someday maybe more. There's nothing you can do in my world, and I don't know if I can leave it."

"I've thought about all sorts of things. I've imagined learning to cook Chinese food in the kitchen of your big house in Georgetown. I've imagined taking the offers I keep getting to run a civil rights organization in Washington, or accepting a serious job in some cabinet department. But the thing I've learned for sure is that I'm not the ideal political wife, or any kind of political wife."

Pausing, she felt tears surfacing in her eyes. "I tell myself you came here for me and our son, so why can't I do that for you? But all these months I've hated what politics was doing to us, and to Malcolm—all the ugliness, all the dehumanizing lies and invasions of privacy until you feel like there's nothing left, knowing it will all get worse year after year. For all that I'm out in public, there's a part of me that needs more space than politics could ever give us…"

"So who says I have to be a politician?" he interjected.

"You, Chase. By running for Congress in the first place. By keeping your career alive. By thinking, like I'm sure you must have since Malcolm went free, that you might still run for the Senate." She looked into his face. "Tell me you haven't, and I'll try to believe you. But I don't think you can put me to the test."

Briefly, Chase was quiet. "I can't," he acknowledged. "But that doesn't mean I have to do it. When I decided to stay here, I was able to put that aside."

"I know," she answered. "I love you for that. But if you still want to run, and I think you do, that's what I want for you." She paused again, searching for answers. "Maybe the price we pay for being ourselves is hard to bear. I know I'll love you for the rest of my life, and I'm guessing that's true for you. But now we've got something more to show for our time together, don't we? Not just caring for each other, but sharing our son."

Allie felt the pain on his face cutting through her. "So we just put how we feel in a corner somewhere?" he asked.

She shook her head. "I know we'll see each other, if you want to. I don't want to ever let go of being part of each other's lives."

Chase touched her face. "Neither do I. But after all this, it's hard to imagine time going by without you."

Despite herself, Allie smiled a little. "But it will, baby, and I'm guessing quicker for you than for me. We both know that it was Jabari and Al Garrett who saved Malcolm. But try telling that to the starstruck voters of Massachusetts. Some morning you'll wake up and realize you're going to absolutely decimate Lucy Battle in the Democratic primary. If that sister has any sense, she'll just get out of your way."

Allie paused again, and then gave in to her desire to kiss him, letting the moment linger. "I wouldn't mind sleeping with a senator, either. But I'm thinking another thing you'll realize is that it's not too late to have a full-time family, and that somewhere in Georgia you found out you want that." Pausing, she felt the catch in her throat. "If you find her, and someday call to tell me, I'll be glad of that as well."

★ ★ ★

It wasn't until she watched him drive away that Allie let the tears flow, feeling the void inside her that only Chase had ever filled.

It wasn't fair.

She imagined trying to explain to her mother why she had let him go. *Maybe I love him too much to keep him, Mama. Or maybe not quite enough.*

It wasn't fair. But at least now she could go home to the only person she had loved even more than Chase Brevard.

Their son.

85

When Chase arrived, Malcolm was waiting near the foot of the road to his mother's and grandmother's farmhouses. Right now, the look of the land where he had grown up, green and rolling even beneath the pall of an overcast winter day in rural Georgia, felt like the only constant in this life.

He felt anxious to see Chase again, and yet apprehensive. Malcolm knew that Chase was leaving for Washington, and he did not know how this last meeting would feel or what their relationship would be thereafter. He was still reeling from all that had happened, and the next months would be consumed with trying to reclaim himself from nightmares, startled responses to random noises, and the oppressive sense that freedom could be taken away from him in an instant. It was hard to see past the day he would enter college, so different than the Malcolm Hill who would have entered Morehouse instead of awaiting his fate in the Cade County jail. Too many people still hated him for the accident that had changed his life, and he was finding it hard to imagine himself feeling safe, or believing in the goodwill of strangers.

But Chase Brevard was no longer a stranger; at considerable cost to himself, Malcolm now understood, Chase had chosen to stand beside him. Watching him emerge from the rental car he had parked at the side of the road, Malcolm wondered why he had not seen himself on the first day this congressman had visited him in jail. It seemed so obvious now—the height, the smile, the cast of their faces, the easy athleticism, none of which had come down from the only family he had ever known. Malcolm had been navigating his almost nineteen years on earth with this man as part of him, helping to define Malcolm the debater, the student, the high school running back, the guy lucky enough to attract girls like Ella.

"What's it like," she had asked him yesterday, "to realize this rich white congressman is your father?"

It was an impossible question, Malcolm had found, with too many possible answers. The best he could do was say, "It's like having to rethink my whole life, and then figure out if I've got room for somebody so different who maybe wants to be what I always wanted."

But were they really that different? Malcolm thought now. They had no life in common. But in certain ways, his mother would have been like his grandmother if the two women had never lived as mother and daughter. It wasn't simply that Chase Brevard wanted to be his father; in so many random things Malcolm did every day, he already was.

Chase stood in front of him, hands in his pocket of his coat, giving Malcolm a cautious, querying look. "How's it been," he asked, "these last three days? Or is that too big a question?"

Way too big, Malcolm knew. But he had no idea when they would see each other again, and he should try to give some kind of answer. Collecting his thoughts, he looked around him.

"I can't really say," he told Chase. "It's like I can't trust anything, like nothing that's happened or will happen is real enough to believe. Being free. Being here. You and my mom. You being my father. Going off to college. I'm not even sure who I am anymore."

To Malcolm, Chase's expression suggested a certain comprehension. "You're going to need time to sort it all out. I didn't go through anything like what you did, and even I feel kind of dislocated. Try as I might, it's hard for me to imagine what it's like to be you."

"Strange," Malcolm answered. "Take right now. I've never had a father. I never thought he'd be somebody like you. Now here we are, and I'm just starting to deal with the ways that *I'm* somebody like you."

"Yeah," Chase responded with a trace of humor, "that must be kind of disconcerting."

For an awkward moment, Malcolm studied the grass at his feet. "Anyhow, I'm thinking I'll just have to roll with it. It's not like back at Harvard you guys could ask my permission before blowing off birth control."

He looked up to see Chase smiling. "Can't help it," Chase told him. "I just caught myself thinking that you sound pretty much like I might, were I in your place. It's just funny to see yourself in someone you didn't raise."

"I guess it must be," Malcolm answered seriously. "But there's something else I need to say. When I was in jail, all I could think about was getting out of there, or dying in prison. I didn't think much about what this was doing to your life, the things you were giving up by coming here."

Chase shrugged. "I didn't expect you to. In your place, I couldn't have."

"But you stayed," Malcolm replied, "even after I lashed out at you. Then you kicked over Congress to be my lawyer. You didn't have to do all that."

"Pure selfishness," Chase said lightly. "I'd rather visit you anywhere than prison." At once, Chase stopped himself. "One of my bad habits is making things sound less serious than I mean. I didn't do whatever I did so you'd be grateful. I wanted you to be free. But if I got a son out of the deal, one I actually spend time with, to me that would feel like some kind of miracle."

It was surprising, Malcolm discovered, to realize how much that last sentence meant to him. "What about you and my mom?"

Chase looked openly sad, as if he no longer cared to conceal his emotions. "They tell me that the kids of divorced parents sometimes have reunification fantasies. Your mom and I seem to have had our own. We'll always love each other, I know. But I don't know that we're going to make it, except as friends for life. That leaves you and me to work this out for ourselves."

So this wasn't about Chase and his mother anymore, Malcolm realized, although they would both see the other in him. Now it was about the two of them, and whether they could become father and son.

"So I guess we're on our own," Malcolm said.

"Sure seems like it," Chase answered. "Driving over here, I started imagining showing up for parents' weekend at Morehouse."

Malcolm could not help but smile. "Now that *would* be something."

"Why? Barging in on their kids' lives at college is what parents do, looking awkward and well-meaning and generally embarrassing. I don't see why you should get a pass."

"You wouldn't be like every other parent at Morehouse, believe me." Malcolm smiled again. "I mean, not all of them are congressmen."

Looking at Chase, Malcolm saw a glimmer of hope in his eyes. "That's something else I started thinking about," Chase told him. "Washington, D.C., is not terrific in the summer. But as far as I'm concerned, the only thing between Cade County and hell are screen doors and some air conditioning. I know you're interested in politics, and I can offer you a summer internship with long hours and rotten pay. You could learn something about Congress, and we could spend time together. You may have heard they've got a baseball team."

Malcolm hesitated, and saw at once that Chase feared that he had overstepped his bounds. "It was just a thought," Chase added hurriedly.

"No," Malcolm responded. "It might be a decent excuse for escaping my mom. I know we both love her. But I'm the one who has to live with her."

This time Chase's smile was rueful. "More days than not, I envy you. But no doubt she's her own person. I keep on learning that, over and over."

Their time was running out, Malcolm realized, and he had to find the words to penetrate the fog of his own emotions. "Maybe things like coming to D.C. would work out," he said. "I've just got so much to deal with right now, and I can't see that far ahead. I'm still trying to see myself in college. So I can't say exactly how we'll do this."

Slowly, Chase nodded. "I understand. I don't want to be one more thing to worry about. That's not who parents are supposed to be."

Amidst his own confusion, Malcolm had the sharp, sudden sense of how hard Chase was trying to be what he needed, and how much that mattered to him. Suddenly, impulsively, he came forward and hugged the man who was asking to be his father, in reality as well as in name.

Wordless, Chase embraced him tightly. It felt good to Malcolm and, he hoped, to Chase. "You came back for me," he murmured. "I don't see how I can forget that."

He never would, Malcolm knew. Ever.

86

The following day, Chase reentered his home in Georgetown.
It was late afternoon, and his housekeeper had turned on the heat to welcome him back. From Jack Raskin's querulous text, he knew that his voicemail was full.

Tomorrow morning, Chase supposed, he'd start caring. Right now, he needed time to reflect, to let his soul catch up with his body.

He sat in the living room, absently contemplating his surroundings while trying to accept the strangeness of being here again, this time for good, knowing that Allie and Malcolm were so far away.

The irony of their situation, which Allie had grasped at once, hit him hard—the gap between private truths and public perceptions was simply too great. In too many false or sentimentalized narratives beyond his control, the media would conjure another chapter in the charmed and lucky life of Chase Brevard—the congressman who had put career and self at risk to save his son from the jaws of racism. But he would do nothing to help them. The truth was that Chase had not saved anyone except for, perhaps, a piece of himself. He wanted Malcolm as a son, not a prop.

But Allie had also identified another truth about him. He had become in reality what she had imagined for him long ago. Knowing why Jack was so intent on reaching him, he had thought yet again of running for the Senate. Love was a hard thing to kill, he had learned, but so was ambition. After all that had happened, what else did he have?

Once again, he found himself alone.

For all that people liked him and he liked them, Chase realized that he had been alone inside himself for much of his life, starting with parents who were emotionally distant from their only son, and from each other. But it was utterly pointless to blame John Marc and Caroline Brevard for who he had become; no one was Adam and Eve, and parents had parents of their own. Nor was it right to blame Allie and their breakup at Harvard for the decisions of the next nineteen years, or to blame her for being who she had always been, and was still. The question now was what he made of his own life—starting with becoming a father to Malcolm—and of whatever he had learned about himself in Georgia.

Pensive, he wondered if it was too early for a gin martini, and decided that he didn't care about that either.

He went to the kitchen, and suddenly thought of the last morning he had spent here with Kara McGuire, exchanging thoughts and drolleries about the world they shared before Chase had turned on the television. Dropping ice in his grandfather Bancroft's martini pitcher, he recalled the exact moment. A yearbook picture of a Black teenager with Chase's smile had taken him places only he and Allie understood.

I'm thinking another thing you'll realize, she had told him, *is that you want a full-time family. If you find her, and someday call to tell me, I'll be glad of that as well.*

The first part of that was true, Chase had discovered. But in the most important way, Allie had been wrong, for Chase had already found her. The last nine months had confirmed for him the hardest truth of all: that Alexandria Hill of Cade County, Georgia, was that rare and forever person, the elusive love of his life.

★ ★ ★

In early evening, Allie sat on the front porch with her mother, quietly watching as dusk settled over their property.

Malcolm was in his bedroom, listening to music before the two women bestirred themselves to make dinner. For the half hour until now, they had observed him systematically shooting baskets from an imaginary arc around the hoop his grandfather had put up for him, one shot after the other, as though repeating this once-familiar ritual would bring him a little closer to who he had been before George Bullock stopped him. After her son went inside, the image lingered with Allie and, she thought, Janie.

Finally, Janie said, "So he still wants Malcolm, even without you."

"Yes."

Janie nodded. "Thought he would."

From childhood on, Allie had learned how to follow her mother's thoughts. So it did not surprise her when, after a while, Janie asked, "So how are you doing without *him?*"

Allie paused, allowing herself to absorb the painful truth of her answer. "I knew it would be hard. But it's so much harder than I thought."

"Funny you hadn't already learned that," Janie observed. "But maybe twenty years is too short a time."

As was typical, Janie just let the remark sit there. Turning, Allie demanded, "Why don't you just say it, Mama?"

Janie folded her hands in her lap, gazing out at their fields with a contemplative expression. "I know you think you asked too much of Malcolm. But right now I'm wondering if we asked way too much of you."

Allie shook her head, resistant. "I've done what I wanted to do."

"And you've done it well, for twenty years now. No one could be prouder of you than I am. What I'm not so proud of as a mother is knowing how unhappy you are, and watching you push all that aside." Her mother faced her. "When I look out at this place, know what I think of? All those years your father and I had together, the family we made with you and then Malcolm."

"I was there," Allie said. "I couldn't have built Blue Georgia without you."

For a moment, the woman who had been with Allie since the dawn of consciousness gazed into her face. "I know, Alexandria. But what else have you built for yourself?"

Stung, Allie wondered if her mother knew how unfair the question felt, and how much the asking of it hurt. But, of course, she knew both things very well. "I can't run away," Allie answered sharply.

Janie took both hands in hers. "You've got your own family staring you in the face, and you've put so much on yourself that you call that running away. I might call it running toward something you've never had, and that Malcolm won't have unless you take stock of things. How do you think the two of them will do better as father and son—with you or without you?"

Allie fell quiet. "With me," she acknowledged. "But that depends on so much else. I told Chase I'm not a political wife."

"Did he ask you to be?"

"He wants to run for the Senate. I want him to."

Janie looked at her intently. "So maybe you can talk it through with him. I'm not saying politics isn't hard on a couple, or that it wouldn't be especially hard on you. But I've met the man, and I can't imagine he wants you to be running after him from one campaign stop after another. He'd want you to have your own life."

"I've already got my own life," Allie insisted, "right here. What would I say to myself if I leave with so much left to do?"

Janie considered this. "That there will always be more to do. That there are other places you're needed. That no one should become indispensable. That sooner or later you'd have to raise up some new Allie Hill to continue what you started." Her voice softened. "You need your own permission to be happy, not mine. But in the way back, maybe it felt like you did. So twenty years ago, if you'd decided to be with him, what would you have told us?"

Imagining this, Allie felt her throat constrict. "That I'll never love anyone else like this."

"And now?"

Allie drew a breath. "That I know it's true."

Standing, Janie bent forward and softly kissed the top of her daughter's head. "Then maybe you should sit with this a while. I'll go see if Malcolm will help me fix dinner."

Alone, Allie reflected.

There was so much to think about, and to remember. The night of Black Juliet. How it had felt to walk out of his life. How much harder it would be now, with all they had become, to make a life for each other. How incomplete, still, was their understanding of the other, and how far Chase and Malcolm had to go. How it had felt to live with him. How it might feel to see Chase and Malcolm at the dinner table during their son's breaks from college. Whether she could ask Chase to give up politics or even his home up north and, if so, whether he would—or could without damaging himself and, with that, her as well.

But there was yet more to consider. Whether she could leave Georgia and still feel true to herself and to the cause that had defined her. How it would feel to start a new undertaking in a city she had once spurned. What might happen if Chase became a senator and heard the final ambition of a gifted politician calling out to him, a thousand voices of altruism or self-interest, the Jack Raskins of this world, urging him on. The good Chase could do for others if he answered, or the harm he could do to them both. How she would feel when Malcolm found his own life, and her life was with Chase—or without him. How it would feel for them to be themselves, free of their fears for Malcolm. How it would feel, at last, to be Allie Hill and Chase Brevard.

There were no clear answers. But so much of this, however uncertain, started with her.

She took out her cell phone, weighing the potential implications for three people of whatever she chose to do, or not do.

For a time, sitting quite still, she studied the illuminated screen. Then she began to tap out a text. "I love you," she said simply. "Please call me."

AFTERWORD & ACKNOWLEDGMENTS

Writing *Trial* was one of my most compelling experiences as a novelist. So I wanted to explain what moved me to do so after nine years away from fiction, and to thank those whose generous help was so essential to the work.

For almost six years between 2015 and 2021, I wrote over three hundred columns or essays on American politics and society—regularly, for HuffPost, the *Boston Globe* and, extensively, The Bulwark—but also for such publications as *The Atlantic* and *USA Today*. As time went on, I realized that many of my commentaries directly concerned America's tribulations of race, or that issues relating to race either or directly or implicitly informed what I was writing. Ultimately, I concluded that there is no problem more deeply interwoven into our social fabric.

Given that, I started thinking about using my background as a trial lawyer, political commentator, and author of twenty-two previous novels to construct a narrative about characters caught in the convergence of several of our gravest issues: voter suppression, discriminatory law enforcement, the political exploitation of racial animus, the rise of white nationalism, and the frequent failure of our legal system to provide fair trials in racially charged circumstances. After some thought, I determined to build the story around an eighteen-year-old voting rights worker's fatal nighttime encounter with a white sheriff's deputy, culminating with his inflammatory and nationally televised trial on a charge of capital murder.

Over time, I conceived of three characters through whose perceptions the novel would unfold—Malcolm Hill, Allie Hill, and Chase Brevard—and a fourth, Jabari Ford, who would carry the principal burden of defending Malcolm at trial. Through these characters, I hoped to provide readers with an engrossing and realistic experience of how it might feel to be caught up in the crosscurrents of a prosecution inflamed by racial antagonism, political ambition, media exploitation, and an ongoing struggle to grapple with the fissures of race.

This was far from the first time that I'd used the courtroom to dramatize complex political and social issues: as examples, *Exile* dealt with the Israeli–Palestinian dilemma; *Eclipse*, with the exploitation of oil resources in a fictional African country modeled after Nigeria; *Protect and Defend* with the corrosive legal and political fight over abortion rights; and *Balance of Power*, with the impact of the gun lobby on our politics and our public safety. So I had no illusion whatsoever that my personal experience was, in itself, remotely sufficient to write responsibly and intelligently about such difficult subjects, or about the lives of those who confront them. Extensive research, interviewing, and travel, I've long understood, were the only way forward.

To prepare for writing *Trial*, I did copious reading, spent significant time in Georgia, and conducted over fifty interviews with a diverse cross-section of people immersed in its subject matter. My primary goals were to incorporate the history and contemporary complexities of a prototypical county in Southwest Georgia, to accurately depict the prosecution and defense of a capital murder case in a racially divided rural jurisdiction, and to render the perception and experience of my disparate characters in a nuanced and realistic way. While there can be no doubt as to where my authorial sympathies lie, I felt it important to explore different perspectives and to avoid the rote and didactic.

First, the setting. After widely consulting among Georgians to identify models for my fictional Cade County, I decided that Sumter County in Southwest Georgia would provide an optimal background on which to build. Here, I must say at the outset that while I incorporated some of its history, geography, and contemporary conditions, in no way do I suggest that *Trial* should be taken as anything like a quasi-documentary reality. Rather, Sumter provided a rich foundation for fiction rooted in realistic imaginings of a representative place. My interviewees there included leaders of voting rights groups, grassroots voting rights activists, journalists, educators, politically engaged ministers, local community leaders, civil rights lawyers, white and Black politicians of different generations, the first Black sheriff in Sumter County, and a woman who, in 1960 at the age of eleven, was jailed with other adolescents under traumatic conditions for attempting to integrate a movie theater—an event now known to history as the Leesburg Incident.

Second, the trial. I interviewed a diverse group of Georgians that included current or former judges, prosecutors, defense counsel, law enforcement officers, and experts in forensics, pathology, ballistics, toxicology, and criminal investigation. I also explored the particulars of Georgia law that would profoundly influence—and sometimes limit— Malcolm Hill's defense.

Third, the characters. Here, a few examples. To help me depict Allie Hill, I interviewed Nse Ufot, successor to Stacey Abrams as the head of the state's seminal voting rights organizations, the New Georgia Project. Because one section portrays the pivotal relationship between Allie and Chase Brevard at Harvard in 2003, I located three Black women who shared their experiences of Harvard during that period. Other interviewees included four prominent Democratic consultants who dissected the challenges to Chase's political career, a psychiatrist who advised on the adverse impact on Malcolm of incarceration pending trial, and prominent African American defense lawyers whose experiences in rural Georgia helped illuminate the particular difficulties facing Jabari Ford. I also did extensive interviewing and reading about other realities that would impact the characters, including Georgia's current political dynamics and the intersection of white nationalist groups with law enforcement.

I'm deeply grateful to all those, in Georgia and elsewhere, who were so generous in giving me their time and advice. Perhaps the first element of gratitude is to say that the novel owes much of its realism and texture to them, and that its errors and omissions belong to me alone. One of the great rewards of my work is the kindness of strangers who share with me what is so important in their lives and, in the process, become friends.

So I'll start with the Georgians, friends old and new, who did so much to steer me to the right places and people: David Lewis, Danica Kombol, Jack Hardin, John Chandler, and David Brand. Dan Berman and Jill Stuckey generously helped me navigate Sumter County; Marc Arnett gave me a riveting six-hour orientation tour of Americus, its county seat; Lorena Sabb shared the remarkable story of Leesburg and other key incidents from her eventful life in the county; Sheriff Eric Bryant shared his observations as its first Black elected sheriff; and Reverends Mathis Wright and Fer-Rell Malone immersed me in the perspectives of politically active pastors. I'm equally grateful to other longtime residents of the county who helped to ground me: former state senator George Hooks, educators Raven Payne and Valerie Trice, civic and business leaders Charles and Kim Christmas, attorney Levi Lyman Barner, and citizen-activist Penny Taft.

Still more Georgians gave me extensive help in understanding the political and social complexities of Georgia. Jim Galloway, the recently retired dean of Georgia's political journalists, gave me invaluable insights and connections, journalist Bill Rankin graciously gave me further advice regarding political and social conditions, and consultant Joe Binns lent key insights into politics. Voting rights leader Rebecca DeHart, Reverend Hermon Scott, attorney Harold Franklin, and activist Lisa Thomas helped me further explore the fight for equal voting rights. Several lawyers helped illuminate the intersection of law and social justice: Attorney Garry Parker provided terrific anecdotes and insights concerning the personal, racial, and strategic complexities confronting Jabari Ford; my friend and law school classmate Judge Herbert Phipps did double duty as a jurist and former civil rights attorney; and my former law school moot court partner, David Walbert, shared his work as a social justice litigator.

Another significant challenge lay in constructing a dramatic and realistic trial rooted in the law and social realities of Georgia. Defense lawyer Don Samuel gave essential advice, one piece of which was to read the wonderfully evocative book *Praying for Sheetrock*, by his wife, Melissa Fay Greene. Retired judge Tom Baxley made important suggestions about the specifics and atmosphere of the trial itself, including a ghost from Judge Tilly's past. As for one of my prior novels, attorney and teacher Stephen Bright illuminated death penalty litigation. And I also got invaluable help from two former prosecutors from outside the state: my old friend Al Giannini, and my new friend Michael McAuliffe.

Homicide trials like that of Malcolm Hill require expert witnesses and investigators. I'm extremely grateful to the experts from Georgia who helped me portray them and their contributions to the case: toxicologist Amanda Cooke, crime scene investigators Todd Crosby and JT Ricketson, Lieutenant Darin Meadows, and ballistics expert Chris Robinson. Further help came from Dr. Michael Ferenc, a prominent pathologist from California.

Of particular importance was constructing the past and present of Allie Hill. Every one of the African Americans I interviewed in Sumter County, male and female, contributed to that portrait. With respect to Allie's work as the leader of a voting rights group, I'm immensely indebted to Nse Ufot. My friend Henry Louis Gates and his colleague Abby Wolf helped connect me with three African American women who would have been her real-life contemporaries during those pivotal years at Harvard, and who gave me rich insights into what Allie might have experienced: Professor Karine Gibbs; businesswoman and lawyer Yvonne Osirim; and former poet laureate of America Tracy K. Smith, whose memoir, *Ordinary Light*, I also read with great pleasure. And my wonderful longtime and very patient friend Cheryl Mills gave me further insights into her life, from delivery to motherhood.

More help came from another friend, activist-lawyer Emily Galvin, who gave me her perspective as a progressive white student at Harvard in 2003, and added some anecdotes of college days on Martha's Vineyard—and whose college acting career inspired me to make Allie into an actress. Dr. Curt Cetrullo helped me get Malcolm born. My dear friend Dr. Charles Silberstein assisted me in considering the stresses stemming from Malcolm's incarceration. Other great friends, crack sailors Jim Swartz and Brock Callan, not only gave me advice but took me out on the water so that I could imagine that harrowing sailing trip that nearly drowned Allie and Chase. As for politics, having written numerous novels and columns about national politics over twenty-five years, I'm just enough of an expert to know when to talk with the real experts: prominent Democratic consultant Stephanie Cutter; seasoned Massachusetts professional Michael Goldman; Elizabeth Warren's presidential campaign manager, Roger Lau; and a key advisor to Congressman Seth Moulton, Aaron Bartnick—all of whose rich knowledge includes expertise in Massachusetts politics.

Anyone who tries to write a novel knows how important it is to have advice, criticism, and encouragement from smart readers. Section by section, I got that from my terrific agent, Anne Sibbald, and my dear friend Philip Rotner gave me penetrating comments that influenced pivotal scenes. My late and much missed agent Mort Janklow read both the outline and the manuscript, and my talented friend Geraldine Brooks made important suggestions about a pivotal scene. And no one did more than my wife, Nancy Clair, who, despite a demanding career of her own, traveled with me to Georgia, participated in a number of interviews, read and commented on every line of every chapter, and did the detailed work of pulling together the final manuscript. For all sorts of reasons, including being my center of gravity and the glue for our family and friends, I can never thank her enough. And, speaking of family, my wonderful youngest son, Chase Kenyon Patterson, was nice enough to lend Chase Brevard his first name.

Finally, there are David Cooke, and the people of the New Georgia Project, to whom this book is dedicated.

I met David through Jim Galloway, and he turned out to be the kind of serendipitous marvel novelists dream of—an extremely talented trial lawyer gifted with a superior fictional imagination. A former district attorney in Georgia now engaged in private practice, David advised on every aspect of the trial, called with further insights that had occurred to him overnight, provided critical suggestions about how to enrich the legal narrative, and reviewed the manuscript for verisimilitude. On top of all that, he's a wonderful guy with a wonderful wife, Rebecca, both of whom Nancy and I deeply enjoy.

It is appropriate that I end this novel with a tribute to the extraordinary leaders and staff of the New Georgia Project.

Put simply, NGP is a seminal force in the fight for American democracy. Their work in Georgia is remarkable. They have created a full-time organization dedicated to putting the power of the vote into the hands of those for whom voting has been made more difficult, if not impossible. They have transformed the electorate of Georgia in the face of innumerable barriers—not only pernicious laws, but the pervasive threat of violence against their leaders and their staff. Their courage and resolve serve as a model for political organizing, not only in Georgia, but elsewhere. And NGP's plan to help seed similar organizations throughout the deep South is nothing less than a "second Southern strategy" that could change the face of our politics.

Protecting the right to vote, and the right to have those votes count, is the essential struggle of our time. If America succeeds in preserving—indeed extending—our democracy in defiance of those determined to tear it down, it will be because people like those of NGP refuse to quit, thereby inspiring others to join the fight. May we all be worthy of their work and sacrifice.